BY DARKNESS SEDUCED

"Poor sweet." Tamlane tugged on her straying hair, forcing her to look up at him. "You have certainly had a surfeit of 'Celtic enthusiasm' this day. There is just one other tradition I would like to share with you—and it needn't tire you. . . . "

Amarantha's heart began to pound. Tamlane was smiling slightly, but she did not think that he was jesting or in any way amusing himself.

"Yes?" Her voice was soft enough to be a whisper.

She knew what he intended and wondered whether she was so exhausted by her adventures as to be totally bereft of reason. Surely it had to be that, for it was madness to allow this man to kiss her. He was leading a double life—one of them quite possibly criminal, whatever his intentions.

At one time, she could not have imagined being attracted to Tamlane Adair. He was somewhat dark and unyielding in nature, while she had been young and gay and feckless. But that had all changed. She was no longer so young and frivolous. Now she found the dedication and even the danger of him to be very attractive.

"What are you thinking?" he asked her. "Your eyes tell me nothing."

"There is nothing yet to tell," she whispered.

Amarantha

Melanie Jackson

LEISURE BOOKS NEW YORK CITY

To Brian

A LEISURE BOOK®

August 2001

Published by

Dorchester Publishing Co., Inc.
276 Fifth Avenue
New York, NY 10001

ISBN 0-8439-4900-7

Visit us on the web at www.dorchesterpub.com.

Amarantha

My very dearest Uncle,

How pleasant to receive word from you of your safe return from Wales. It was a delight for me to learn that you are well and escaped the grippe. I myself am still suffering from a certain lowness of spirits, but such is not to be marveled at, as London has of late been filled with much sickness for both the poor and the well-born alike due to the extended cold weather that afflicts us still.

I am well enough, which is a matter of mixed fortune since Mister Delderfield is also in strong constitution and, being deprived of other amusements, is again determined upon a courtship. The rumor in town is that his finances have reached so serious a pass that he can no longer put off the disagreeable task of finding himself a wife. Since I am the only heiress of his acquaintance at present healthy enough to receive his address, he has again been importuning me with unwanted proposals. As his heart (and mine own) are in no way involved, I have had no hesitation in rejecting his latest offer. Indeed, if you will forgive the vulgarity and unfeminine nature of the topic, I will reveal to you that I have rejected this proposal and two others since my parents' demise. I cannot but feel it is my new fortune and not my face that attracts these men. It is understandable that they should be drawn to me for this reason—I also thoroughly enjoy the possession of such ample funds. However, I am most disinclined to share my inheritance with wastrels and have lately resolved against entering the married state.

And so, thanks in large part to Mister Delderfield's stubborn nature, good fortune has devolved upon you. I am quite at liberty to join you in Cornwall after the end of March when I have the last of my engagements here in town. I shall shut up the London house on the thirty-first of the month and begin my journey. Allowing for two nights upon the road, I should be with you no later than the third of April, if that is convenient. We shall begin at once to untangle your affairs and set your notes into order.

And so, until April, I remain,

Yr loving niece,
Amarantha Stanhope

Prologue

Arthur was dead! His body lay on the field of battle, cut down at Camlann by a rebel's sword. Enchanted Excalibur had been drowned in Drozmary Pool. The King's loyal knights were disarrayed and fled toward the holy city of Lyonesse, shocked and disbelieving that their beloved King was truly gone.

But wicked Mordred and his men were behind them as close and unshakeable as their own shadows, chasing them up the sanctuary mount of blessed Scilly where the loyal knights would be forced to make their final, futile stand against the men who had once been their brothers under the sword.

There was a flash of lightning, which split the sky in twain and divided the black horizon and light poured through. A horse screamed in sudden terror and shied away *from the apparition that appeared in their path. Other mounts farther down the hill, reared in agitation, nearly unseating their riders. The men, fearless in the face of any mortal foe, were struck dumb, awed at the sight that coalesced before their eyes. It was a ghost, a thing of dread and power that in life had been the most powerful of magicians. It was gray-cloaked Merlin who rushed over them in an icy gust and sped down the wooded hillside to chastise the evil Mordred's men.*

The last rider in the fleeing train was a stranger—a raven-haired woman disguised in a man's clothing. She turned about on her steed's back and watched with alarm as the ghost raised high his staff and called down lightning from the sky. Thunder roared and the very earth beneath her shook as though being torn by the giants who had long slept under the crust's stony mantle but, roused by the magician's call, were now vigorously seeking the open air.

There came another burst of lightning and the odor of burning rock filled the air. Her horse staggered once and then fled after his panicked brethren, but still the woman did not turn forward. Her eyes were fixed in fascinated horror at the sprays of pulverized stones that flew up into the air, blasted by some force deep within the earth. She stared with her eyes wide and unblinking until a terrible wind forced the cruel gray rain upon her. It was a shower of stone that scored the flesh of man and equine alike as it fell back upon the earth in a punishing, wind-driven stream.

Then the very sea around them reared up, and on its crest rode the hordes of rebellious Albion. With a roar, it hurled itself upon shining Lyonesse. The briny onslaught swallowed the city's hundred and forty churches in the blink of an eye. Wicked Mordred was swallowed, too, sucked forty fathoms below the waves. But still the oceans did not stop. On and on the shrieking waters came, racing toward the mounts of Scilly where Arthur's men had taken refuge.

The woman screamed in terror, but, before the sound could escape her lips, the icy waves were upon her, pressing her agonized voice back into her throat, swallowing her up in its watery maw.

Water foamed whitely. Desperate, she and her mount clawed toward the moonlit sky that shone bright above her like a beacon through the churning waves. Around her there came the deafening clanging of bells, as every church in drowned Lyonesse began to peal her death knell. . . .

Amarantha sat up straight in her generous bed, gasping for air as though her lungs had truly been deprived of breath by a vengeful ocean. She did not need to strike the candle on the night table to see her surroundings because a baleful moon, wholly as bright and full as the light in her dreams, had crept up over her coverpane and bathed her room in its cold, silver beams while she slept.

"Bloody hell," she muttered profanely, taking another deep breath and then throwing back her covers so she could close the shutters upon the unpleasant light. "I'll not listen to any more of Uncle Cyril's tales before seeking my bed. Who could have imagined that such nonsense would be upsetting?"

But she should have guessed it. Of late, much of life had been upsetting, she thought, looking down at the vast Bodmin Moor, the view distorted by the tiny panes of old glass. She shivered, though the spring night was not especially cold. It was remembered chills of unpleasant things past that crept over her skin and into the marrow of her bones.

11

She had lost her parents and a fiancé two years before. First her gentle mother, then her father, and finally Ian—though in many ways he had been dead to her for months before that. He had ceased to be hers when he had left to embrace the Jacobite cause. His last, dramatic words to her had been from a Lovelace poem—" *I could not love thee, dear, so much, loved I not honor more.'* "

Of course, she could not argue against that sentiment, but it had not lessened her exasperation or made his abandonment any less painful.

Faced with the loss, she had done what society expected of her: hired a respectable companion, gone into seclusion and grieved privately—especially for Ian and the death of her innocent dream of romantic love. She never spoke of him; it was too difficult a social situation for her friends, who were uncertain whether to express condolences on the death of a man who had died fighting in a rebellion against their king.

Amarantha hadn't noticed her loneliness at first. She had withdrawn to a place in her mind where she was comfortably numb and insulated from the facts of her life's permanent alteration. But time had eventually passed, grief and insulation alike wore off, and she'd begun to feel the pangs of social isolation. Blaming boredom for her continuing unhappiness, she'd obeyed societal dictates that said her time for mourning was over. She rejoined the social order of her peers and took up old diversions, which she now pursued with deliberate will. She performed her role of carefree heiress well and kept so busy that she could often completely ignore the pain lurking in the familiar background of the now sentiment-empty London.

But she was not always successful in avoiding old memories. They came whenever she was alone. Sometimes she was plagued by dark thoughts when she deliberated endlessly about Ian, and wondered whether she was not in some way sorry that they had not become lovers as he wished. He had pleaded to know her physically before he left for Scotland—he'd said that it was a memory that would carry him, that would sustain him through any turmoil or pain.

At first, she had not regretted withholding herself from her fiancé. It had been the wisest—and expected—course for a maiden of good upbringing. How much worse might be her grief, she considered, if she had surrendered not only her heart but also her body before being abandoned for the Stuart cause?

Ian had sworn that he would return to her by summer and they would marry, but angry and hurt, she had still refused him.

Her parents would have agreed with her decision. But in the dark stretches of the night, when she was alone in her chamber and could not sleep, Amarantha had to wonder whether Ian would have gone north had they been tied by bonds of physical intimacy. Might she have prevailed upon him to stay with her instead of joining the Jacobites? Might he now be alive? Over time, she had begun to feel that she had made an unfortunate decision in denying Ian—that his death *was* in some ways her fault.

She began telling herself that if she were faced with the same situation, knowing that the angel of death was hovering nearby, she would choose differently. Perhaps it made her wicked and defiant, but society's morals were proving to her newly opened eyes simply tedious hypocrisy. She'd come to view its regulations of behavior as church-sanctioned convenience; it supplied order to the common man but went largely ignored by the members of the *ton*. And since she had inherited her fortune—and she had no plans to surrender her new wealth and freedom—there was no need to preserve her innocence as barter for some future husband. If she loved again, and chose to give herself to some man, there was no one of consequence left to be hurt by her defection from her childhood morality.

But though resolved and even searching for a someone to bring her from darkness, there was no one who attracted her. No one at all. In need of distraction, she searched diligently, but there wasn't one man in the whole of London who stirred even a vague interest in her breast. They were all of the same stamp: shallow, pleasure-seeking, often stupid—and always arrogant.

After months of futile searching, her thoughts had grown more discouraged and unhappy. She'd managed to finish the season with a pretense of enjoyment, but it required constant simulation. However, it was not until winter that her deep frustration with her town life took complete hold of her and tried to drown her in cynicism. By December, there was no talk in London except of the consequences of rebellion in the north and how many traitors had been hanged or beheaded.

It had been exceptionally cold as well from November onward, confining her much of the time to her home where her only socializing was with such friends as who felt hardy enough to venture into the sleet and rain to share the unhappy news of other acquaintances in the north—or with the impoverished predators who were searching for a wealthy wife to rescue them from monetary misfortune and could not wait for the start of a new season.

Her feeling of imprisonment had grown until she began suffering from headaches and a persistent lowness of spirits that had not passed even with the calendar's firm insistence that spring had returned to England. She'd walked in the park, daring the chill breezes, but the new daffodils did not please. She'd attended the theater, but the new plays did not amuse. She'd avoided Tyburn Hill, but still the news came to her of how many unfortunate men were hanged there.

When the letter from Uncle Cyril arrived, complaining that he had lost his third secretary in as many years and his notes were growing too jumbled to sort out the Irish tales from the Welsh, she'd seized upon the excuse to pack her bags, dismiss her companion, close the London house and depart from the cold gray city for the comparative warmth and quiet of Cornwall.

For the most part, she was content with her decision to vacate London, though it meant leaving friends behind and taking up an outwardly more lonely existence. There was little society to be had in their remote corner of the moor. A few isolated hamlets and farmsteads were scattered about, but many had been abandoned long ago. Their nearest neighbor was one Rector Tamlane Adair, a man who supposedly lived in a strange cottage not far from the hamlet's only church. She hadn't met the rector yet, but was looking forward to making his acquaintance. He had quite a reputation among the superstitious farmers for being an opponent of the evil demons and malevolent spriggans that plagued the area. Since they no longer had Merlin to protect them, the locals had turned to Rector Adair to keep them from otherworldly wickedness.

Which was utter nonsense, of course. There was no magical influence at work on the moor. But perhaps the natives' beliefs were understandable, for they had always lived in this strange country of wild tales and monuments, and were not exposed to the enlightening educations of logic.

Amarantha shivered again. Painted in moonlight, the moor truly seemed a place of dead things—an eerie land where the vast and ancient stones that towered over the scenery had been erected to the dead by a long-forgotten people, and where even the innocent stalks of the stark marsh grasses looked like heaps of brittle bones when bleached of their daylight colors. And there was an eerie wind that muttered incessantly at her tiny casement.

In morning light it was otherwise. Then, one might see the moss growing green and succulent on those ancient stones. And beyond the rock outcrop that guarded her uncle's front door from the wind, there was a stretch of spring bluebells that blazed an astonishing assault on the eye under the midday sun. And there were always sea birds flying inland to visit the marshy heath, filling the sea-swept air with their harsh-voiced songs and graceful beating wings.

But that was for the morning. It was still night, austere and silent but for the wind, and the giant moon above brooded as she did.

Amarantha firmly closed her shutters against the bespelling moon and the empty, dead moor. Both of them would be improved by a few more hours of peaceful slumber and the light of new day.

Chapter One

"Slept well, did ye, dearie?" Mrs. Polreath asked, beaming cheerily as she poured the morning tea and set the fragile cup in front of Amarantha.

"Very well, thank you," Amarantha lied with a polite smile. The apple-cheeked Mrs. Polreath was too kind to upset with talk of disturbing dreams. Her happy countenance was an antidote to all the heavy gray granite that surrounded them, and Amarantha had no desire to see it banished by concern over evil portents, which the superstitious lady was certain to think bad dreams were.

The Talland House was called *Lorelei* by her uncle because of its uneven twisting stair that threaded its heights from cellar to attics. Like the siren of German myth, the ancient staircase was beautiful but rather

18

treacherous—with slippery and uneven treads and newel posts that more closely resembled spears than handholds. The house itself was some four hundred years old and constructed in the days when vast fortifications were considered by the gentry to be a reasonable necessity. The house had, in fact, been attacked by troops sent by Henry VII to quell an uprising in the district when the more passionate natives had backed the pretender Prince, Warbeck, and gotten involved in Flamank's fifteenth-century tax rebellion—but no real damage was done to the house then or by the corrosive sea winds that blew centennial after centennial upon the high moor.

Of course, nothing short of cannon shot would have been able to mar the massive stone structure. The exterior ground floor walls were in places an arm's length in breadth, and the interior walls nearly four hand-spans. The lintel over the heavy plank door that led into the dining room was of itself a massive piece of masonry, likely looted from some ancient tomb, Amarantha thought, with a small shake of her head.

Such re-use of stones was common in Cornwall, but made her uncomfortable. It wasn't that she was superstitious about vandalizing pagan graves but ... such was still desecration of someone's final resting place. And it seemed unwise to build tombstones into the very walls of one's home. Though there might be no danger of contagion from ancient ills, at the very least, such reminders of the deceased depressed the spirit. And yet few persons shared her distaste for the habit. Granite was hard to carve, and it was asking a

19

lot of people to ignore these conveniently quarried stones available on the moor.

Amarantha glanced to her right where she knew another borrowed stone to be. The entrance to the house was likewise framed by the irregular curved granite quoins of darkest gray peculiar to many of the moor tombs. It was so wide that a mounted steed might be ridden through it straight into the never-used fireplace, which was roughly the size of a horse's stall and rather better decorated, though less warm than Talland's small barn where the gardener and groom lived with Uncle Cyril's one fat pony.

It was unfortunate that she was obliged to pass under the stones whenever she left the house, because it felt rather like she was walking into and out of a mausoleum, but Mrs. Polreath and the cook, Pendennis, were adamant that she could not come and go through the kitchen like a servant, so she had little choice but to pass beneath the shadowy granite arch whenever exiting or entering the premises.

To be fair, the shadows in the entry hall were unavoidable, regardless of its stone's origins. Casements in Talland House looking outward toward moor and sea were small and narrow—only wide enough for an archer to shoot through—though they were rather larger in the enclosed courtyard at the south side of the house, which had a generous suntrap where the cook's herb garden grew.

The house had eight bedrooms on the second floor and as many rooms below, so it was not confining in size, but sometimes the lower rooms appeared smaller than they were because of the poor light. The ceilings throughout *Lorelei* were dark and timbered and high trussed, which made them rather cold and dark. An effort had been made to relieve some of the gloom by white-washing the walls with a mixture of unslacked lime and Spanish whiting, but it was not wearing well under the onslaught of sea air, and the walls had taken on a peculiar shade of shadowy gray more suited, in Amarantha's opinion, to a fortress dungeon than a home.

The whole imposing edifice was topped with a heavy scantle slate roof inset with tiny gables where pigeons roosted in the spring and summer. The stair and gables were the only touches of architectural frivolity. In all, it was an impressive residence but long neglected, and it needed some smartening. Amarantha made a mental note to inquire about paint and plaster on her next trip into the village. The house had the potential to be a dignified, if somber, masterpiece, and she intended to assist it to its full potential.

"Uncle Cyril?"

"Hmm?" Cyril Stanhope looked up from his sheaves of notes and peered at his niece across the table. "Oh, good morning, Amy dear. Slept well, did you?"

"Yes, indeed." Perhaps repeating the lie would make it so.

"Good. Very good. The fresh moor air is just the thing for putting color in the cheeks."

The Bodmin's air, or something, had certainly rouged his cheeks into apple brightness, though he looked less jolly than Mrs. Polreath, as he was cadaverously thin, tall and long-limbed. His attire was also very much haphazard in its style and color, where

21

Mrs. Polreath was always scrupulously tidy in her dark brown gowns.

"I am certain that is true," she agreed politely before going on. "Uncle, I was thinking that perhaps we should attend church this Sunday."

"Church?" He blinked at her. "But there is no need to go there. It is not at all ancient and has no associations with the Mabinogion tales. Perhaps later we can visit St. Catherine's. And certainly you must see Tresco."

"I know the new church has no Arthurian legends associated with it, sir. But I was not thinking of Arthurian romanticism just now."

"You weren't?" he asked vaguely, clearly wanting to return to his papers.

"No, I was thinking that it was time that I made the acquaintance of the illustrious Rector Adair. He is our nearest neighbor and only likely society. We have an obligation to call upon him."

"Needn't go to church to do that," he assured her, relieved. "Just follow the path that goes right from the door. It'll take you straight to Tamlane's cottage. It is called Penrose by the locals. You can't miss it. It has this damned topsy-turvy roof upon it—a great ugly pigeon house, too, patterned after some bloody heathen palace in the Holy Land seen by a Penrose crusader who left a drawing to inspire his descendants or some such rubbish. There's a large mounting block plopped square in the lawn like it was dropped by a giant and never taken up again. Should have been moved years ago, but the Penroses were always a superstitious lot. The whole place is an abortion of bad taste. Women think it charming. You'll know it at once."

Mrs. Polreath snorted as she laid a platter of toasted bread upon the table, but Cyril did not apologize for his language and Amarantha didn't expect him to. He had made it plain upon her arrival that he was a bachelor and too old to learn new ways. He kept early hours, was largely antisocial, drank immoderately upon occasion, did not attend church and used profanity whenever he felt so moved. Mrs. Polreath had told her that before the new rector had settled into Blesland's parish, Uncle Cyril had been fined regularly for such defiance, as well as for breaking the eight-bell curfew by burning house fires late into the night—it was his house, after all, and if he chose to burn it down it was no one's business but his own. As he had money and a great deal of arrogance, these fines had not troubled him, and Cyril had managed to outlive his nemesis.

There was a new rector now, and Tamlane Adair did not bother the country folk with town laws, so harmony had been restored between town and church. In fact, the only thorns left plaguing the neighborhood were the excise men imported from Sussex to collect taxes and ferret out smugglers, and a small band of soldiers posted at Bodmin Town who were only rarely seen. The current holder of the unenvied position of chief tax collector was a pompous upstart named Percy Aldridge. He was, without argument, the least popular man on Bodmin Moor.

None of her uncle's habits bothered Amarantha. She too had always used profanity when it suited her and occasionally joined her father in an after-dinner brandy when he was feeling lonely or garrulous, and she attended church only when she felt the need to socialize. Other than Cyril being in her father's place, drinking a little more heavily and often, and their having fewer guests in to dine, nothing had changed from her early life.

"But, Uncle Cyril, don't you think it might present a better appearance if I met the rector in church?" Amarantha suggested. "One does not usually just call upon a person without some previous acquaintance."

"Don't be a mealy mouthed maledisant, girl. Visit Tamlane if you want. No one will think a thing of your visiting the rector. I do it once in a while myself. The man consorts with all sorts of unsavory specimens—why would he object to you?"

Amarantha gave up her appeal for traditional decorum as it was plainly falling on deaf ears and deadened sensibilities. There were better uses for her breath.

"Then I shall visit him today and invite him to a meal on Saturday evening—if Mrs. Polreath is agreeable," she added.

"Fine, splendid," Cyril answered with indifference.

"That would be lovely, dearie," the housekeeper assured her. "I'm sure that I always feel better when Rector Adair is near. He was gone nearly a week this time. That's time enough for the devil's beast to start stalking the moor again." She *tsked* and shook her head.

It was Cyril's turn to snort.

"Superstitious nonsense! I have told you a dozen times that the devil does not go about in a sable coach pulled by headless horses. Why, the roads around here are a penance! He'd break an axle if he tried trundling over the moor even with horses that had their heads firmly attached. And the so-called Beast of Bodmin is just a large, feral cat."

"The devil has great powers," Mrs. Polreath said, nodding significantly. "The only reason he and the beast trouble us not is because Rector Adair is ever vigilant in the neighborhood. I shall ask Pendennis to make him a pig's head pudding to celebrate his return."

She turned and beamed at Amarantha.

"Now, Dearie, if the rector is out this morn, you just leave word with his man, Trefry. The creature is quite stupid and illiterate, but will give the rector your message. And you needn't wait for your uncle to attend church. Pendennis and I always go. We shall walk you down to the village so you will not get lost."

"Thank you," Amarantha said, not betraying by so much as a flickering of an eyelid that she found the notion of getting lost on the way to the village amusing. There was but one path to Blesland and it was well marked.

"Speaking of the devil," Cyril muttered. "Trefry looks like a lesser demon. They should hang him from a parapet to scare away witches."

"Trefry at least attends church on occasion! If the Evil One has not visited this house, it is only because you are already *His*, and he needn't bother to make greater effort," Mrs. Polreath scolded boldly.

"Confound it, woman! There is no devil on the moor. He's too busy in Scotland murdering Jacobites to bother plaguing Cornwall." Cyril, suddenly recalling Amarantha's unhappy associations with the North, cast his niece an apologetic glance.

She lowered one eyelid in a quick wink to reassure him that she was not hurt.

"The Evil One is everywhere looking for sinners," Mrs. Polreath, oblivious to Amarantha's past sorrows, contradicted her employer. "He cannot still be in Scotland, for he has been seen more than once riding on the moor when the moon is small."

Amarantha sipped her tea but said nothing. She did not wish to hurt Mrs. Polreath, but she did not believe the story of the devil and his headless horses either, though her skepticism had nothing to do with potential broken axles on mythical coaches, but rather with the knowledge that smuggling was a favorite occupation of the locals and had been from the time of the Killgrew pirates. Without a doubt, there were strange things happening on Bodmin's moor at night. Their little hamlet was too well stocked with brandy, milled soap and even tea—items not commonly available to small-town folk. Even in London the price of these items was dear due to the taxes levied upon them and many merchants did not carry them.

"No!" Cyril looked up from his notes and frowned. "I mean, no, don't prepare pig's head pudding. Make a pilchard and leek pie and pease pudding. And some oyster soup. And do it quietly for I am occupied with some translations and this ridiculous babble is interrupting me!"

Mrs. Polreath sniffed as she left the room, but did not take offense. She had been with Cyril Stanhope long enough to grow accustomed to his ways. She saw it as her Christian duty to persist in her attempts to make him see the error of his heathen habits, but she had long abandoned any real hope of converting him to the path of righteousness.

"I, too, shall leave you in peace," Amarantha said, putting down her cup and taking a piece of toasted bread so that Pendennis would not be offended by her failure to eat. She didn't want the coarse bread, but the pigeons had come to expect some scraps tossed into the bushes at the time of her morning walk and were apt to follow her until they got it.

"Thank you, dear," he said without irony or intended offense, then returned to his scribblings. "This afternoon I shall be going out to Trethevy Quoit if you would care to join me."

"If I have returned from the rector's by then, I shall be happy to."

"Good. It is an amazing portal dolmen. Quite antique."

"I shall look forward to seeing it," she answered with more politeness than truth. The ancient tombs all looked rather alike to her, their carvings of forgotten centuries buried under years of lichen and moss, but she did enjoy the long walks over the moor with the wind blowing through her hair, which she mostly left unbound these days. It made her feel free, and freedom was a commodity she found that she valued dearly.

The air outside Talland House was still crisp but warming rapidly under the golden sun. Though inland from the coast, the breezes carried the clean scent of the sea overlaid with apple blossoms and gorse and a distant smell of burning peat. The cold and damp—and futility—of filthy London couldn't have been farther away from the sun-washed land on that spring morning.

Tregengon, the groom, was out in the garden polishing a bit of tack as he visited with Penkevil, the gardener. They nodded politely as Amarantha passed, smiling benevolently as she rid herself of the pigeons' breakfast. The two men rarely spoke to her as she did not speak their native tongue and their English was minimal.

Following her uncle's instructions, she soon reached the rector's quaint house. To a man who appreciated living in a squat, gray square, the rector's residence no doubt appeared wildly whimsical. But Amarantha was not so fond of the traditional moor buildings, and she rather liked the cottage's uneven angles and roofline of random rag and slate that rose above the small wooded hillside in fanciful fits and starts.

She pushed by some exuberant greenery that blocked the path from Talland House to the cottage and came to the side garden. There was not a great deal to the plantings: a small patch of grass before the house, trimmed carelessly, especially about the mounting block that offended her uncle's aesthetic taste, and there were a great many shrubs that had not known a gardener's shears for a decade or more. The grandest of the bushes was giant lilac whose new blossoms perfumed the air with a thick sweetness as she brushed by it and set its bruised blooms dancing.

She paused for a moment to watch some silly butterflies gamboling about a stray vine of twining honeysuckle that had wandered onto the lawn and over the giant stone. They disported with its golden flowers, careless of the lazy bumblebees that filled the air with a sleepy drone as they gathered their nectar. It was a wonderfully peaceful sound.

Uncle Cyril was correct; the rector's house, at least from the exterior, was delightful to her. It was so much more welcoming than Talland House.

She turned from the flowers to face the building itself. The disheveled air of Penrose Cottage was charming on that bright morning, though Amarantha rather suspected that it would appear altogether more forbidding on a winter's night with the cold wind stirring the overgrown bushes, which gave its walls the semblance of life. If she lived there, all the shrubbery would be pruned back a pace so that it did not abrade the wall.

But perhaps the ghostly tapping would not trouble a man who routinely met and rebuked the devil. She grinned. Whimsical and mysterious, it was the perfect residence for the illustrious, ghost-hunting Rector Adair. She could not wait to meet the old gentleman.

Taking a deep breath of the sweet air, Amarantha dusted the last of the crumbs from her hands and stepped up to the front door with all the brazen confidence of a mannerless gypsy. Country ways were still odd and new to her. In London, she would never have performed this task—a coachman or groom would have done it for her. Of course, in London, she would never have gone alone, on foot, to call on a gentleman—or anyone—before noon. Smiling at the notion of the figure she would make, could her Metropolis acquaintances see her, she grasped the heavy knocker and applied it enthusiastically, expecting the same hollow thud of summons made by the *Lorelei*'s door.

The knocker rang out like a cannonade set off in the interior of a drum. There was a brass strike plate mounted beneath the giant knocker. The sound was so loud, Amarantha winced at the percussion's long-lived echoes and stepped back a pace to save her ears from the din.

Before she could recover herself, a very ugly man, who she assumed from her uncle's unflattering description was Trefry, answered the summons. He appeared with alacrity on the shallow step, throwing back the door with a heavy fist and looking about in some alarm.

Amarantha sighed. Doubtless, her knocking had sounded like a summons to judgment day, or, at the very least, a frantic command for assistance. She made a mental note to be less forceful in the future when she visited her neighbor. She did not want to give the old cleric a spasm.

The rector's man was not actually scowling, but appeared rather taken aback to see a strange female standing upon the step instead of someone he knew. He squinted at her and slowly beetled his brow.

"Deth da!" she said boldly, offering a smile in apology. She had been paying careful attention to the locals' conversation and thought that she had learned the basic Cornish—or *Kernowek,* as they called it—greetings.

The gargoyle made no reply to her salutation and continued to stare out of suspicious, slitted eyes. Deciding that perhaps she had not quite mastered the local dialect after all, she tried again in English. "Good morning," she announced pleasantly, if with slightly less enthusiasm than her first greeting. "Is Rector Adair at home? I am Cyril Stanhope's niece."

The man stared a while longer, then finally muttered: *"Ez."*

Amarantha was relieved to discover he wasn't mute. However, he appeared quite deficient in mental capacity as he continued standing in the doorway and staring blankly.

"The rector," she prompted. "I would like to see him."

Trefry studied her a moment more and then jerked his head, seeming to indicate that she should enter the house. Amarantha hesitated a moment until he jerked his head more emphatically and added: *"Bettergogitun."*

Amarantha had also been pursuing the local *patois* dialect of Cornwallian English and thought she understood that he was saying that he would fetch the rector, so she smiled again and stepped into the entry hall.

Though suddenly feeling a bit awkward about intruding upon their neighbor without notice or even a calling card, she was pleased to finally see the house's cheery interior. The floors were neatly laid with a marble the color of a blue-green sea, and the walls were recently white-washed to the healthy color of pearls that showed no sign of disintegration. Perhaps it would be possible to find someone to do something with Talland House's flaking fortifications. She would ask the rector for a recommendation.

The butler started to leave, but then, as an apparent afterthought, Trefry pointed at a carved bench and said sternly: *"Ullonaminit."*

"Certainly," she said, seating herself with care. She had discarded the panniers of her skirts upon departing London, and without the metal frame to hold them out they were overly long to wear with out tying up. Unfortunately, she had not found the time to securely stitch all her dresses' alterations, and the one she was wearing was only haphazardly pinned into place.

The bench, she discovered while trying not to squirm under Trefry's squinty gaze, was worked end to end with sharp, clinging curlicues that made it hazardous to cloth and uncomfortable to the unpadded body. She began to hope that Rector Adair was not the sort of minister who believed in the mortification of the flesh, who would keep her waiting as punishment for her early call. Rector Adair was respected at Talland House, but she could place no reliance upon her uncle's or Mrs. Polreath's taste in company.

Trefry snorted and shook his head, either in disbelief, disapproval, or to rid himself of the lingering ringing in his ears caused by the knocker, and disappeared through a narrow, foreshortened doorway that led into the interior of the house. Belatedly, it occurred to Amarantha that elderly Rector Adair might still be abed resting up from his week of travel.

The bench truly was an instrument of punishment not meant to be long endured, and Amarantha was relieved to hear brisk footsteps returning down the narrow corridor. She rose thankfully to her feet, shaking out her skirts and retrieving a polite smile for her host.

The man who entered the room was not at all what she anticipated. To begin with, she had expected a gentleman of mature years: small, wiry, stern, gray-haired as many of the village fishermen were.

But the famous rector was none of these things. He was tall enough to have to duck under the low doorway, and he moved with a sort of careless grace that had to be deliberately cultivated, as he was too tall and muscled to have achieved such languid movement without practice. He was also possessed of a thick mane of dark hair that was unbound and unpowdered. Though there was no reason for it, she was pleased that he wore his own hair and not a wig, and that he had not tortured it with curling tongs. His eyes, she saw at once, were not a common watery blue but the light green of a cat. He did not look Cornish.

He didn't look like a rector either.

Though she should have guessed it from his name, she had not until that moment realized that Tamlane Adair was a Scotsman.

Unbidden, there sprang to mind a verse from an old folksong.

> *O I forbid ye, maidens a',*
> *That wear gold on your hair,*
> *To come or gae by Carterhaugh;*
> *For young Tamlane is there.*
>
> *There's none, that gaes by Carterhaugh,*
> *But maun leave him a wad;*
> *Either gold rings, or green mantles,*
> *Or else their maidenhead.*

"Mistress Stanhope?" The voice was soft and deep as velvet and twice as appealing. It hadn't a trace of fiery brimstone in it, just the familiar, melodious brogue of the highlands that was all by itself a seduction.

Amarantha blinked twice. Faced with this unexpected vision of a childhood legend, she had a sudden horror that she might, like the "fair Janet" in the folksong, have lilac blossoms scattered in her hair—which was also unbound and likely snarled from the breeze that blew constantly over the moor! It belatedly occurred to her that she was hardly properly attired for an ecclesiastical visit.

Amarantha suppressed a moan, thinking unkind thoughts about her uncle for failing to mention that the rector was so very young and handsome, and regretting her disorder keenly. She could only hope that it did not give him a permanent disgust of her.

"I am Amarantha Stanhope," she said finally, then paused, shocked that she had presented this stranger with her given name. She began to color. Off-balanced by her mistake, she blurted out: "I am Cyril Stanhope's niece. I am sorry to intrude upon you without warning, but I was feeling remorseful that I have been so slow to make your acquaintance and decided to chance finding you at home to visitors."

He laughed softly, apparently not offended by her words or person.

"But surely that apology should be mine," he answered. "It is, after all, my duty to greet new parishioners. I hope you will excuse me on this occasion. I have not been remiss without reason. Please come inside. I can't imagine why Trefry left you in the drafty hall, and I hope you did not try and sit on that ghastly bench. It leaves bruises. Trefry sometimes lures people into waiting there. It is some perversity of humor that makes him pull these tricks."

"It is revenge, most likely," she muttered beneath her breath, resisting the urge to rub at those bruises.

Tamlane smiled. Evidently his hearing was excellent.

"If it wasn't a relic of my grandfather's, I would burn it. Or perhaps I should use it in place of the stocks. It would surely cure the most recalcitrant sinner."

"That seems too cruel a punishment."

"Indeed."

The rector gestured toward another doorway, and only then did Amarantha notice that he was coatless and his cuffs were tucked up his sleeves, as though he had been engaged in some physical task and had not spared the time to dress himself before coming to her.

She damned the doorknocker for raising such a din of false alarm.

"If I've come at a bad time," she began apologetically, gesturing to the front door in an offer to depart.

"Is this familial belief in magical intuition? Ah—no! 'Tis observation," he said, grimacing as he also took notice of his unfinished attire and began untucking his ruffles. "Please, don't give the matter another thought. I have only just returned from Penzance and Padstow. It is market day there, and since the carter is ill I took the opportunity to bring some supplies for the village."

"Penzance and Padstow? Has the devil been abroad there too?" she asked without thinking.

The rector's green eyes returned to her face. They were amused.

"Indeed. However he did not follow me home, so it is quite safe for you to step into my library. Trefry did not say why you have come to call, but I should be happy to assist you in any manner that I am able. I trust that your uncle is well."

"Very, thank you. I do not actually require any assistance—*at present*," Amarantha answered, allowing Rector Adair to escort her though the low door into his library. It was a pleasant room, a bit small with some oddly angled nooks, but with the friendly piles of books and folios, and a small, blackened fireplace with an over-mantel carved with sea creatures and mythical beasts; it had a definite fairy-tale charm.

"Then this is a social visit?"

"Purely." Her eyes returned to the rector's face. Charming as the room was, it could not long compete with its owner. "I am sorry if I caused you alarm. I was not expecting the door knocker to be so loud."

" 'Tis the brass strike-plate. I installed it so that we would be able to hear the knocker from anywhere in the house."

"I imagine you can hear it, and from the village as well," she muttered.

The green eyes gleamed.

"Ah well, so this is a neighborly call. I supposed it was too much to hope that your uncle had had a sudden conversion of faith and required my immediate presence to witness." His smile was swift and did wonderful things to his already handsome face.

"That would certainly be a remarkable conversion to witness," Amarantha agreed, knowing that she shouldn't say such things to a stranger, but finding herself completely disarmed by the lack of formality in this most unrector-like minister. Her first unforced smile in six months curved her lips and brought a sparkle to her usually sober gray eyes.

Rector Adair blinked twice and then cleared his throat.

"Won't you take a seat?" he asked, gesturing to the two chairs that flanked the cold fireplace. "These are quite safe, I assure you."

"Thank you." Amarantha again seated herself with care. A quick peek told her that there were no stray blossoms on her bodice, though the dark hair resting on her bosom was definitely not neat. She resisted the futile urge to restore order to her tresses since unkempt informality seemed to be the order of the day, and she did not want to call further attention to her disorder of dress by fussing. Perhaps the rector was one of those men who did not notice female attire.

The rector joined her immediately. His booted legs were long enough to brush up against her skirts as he settled into his chair, but he seemed not to notice the contact.

"I have come to plead with you for company on Saturday evening," Amarantha said honestly. "Mrs. Polreath and I are in need of spiritual comfort and deliverance from great mental anguish."

"Indeed?" It was too much to say that he was startled, but she knew that she had caught his attention.

"It isn't that the ancient portal dolmens of the area

are not stunning," she went on, keeping her mouth prim, though she felt sure her eyes were giving away her lack of seriousness. "But I do rather feel that I have explored this area of conversation—in depth. And poor Mrs. Polreath has begun speaking fondly of the Evil One coming in person to take Uncle Cyril away in his sable coach. Something must be done to restore accord. Congenial company seemed the easiest and safest recourse, so I have come to intrude upon your good nature."

As she had hoped, this flight of fancy brought another swift smile to the rector's mobile face.

"I understand completely." But though he smiled, she had the feeling that he was calculating some difficulty. He added, almost randomly: "Cyril is much given to scholarly conversation. I imagine that it can grow tedious after a time for those who do not share his passions."

"Quite so. I am glad to find you sympathetic. But perhaps you have a previous engagement for this Saturday? I realize that I have not given you much warning," she said, breaking every rule of propriety her mother had taught her by pressing for an immediate answer.

"I have no other engagement for dinner on Saturday evening," he assured her swiftly, apparently putting inner thoughts aside. "I am most happy to be intruded upon and will gladly join you in this mission of mercy."

Amarantha felt oddly relieved to hear it. Perhaps she was more bored and in need of company than she realized.

"I am sorry that there won't be any pigshead pudding," she said, feeling at once more gay since the invitation had been accepted.

"What?"

. A dimple appeared in her cheek and Amarantha found herself chuckling. "Very well then, if you must have the truth—"

"Certainly I must," he interjected, his eyes again laughing. "It is my professional duty to encourage the daily use of honesty amongst my flock."

"Then I am not the least bit sorry that we shan't be having pigshead pudding. Instead we are to have pilchard and leek pie. And pease pudding."

"And oyster soup?"

Amarantha chuckled again.

"You have dined with my uncle before?" she guessed.

"Many times."

"And you like pilchard and leek pie?"

"Almost as much as star gazy pie."

"What is that?" she asked, intrigued by the pretty name.

"Mackerel with tarragon and parsley."

"Oh, more fish," she said, disappointed. "I thought it was bad luck to bake fish into pies."

"Only into pasties. And that is on account of the *knockers*."

"Knockers?"

"Has your uncle not told you of them?"

"Unless they were contemporaries of Uther Pendragon, I am afraid that Uncle Cyril probably won't discuss them with me any time soon. Arthurian legends are his current preoccupation."

"Then I feel it is my duty to tell you of them, lest

you betray your ignorance in company. The *knockers* are the wee folk who live in the mines. The miners often leave a portion of their pasties for them as a bribe for good fortune, and I believe that they have no taste for mackerel or herring."

"The wee folk are notoriously finicky about their food. Many in your own land are said to dine on nothing but white milk and cake."

"My land?" The rector asked. He did not visibly tense, but his mobile face stilled and he leaned back in his chair.

"You are Scots, are you not?" Amarantha asked, feeling suddenly timid that she had blundered into forbidden territory. More than anyone, she knew that some subjects were too painful for casual discussion. She said diffidently: "Tamlane is a rather famous name in the north . . . from the ballad?"

"Ah, so you are a folklorist also?"

"Hardly. But my mother was a Cameron of Erracht," she admitted with a small lift of her chin. "Though I have never lived in Scotland, I know the northern accent and stories well. And this particular poem is quite famous."

An eyebrow flew upward, telling her that he was aware of the Errachts' role in the failed Jacobite uprising.

"That would explain your knowledge of Gaelic names. My maternal grandfather was Scots—a Gordon, in fact—and my father, obviously, was an Adair. But my mother was a Penrose, born and bred here like all the Penroses before her to the beginning of time. This has been my residence for some time now. I consider it my only home. In spite of my famous name, I am a Scotsman no more. It might be best for you to also reconsider advertising your connection to the Camerons—at least for the time being. Even in Cornwall, there are those who are not sympathetic to the rebellion."

Amarantha colored, half embarrassed that she had introduced the subject and half angry at the rector's suggestion. It was perfectly sound advice, but she hated that such deception was necessary even in this place. It made her feel cowardly and disloyal to her family though she had not herself embraced the Cause.

In a second effort to break the new tension between them she grasped at a seemingly safe topic. "So this is a family home, unconnected to the church? I had heard it called Adair House, but Uncle says that it is Penrose Cottage after your mother's family?"

He inclined his head formally, lacing his long fingers.

"The vicarage burned some years ago during the residence of my predecessor's tenure."

"How unfortunate."

"Hmm." The sound was neither agreement nor disagreement.

She said after a moment: "It is lovely and refreshingly informal after Talland House. So much of Cornwall is charming. Very different from London. I believe that Talland House was built by one of King Richard's appointees. It has a very defensive flavor about it. I don't think Cornwall agreed with the architect."

"Likely not. He was English after all."

41

"But your family must have loved it here to build such a house."

"They did. And I am likewise fond of the old sod, in spite of its inconveniently short doorways," the rector admitted, his expression softening slightly. "I was gone for some years in the north being educated to other tastes, but this cottage and I rather suit one another now that I have grown and settled into my occupation."

Before she could answer, there came a familiar heavy footfall from the entry hall. Trefry appeared almost at once. He thrust his heavy jaw halfway through the door and said: *"Goynary?"*

"Awright'n aree?" the rector asked, a slight frown forming between his brows.

"Ez." The gargoyle also frowned at her and retreated.

Amarantha stood up. The mood had turned serious at the mention of Scotland and the earlier playfulness was not to be retrieved. Plainly, the rector was busy and it was time to leave.

"I must be going," she said, retreating into formality. "The dolmens and Uncle Cyril await."

The rector also rose. Standing so close together made his unusual height very apparent, and it seemed to her that she could almost feel the heat of his body.

"Thank you for the invitation," he said politely, making no effort to detain her and giving no apology for speaking in a foreign tongue without translating, even though they both knew that it was very bad manners. "Seven o'clock?"

"You do know my uncle," she answered wryly.

"I shall be there. And tell Mrs. Polreath that the catch in Penzance was a good one. I shall bring her a mackerel."

"How thoughtful of you to carry a fish all the way from Penzance." Amarantha knew she sounded disappointed and didn't bother to hide her expression of skepticism about what sort of *catch* the rector referred to. Penzance was notorious, but not for its fish. And the only thing Mrs. Polreath had expressed a desire for was more tea.

A black brow lifted in question at her censorious tone.

It wasn't that she entirely disapproved of smuggling. She could well understand why people engaged in it. But it was still an illegal activity, and she thought it ill became the rector to set such a poor example for his flock. And she certainly did not approve of Mrs. Polreath engaging in such unwise enterprises. It could lead to trouble for uncle, who was too unobservant to have any inkling of what was afoot in his household—and, one had to admit, too cantankerous to care if he did know.

"You disdain our local sea economy?" he asked as she turned to leave the room.

"I think it is perhaps a very foolish fisherman who goes to Penzance at this time," she said without turning. She felt ridiculously disappointed in Rector Adair. "I have met this Preventive, Percy Aldridge. Your local excise man does not have the finest of minds, but he has ambition and he is certainly determined to—"

"Put an end to poaching and untaxed importation?" the rector suggested.

"Precisely." Amarantha stopped when she reached the front door and turned around to face her host. She had to tilt her head as a child to an adult to look into his face, but she did not let this deter her. "The man is pompous, pretentious, dull-witted, officious, and has a face like an old suet ball—"

The vicar laughed. It was an appealing sound, hard to resist, but Amarantha remained firmly on topic.

"You are harsh, Mistress. Surely he has some fine qualities lurking in his interior. Most humans do have one or two, if one is inclined to search for them."

"Perhaps." She shrugged. "I have not seen any evidence of virtue—however, there is ambition aplenty. And only a fool would fail to comprehend that he is determined to better himself swiftly, and I do not believe that mercy and understanding for the local people's tax burden are any part of his plan or character," she warned.

"You are a very observant woman, Mistress Stanhope, to have seen this all in the weeks since your arrival." His mocking green eyes laughed down at her. "But you may rest at ease. I assure you that I returned from Penzance with a crate of salted fish had from a lawful Cornish fishing vessel that has paid its taxes. There were witnesses."

"I have no doubt that you did and there were."

Annoyed that he was playing games with her when she was serious about her concern, Amarantha turned abruptly and reached for the door's latch. But the rector's long fingers were there before hers, his chest brushing against her shoulder as he trapped her in the small space between his body and the plank door. He smelled betrayingly of lavender soap, not brine, and as she had thought, his body was hot to the touch.

"If you please," she said without turning. His voice was not entirely steady, and she could feel a flush stain her cheeks as awareness of his maleness returned.

He hesitated for an instant before opening the door, but in the end merely said: "Thank you for the invitation, Mistress Stanhope. I shall look forward to continuing our conversation on Saturday night."

There came a fleeting touch on her arm, too brief to be a caress and yet too intimate for indifferent politeness.

Amarantha nodded and walked away without looking back, though she was convinced that she could feel the rector's catlike eyes focused on her spine until the sprawling lilac hid her from his gaze.

She wandered slowly along the path toward Talland House, her hand protectively covering the place where Tamlane's fingers had briefly lain. In the back of her mind a notion was born. It was a half-formed idea, vague about the method of execution, but the seed of conviction had been firmly planted. The rector was going to go on denying his—and Mrs. Polreath's—activities until he was caught under circumstances where such denial was impossible.

It was her duty to discover him and put an end to such dangerous foolishness before he—or Mrs. Polreath—was caught by someone else.

The natives to the south did not understand the mood of the government, she thought, worrying at her lower lip. The regime in London was daily growing more angry and vengeful with those they perceived to be lawless, disloyal people. Parliament, at the urging of the king, had this last year passed a number of Draconian laws designed to suppress "acts of sedition and rebellion." The wrath that had fallen upon poor Scotland could easily be visited upon Cornwall.

Amarantha shuddered at the thought of the destruction of her haven.

Chapter Two

"Of course, the Celts under Vercingetorix finally made a stand against Caesar's Romans in 52 A.D., but by then it was too late. For too long they had relied upon personal magic to ward off the tides of change, and political and military unity could not be achieved in time," Cyril Stanhope lectured as he sketched.

"Magic, unless on a grand scale, would not have been effective against the Roman legion," Amarantha replied absently. "They were bred to war. Even Merlin could not defeat them."

"Indeed. Organization and logic was needed to carry the day, not bravery and belief. It happened with King Arthur and again at Flodden Field."

"And Culloden."

She was studying her surroundings carefully. Not

the tomb her uncle was admiring. That had rated no more than a quick glance. But the crushed bluebells and scuffed moss at its massive base seemed rather significant. Many things might disturb the moor's vegetation, but most of those creatures would also have eaten the tender shoots. The uncropped greenery was a sign that someone had been there lately, perhaps even occupying the stone chamber for a time.

The Trethevy Quoit was certainly large enough to house a man, or even two, along with any number of barrels or crates. One of the supporting stones had toppled, but that left six still firmly in place holding up a ceiling more than twice the height of a man and a length nearly as long. It would be a drafty place to reside, but not so uncomfortable in spring as long as it did not rain.

However, it was entirely possible that lovers had been trysting here. She knew from her uncle that many of the ancient sites were supposed to be places of pagan fertility worship. It was possible that more than one party had been paying calls on the dolmen, so such a sign of visitation didn't conclusively prove that supposed smugglers had been that way in recent days. Or ever.

And even if there had been smugglers here, there was no way to prove the rector knew of it, she thought, piqued. *It would be enough to needle him with, but some other undeniable proof would have to be sought.*

"True, niece, very true. But you must remember that the ancient Celts were a superstitious people— why they are still, in large measure, to this very day! Witness Mrs. Polreath," Cyril said in exasperation, interrupting her thoughts. "In every other way, she is an intelligent woman, but bring up some legend and she is warding off the evil eye. Still, we must be understanding, I suppose. Where there is dread, there will always be rituals and religions to chase away the unknown. And there has certainly been dread in this place from the beginning of time—or, as the locals put it, from the *days when swallows built nests in old men's beards*."

"And where there is religion, there are sacrifices and war," Amarantha said softly. "I suppose 'tis the natural way of things. And if not war for this reason, then 'twould be for profit or power."

Cyril sent his niece a piercing glance.

"You are speaking of the recent troubles in the north?"

"I am speaking of pagan sacrifices," Amarantha said firmly, turning away from the dolmen. "Did the Cornish drown their sacrifices as the Scots and Irish did?"

"I believe it to be possible, though I have never discovered bodies in any of the local bogs," he answered, willing to be diverted from an unpleasant topic. The ancient dead were easily discussed. More recent tragedies left him uncertain of what to say to his troubled niece. "I have looked for evidence that the cult of the severed head reached this area, but the artifacts are not conclusive. Certainly they made offerings but . . ."

Amarantha let his words fade from her thoughts as she looked into the blue sky and marveled at the beauty of the wild curlews that soared there. They never ceased their flying and muted singing as they caroled to the endless sea. She envied them. Unlike people, they were not halted by the gray wall of the ocean, but could go on flying forever—past drowned Lyonesse and to the very ends of the world, if that was what their hearts commanded.

Saturday came without any additional proofs of perfidy on the rector's part, or even inspirations for finding such facts. Amarantha should have been piqued at her failure but instead found herself humming happily as she prepared for their dinner guest. Her brocade gown—which she had managed to lace herself into unaided—was a little grand for a small, country gathering, but it was quite pretty and the pale, silvery green of new willow was flattering to her and rather neatly matched the rector's eyes.

"Rubbishing thoughts," she said to the image in her glass as she twitched her lace into place. The reflection only smiled back. She did not notice that the tune on her lips was the old Gaelic ballad of Tamlane.

A knock fell upon the front door, and presently there came the murmur of voices. Mrs. Polreath spoke, then the rector and then Uncle Cyril. It was time for her to go downstairs—past time, in fact. She had fussed long enough.

Amarantha stepped carefully on the poorly lighted *Lorelei* stair, not raising her eyes until she was safely at the bottom of the worn treads. It did not amaze her that Uncle Cyril had disappeared into a parlor without her, and Mrs. Polreath to the kitchens to harass Pendennis, but she was surprised and pleased that Rector Adair had remained politely in the hall to offer a supportive arm to his tardy hostess.

"Good evening, Mistress Stanhope," he said politely. "I hope this evening finds you well."

Amarantha was very glad that she had taken pains with her appearance, for the Rector had certainly dressed for the occasion. His coat was of a sober brown, but the uncut velvet was most elegant in its austere design and the embroidered waistcoat beneath was a true work of art. Painted by the light of the candle branches flanking the narrow board, he looked as elegant as any gentleman in London—and more than twice as appealing. It was ironic that after searching out the eligible males of the capital and finding none who appealed to her, that she should come to remote Cornwall and discover a man in religious orders who would probably never consider entering into even a light dalliance.

Of course, she was not considering him as a lover, but rather as an opponent—and for this, his calling was of no consequence.

"Good evening, Rector," she replied, accepting the proffered arm with a cool smile. The battle was joined, and she was prepared for the skirmish. "My apologies for tardiness. I should have been here to greet you."

"Tardiness is the prerogative of ladies," he answered with a small smile of his own. The tone was polite, but she suspected he knew well that the answer would be aggravating. Therefore she resolved not to display any irritation, nor any discomfort when he covered her hand and gave it a light squeeze in a most familiar manner.

"Very true," she agreed airily, as they strolled toward the parlor. "That, and the fact that a gentleman should not contradict a lady are our two greatest advantages in social intercourse with gentlemen. With

51

them, a woman of less than needle wit and education may still enjoy herself in masculine company."

"I am not sure which is more painful, the sharp tongue wielded by the dull-witted or the stinging barbs of the quick humor."

"One is a slow death. The other swift and sure."

The rector laughed softly and withdrew his hand, leaving her own suddenly naked.

"Tell me, Mistress Stanhope, which are you this evening?"

"Neither, sir. Behold! I am a lady."

Tamlane's eyes danced, but before he could reply, Uncle Cyril interrupted. "Ah! There you are, Amy, and not a moment too soon. Mrs. Polreath shall have dinner served in but a moment. We should go in."

As if to confirm his prediction, Mrs. Polreath's light step could be heard coming toward them. The rector, not waiting for a summons, turned his charge about gracefully and the three of them started back across the entry hall toward the dining room. Uncle Cyril found the hobbling pace required by Amarantha's dress to be awkward, but it did not disturb Rector Adair.

"Well, aren't you a grand sight, dearie," Mrs. Polreath said happily, meeting them in the hall. "I am sure I have never seen a gown half so elegant in all of Cornwall. It must have cost the earth."

"Nor have I seen such a gown outside of London. There is enough cost in the lace alone to clothe any ten women in muslin. Unless of course it was not subjected to duty." The tone behind the rector's words was more mocking than complimentary.

"Thank you," Amarantha answered, refusing to

blush as she met her escort's bland gaze. "It was a gift from my father. He sent the fabric and lace from France. Of course, the duties were dear. But what is a *law-respecting* person to do?"

"I imagine the taxes rivaled the cost of purchase."

"Or rather more. But Alistair always was foolish about such things," Uncle Cyril said with tactless vulgarity, taking a seat at the table without waiting for his guest or niece. "He loved fripperies."

"So, too, do I," Amarantha said, showing teeth.

"What lady would not?" Mrs. Polreath asked as she disappeared again. She knew that Cyril would begin bellowing for his soup if it was long delayed.

"That is all well and good, but many of the recent tax laws are a disgrace," Cyril Stanhope complained. "I can't imagine what Parliament was thinking enacting so many new tariffs."

"I think we are all aware of their thinking. The present Parliament has been prone in recent months to passing legislation that will subdue the North. Unfortunately, it takes no account of the suffering of common people," Amarantha said without inflection, as she arranged her nappery. Mrs. Polreath had set an attractive table. It was well that it was not an over-large board as the seating was imperfect with Uncle Cyril at its head, Amarantha at the foot and the rector midway between them. As it was, it took three branches of candles to light it and conversations needed to be conducted in a slightly raised voice if messages were to travel its length, for the room had an odd acoustic and swallowed up most sound.

"That is a tragic fact and much felt in the village . . . and elsewhere." The rector's voice was equally uninflected as he took a chair after seating Amarantha.

"It is not the first time that we have had rule by the insulting, unjust and unkind. It is the way of things that the victor is allowed to decide the rules. We should be grateful that it is London and not Rome that triumphed this time. I understand Caesar was not terribly merciful with those he conquered." Her attempt at humor did not succeed, and Amarantha closed her eyes briefly as she swallowed at the lump in her throat. This would never do! She had to regain her calm.

"Unfortunately, that is true. And many would argue that our present leaders are concerned more with private profiteering than with the safety of the realm. It seems we must needs look elsewhere for morality, justice, kindness and so forth." The rector met Amarantha's eyes and added: "Fortunately, the Cornish are a godly people and blessed with many churches where they may seek spiritual comfort and guidance."

"One might have to seek a long while to find such a list of virtues anywhere—honesty, particularly," Amarantha said pointedly, glad to have another, and more interesting topic to pursue. She bared her teeth in what might pass for a smile. "And they seem to be seeking more than *spiritual* comfort."

The rector's left eyebrow flew up. His eyes, as they held hers over the flickering candles, held the miniature lights of a dozen dancing flames. They seemed to sparkle with impish delight.

"Is that a challenge, Mistress Stanhope? An aspersion cast upon the morals of my parish for avoiding privation and suffering?" The voice was calm, even mild.

"Merely a general observation. And it was not the morals of the parish I questioned." Amarantha looked away and smiled at Mrs. Polreath as she entered with a large tureen and went carefully to the sideboard. She then nodded her consent to Uncle Cyril, who had risen and was offering to pour the wine. Cyril refused to have a butler, and Penkevil and Tregengon had proven hopeless at the task of waiting table so Cyril now performed the office himself. For good or ill, his casual manners forbade any real formality at the board.

"Think you that we are all godless heathens here in the south? Self-involved and uncaring because we choose to be cheerful and accepting about government-caused penury?" the rector inquired.

"Oh, surely not *godless*," she answered. "And I have *never* advocated accepting poverty. However, I have nothing against being cheerful. Good manners cost nothing, after all."

"That is an excellent point, Amy dear. And it is one that we should all endeavor to remember."

Amarantha looked at her uncle, pleasantly surprised that he had an opinion on this subject. He had never seemed particularly interested in the plight of the poor. She did not remain deceived for long. As usual, Cyril was thinking in terms of ancient history rather than his neighbors.

"Pagans were not godless people. Far from it. That is something which modern man has failed to understand." Uncle Cyril continued down the table to the rector's empty glass. "Of course, it has not helped that the legends have gotten so muddled up—the Irish with the Welsh and tales from the Crusades—

until one can barely sort them out. It is easy to forget that there was a profound belief in God before the Saxons came. Many of the ancient ruins suggest a great attachment to a deity not unlike the Christian savior. The Trethevy Quoit, for instance . . ."

Amarantha turned unwillingly to her guest and met the rector's twinkling eyes. She was obliged to hide a smile behind her napkin as Mrs. Polreath placed a bowl before her. Had the rector not been there, she would have been seized by irresistible sleepiness at the renewal of the topic of pagan tombs, but with Tamlane Adair present, it was impossible to feel such dull quietude.

"And have you been to see the Trethevy Quoit yet, Mistress Stanhope?" The rector asked maliciously as Uncle Cyril returned to his seat and paused in his lecture long enough to taste his soup.

"Indeed. And I found it most interesting," she answered cordially. "One would think that such old places would hold terrors for the villagers, and yet there was plain evidence that some have been visiting the site."

"Indeed." The rector's voice gave nothing away.

"Naturally, I was reluctant to suspect the worst," she said pointedly. "The Cornish are such moral people after all."

" 'I know a bank where the wild thyme blows,' " the rector said softly, yet cheerfully. He seemed impervious to her barb, just as she had feared. "I do not approve of hand-fasting, of course, but there is an old tradition of it here, and the quoits are built well away from the quagmires so are fairly safe for lovers to visit."

"I thought of that as well," Amarantha agreed amiably, earning a strange look, but no comment, from her uncle. The entire conversation was, of course, entirely beyond all social acceptability. Pagan fertility rites were quite outside the polite boundary, and to discuss modern ones was downright scandalous. Even her uncle was aware of that territorial border.

"I shall have to warn my flock to be cautious now that there is a Puritan come among us," Tamlane said.

Uncle Cyril seemed to choke on an over-hasty spoonful of soup and disappeared behind his napkin. Amarantha narrowed her eyes at the provocation. *Puritan!* There was no greater insult as far as she was concerned. She detested the joyless reformers.

"That is more sensible than terrorizing them with tales of the devil posting about the moor with a team of headless horses."

"You have no fear of the Evil One?" His manner was one of unruffled amiability. "How brave of you. It is a wonder to meet a soul so pure that it has no fear of the Father of Lies."

"Not at all. I have a lively fear of Evil, but I am unable to believe that the devil is out on the moor on moonless nights—tooling about in sable carriage drawn by decapitated horses. *Sable!* Why not ebony? Why not fiery red?"

The rector continued to smile, but said with a sudden note of true seriousness: "Believe me, Mistress, whatever the color or conveyance, there is danger abroad at night out on Bodmin Moor. This month particularly. If you do not fear the devil, then fear men. There have been some escapes by prisoners from the gaol. The poor souls are often quite mad.

57

They have likely fled the area, but caution is in order. It would not do to set your pretty nose to the wrong grindstone and end in jeopardy."

Amarantha looked again into Rector Adair's eyes and answered with equal seriousness. "I believe that there is danger, and shall use all care while investigating the *historic antiquities.*"

Cyril pushed his empty bowl away and rejoined the conversation in a determined manner.

"April is a notorious month for witches and wizards and others of that ilk. The calendar is full of strange events. There was the burning of the Scottish sorcerer, Major Weir. That was in 1670. The daft creature confessed to the authorities of his own accord, they say. Then there was the confession of Isobel Gowdie in 1662. She was another one who confessed without being put to the question. This was also the month of the witch trials in Chelmsford in 1579. Unpleasant incidents, all of them. Perhaps they were caused by all the pre-Beltane fervor that leads Celtic people astray. Why there is madhouse right here on Bodmin Moor where the gaol sends its more violent prisoners. That is likely when they made their escape. They are sometimes careless during transport—Do eat your soup before it gets cold," he recommended. "Pendennis has outdone himself."

Amarantha and the rector stared at Cyril in consternation. Unable to believe her ears, Amarantha looked down at her bowl and then at her guest. Even the rector appeared taken aback by the turn of the conversation.

"Niece, you shall have to take part in the Beltane celebrations. They have such quaint customs here.

One that is quite unique to Cornwall is the Obby Oss. It is based on the old Trojan Horse legend, I believe, but somehow the creature has become a sort of sea monster who parades through the streets to the banging of drums. Then there is the furry dance of Helston. Though that is sometimes more of a drunken revel—people galloping about in costume and making a deal of noise."

"It sounds like a night at the theatre."

"*Hmph!* London!" Cyril said with loathing. "That is another matter entirely. Nothing historical about those carryings-on!"

"Indeed, you should come to the celebration and see the Obby Oss. Though you must have a care not to be captured by it, Mistress Stanhope. It would not do for a Puritan to end as a virgin sacrifice to a sea monster."

"Far more likely to happen in London," Cyril stated. "Degenerates—all of them! It is a good thing that you are gone from there, dear. You might have come to a bad end now that you are wealthy. Fortune hunters will resort to desperate means in order to get a wealthy wife."

"The love of wealth is indeed the root of all evil," the rector agreed.

She sent first Tamlane and then her relative a withering glance.

"There is little danger of anything like that happening, I assure you. I am not so stupid as to be caught and seduced at the theatre—or anywhere else." Amarantha turned back to her plate and noticed the wax that spattered its rim. "Uncle, there is a decided draft in this room. We must have the windows examined. The candles are shedding more wax than they burn. And, Rector Adair, I have been meaning to ask you about hiring someone to whitewash our walls. Is there a local person that we might engage for the task?"

Tamlane smiled but accepted the change of subject.

"I shall inquire. This is a busy season for farmers but, for the proper wage, I am sure someone can be found."

"Thank you, I am certain that we can arrive at a fair price. My! This soup does look excellent." Amarantha took up her spoon and began eating the tepid broth with more determination than enthusiasm.

"It certainly does." Rector Adair meekly followed her lead. Amarantha was suspicious of his conversational docility and remained on guard.

"It is going to rain. Perhaps you should stay the night and not venture out into such danger," she suggested cynically as the rector consulted his timepiece for a second time. He pocketed his watch, pulled on his cloak and prepared to depart. "After all, what profit a man to gain the world but lose his freedom? Or even his life."

"I should hate to contradict a lady, but this is rather my realm of expertise, Mistress. The quote is '*what profits a man to gain the world if he loseth his soul?*' But you needn't be concerned for me. I have the strength of ten because my heart is pure. And, in any event, it is my duty to go. I cannot be deterred by weather." Tamlane set his hat upon his head, and possessed himself of her hand. His salute was too perfunctory to suit her.

Amarantha knew he was not jesting and had a moment of baffled frustration. Surely he could not believe all this talk of the devil out on the moor! If only there had been time for private conversation, she might have ferreted out his plans, but Uncle Cyril had kept their guest long over their port and now he was anxious to depart so would not stay for the tea tray brought in by Mrs. Polreath only moments before.

"Good evening, Mistress. I shall hope to see you on the morrow. Then you may judge for yourself about the villagers' morality," he said, opening the front door, making a small bow and disappearing quickly into the black night. She had not even had time to offer him the use of a lantern. Or to think of a reply to his parting verbal sling.

"Tomorrow." She would see him on the morrow— certainly—but she could also see him before then.

Amarantha was certain that he had an assignation. Since she could not imagine him calling on any respectable person at this hour, that left only various nefarious persons and occupations for him to be engaged with.

Of course, there was only one way to know for certain. Should she follow him into the dark where possible danger and certain dampness awaited?

She hesitated for only an instant. The impulse to follow the rector was not a cautious one, but she could not believe that there was anything in the way of spiritual danger waiting on the moor. Such fairy tales as Tamlane Adair told the incredulous revolted the common sense of any rational person. She would not—could not—believe that such things existed until there was evidence placed before her own eyes.

And if he was not going to meet and rebuke the devil, then he was off to meet with some human agent. And as long as the rector was present, she could not imagine him allowing any harm to befall her.

She took a deep breath and looked up at the heavy stones above the door while she debated.

Her uncle had retired to his study with a bottle of brandy, and Mrs. Polreath to the kitchen with the soiled crockery. There was no one but the stolen rocks to notice if she slipped outside for a few minutes, and they would never betray her.

Determined to discover an answer to the riddle of the rector's activities, she caught up Uncle Cyril's walking cloak, habitually left by the entrance, and pulling the door shut softly behind her, began to follow the rector home.

She had not been out walking after sunset in the country for many years and was astonished at the darkness that made up the night. It was not that she could not see, for there was nearly a half moon and the stars were very bright overhead, but after the light and order of the city, the uneven landscape seemed very open and wild and oddly unfamiliar to the eye.

There was a decided nip in the air, and Amarantha could smell a storm wind rising even before the breezes shifted and began running overland. In the dark, it was easy to imagine monsters hiding behind every stand of rustling gorse, which seemed to loom in a new and ominous manner. The path seemed distorted, too, and steeped with hidden menace. Every gruesome legend she had ever heard of Bodmin Moor presented itself to her mind, and she almost believed that the devil *could* be near.

Left on her own, she might have given in to the growing superstitious dread and turned back to the comforting light of Talland House still visible behind her, but the rector's distant yet solid form remained to guide her through the night perils. And, though her mind was overtaken with unease, her stubborn curiosity about his destination remained too strong to ignore.

Curiosity won the battle with superstition and cold. She kept on.

Presently, her intrepidity was rewarded, for rather than continuing up the drive to Penrose Cottage, the rector turned onto the path that led toward Trethevy Quoit. The way was rough, not even fit for a pony trap, and she hesitated a moment at exposing her gown and her uncle's dragging cloak to the rigors of the open moor. Some of the plants were quite sharp enough to shred her tender brocade on their briars and everything would be horribly stained.

But curiosity had been given some encouragement by the rector's actions, and was not to be denied an answer when the solution was nearby, so Amarantha held up her billowing skirts and stepped carefully after the rector's vanishing form.

The wind, as though protesting her decision to proceed, gusted suddenly and blew her straying hair across her eyes and tore her skirts from her grasp. She quickly pulled the blinding tresses away, not caring to be sightless when that unfortunate wind was

63

moaning like some lost soul forbidden from Paradise and might prevent her hearing someone coming upon her.

A quick look at the sky told her that a canopy of black thunderclouds was building in the west. Worried now that she would lose the rector if the moon was overshadowed, she hurried on her way with less concern for her clothing.

Something scuttled into her path and turned to stare at her with luminous eyes. For one moment her heart stopped dead with her feet, convinced that she was being confronted with the beast of Bodmin Moor. But then the shape gave a small mewling chuff, identifying itself as a common cat.

"Bad puss!" Amarantha scolded at a whisper. "Go back home before you are rained upon."

The cat looked away, ignoring her hypocritical advice. It sniffed at the creeping damp rising from the soggy ground and went slinking into the bushes, intent on some nocturnal activity.

Amarantha looked about after the cat was gone and discovered to her dismay that the rector had also departed. In the night and dark, his disappearance had the air of a magical vanishment.

She shivered as a particularly cold gust of air found its way beneath her borrowed cloak and brushed the base of her spine.

"Bloody hell!" she muttered, borrowing from her uncle's store of curses. She had not been in his household long but was glad to adopt his extreme candor of speech. It was so much more satisfying than muttering ladylike *luds!* on the occasions when one was truly exasperated.

She pondered a moment what course to take. The intelligent thing to do, now that her guide was gone, was to return home before she was lost on the moor and overtaken by rain. But that was also the spiritless thing to do, and she was fairly certain that she could find the trysting quoit on her own.

If it happened that the rector was not there after all, she could abandon her search and return home with her pride intact and no harm done.

But even with this decision resolved upon, it took an effort for her strike out on her own. The moor was vast and unprotected from the weight of the boiling sky, and she had never felt quite so frail and alone.

Her instincts, as usual, were found to be sound. She reached the tomb shortly after parting from the cat, and crept up to it silently. At first, she could hear nothing above the muttering wind, but as she rounded the north corner, she heard the rector's voice come plainly out of the dark.

"Show yourself. I dislike people skulking in the shrubbery."

Amarantha jumped, feeling shocked and then embarrassed at being caught spying. She made to rise, an apology on her lips, but then another voice spoke out of the night.

"Je suis ici en lieu d'ami," the other voice said reassuringly. A lantern was unshuttered, bathing the west face of the quoit in a welcoming light.

Amarantha crept as close as she dared without entering the betraying, golden pool and hunkered down in the rustling shrubbery. She peered out at the silhouettes, feeling both thrilled and vaguely terrified that her suspicions of the rector's destination had been proven correct.

"You have any cargo for me?" the rector's new friend asked. His shape was thick and stooped, and he appeared neckless. Or else he was highly muffled against the cold—and recognition.

"Not yet. On Sunday after next, if all goes well," the rector replied in French.

"*Bon.* I shall have some new deliveries then, so we may transact."

"*Oui*, but we must change location for the meeting. You might send word to the good brothers to have a care. This place has been noticed."

"By the stupid Aldridge?"

"No, by a curious female." Almost, the tone was affectionate. It was certainly amused.

"That is worse—unless she would perhaps like some bauble? A bit of lace maybe?" The rough voice was hopeful.

"I don't think that this one can be bribed with pretty trinkets," the rector replied. His answer pleased Amarantha. She did not want him to think her bribable.

"A pity. That is so much more pleasant. Shall we have to do something with her?"

Amarantha's breath froze as she awaited Tamlane's answer.

"No. It is not a great matter—simply a precaution. If the woman found this place, so may the Preventives. We shall meet in the old location at the wood by the standing stones at eleven o'clock on Sunday."

Amarantha began breathing again. She doubted that the rector was speaking of the Sabbath morning when his presence would be required in church. Besides, whatever he was doing needed the cover of night. Obviously. If this were a straightforward business transaction, the Frenchman would simply call at Penrose Cottage at a more conventional hour.

"*Bon.* 'Til Sunday then, *mon ami.* And do not catch an inflammation of the lung. This cursed winter weather lingers on."

The lantern was again shuttered. The men wasted no time in parting as the first drops of water were beginning to fall. The rector turned back toward Penrose Cottage and the Frenchman toward Camel River. Both were walking briskly.

Amarantha did not move, but stayed huddled in her shrub until the sound of footsteps faded. Her mind was buzzing like an overturned wasps' nest. The rector was sending *out* cargo? But what could that be?

Instead of answering her questions, this conversation had only raised more in her brain. And to find those answers, she would have to again follow the rector out onto the midnight moor. This time to a place she did not know.

"Bloody hell," she said, as the drops of rain began coming in earnest.

A smart woman would abandon the entire notion of repeating such an unpleasant task at the small of the moon. But she already knew that she would not make the intelligent decision.

Chapter Three

Amazingly, Amarantha slept the night through with never a dream to disturb her. She awoke late the next morning to the cooing of hungry pigeons, feeling much invigorated in body and spirit, and very pleased that she had not contracted the prophesied inflammation of the lung during the night.

Her abused brocade, when examined in the light of morning, was found to have fared less well than her person and was quite soiled about the hem and knees where she had knelt on the ground. Amarantha cursed the distinctive colored mud, which was as good as a confession of her whereabouts. Mrs. Polreath would have questions about this damage. Having no time to spare for attempting to clean it before breakfast, she thrust the stained dress in the back of the chest where Mrs. Polreath wouldn't immediately find it.

The sun was well up by the time she completed her ablutions, and there was no occasion for a morning constitutional if she intended to attend church with Mrs. Polreath and Pendennis. It was a shame that she had slept so late and could not take her lonely ramble, but she still found time to open a casement and throw a crust from her tray to the clamoring pigeons. They had become her pensioners and vociferously protested any change of routine.

Modesty and vanity had a brief skirmish when she opened her wardrobe and went to select an ensemble for church. Vanity won, but on terms. The bodice of the gown she chose was reserved enough for any but a puritan, and the fabric a modest muslin. But the dress was also trimmed in ornamental braiding, and the pale peach color was most fashionable as well as flattering. Amarantha debated briefly about wearing panniers, but as the gown had already been altered for wear without the wire foundation, she decided not to bother. Mrs. Polreath did not wear panniers either, finding them a burden to her chores, and she saw nothing amiss with Amarantha shedding hers as well. No one else in the village wore them either, though they were seen sometimes in Padstow in the wealthier households.

The demure gown proved a good choice. Mrs. Polreath, who was summoned to help with the lacing of the dress, approved it in her usual, uncritical manner saying that color suited her.

The two women scurried down the stairs, taking a care not to trip in their skirts until they were safely past the narrow landing with its wickedly sharp newel post and onto the broader treads of the main stair where they could walk two abreast.

Uncle Cyril's stained cloak was hanging near the front door as a reminder to Amarantha of her night outing. Mrs. Polreath *tsked* loudly at the stains and grumbled at Cyril's carelessness. The garment was not damaged, but the hem would certainly require some cleaning, as would her concealed brocade gown. Fortunately, Uncle Cyril wasn't likely to realize that he wasn't the guilty party on this occasion and would ignore Mrs. Polreath's fussing.

Feeling culpable, Amarantha resolved to attempt a clean-up of her own gown, though she had no clear notion of what needed to be done, not being commonly in the way of attending to her own clothing. It was most vexing. She had not thought that she would require the services of a maid in Cornwall once she rid herself of her more extravagant town fashions and had let her own dresser go. But the matter of having regular assistance with her dress might require some further consideration. Mrs. Polreath could not continue as her dresser, yet she was reluctant to hire any of the village women who would doubtlessly gossip about the household until the matter of Tamlane Adair's activities was solved.

"Are you ready, dearie?"

"Certainly."

It was the Sabbath, but Amarantha's thoughts were not pious as she wended her way toward the village, though she maintained a thoughtful silence as she walked the road to Blesland's church under Mrs. Polreath's guardian eye. Pendennis strolled with them as well, but as he was extremely retiring and disinclined to stay abreast of the two women, it was easy enough to forget about him for stretches of time.

The hamlet, being a few leagues inland from the coast and on level ground, was of an unusual pattern for Cornwall and laid out in the style of a squared Saxon green more common in the English north. The greensward was the villagers' meeting place and where markets were held every Monday and fairs twice a year on Beltane and Saint Stephan's Day. The four sides of the green were bounded by buildings. On the east, it was enclosed by a row of neat cottages and a tiny shop, which sold sundry household goods. A forge attached to an inn bordered on the south, and a small tavern where the weekly coach stopped for refreshment was built to the west. The north side of the green was dominated by Blesland's only church and burial ground, and the charred remains of the old rectory, which were mostly overgrown with honeysuckle and brambles.

The holy edifice Uncle Cyril reviled was unornamented. Being wholly subjugated by a square, perpendicular tower of no particular beauty, historic significance or even age, the builders had apparently seen the futility of appending any artwork to the edifice.

The graveyard was likewise of recent date and as equally unremarkable, boasting of no great monuments for the wealthy or illustrious dead. The era of the great tombs had passed hundreds of years ago.

It was not strange that Uncle Cyril scorned Blesland. The entire village was architecturally insignificant, having no buildings older than the mid-sixteenth century, and those from that era having escaped any architectural inspiration. Indeed, the scene would have been an utterly forgettable one but for the vernal eruption of golden daffodils, which pierced the velvety green in exuberant patches of color. They made the narrow gray church and its modest dead seem almost pretty.

Amarantha paused a moment to take in the floral sight and allowed herself a small smile.

"Immodest flowers," she said softly. Did daffodils enjoy thrusting themselves out of the cold ground and into the spring sun where they were nipped with frost and chased by strong breezes? Or was their beautiful show an act of painful vanity? If that was the case, then she could sympathize. They were not the only ones who endured discomfort that they might be pleasing to the eye. She had once been so young and foolish as to think that the most important thing in the world.

But surely there was more to them than that. After being buried in the cold and dark all winter, whatever waited above them must seem better. Air and light—even if filled with late snow—would have to be welcome, else the world would never rouse itself from its hibernal slumbers and life would end.

If this were so, then these spring bulbs were her kin.

Pendennis cleared his throat, reminding Amarantha that the time for services was drawing near.

"The flowers are beautiful," she excused herself. "They never seemed as lovely in London."

Pendennis beamed.

"Ezyau," he said softly.

"Yes, dearie, they are a sight." Mrs. Polreath frowned at Pendennis. She did not approve of the use of local vernacular and was always after the men to watch their language in Amarantha's presence. "But we mustn't be late."

"No," Amarantha agreed, finally turning away from the narcissus. "I would not want to miss Rector Adair's sermon. I am quite curious as to what he shall speak about."

Mrs. Polreath beamed happily at her words but Pendennis, apparently hearing something else in her voice, sent her a quick look. Amarantha quickly arranged her face into a vacuous expression, which was as close to piety as she could come, and followed Mrs. Polreath into the dark house of worship.

Much to Amarantha's embarrassment, Mrs. Polreath hurried her to the front of the crowded church and slipped into a pew that was the first but one. From there, Amarantha could feel the weight of curious eyes resting on the back of her head, which she quickly bowed. Prayer eluded her that morning, so she studied her hands, which were growing rather tanned, and thought about what Rector Adair might be doing with the Frenchman he had met out on the moor.

So absorbed was she in avoiding conversation with the curious villagers and speculation about her handsome neighbor's activities that the rector's voice welcoming the faithful to services came as a shock.

Her head jerked up at his ritual words of blessing and their eyes met briefly. Not a muscle in his face betrayed any particular recognition of her as he started his weekly sermon.

Amarantha studied the rector without reservation, as any staring would be construed as attention to the sermon rather than bad manners. His dark hair was restrained this morning, drawn back in a tidy queue. His face was strangely inanimate as he addressed the congregation, and his clothing was as somber as his expression.

His voice was rich and beautiful, though, and it seemed to cast a spell over the congregation. Even the restless babes quieted when he spoke.

" *'Woe to the inhabiters of the Earth and the sea, for the devil has come down to you.'* "

So gentle was his tone that it took a moment for the meaning of his words to penetrate her cloud of thought, but when they finally did, it was all she could do not to let her jaw drop. She had possessed no particular notion of what sort of sermon her charming guest from last night might preach, but the morning's topic had never entered her imagination. The verse from Revelations was one worthy of the sternest Scottish Calvinist and not one that she had ever heard in a church in London.

"... As He is the Judge of the earth, He doth exercise strictest justice. He will not acquit the guilty, nor spare the wicked His judgment. Yet how wonderful and infinite is His mercy toward the sinner. Though He be the Judge of the earth, yet still is He its Savior. Though He be the all consuming fire of sin, yet he is the light of salvation. In Romans, chapter Five, verse Ten. *'When we were enemies, we were reconciled to God, by the death of His Son.'* "

Amarantha sat in shock, amazed that such stern

and moralistic views would be embraced by the parish.

Yet perhaps it was not so amazing. Blesland was remote and its entertainments few. Too, the Church of England had been harsh with the Roman Catholics of Cornwall, confiscating church lands and rousing the ire of the people. Most of Cornwall had reached an accommodation with the English and her episcopal king, but the Church would not have made as great inroads among the secluded populations where the leanings toward rebellion still existed. Such Calvinist preaching, though not of itself popular to the village folk—and in its own way, quite as hostile to Catholics—might seem like a minor defiance of the overlords who had taken over their lands. It would therefore be appealing to the villagers.

Amarantha's lips curled in a cynical smile. There was also the matter of the rector being the only minister in Blesland. His audience, ever fearful of the evils on the moor, was fairly well assured.

The sermon was over quickly and the church emptied immediately as the villagers, unaffected by the dark sermon, returned happily to the sunny green to converse and enjoy the fine day.

Mrs. Polreath wanted to visit with her sister, so Amarantha sent her away, saying she would find her later. Amarantha remained inside the church, head bowed as though in prayer, waiting for the humble place of worship to empty. She spent the time considering what she had just learned, and feeling that she was coming closer to an answer about the rector's activities. Her speculations were troubling. Back and forth her mind went. Was Tamlane smuggling for personal profit or, to be fair, to help the poor of the village? Or was he involved in something more dangerous?

Amarantha hands clenched. She hoped it was the former venal notion that would prove true. She did not want to become involved with another rebel sympathizer. The Stuart cause had failed. It had failed in '15 and '19 and again in '45. To continue clinging to the futile struggle was a sure path to bitterness, and she did not want to think that Tamlane was raising money for this cause by smuggling and perhaps selling information to the French.

"Ah! I knew you were a pious woman, Mistress Stanhope," Tamlane said quietly as he approached her down the aisle.

Amarantha rose slowly and turned to face the rector.

"I was not praying, but rather contemplating your sermon," she said.

"And was it instructive?" he asked politely, offering his arm.

"Most revealing," she answered, laying fingers on his sleeve, pleased—in spite of her troubled thoughts—that she had a reason to be close to him.

"I am so glad." His shadowed face betrayed no smile, but his voice suggested amusement. "If you have a moment, I would like to introduce you to someone."

"Certainly," she said, but her heart sank. She did not feel ready to meet anyone. She was still reveling in her solitary existence, and though she was enjoying the rector's company, she did not wish to have village society pressed upon her.

As though guessing her thoughts, Tamlane said: "Most fortuitously, I have found someone to white-wash your walls for you."

"Indeed?" She didn't bother to hide her surprise.

"And as your good fortune would have it, I have the proper supplies for making a long-lasting white-wash that can withstand the corrosive sea air, so he may begin work at once. If you are agreeable."

They emerged into the light of the late morning bustle, which seemed blinding and quite loud after the dark quietude of the church.

"Certainly I am agreeable. The sooner the better."

"Excellent. Maxwell Taxier is from York, but has come for a visit with kin. Unfortunately, he did not wait for a reply to his letter before journeying south, and he arrived only to discover his aunt and uncle have died."

"How distressing," Amarantha said politely. The story was not improbable, but for some reason, she did not believe it. There had been a rumor in London that some of the more fanatical Stuart adherents were again attempting to recruit an army out of the sympathetic people in the south. The notion had sounded ridiculous then. Now she was not so certain.

"He has not decided whether he will remain in Cornwall for the spring or return to the north. In the meanwhile, he must find work. He has had experience with building and all manner of carpentry work, so should prove quite useful to you if you mean to make repairs to Talland House."

"Does he require lodgings?" she asked directly, as they walked slowly toward the inn.

Rector Adair paused. Her question seemed to take him by surprise.

"It would be most convenient if he could lodge in the stables with Tregengon and Penkevil as the inn is rather beyond his means as a permanent abode, as well as having another—unfortunate—guest. But, if that is not convenient . . ."

Amarantha did some quick calculating. She might be bringing a viper to their bosom if Taxier was attempting to recruit rebels. But, on the other hand, she would stand a much better chance of knowing what was afoot if the man was kept close at hand.

"It will not inconvenience me," she told him. "Uncle Cyril won't notice anything. Mrs. Polreath is the only one likely to be put out, but as she is your most devoted admirer, I doubt she will raise any protest. And I certainly will not."

Tamlane's brows twitched together, but before he could reply, a shrill young voice cut through the air.

"Where's my basket of cabbages? Did you hide it, you cloth-head?"

"Why? Are you looking for sisters? They went home with the other vegetables," another voice answered insultingly.

"Ullan yaw! Leebm lawn!" the first voice yelled back.

Amarantha turned her head and watched the two short combatants squaring off. She didn't need to see the out-thrust jaws and raised fists to understand that a challenge had been issued and accepted. She paused, giving the rector a chance to intervene.

"I believe that those boys are about to engage in a bout of fisticuffs," Amarantha pointed out when the rector also paused but did no more than lift an inquiring brow. She gestured. "The boys over there."

"I believe you are correct," Tamlane answered after a moment's study.

"Shouldn't you do something?" she asked, a little shocked that the man showed no sign of stepping between the tussling boys.

"Well, they have been in church all morning. And 'tis nearly May Day. As your uncle explained, this holiday seems to loose a great deal of Celtic passion among the populace. It is kinder to their mothers to let them have some fun before they return home." He tugged gently at her arm and continued strolling toward the inn.

"You are a very *strange* rector." Amarantha was aware of being the cynosure of a dozen curious gazes and strove to keep her expression neutral.

"I do try not to be completely ordinary," he answered, ushering her inside the inn. Again, due to a low threshold, he had to stoop slightly to enter.

"You are not ordinary at all," she assured him.

Tamlane only smiled.

Taxier was found in the common room enjoying a cup of coffee while seated in the sunlight of a narrow casement.

As her eyes adjusted to the gloom, Amarantha also saw that the space had a second occupant—the excise man, Percy Aldridge. He would be the other unfortunate guest Tamlane was referring to. Taxier might not be a smuggler, but he would still attract the attention of the Preventive if he behaved at all suspiciously.

Aldridge did not rise as they entered the room, but jerked his head in a greeting that was just barely cordial. In fairness, she could not blame him for being curt. Uncle Cyril had been anything but polite about the Preventive's men tramping over what he considered to be his private preserves and disturbing his work. Normally, she would have gone to some length to propitiate the insulted man, as he was—for better or worse—a representative of governmental authority, but Amarantha found that she also simply could not like, even a little bit, the wood-headed, humorless Preventive. So she, in turn, made him only a barely polite nod.

"This will not take long," the rector promised, sotto voce. "Simply smile and hold your breath and tongue."

"Why isn't he off harassing the tanner or the chandler?" she whispered, averting her face.

"Because it is the day of rest—and he was gone all of yesterday to Padstow interrogating the maltster, the tobacco dealers, the victualler and any number of fishermen."

"Good morrow, Rector," Taxier said, rising politely and putting an end to their low-voiced conversation. The Yorkshireman's voice was pleasant, if gravelly, and devoid of the expected northern accent.

"And to you also." The rector urged Amarantha closer to the table so that they might speak in private tones.

The Yorkshireman was not much taller than her, but his compact body suggested great strength. His face was also strong and not one that had been spared by time and elements. It was deeply tanned and no longer young. But the lines upon it were not all from pain and ill humor. There were many caused by the wide smile he was showing them now.

In spite of herself, Amarantha liked him immediately.

"Taxier, this is Mistress Stanhope, the lady I spoke of who needs some work done at her uncle's home." The rector did not bother to lower his voice.

"Mistress," he said, making a slight bow. His movements were a little stiff, as if he had an injury or suffered from mild rheumatism.

Amarantha nodded back and smiled.

"We are fortunate to find you. I fear that our walls are in dire need of attention." Following his lead, she did not try to hide their conversation from Aldridge, though hers was probably too warm a speech for a hired hand. Amarantha shrugged mentally. Somehow, Maxwell Taxier did not seem like a common laborer. Perhaps it was his educated tongue.

A smooth speaker would be needed to find any converts for his cause.

Also in Taxier's favor, she could sense the excise man's scrutiny and disapproval of their conversation, and though she might have suspicions of this man's reason for coming to Cornwall, it made her inclined to favor Maxwell Taxier on general principle.

"I am grateful, Mistress, to find work and a place to stay. My aunt's death was a sore surprise."

Percy Aldridge snorted loudly. No one turned to look at him.

"We are both fortunate, Mister Taxier." The rector nipped her arm. Responding to the prompt, she added: "Until tomorrow then. Will eight o'clock be convenient?"

"Aye, that will do quite well."

"Good day, Taxier." Tamlane said, taking Amarantha's hand and placing it back on his arm.

Amarantha was a little surprised, but did not protest the interview being cut short. No doubt the rector had a reason for his actions, and Amarantha decided that prudence might be the order of the day until she knew more of Tamlane's plans.

"Good day, Rector. Mistress Stanhope."

"Good day." Amarantha caught a glimpse of Aldridge's pinched face from the corner of her eye, but pretended not to notice the Preventive as she made her farewells.

Taxier politely remained standing until they had left the room, showing again the manners of a gentleman.

"That was a short interview," Amarantha commented softly as Tamlane led her back to the inn's door. "We have not discussed a fee for his work. Or does he not care about that?"

Tamlane said: "There wasn't any more to say, was there? Do not worry about his wages. I will settle it later with your uncle. I simply wished to make you acquainted with Taxier before he arrived at Talland House."

"Thank you. My nerves, you know, are of a most delicate nature, and might not withstand the shock of finding that Uncle Cyril had hired someone to repair the whitewash," she agreed blandly.

"Your nerves may be delicate—I certainly would not say otherwise," he answered as they paused at the edge of the green. He glanced down at her with a half-smile. "But you are also curious as a cat and, I suspect, inclined to be overly imaginative. I thought

I would save you an afternoon of alarmed investigation of Taxier's background."

"Ah! Then I must again thank you for the thought. But, truly, I enjoy investigating. It is a way to test one's critical faculties. To assess the validity of one's beliefs and assumptions."

"So true—assuming one has critical faculties rather than an overdeveloped imagination."

"Of course. But you have forgotten to mention that you have also saved the Preventive a deal of wondering and investigating by giving him knowledge of Taxier's whereabouts and occupation on the morrow."

Tamlane drew in a quick breath, and said in a tone of mild exasperation: "I was rather hoping that would escape your notice."

"I am certain you were. You are playing a very dangerous game, Rector."

"As I said, *an over-developed imagination*. Never fear, Mistress. I am not imaginative and never play games of chance unless I am certain to win."

Amarantha spotted Mrs. Polreath advancing purposefully across the green with Pendennis in tow. "Unfortunately, I believe that this discussion will have to be continued later. Mrs. Polreath has just recalled Uncle Cyril's midday meal and will wish to return home immediately."

"I shall bid you a good day then. And thank you for your assistance with Taxier." The rector bowed over her hand, then surprised her by lifting it to his lips. Saluting the hand was not an uncommon courtesy among the gentry in London, but Tamlane Adair had not previously used it. He straightened and calmly added: "I shall stop at Talland House tomorrow to speak with your uncle about Taxier's wages so you may put your mind to rest about ill-using the laborer."

Amarantha couldn't think of a thing to say until the rector was out of the range of polite greeting. This was getting annoying. He always seemed to get in the last word in their skirmishes.

"There you are, dearie. We had best be getting back home."

"Of course."

"Did you and the rector have a nice visit?" she asked with a touch of slyness as they turned toward Talland House. "You certainly spoke together for a long while. I wondered why you had gone into the inn."

Pendennis fell in step behind them.

"Certainly the visit was pleasant. The rector took me to see the man who will be doing the whitewash on the house. He is residing at the inn at present. His name is Maxwell Taxier and he is from York. He will be staying in the stables from tomorrow onward with Tregengon and Penkevil." Amarantha tucked her tingling hand under her cloak.

"Oh." Mrs. Polreath was plainly disappointed in her answer.

Amarantha hid a grim smile. Her explanation certainly sounded unromantic, which was what she intended. Gossip was a fact of village life, but she had no intention of fueling any speculation about her relationship with Rector Adair. If the rector was doing what she suspected, gossip was the last thing they needed! She would have to steer him from his present course before he ended in disaster.

Chapter Four

Amarantha stepped out into the suntrap, a smile of welcome in place. Uncle Cyril had informed her over breakfast that the rector's man had already arrived and was cooking up a batch of whiting out in the garden. Curious about this supposed Yorkshire carpenter, she decided that she would have a private word or two with him. Perhaps she could discover some proof of her theory that he was wanted by the Preventives up north for smuggling. There were really only two reasons that she could think of for him to have come south. The people of Cornwall were certainly not the only smugglers in the land, but it was her experience that the odds of it being the Stuarts who were the cause of a man's disenfranchisement increased as one approached the Scottish border. York was in the very north of England.

"Hello—" Amarantha drew in a single breath of gusting air and then recoiled, coughing. She understood now why for the first time in a week the birds had flown off without their morning crusts.

"Bloody hell!" she wheezed, tears starting in her eyes. Whatever Taxier was cooking up in the giant cauldron, it was not the standard whitewash. She fumbled for a handkerchief to press over her lower face before approaching the pot where Taxier was standing slightly bent, propped up on some sort of paddle, which looked like a crutch. Had he not been upright, she would have assumed that he was overcome by the noxious fumes, so still was he standing. But since he was more or less vertical, she had to presume that he was merely resting and keeping a close eye on whatever brew was in the giant cauldron.

"Good morning, Mister Taxier." Her words were rather muffled.

"Good morning, Mistress Stanhope." Taxier's words were also muffled. He turned toward her slowly, showing her a likewise stifled face, though his kerchief was larger and darker than her own and secured by a knot beneath his hat. Somehow, she doubted that the covering was sufficient to remove all taint from the air and had to admire his fortitude. "Was there something you needed? I fear that I cannot leave this batch just now. It must be applied to the walls while still hot."

"No, I require nothing. I am merely here to say welcome."

Taxier's eyes crinkled up above his cloth mask.

"Thank you kindly, Mistress. That is brave of you."

"That's the famous whitewash, is it?" she asked with some misgivings.

"That it is. Vile stuff, isn't it?" Taxier turned and plunged his paddle into the hell broth, giving it a vigorous stir. "It is not the standard recipe, but never fear it. The smell dies once the wash has cooled."

"So I should hope! What *is* it made of?" Amarantha bravely came a step closer and peered into the cauldron.

"Well, it is one part unslacked lime, to five parts boiled sea water, one part milled oyster shell, part glue, and a bit of dried, ground furze."

"Furze?" she asked, momentarily diverted.

"Gorse—that yellow flower out on the moor. The same as is used to dye cloth."

"But, why furze?" she asked stepping back from the thickening concoction in an effort to catch a breath of unpolluted air. It was difficult as the wind-borne scent was omnipresent.

"It gives it a bit of warmth. Keeps the stuff from looking so gray."

"Ah."

Amarantha noticed a square of hessian cloth lying low to the ground near the cauldron. It appeared to be smoking. She took a cautious step forward and encountered a strong fish smell.

"And what is that?" she asked warily.

Taxier looked down.

"A smoking barrel. Or, more rightly, a smoking pit, as they use rock instead of wood in these parts."

"I see. And why is it smoking? One doesn't put fish

on the wall as well—*do you?* I mean, that isn't York-shire tradition, is it?"

Taxier turned fully to look at her, his reddened eyes beginning to twinkle. Though he did not laugh aloud at her question she could not see beneath his neckerchief to know if he was smiling.

"Nay! That it is not. The pit would be fired because Mrs. Polreath asked me to lay on some sticks. The rector brought her some fish from Penzance, and she had a mind to have some pilchards and pleated meats laid on for later. And since I was building a fire any-way . . ." He shrugged.

Amarantha could well believe that Mrs. Polreath had asked Taxier to make a second fire. He did not know it, but if he stayed, he was likely to be asked to do any number of additional chores that bore no re-lationship to carpentry. Mrs. Polreath was a great be-liever in putting by, particularly with things that could be collected freely. Poor Pendennis was forced into making jam and conserves all summer long—first from damson, then red raspberry, and last blackberry and crabapple, all from fruit gathered on the moor.

In theory, it was a sound notion, for in the winter and early spring there was little sweet produce avail-able, a few fall apples only. Their own garden boasted a fine crop of turnips, carrots, potatoes, parsnips and leeks so their diet was varied, but it was too early for new fruit. Still, Pendennis felt that putting up pre-serves was beneath him, and there was, her uncle said, a great deal of unhappy rumbling from the kitchen during the summer months.

She wondered whether Taxier would eventually feel such jobs were beneath him. That would probably depend on how desperately he wished to remain in Blesland, she supposed.

Footsteps approached from the stables, and Amarantha turned to find Penkevil and Tregengon waiting a small distance from them with large brushes in hand. Though it was a fairly warm morning, both men were wrapped in mufflers to just below their eyes. They did not look entirely happy, but then the wind was blowing mostly in their direction and that could be causing them to squint and grimace.

"Good morning," she said anyway.

The two men nodded and mumbled something. She nodded back and then turned again to Taxier, frustrated that their time for a tête-à-tête had been cut short. Curiosity could not be assuaged now without possibly betraying Taxier, something she had no intention of doing—whatever he was up to.

"Has the rector been to call this morning?"

"Aye, but he could not stay. He was needed in the village. But I believe he intends to call in here again this afternoon. He and your uncle have some outstanding business to discuss."

"Excellent. Well, I will leave you to your work." She nodded at the men again and retreated back into the house where the air was as yet uncontaminated.

Her footsteps were slow as she ruminated on Taxier's words. *Outstanding business?* The rector's only legitimate business was affairs of the soul—something that her uncle did not admit to having. That left Tamlane's sideline of smuggling—and possibly recruiting men for a new rebellion—as a possible reason for a second visit.

89

Unless the rector truly meant to ask about Taxier's wages?

But surely there was nothing to discuss with Uncle Cyril. It must have been agreed upon already or the man would not have started work, and in any event, the rector did not need to be involved in the matter of negotiation. Taxier could speak directly to her uncle. Such would be the normal course.

Amarantha paused and worried at her lip. An unpleasant notion had inserted itself in her mind. Could it be that her uncle was knowingly sheltering a law-breaker? That perhaps he did it all the time? She had not been a part of the household long enough to know whether this was true.

Surely Uncle Cyril would have better sense than to get involved. . . .

Of course he had! She was behaving like a hysteric. Suspicion had made her overimaginative. Taxier's presence at Talland House was a single, never-to-be-repeated event. She needed to put all these fears from her mind and seek some meaningful occupation. Worry aided no one.

There certainly were a great many things she needed to do. Her uncle's papers, for instance. They were still desperately in need of ordering, and it was a task that she fully intended to get to—soon.

Amarantha looked over at the library door and the dark gloom beyond where the untidy piles of vellum waited. She shuddered in distaste and turned away. She was too agitated to work on papers.

What she needed was some physical activity. Really, it seemed a perfect morning for a long walk—a bit breezy perhaps, but with no threat of rain. Perhaps she should go out for a while. The men would be working in the house soon anyway, and the fumes from the whitewash would surely drive her away from the library.

Amarantha tapped her foot as she considered.

She could—she *should*—ask Uncle Cyril to take her to see the standing stones by the wood the rector had spoken of.

But not today. She wished to have some privacy for thought. And Uncle Cyril said that he was *quite* busy that morning with his correspondence. She shouldn't disturb him now. There was plenty of time to investigate that site later. After all, there wouldn't be anyone or anything there to see at present. . . .

The village then! That seemed a likely destination. She needed some thread and could have it from the shop there.

Of course, Mrs. Polreath probably had a supply of thread as well. . . .

But, Amarantha thought, *Mrs. Polreath was occupied with removing the stains from her brocade gown—her own attempts at cleaning having failed completely and the gown being discovered by the thorough housekeeper. She couldn't disturb the poor woman with another request. No, she would have to take a walk all alone and buy some thread.*

The course and excuses for her walk decided, Amarantha went up to her room to fetch a cloak and a few coins. She took a moment to study her glass and be sure that her hair was still tidy and that her dress did in fact become her. Eventually satisfied all was in order with her appearance, she went carefully down the stair and scurried out into the morning before she could be delayed by anyone.

The rector's home was fortuitously located on the way to town—or nearly so. To visit Penrose Cottage was only a small detour, and the path so very pretty that she did not mind the extra distance a diversion would cost. Taxier said that the rector wasn't at home to receive callers, but Tamlane wouldn't mind if she just had a little walk through his garden looking for . . . birds and flowers.

And concealed sheds and perhaps people.

Amarantha shook her head, trying without much success to dismiss the ridiculous notion that she would find something incriminating there.

"I can't do this. There is no one there. And what would Tamlane think if he saw me peering through his shrubbery? He could return home at any time."

She stared at the sky, studying the heavens while she listened intently. The blue overhead was full of movement. Birds and clouds were on the wing, filling the space above her and all the way to the line where the moor met the sky. The hedge-parsley along the rising path danced in the breeze, and the wild carrots swayed gracefully at whim of the wind, sounding a bit like whispering voices when the stalks rubbed together.

But there wasn't a human voice or footstep to be heard and no evidence of any human activity. No one was about to see her if she detoured.

Amarantha exhaled slowly and ignoring the manners she had been taught by her parents, she turned aside onto the cottage path.

The giant lilac in the yard was found shedding petals in a pale violet rain, its heavy perfume circling the yard with the cyclonic breeze. Amarantha entered the garden quietly and likewise walked with her back to the wind, traversing the wild grounds with an attentive eye and ear.

Her review was unenlightening. She was uncertain how to feel about her inspection of the gardens revealing nothing that might be used as a place of concealment for brandy or other large cargo. It was a sorry fact that smuggling now seemed the most innocent activity that Tamlane could be engaged in. It would be something of a relief to know that that was all the rector was up to.

But if smuggled goods were being kept at Penrose Cottage, then they were concealed within the house— possibly in a hidden cellar. They couldn't be far away, not if Tamlane was bringing something to Uncle Cyril that afternoon.

"Bloody hell. Let the notion go."

After all, there was no proof that he was actually doing *anything* illegal. She had probably formed an incorrect conclusion based upon worry and an over-developed imagination. With a few snips of imaginative threads and scraps of gossip she had constructed an entire cloth of conspiracy and illegal actions for the rector, her uncle, Mrs. Polreath and Taxier. After last Sunday, she had been fairly certain that smuggling was not the rector's hidden vice—now she was sneaking about his home, looking for illicit cargo. This was proof that she was not behaving reasonably.

Perhaps, she thought with hopeful contradiction, if he was doing anything, he was only aiding men in their escape from harsh punishment in the north. It was the sort of thing a good Christian would do— particularly for a friend. And Taxier might have done any number of trivial things to get himself in trouble with the law. She was imagining conspiracies. Jacobite recruiters in Cornwall—forsooth! The notion was daft. If there were any left, they would be with the prince and applying for help in France or Sweden— or even Spain—but not in Cornwall.

"Admit it. You were imagining things—just like Tamlane said. Now you need to put this whole notion from your mind," she scolded herself. In any event, hunting for a cellar was out of the question. She should leave at once before Tamlane came home and found her there or she met up with Trefry. A reunion with the rector would embarrass them both since she had made her suspicions of him so plain. Instead, she would behave properly and send round a note asking him to visit her—and Uncle Cyril—for tea.

A relieved Amarantha decided to depart using the main drive to the west of the house and started briskly in that direction.

Her mind, after the scolding, was almost made up to completely abandon her reservations about the rector's activities, and she was therefore rather unpleasantly surprised to reach the front of the house and find the door standing open in mocking invitation.

"Oh no." She stopped walking and looked round hurriedly. There was still no one in sight.

She closed her eyes and counted to ten, but when she opened them the yard was still vacant and the door still conveniently open. Temptation beckoned.

"Rector?" she called. Receiving no answer, she reluctantly added, "Trefry?"

No one replied.

Perhaps Trefry was down in the cellar and that was why he couldn't hear her.

"I can't do this," she whispered, even as she stepped toward the door. "It would be so wrong of me."

Amarantha's pulse quickened as she climbed up onto the flags just outside the entry. She deliberately did not look at the knocker of doom waiting on the door for her use. She instructed her brain to forget the instrument of certain summons was even there.

"Rector Adair?" she called once more, but this time in an even softer voice. "Is anyone home?"

When no answer came, Amarantha took a quick look around and advanced a cautious step over the threshold. It was a violation of hospitality, and she waited apprehensively in the entry for someone to appear and challenge her presence in the house. She felt a little ill.

But no one came to ask what she was doing.

She edged closer to the door that led to the back of the house and laid her ear against the thick panel. It took a moment for her thundering heart to subside sufficiently enough to listen for sounds of occupation. But once her pulse and respiration had calmed, she found the silence remained reassuringly unbroken by any human sounds.

"I should leave right now," she whispered.

But perhaps she could have a quick look in the library—in case the rector was there and simply hadn't heard her call.

Amarantha did not allow herself to think of the words *trespass* or *spying* as she stole down the narrow corridor toward the rector's study.

The small door was open. The room beyond was as she had remembered it—whimsical, exuding charm and welcome—even to her, even when her task was an unfriendly one. Standing in the doorway, she noticed many objects that had eluded her attention on the first visit, the details of the room's furnishings being obliterated by the rector's distracting presence.

For one thing, she had never noticed the tiny door in the back of the room; it was really only a panel set into the wall by the fireplace. It wasn't a precisely a secret cupboard, but the opening would not have been noticeable if someone had not carelessly left it ajar.

"Rector? Are you in there?" she called again for form's sake, her voice hardly louder than a whisper. It was unlikely that the rector would actually squeeze himself through the narrow opening should there be a room beyond.

Unlikely, but not impossible.

"You have to look." Three more cautious steps brought her to the cupboard. Her hand shook slightly as she touched chilled fingers to the panel and nudged the old door open a few more inches.

She let out a pent-up breath. Having expected to find an abandoned skull, or a cache of treasure—or, at the least, a cask of brandy—she was disappointed to discover only a collection of swords and pistols mounted on the walls. They were all rather ordinary dress swords, except one, which was larger and brighter than the others and hung beneath a canopy of tartan wool.

Peering into the gloom, she could barely make out

the sword's details, but what she saw was intriguing.

This time, Amarantha did not call out before taking action. She opened the door wide, and using both hands, she lifted the heavy sword and carried it to the window.

The weapon was a work of art—a broadsword, double-edged and unusually long, more like an antiquity of the type used in Scotland centuries ago. Her grandfather had possessed just such a sword, and it had come down to him from his own grandfather. It was a warrior's weapon.

She turned the sword over, admiring the ironwork. This was an old sword, but not a relic. The blade was polished, sharpened and gleaming. It had a basket hilt with black varnish and some faint pattern incised on the pommel, which was much worn from use. In the sunlight she could make out a crest coronet with a buck's head rising out of it. The sword was from the Gordon clan.

She peered closer. There were three spikelike fullers on each side of the blade, and within them was inscribed the name *Andrea Farrara.*

"Farrara," she whispered, in shock.

"He murdered his apprentice for spying before fleeing to Scotland," Tamlane said from the doorway.

Amarantha jumped and nearly dropped the weapon on her foot. Her heart leapt into her throat and attempted to squeeze through the narrow opening.

"After that, he made all his swords in the highlands for the chiefs who protected him. Do have a care. The blade is quite sharp and would pierce your shoe like a headsman's axe. Though it might be a fitting pun-

97

ishment for playing with a man's sword, I should still hate to see you truly hurt."

"I can see that it is well cared for. A truly remarkable artifact," she said after clearing her throat and sending her heart back where it belonged. She pasted on a smile and turned to fully face the rector, hoping he would not notice the flags of embarrassed color upon her cheeks. She added brazenly: "It seems particularly long, even for a broadsword."

Tamlane was leaning against the wall, a study of casual repose, but Amarantha knew he was about as relaxed as a cat on the hunt.

"It is indeed. But my family has always been endowed with greater than usual height and long limbs—and corresponding short tempers." He pushed away from the wall and came into the room. A single pace brought him to her side, and he gently relieved her of the weapon. He matter-of-factly returned it to its cupboard and closed the panel tight.

"How fortunate that you are a man of God and not given to violence."

"Yes," he agreed gently. "That is most fortunate."

"And how are you today?" Amarantha asked, still striving for normalcy in their conversation.

"Irritated."

And he was, primarily at himself for leaving the cupboard ajar. Tamlane was also dismayed to discover that he was rather more pleased than not to see his nosy neighbor, even if she had come to call for the purpose of rifling his library for proof of her suspicions.

Of course, his sensible self knew that his growing attraction to this woman was distracting him from serious tasks, but this strange magnetism she had worked from their first meeting fought determinedly against all reason and willpower, and he was growing ever more fascinated.

But more distressing still than the beguilement of his senses, she was dangerously willful. Her stubbornness and curiosity could put everyone in jeopardy. For her own safety, he should repulse her—at least for the time being—and find something to frighten her away from the cottage before she was hurt by her own curiosity.

The thought of her being caught in a clash between The Brothers and the excise men made his gut clench, and he wanted to shake her for being so foolish. True, she had no proof that there were actual smugglers on the moor, but he had warned her that there were dangerous people about!

"Oh? How unfortunate," she said, peeping up at him from under those dark lashes.

"Any normal person would shrink up like a salted snail from the shame," he informed her sternly, resisting the appeal of her gaze. It was not an easy task, for hers were eyes that begged a man to drown in them, but Tamlane suspected that there was a deal of truth in that old adage about *beginning as you meant to go on.* "Have you nothing to say for yourself?"

Amarantha shrugged with apparent carelessness.

"And how would you know about the effect of salt on snails?" she asked, choosing to ignore the main thrust of his observation and question.

"I had an elder cousin who liked to torture the weak and vulnerable. It is a family trait." Only he did not want to torture Amarantha. His impulses were violent, but not in that manner. Tamlane exhaled, striving to get a grip on his willpower and his good sense. It was difficult with the sweet scent of her violet water filling his head. "How do *you* know about salted snails?"

"Oh—I, too, have an elder cousin," she answered, face tilted back as she studied him to see whether he was truly angry. Tamlane knew his expression was intent, frowning even, but not thunderous, and she was plainly relieved to see this.

"And why are you here?" he asked again, annoyed that he couldn't find the will to truly frighten her.

"I merely stopped in on the way to the village. I am off to buy some thread for mending."

"I believe, Mistress Stanhope," he said slowly, still looking into her eyes, "that you may be a liar as well as a trespasser."

She colored delicately and glanced away. She had to work at suppressing some emotion. He could not tell whether it was hurt, shame, or alarm. It took an act of will not to take her chin in hand and turn her face up to the light. But, he wisely realized, if he ever began touching her it was likely that this conversation would end in kisses and not lectures.

She had to leave at once!

"Rector! I assure you that I do indeed have an elder cousin, and I most certainly need thread."

"That is not what I meant, and you are well aware of it." Tamlane's itching hand snaked out and took her about the wrist. Before she could utter a protest at the treatment, or he did something both unforgivable and foolish, he pulled her toward the door. "You are also imprudent. I am walking you home now. If you are sensible, you will follow me without argument."

"I shall follow you like a shadow," she agreed, as she was dragged along. "But it might be more pleasant, don't you think, if we walked side by side? It is so much easier to converse."

Tamlane muttered beneath his breath as he marched toward the front door.

"What was that? I'm afraid I didn't hear you."

"I said *'all wickedness is but little to the wickedness of a woman.'* I should tell your uncle about how you are spending your days and let *him* deal with you."

"*Hmph!* I have never cared for Ecclesiastes—or Proverbs." She continued to ignore the more unpleasant of his observations, probably hoping he would recover his sense of humor.

The shame of it was that he would forgive her. In fact, he already had pardoned her. Annoyance had evaporated like mist before the sun of her smile, and all that remained for him was an ever-growing attraction that quickened his pulse and fogged his brain— and he knew that though he should put her completely from him until his work was done, he probably would not be able to do it.

"I am amazed to learn that you have even read them," Tamlane answered, pulling her out of the house with ungentlemanly speed and roughness just to prove that he could be stern. "You certainly have not profited from the lessons there."

"And have you? *'Be not forgetful to entertain strangers.'* "

Tamlane pulled up short and glared down at her

in aggravation and disbelief. Her boldness and daring knew no bounds!

"What? Are you actually quoting Scripture—*at me?*"

"We are the only two people here. Obviously I was addressing you. That was Hebrews, chapter thirteen, verse one." Amarantha actually giggled, but it was nervousness and not humor that colored her voice. "Can you be certain that I am not an angel visiting in earthly disguise?"

The rector stared at her for a long moment of inner debate, than his own features relaxed. He managed not to sigh, even though he wanted to.

"An angel? You are too earthly in your guise. I think, for example, that you are perhaps more concerned with manners than morals. That is not angelic."

"At this instant, yes, I am concerned with earthly matters rather than heavenly ones. Should you not at least hear why I have come to visit you before dragging me away? I hadn't time to leave you a note."

He thought about it for a moment and had to concede the point, at least to himself. Perhaps she had a valid reason for being in his home. He had not stopped to ask Trefry if he had shown her into the library. If that was what had happened, then he had behaved abominably.

"Very well. I apologize for my inhospitality and impatience. Please tell me why you are here."

Amarantha smiled up at him.

"Thank you. And I apologize for—" she stopped, trying to decide how much to apologize for.

"*For?*" he prompted.

"Everything." Amarantha waved airily with her left

hand, her right still being shackled—though less tightly than before. "I didn't come with the intention of—"

"Spying?"

"—quarreling," she corrected. "Taxier said you meant to call this afternoon and I thought that you might like to stay for dinner."

"Dinner?" he sounded skeptical. "You came to invite me to dinner?"

"Yes, *dinner*—as in *to dine.* It is that large meal consumed in the evening after tea and before bed. It is sometimes referred to as *supper,* though around here supper seems to be mainly eaten earlier in the day." She held his gaze, waiting anxiously for a reply.

Had she really come only to ask him for dinner? If so, he should be flattered and pleased with the encouragement.

"Are you ever serious?" he demanded at long last. He was puzzled by her, and the lack of understanding was every bit as frustrating as it was fascinating.

"The invitation is sincere." And it was, even though she had only that moment thought of it. A moment's contemplation of that depressing large table and its vacant seats convinced her that company was needed. "As for being serious—well, need dining be solemn? Could we not break bread for some frivolous reason—perhaps pleasure at one another's company?"

For a moment, her face was shadowed by old hurts and Tamlane mentally cursed himself for being so gruff. Of course she was serious. Too much so, if half of what Cyril Stanhope had told him was true. She had even told her uncle that she had turned her face against marriage. That was surely an overstatement, but there was no denying that she had been badly hurt and if she was beginning to seek out company again, he could not refuse her. To do so would be unkind. It was also against his own long-term interests.

"No. It needn't be solemn." Tamlane looked down, and seeing that he still had hold of her, reluctantly released her. His hand felt very empty without the warmth of her wrist clasped to his palm. He said more gently: "Come. I will walk you home now."

"But I still need thread," Amarantha said tentatively.

"It will have to wait until you have someone to go with you. Amarantha, you must not go out on the moor alone. Another prisoner has escaped from the goal. The man is violent—quite insane. He has already attacked one of the farmers near Blesland and stolen a horse. I have just come from the farmstead that was robbed, and I assure you that there is danger. You must promise not to go out unaccompanied until he is recaptured or we are certain that he has left the area."

"I see." And she thought she did. A large part of Tamlane's anger could be explained. Fear made people behave quite irrationally—particularly men, who did not take kindly to being frightened. And witness her own actions! Worry had made her behave reprehensibly and suspect Tamlane of dishonorable dealings—and that suspicious behavior had nearly destroyed her friendship with this man before it had a chance to blossom.

Half chastened, but also relieved that the storm had passed, Amarantha said, "Tamlane?"

"Yes?" He did not comment on the use of his given name. Perhaps it felt as natural to him as it did to her.

"I wish—" she began, but couldn't think of what to say. His expression was still rather forbidding. His mobile lips were firm, his lovely eyes devoid of their usual humor. He looked stern and Calvinistic. Perhaps now was not the time to explain about her irrational fears of Taxier being a Jacobite recruiter. Amarantha sighed. " 'Tis naught."

For some reason, this response amused him and some animation returned to his countenance. This signaled the end of end some inner debate, and he entirely let go his remaining anger and distraction. Finally he smiled upon her in his usual manner, and the cold fist about her heart unclenched.

"You may fetch your thread tomorrow. In Padstow. I will arrange with your uncle for you two to accompany me to town."

She blinked.

"Padstow?"

"Yes. For the Beltane celebration. Tomorrow is May Day. We shall go and participate in some of that *Celtic enthusiasm* your uncle likes to study."

Amarantha beamed up at him as though he had offered her a treasure rather than a ride to town, and it was Tamlane's turn to blink in surprise. He found it a little frightening, the power she wielded with her lips. He had not made any provision for such a temptation in his life. Caution said that he should not rush heedlessly at this new feeling. Attraction that flared so swiftly could surely die just as quickly. Poets and wise men had both warned against it.

However, he was discovering that it was not in his heart to be wholly reasonable about this matter. And just this once, he would allow his heart's wishes to be placed—not above his head—but beside it. Though there was still more work to be done, as soon as Sunday was safely past them, he would turn his attention to this woman and decide how best to woo and win her. Instinct told him that it might not be any easy conquest. She was suspicious of him for some reason—though how she had guessed his sympathies, he did not know—and she was also haunted by an old tragedy that would make her wary of trusting her heart again to anyone who had served The Cause.

And in the meanwhile, it could do no injury for them to better their acquaintance in harmless ways, such as having conversation over dinner at her uncle's home, or witnessing a public festival in the company of a chaperone.

"Come along now, lass." This time he offered his arm instead of taking hers.

Without any hesitation, she placed her fingers on his sleeve.

"I am afraid that we will be having pilchard and leek pie again."

"Yes?"

"It is your own fault for sending Mrs. Polreath fish. She has poor Taxier cooking them even now. She'll be at Pendennis the moment I tell her that you are coming to dine."

"Has she commandeered Taxier? I thought he was to begin whitewashing this morning."

"He has started, but you know how Mrs. Polreath is."

Tamlane smiled wryly and nodded.

"Yes, I know Mrs. Polreath very well."

Chapter Five

Tamlane Adair watched the thin line of wavering smoke rise into the clear morning air above Talland House and again questioned his sanity. He had not meant to volunteer himself as Amarantha's escort to Padstow for the May Day celebrations. He had, in fact, resolved after their dinner last night to revoke his invitation and to not think of Amarantha Stanhope again until his business with The Brothers was completed on Sunday next. But for all his good intentions, here she was again—cluttering his judgment with her pretty shade. She dogged his thoughts as persistently as his shadow followed his footsteps. Hadn't she even said that to him, *I shall follow you like a shadow. . . .* She was an endless, dangerous distraction. Surely there was some embrocation—some cure—for this annoying malady!

It would have to be a comprehensive potion though, he thought gloomily, for everything seemed to remind him of her. Even last evening when he had carelessly allowed himself to be caught on the thorns of that wicked vermillion rose running amok in his garden, its spicy fragrance and velvety petals had called Amarantha to mind and stayed his pruning knife when he pulled it from his boot and prepared to sunder the offending stalk.

What sentimental rot he was spouting these days! Shaking his head in self-disgust, Tamlane dismounted from the pony trap and approached the front door. He made his knock brisk.

Mrs. Polreath answered the summons, glowing with vigorous color and adorned with a knowing smile. The faint scent of cooked oyster shell and the change of color made to the entry walls soon explained the housekeeper's healthy hue. Gone were the gray walls with their flaking whitewash. In their place there was now a pale gold plaster, which lustered warmly in the morning sun spilling in the opened door. Taxier had managed to do the trick and make Talland House feel warm and light.

Tamlane was glad, for it somewhat compensated for the dishonesty he had perpetrated on his fair neighbor.

Or the deception he was attempting to perpetrate. Mistress Stanhope was a deal sharper of wit than he had expected. Trefry had been questioned, and Tamlane knew now that Amarantha had let herself into his library uninvited and somehow discovered his cache of arms. What she made of it he did not know, for she was holding her counsel. All she had done last night was watch him with thoughtful eyes while they worked their way through soup and pie. It was not the sort of expression he wished to see on any woman's face when she contemplated him—and particularly not on Amarantha's.

"Oh, Rector Adair! Such a wonderful day!" Mrs. Polreath enthused.

Of course, he thought, the new whitewash might not be Mrs. Polreath's only cause for high spirits. She could be wearing a mask of glowing cheerfulness because she—like the rest of the village—was dreaming of bridals for him. It seemed that she might well be, having told him more than once that he should take a wife. And he had to excuse her for reaching the conclusion that he was courting Amarantha for they had been much in each other's company since his return to Blesland. And, of course, he was courting her, after a fashion.

However, that did not mean that he had to confirm Mrs. Polreath's speculations or add any encouragement to the idea at this time.

"The sun is certainly with us this morn," he said repressively. "Is Mistress Stanhope ready to depart?"

"Yes! I believe she is with her uncle. I'll just go and tell them that you are here." Mrs. Polreath chuckled—giggled like a maiden actually—and then retreated down the hall.

Tamlane sighed.

Amarantha did not keep him waiting that morning. She came out from Cyril's library, drawing on a pair of gloves, a light cloak of fawn laid over her arm. Though dressed in a gown of a shade of festive goldenrod, she seemed subdued, not meeting his eye as she made her greeting and then offered her uncle's apologies for not attending the celebration with them.

Cyril's sudden decision not to attend the festivities of Padstow was not news to the rector, as Amarantha's uncle had sent around a missive that morning acquainting Tamlane with his intentions to remain at home while the youngsters had their fun. But Amarantha had apparently not received advanced notification of her uncle's change of plans and was mildly perturbed and discomfited to find that they would be alone on their journey.

Tamlane was grimly amused by her reaction. Did the minx actually suffer from embarrassment at the thought of the social speculation, which was bound to be raised in the village when it became known that they had traveled together—unchaperoned—to Padstow? Almost, he laughed to finally see her discomfited.

But rather than tease, he would look on this unexpected modesty of mind as a positive sign for their afternoon by the sea. Perhaps her behavior would not be too outrageous and questioning as in the past. After her actions yesterday, he would not have wagered any great sum on her instincts for discretion.

In fairness, he also would have been bothered by this abandonment of Amarantha's uncle, and the resulting gossip, had he not already resigned himself to the fact that Amarantha Stanhope was going to be in his life from here forward. Like it or not, his emotions were stampeding him toward the altar. Cyril had obviously arrived at the same conclusion about their destiny, and being unaware of Tamlane's more pressing obligations, he was happily playing matchmaker.

Tamlane smiled slightly. So the two men in Amarantha's life—and Mrs. Polreath—at least agreed upon her future. Amarantha's own feelings were, as yet, unknown to him—and probably her uncle too. She did not seem inclined to confide her thoughts on this subject either.

Marriage! Tamlane shook his head. He had never thought of it until the last few days. The pleasures of a hearth fire and a woman to share his life had been forbidden when he was at war. But things were different in Cornwall, and now that the seed had been planted and taken firm root, he was certain that he'd have no peace until the deed was done. It was, of course, a drastic palliative for the illness he suffered, but then so, too, was the ailment of a particularly violent nature. Nothing short of marriage would do.

It was annoying, though. Amarantha Stanhope was not the only person who had thoughts of avoiding the institution. It wasn't as if he *wished* to marry. Far from it! A wife would greatly complicate his life and his work, which was so often a balancing act between varying obligations. A spouse was a hostage to chance—an Achilles heel. And there would be the risk of her disapproval—though surely not exposure, given her family ties—when he revealed his true occupation to her. He had no wish to bring another into his dangerous activities by forcing knowledge upon her, but he could not in good conscience marry Amarantha and not explain his past—and present—

undertakings to her, for some day that dangerous past might well catch up with him and they would have to leave Cornwall.

But this was all for the future. He could not risk making any revelations to her until The Brothers departed the neighborhood with their dangerous cargo. Too many of the Frenchmen were in the business of seeking information about the various garrisons' movements now that war with France looked inevitable. Such men would be unscrupulous enough to hold someone hostage to extort such information. No, he could not take any chances with her well-being. Her curiosity, once given a target, might take her into danger, and the very thought of her left in The Brothers' ruthless clutches made him break a sweat.

After Sunday he could explain everything and lay his heart at her dainty feet. He might as well—the poor infatuated organ was useless for all other things. Odd, that at his age, he should suddenly develop a violent and poetic infatuation. Yet the symptoms were all there—chivalrous impulses, disturbed dreams and a ridiculous desire to compose verses in her honor.

"Tamlane?"

He made an effort to shake off his distraction.

"Shall we be off?" he asked politely, assisting Amarantha into her cloak under Mrs. Polreath's giggling supervision. The housekeeper's presence meant that he firmly resisted the inclination to rest his hands upon Amarantha's white shoulders as he settled the fabric around her.

Apparently she was ready to depart, for the sudden lack of a chaperone—and Mrs. Polreath's prurient interest in their plans—did not deter her from traveling with him. Tamlane concluded that she was either very determined to see Padstow or she had an intense desire for private conversation with him. Mayhap she wished to berate him for being a dastardly scoundrel who evaded lawful taxes. He supposed that it was too much to hope that she was likewise smitten with a need to write verse and whisper sweetly in his ear.

Ideally, he supposed that he should try and coax some confidences from her, for he very much wanted to know what she was thinking. However, looking at her closed expression, he did not hold out a great deal of hope for this endeavor.

Tamlane gave into whim while they were mounting the trap and rather than lending only a hand to assistance, he lifted Amarantha up onto the board. Her body was supple and—he was shocked to discover—uncorsetted. Apparently it was not only panniers and bonnets and bound hair that she had abandoned in London.

Displeased with his body's strong reaction to the woman's soft heat, he released his fair burden at once and went to check upon the pony's rigging until calm returned to his senses. It took a long moment, because he could feel Amarantha's unwavering gaze upon his back demanding that he turn and look at her.

He resisted, but the struggle was more difficult than he liked.

The road to Padstow was at first smooth and pretty. They passed through Blesland where the fair was in progress and the giant Maypole was being erected.

Piles of wood for a balefire were being gathered upon the green.

To her credit, though obviously uncomfortable with the attention, Amarantha did not attempt to hide herself from the revelers beneath her drawn hood, though she did no more than smile and nod at the greetings thrown their way.

Tamlane wondered whether she would comment on the erection of the Maypole and the rather crude invocations the villagers sang as they worked, but she did not say anything about the call to the mother earth to *open to the seed*. And he could not know whether the color in her cheeks was from embarrassment or sunshine.

Once the busy hamlet was departed, the road took a downward turn toward the coastal elevations. The mossy beds of new spring grass that decorated the way were a verdant green and bordered with a flush of pink and yellow wildflowers and new saplings of hazel, rowan and ash. His companion, though now presented with ample privacy, seemed absorbed in the scenery and disinclined to begin conversation.

Tamlane waited patiently and amused himself by counting the thrushes that darted in and out among the shrubbery.

"Lad's love," Amarantha said tenderly into the silence, which was broken only by the soft clip-clop of the pony's feet.

"I'm sorry," Tamlane answered. "Did you say *lad's love?*"

"Yes, that is the name of those flowers you are admiring. The purple ones are lavender, and those to the right are sage and wild thyme. I think they must

115

have escaped from someone's garden, for they do not usually grow here." She smiled at him for the first time that morning.

Tamlane blinked and answered at random: "Mayhap, but if they did escape it was long ago. The house that used to be here was burned during the Warbeck affair. All that is left are some flags and a staircase— some crumbling walkway as well, and a bit of an orchard grown so rank that it hardly bears fruit any more."

"Ah. The flowers are orphans then." She sounded suddenly sad. "So many have been displaced by careless men."

"There have been other victims more deserving of pity," he answered. "Many were obliterated."

"I am aware of it." Amarantha averted her face. "But then what is a victor to do with the survivors of a lost cause, but fling them away? Mercy was never truly the way of kings."

"Sometimes they do not fling them away—sometimes they bury them. But unlike the Trelawnys, these flowers have survived and seem happy enough in their freedom. You should rejoice for them. Perhaps being displaced may be the best event that occurred in their lives. It might well have been both their salvation and liberation."

"Do you think so? That they are happy being tossed into new ground?" she asked seriously. "I wonder sometimes if all this bright show does not pain them. Perhaps it is all pretense—just the carrying on of a tradition because they know no other way to live. That if someone showed them another way, that they might not prefer it."

She spoke not of flowers or Cornwall's ancient rebellion, but of affairs more immediate. Tamlane
thought of the scourging of the highlands that had
come after the second Jacobite Rebellion and the
people driven from their homes and even from their
country's shores. Some went to the New World voluntarily to seek their fortunes. They at least were not
unhappy in their exile—but many, most even, were
in a pitiable state. But since she seemed as yet unprepared to speak of such things, he answered her meta-
phor indirectly.

"What a morbid thought, and not at all correct,"
he rebuked mildly. "All God's creatures act as they
must. They will follow their charted course—even if
it leads to destruction—if that is their will. Some will
learn new ways and thrive—others will not. What
must be remembered is that no blame can ever attach
to another for the actions taken by someone else. Not
even by those nearest in our affections. We are responsible only for ourselves."

"Blame? But I should think anger and sorrow are
closer to the heart of those who are abandoned."

"You were not abandoned," he told her bluntly, for-
saking indirection. "The parting was never intended
to be permanent."

After a moment she said, "I see that you have spoken with Uncle Cyril."

"Aye." He added quickly, "Your uncle cares very
much about your welfare and wanted me to know the
particulars so I did not accidentally cause you pain."

"I know this was his intention. Cyril does not gossip
idly. But he does not entirely understand what happened. I don't think any man can know what it is to

117

be placed second in their love's affections—displaced not by another person, but by politics."

Tamlane gave this a moment of consideration.

"Perhaps that is true. But I do know that you must have a care with this sort of thinking, Mistress. If you invite sorrow and regret into your heart, it will take up residence and feast until all joy is devoured," Tamlane was surprised to hear himself say. He *never* spoke of such things. It was a rule he had made for himself. He had surrendered all emotions and recriminations after he entered the Church and did not allow himself to think on those dark times in the north. On the other hand, it was his calling to offer spiritual comfort, so he continued: "You are too young to shut yourself away from life that way. Let it go. Give it up to God and heal."

Amarantha turned and looked full into his eyes for the first time that day. There was no veil of speculation in her gaze, and when she spoke, her voice was intent.

"You speak from experience, do you not?"

"Of a sort." Tamlane smiled wryly. Had he truly worried about being tempted into courtship and lovers' talk with this melancholy waif? "In my case, it was anger I invited in when I was young and impulsive. And that not only consumes all joy, it also breeds hate. Most unhealthy and uncomfortable I found it to be. It took me a period of time—years—to make that anger into my servant rather than my master. And during those years, I thought that my faith had been destroyed."

Her eyes studied him.

"That is very sad, Tamlane. I am glad that you kept

your belief. But if you were so taken up with anger, what saved you from despair?"

"Realizing that the Lord had a plan for me after all. That all I had worked for was not in vain—that my training as a warrior and a man of God could be put to a practical use. I am not a passive person by nature. Meaningful occupation was the answer. It replaced the parts of me that had been given to anger and despair."

Of course, he realized now that this was not all which made him feel whole. Tamlane had only just come to understand that he had been existing in a sort of emotional limbo for many years, living every moment as it came and discarding them swiftly before they accumulated into another painful memory, or became some inevitable plan for life. Most of him had gone rather cold and numb, but there had been a small piece of his heart that had been waiting, biding its time until something of great meaning reentered his life.

He was not pleased to think of the years that had flowed by him while he waited to reawaken to joyous things, but that was what happened to a man who was not willing to release his past memories, and yet was not ready to contemplate a future without them. He simply went on from one day to the next, content with life but not hopeful.

Tamlane exhaled slowly. Though he rarely allowed himself to look back on his previous existence, he could still recall vividly the day that his life had changed.

It was late in the spring. The prince had retreated into Skye with the dogs of war howling after him. Culloden had devastated the clans, and the survivors were in disarrayed retreat. Numb with shock and a wound to the head, Tamlane had wandered for a day after the battle, and finally when the itching on his face had become unendurable, he had taken his sporran and *sgian dubh* down to a quiet pool where he might wash off the stink of battle and shave off a week of whiskers.

Without thought, he'd laid out his knife, then the tiny shard of glass he had salvaged from the battlefield and prepared to scrape his face clean. It was then that he had looked into the glass and seen the anguished eyes of a lost soul staring back at him from the broken shards.

His face was gray and nearly unrecognizable. Not merely battered and transformed by privation, it had become the countenance of a man who believed in eternal damnation, who understood that demons of hell were waiting to consume him and all he held dear.

The revelation had shaken him to his soul. With a cry, he had thrown the shard of glass into the brown water and fled into lonely moors. It was only later when he lay cold and exhausted and starving that he had recalled there was a message of salvation—rarely spoken of in those dark days—that was part of the message of faith. It was a basic tenet of Christian faith that salvation was always possible whatever one's situation or sins. One simply had to return to a state of grace, to accept God's will, and one would heal.

And that was what he done—lying there in the rough gorse and mud—he'd given his hate and fear to God. But not his trust that there would be a better future. And so the healing that followed was only a partial one. For while in giving up his horrible feelings of defeat and loneliness so that he could find the strength to live, he had not replaced his smashed dreams with a new vision. He had not made any plan for the future beyond vowing to help his fellow Scots to escape the hell of war in which he had so long been trapped.

But Amarantha's arrival had changed his course of action and he finally had something for which to anticipate and plan. He was awakening again to the wonder of life and the possibility of happiness. Of course, his reawakening senses pained him much as a waking limb that had gone to sleep and then was called to prompt action. Though it would come right in the end, at first he had to endure a time of sharp prickles and unpleasant tingling.

"Doubtless you are correct and I need occupation. And I am seeking it." Amarantha looked away again and Tamlane realized that silence between them had grown extended and uncomfortable.

"You shall have it soon enough. We will make it an urgent priority," he said encouragingly. Their life together would doubtless be a full one.

"Yes. I believe I shall find it in Cornwall." But she sounded doubtful and did not turn to look at him when she answered.

Seeing her unhappiness, it was all Tamlane could do not to tell her of what he was planning. The only thing that forestalled him was the knowledge that she would likely insist on aiding him. He didn't believe that he could count on her to remain passively by while he did his work, and he was not ready to place her in the path of danger. Still, something more needed to be said—some declaration of serious intent.

"Amarantha—" he began, but found that he could not make any coherent pronouncement. He was awakening to thoughts of the future, but was unprepared to articulate them. And Amarantha was hardly likely to accept his declaration without some explanation of why they must wait to pursue their friendship.

She turned her eyes upon him and waited. When he didn't speak, she smiled politely and said: "Sorrow doesn't own me any longer, Tamlane. I have resolved on a new course. This mood is just an old shadow—a memory. And it is made as much of frustration as sadness. But on such a beautiful day it is easy to put the cold memories aside. Let's neither of us hate nor sorrow this day. Tell me instead about the celebration we shall see. Why a sea monster?"

Amarantha looked down and smoothed her skirt. Confidences were at an end for the time being.

Tamlane studied her averted cheek, then nodded. Perhaps a delay in a declaration was for the best. He knew some of her history from Cyril—though obviously not all of it—and he did not believe that her emotions for the dead man who she supposed had abandoned her for the Stuart cause were as lifeless as she claimed. But they were nearing decease, he believed, and he was quite happy to distract her from their death throes with lighter matters.

"I haven't Cyril's interest in old legends, but I can tell you what I do know. The Obby Oss is really more of a horse. A sea horse, if that makes sense, though

I do not understand at all why your uncle thinks of it as a Trojan Horse survival. As for the connection of the village to the sea, Padstow is a coastal town. The sea represents many things to the people who live there. It is their livelihood, the place where they see miraculous rebirth—and a place where some go to exile and even death. It is everything to them."

"Rebirth? From the sea? You surely do not mean like Jonah from the whale?"

"Yes, in a sense." He smiled. "For the farmer who lives inland, the Beltane fire is about renewing the land. But in Padstow, they must renew the sea as well. They do not sacrifice to an earth mother, but rather to the waters of the ocean that feeds them—hence the virgins given to the sea monster."

"Why a virgin girl, though? It seems so unfair. Why not a boy? Or a warrior? Or someone old and wise? Any of these would be a sacrifice."

"Because a virgin woman is a thing most precious and rare—and the most desired by the gods of renaissance. Only women can create life. Fair or not, that is the way of it. And the beast must be fed."

"It seems to me an excellent reason to lose one's virginity as immediately as possible." Amarantha's eyes were turned back to his face. A quick glance told him that she was smiling now with genuine warmth rather than mere politeness. "You are very calm about all this paganism in your midst, Rector. Does it not offend you and your faith?"

"No, oddly enough it does not. The Christian faith is also about rebirth. This is just another aspect of the miracle that survives from the era before Christianity came to this land. And these days, they do not actu-

123

ally throw maidens into the sea—nor are they ravished in the village. Unless they are willing, of course."

"I should hope not!" Amarantha cocked her head. Tamlane noted that she did not blush at their conversation about ravishment and detected Cyril's fell hand at work. The topic of virgin sacrifice was likely discussed over tea every afternoon and held no terrors for his outspoken niece.

"I think that I am not the only unordinary person here," he grumbled.

"This thought has only just occurred to you?" Amarantha shook her head, pretending sorrow. "I fear you are not very observant."

"No, I am observant enough, and have thought this on several occasions," he answered. "In fact, I believe I thought this only yesterday when I found you in my library."

"Hmm . . . I hear drums," she said, prudently changing the subject. "Or is that thunder? Or perhaps the sea? I can smell it now."

"Yes, there are drums. There will be a great deal of music today—flutes, whistles, fiddles and bodhrans. But above all, there will be drums." Tamlane listened for a moment. "I know this song. It is an ancient *Kernow* verse."

"What is it about? It seems a bit frantic."

"It is. Oddly enough, though, it is a love song."

"Sing it for me."

Tamlane cleared his throat and then began to chant:

Gold will fade. Silver will fade,
And velvets and silks, too.

Every known cloth will fade,
But not so my longing.

The sun will rise. The moon will rise.
The sea shall rise up, too.
Winds will rise, and grass will rise,
But not the heart that's longing.

"That's beautiful! But the music is still so——" She hunted for a word but could not find one to precisely express the mood the drums conjured. She threw up a hand in vexation. "It is most disturbing."

"Much of the ancient world was frightening. But then," he added to himself, "so is much of our world, too."

"Yes, but *you* are not so fearful after all. You have a lovely voice." She added carelessly: "So did your namesake, or so legend says. Do you think your mother knew of your gift at birth and named you accordingly?"

Tamlane was annoyed to feel himself redden. His name had through the years been more of a burden than a benefit.

"That is nonsense—superstition. After all, did *your* mother know that Lovelace's poem would suit you?"

Amarantha chuckled and then quoted:

Amarantha, sweet and fair,
Ah, braid no more that shining hair. . . .
Every tress must be confessed
But neatly tangled at the best

Like a clew of golden thread
Most excellently ravelled.

125

"Was that what you meant?" she asked him. "But I am not golden-haired. Anyway, mother did not read poetry. I was named for the flower."

"The verse still fits you well. '*Do not wind up that light in ribbands. . . .* ' "

"That is a pretty compliment, sir. I did not know that you had the way of flowery speech. You are a lover of cavalier poetry?"

"Some of it. But the compliment was from Lovelace."

"No. I don't think so. After all, Lovelace is not here." Suddenly she looked truly happy.

Their arrival in town put an end to their intriguing, but also rather painful, conversation. The pony and trap were put up at the local stable where much of the transaction was done with gestures because of the noisesome music in every corner of the village.

It was apparent to Amarantha that Rector Adair was well known in Padstow, as many people smiled in greeting or shouted jests in Cornish as they slowly traversed the streets. It was also apparent that her presence was causing a great deal of startlement and aggravation among the females of the coastal village. They glared at her with angry suspicion and pouted rather than smiled when Tamlane's handsome head was turned away from them.

At another time, she might have been pleased or even amused by this reaction, but something uncontrolled and perhaps even dangerous was riding in the air that day. Feeling shy and somewhat overwhelmed by the foreign sounds and press of bodies, Amarantha made certain that she stayed by Tamlane's side, arms linked as they pushed into the crowds so that they might have a close view of the parade.

Amarantha would have liked to know more of the dancers in the procession—the Teazers, her uncle had called them—but there was no chance to talk for the percussive beat of dancing feet and pounded drums filled the air and made the very earth beneath them seem to tremble at the blows.

Suddenly, the mob about them cheered and then began to sing, adding their voices to the musical din.

"What are you going to do?" the women asked.
And the men replied: *"Kill a little fish."*
"How will you take it home?" the ladies cried.
"In my belly!"
"How will you eat it then?"
"With my teeth and hands!"

The mob surged swiftly and renewed its wild cheering, waving long sticks in the air. Amarantha was pushed away from Tamlane's side by a band of women, her hand jerked from his arm before she could catch a firm hold. She felt many hands in the middle of her back shoving her out into the cobbled street.

"Stop!" she commanded. Amarantha turned her head all about, but the masked and cloaked revelers were too close to permit her any view of her guardian.

"Tamlane!" she shouted. Her voice was barely audible even in her own ears.

The music changed, grew hypnotic and deafening. The mob began to chant.

Earth and water and fire and air—
Wind and flame and sea and stone—
Bold and black the Obby Oss comes!

Other young girls, these decked as sacrifices with wreaths of bluebells and hazel twigs, were herded out into the street and ringed with chanting dancers. They were giggling so Amarantha assured herself that there was no need to be alarmed, but the rabble of grotesque masks and caped bodies was drawing in tighter and tighter, threatening them with pointy sticks, and the shrieking voices were all but piercing her ears.

It was like a hanging day at Tyburn Hill when the mobs came to see off their favorite criminals, she thought, feeling suddenly ill. She needed to get away—to find a breath of clean air.

The Obby Oss comes!

"Tamlane!" she shouted again. But she couldn't hear her own voice above the dancing rabble.

Amarantha turned about. Not all the faces in the circle were friendly as they stared at her and she was more than once pinched on her arms by hidden tormentors. Disgusted with the riot and growing more fearful, she fought her way to the edge of the laughing girls, determined to push through the dancers and regain her place at Tamlane's side. She could see him now, standing a good head taller than the rest of the crowd. His face was turned away as he searched the crowd for her. His mouth in profile looked vexed but unalarmed.

"Tamlane! Here I am!" She waved an arm, trying to attract his attention. "Bloody hell!"

Spurred by another nip to the arm, she began pushing and shouting with an appalling lack of verbal manners and brutal inconsideration for the revelers' feet.

"Let me go, you oaf! Tamlane!" She was nearly free of the laughing maidens when the crowd suddenly pulled back from them. A hundred masked fingers pointed and began a sinister laughing.

The Obby Oss has come! Choose! Choose!

Something dark blotted out the sun. Amarantha spun about and was confronted with a midnight black monster.

"Bloody hell!" she said again. She had one moment to take in the fact that the beast looked a bit like Uncle Cyril's drawing of the horse god Epona and then the creature reared back and she was engulfed in its tattered, smothering skirts and a tangle of legs.

Amarantha screamed as rough hands grabbed her and dragged her inside, but it was a waste of breath, for nothing could be heard above the cheering crowd.

"Hello, pretty," a drunken voice breathed into her face, bathing her in noxious fumes. An arm encircled her bent waist and she was pressed against a sweaty body. A rough hand fumbled at her breast and she could feel the fabric of her bodice giving way.

Suddenly more enraged than frightened, she lashed out and was pleased to feel her elbow connect with something solid. She then pulled away with all her might and snatching up her skirts so she wouldn't trip, she scurried at a crouch though the forest of bodies beneath the monster for the ray of daylight that showed the break in the creature's bunting. She ran out into the daylit din of hideous masked dancers and banging drums and straight into Tamlane's arms.

The rector also laid rough hands upon her person as he secured her to him, but this she did not mind. She laid her face against his waistcoat and waited for the remainder off the mob to rush after the monster.

Once it was quiet around them, she lifted up her head and took a shaky breath.

"That was—I assume—the Obby Oss." Her voice was unsteady.

"Yes." For one instant Tamlane sounded angry, but then he looked her over and smiled. He touched her now very wild hair and then shook his head saying: "You look a complete gypsy. I feel I should say something reproving about the evils of virgins rushing out to be seduced by monsters."

The teasing was an effective restorative. Her pale face flushed with color and Amarantha stepped back from the shelter of his arms. She pulled her cloak about herself and began to inventory the damage to her person and clothing.

"Please do not start being an *ordinary* rector now. In any event, that wasn't seduction—it was rape. And I didn't rush to the monster, I was pushed." She glared down at the smudges on her skirts and made an effort to gather up her loosened hair and tuck it beneath her hood.

"I fear the results are the same. Legend says you shall have a child before the next Beltane," he said lightly. "I predict that this shall come to pass."

Amarantha glared at him.

"It might have happened at that," she said tartly. "But an elbow to the nose seemed to discourage whichever one of those inebriated bullies had a hold on me. I just wish that I had hit some of the pinchers as well. I shall be bruised for a week."

Suddenly Tamlane was not smiling.

"Are you saying that someone *touched* you?"

"Wasn't that the point?"

"No! Certainly not."

"Then you can better spend your time reproving the monster. I surely do not plan to repeat this experience. Look at this!" Amarantha opened her cloak and pointed at the torn ruffles of her bodice. The damage was minor, but annoying. Soon she would have no nice dresses left to wear.

She was about to add another scathing comment about the local traditions when it dawned on her that Tamlane wasn't just stunned—he was blindingly angry. His bronzed skin was drawn taut over his cheekbones and his lips were compressed into a white line.

"Are you hurt?"

"Definitely not. Be at ease," she said instead, abandoning her complaints in the face of his rage. "I have already defended my honor. I wasn't harmed. Only my gown is hurt, and it can be mended."

Tamlane took one deep breath, then another. Trembling hands were clenched behind him. Amarantha belatedly recalled stories of Scotsmen of the Gordon clan going into berserk rages on the battlefield, and though rather flattered at his protectiveness, she regretted mentioning the incident. Tamlane in a berserk rage was not something she wished to witness.

"Tamlane?" she said uneasily. "You aren't going to

go off and leave me here alone while you chase the monster. Are you?"

"No, though I should deal with the brutes now."

"No, you should *not*." Amarantha was emphatic.

"You should not have been molested—and had it happened, you should not have had to defend yourself," he said shortly, through clenched teeth. "This was a terrible breach of hospitality, and be certain that I shall *reprove* the sea monster. Harshly."

"Please don't. Truly, I think I broke the man's nose. See, there is blood on my sleeve. The dress was probably an accident. It was very close quarters under there." Her excuses sounded lame, but she persisted.

"Come along. I will take you home."

"You said that yesterday," she sighed.

"So I did, and it was a sound notion then as well."

"Tamlane, there is no need—"

"There is every need!" He took a breath and said more mildly: "The gods apparently do not smile on this celebration. There will be a storm soon."

"What?"

"It is going to rain." His tone was still clipped, but his hands as he wrapped her cloak back around her no longer tremored with rage and were as gentle as she could wish.

Though Amarantha had no desire to be hurried home, she decided that removing Tamlane from the village until he had calmed might be the most prudent course to take.

"Tamlane?" she asked as they walked toward the stables. "Do you know who was inside the Obby Oss?"

"No, but I shall."

"You aren't going to do anything impulsively idiotic, are you? Truly, I am not hurt. This was just high spirits run amok—too much Celtic enthusiasm and drink."

"Don't concern yourself, Amarantha. I am never impulsive."

"That is not much reassurance, for I know that is a patently false statement," she scolded, her teeth beginning chatter. The wind was rising off the sea, and daylight was taking on a strange yellow-green color that gilded everything from the waves to the stone of the buildings with a tarnished glow. There was indeed a monster coming from the sea, and it was not the Obby Oss.

"It is all the assurance you should need," he said, pulling open the stable door and ushering her inside. "I have never lied to you."

"Ha! You haven't told me the truth either. I like you better when you aren't angry," she muttered. "You are quite frightening when you get like this."

"I am sorry if I have frightened you. I prefer myself in a calm state as well, but I fear that we are about to be caught in a downpour and must make haste. It is bad enough that you have been manhandled. I should like to return you without an inflammation of the lung as well. Your uncle will think me unsuited to have care of you. Have a seat while I hitch up the cart." He did not precisely shove her onto a roll of hay, but he was definitely sacrificing manners for speed.

"If rain upsets you so, I should hate to see you in a snow storm," she mumbled.

Tamlane didn't answer her. Perhaps he hadn't heard.

*　　*　　*

Though it was but early afternoon when the cart mounted the upward track to the moor, the sky outside had darkened to twilight levels. They reached Blesland ahead of the storm, but not by much. The green was covered over with lilac shadows. It looked cold and forbidding even with the light from the smoldering bonfire.

"I am glad they lit the fire early," Tamlane said. "It would be considered an ill omen if rain ruined the ceremony. For the next year, the farmers would go in fear of their crops and livestock."

"May we not stay and watch for a while?" Amarantha asked. "The rain has held off. Perhaps it will not come at all."

Tamlane looked down at her and shook his head.

"You are pinched with cold," he objected.

"But we could stop at the tavern to dine and warm ourselves."

His familiar smile finally eased onto his face.

"Poor Amarantha. You have not had a pleasant day. And we forgot your thread as well. Very well. We shall stop for a meal and watch the sheep being driven through the fire."

"They drive the sheep through the fire?" Amarantha was appalled.

"There are really two fires. There is a narrow gap between them where the sheep—and people—may pass."

"People too?"

"Those wishing for children, yes. That is what the Beltane fire is for. The insurance of fertility and protection from disease."

"Better the fire than the Obby Oss, I suppose."

Their arrival at the tavern was met with little comment, as it was largely empty. The anxious boy who waited their table spent a goodly portion of his time staring out the casement and the rest watching Amarantha. She could not take offense at his behavior, however unnerving the attention, as his expression was so unabashedly admiring. Still, she wished that they were left completely alone over their meal.

Since there were no other diners that evening and the tap room was empty of customers, the villagers all being outside with the fire and rising winds, they were able to secure a table near the hearth and its dying fire that also gave a view—though a very restricted one, which was often obscured by their curious server—of the darkening greensward and its balefire.

Amarantha did not remove her cloak, for it would betray the state of her dress, but as the weather was chilly and the fire plainly being allowed to die, such behavior was not unexpected.

Seeing Amarantha's confusion at the neglected hearth, Tamlane explained: "It is because of the balefire. All other fires must be put out before full dark or it dilutes the magic."

There was a limited selection to be had from the kitchen that day with most of the staff out at the bonfire. But they made a good meal of under-roast kidneys and potatoes, and an adequate but somewhat cloudy hock. They finished the simple repast with *mahogany,* made with treacle and some strong spirit, which made Amarantha's blood race and brought color to her cheeks.

"Awright 'n aree?" their server asked Tamlane, with a longing look at the flames outside the tavern's small window. The words were unintelligible to Amarantha, but the meaning was not.

"Ez." The rector waved the boy away, and the lad rushed off without clearing the table.

Tamlane stood and offered his hand.

"Come to the casement and view your fire." He drew her to the window and placed her before him, caging her with his body. One hand settled at her waist, the other pointed over her shoulder. "This is not just any jumble of sticks you see before you. It has been started from nine pieces of wood gathered by nine men who neither wore nor used iron while collecting it. Next, the bones and skull of a horse were thrown in. That will transfer the horse's strength to all animals passing through the fire."

Amarantha looked at the tall pole in the middle of the fire, its tattered streamers badly charred and being whipped by the wind.

"They are burning the Maypole," she said in dismay.

"Yes. It has served its purpose. Now it must be sacrificed, too."

Sacrifice! How she hated that word! Amarantha shivered in spite of the heat of Tamlane's body pressed to her back.

"Suddenly I am very tired," she said quietly. "And it has begun to rain. Let us be off before Uncle Cyril worries."

"Poor sweet." Tamlane tugged on her straying hair, forcing her to look up at him. "You have certainly had a surfeit of *Celtic enthusiasm* this day. There is just

one other tradition I would like to share with you—
and it needn't tire you. . . ."

Amarantha's heart began to pound. Tamlane was
smiling slightly, but she did not think that he was
jesting or in any way amusing himself.

"Yes?" Her voice was soft enough to be a whisper.

She knew what he intended and wondered whether
she was so exhausted by her adventures as to be totally bereft of reason. Surely it had to be that, for it
was madness to allow this man to kiss her. He was
leading a double life—one of them quite possibly
criminal, whatever his intentions. And had she not
been glad when her feelings for Ian had finally died?
She knew well that it was madness to care for a man
wedded to some political quest—and the Church as
well!

At one time, she could not have imagined being
attracted to Tamlane Adair. He was somewhat dark
and unyielding in nature, while she had been young
and gay and feckless. But that had all changed. She
was no longer so young and frivolous. Now she found
the dedication—and even the danger—that was part
of this dark side of Tamlane's business to be very attractive.

"What are you thinking?' he asked her. "Your eyes
tell me nothing."

"There is nothing yet to tell," she whispered.

Had she not said that she would not repulse a new
love if it came to her? Here he was at last—a man
whom she liked and found fascinating. If he could
reconcile his holy calling with his impulses, she need
not argue with him—she would not turn her head
away.

"Ah, lass." The gentle brush of his lips across hers evoked a tender sigh and a tell-tale softening of posture.

Tamlane shuddered with pleasure and set her from him. As much as his body clamored, he did not permit himself to linger with Amarantha in his arms. The brief meeting of their lips had told him all he needed to know. His physical passions for this woman would burn hotter than a balefire—and much less safely.

The only sensible course of action was to see as little of her as he could until his business with The Brothers was done. And after that, he would make all haste to the altar. *Better to wed than to burn.*

Chapter Six

The night rain had quickened the earth, and the moor was bursting with life. Overnight the asphodels had leapt from the ground and unfolded into bloom. The somber mood of yestereve had fled. Looking about at the rain-washed bluebells—glorious after the storm—it seemed impossible that the sort of political chaos that had engulfed Scotland could ever come to the moor.

Amarantha walked slowly away from the house, shredding crusts for the birds that lined the roof's gables in an uneven row and were staring at her in greedy anticipation. Her hair was once again loose. She had followed Tamlane's advice and not bound it, or herself, up in feminine shackles. Though she had gone about the moor unfettered before, it had been

Melanie Jackson

a small act of protest. That morning she had awoken feeling curiously liberated and free. There was no need to envy the fowl their wings. Her soul had finally escaped its cage.

A green softness lay over the land. It was early yet, but the sun's heat fell out of the sky—a radiant benediction that warmed her bones and flooded her soul with joy as she lifted her face to the light. Of course, it was not the sun alone that warmed her. It was an emotion that she had thought forever dead and buried with an old love. It was hope and attraction and—many wondrous things all bound up together!

Tamlane had kissed her!

A small thrill shook her as it raced through her body, leaving her blushing and shaken. So moved had she been by the kiss that that night she had dreamt of him. He had appeared to her, striding from the heart of a balefire, a long green cloak of enchantment falling from his shoulders, his hair loose and wild, eyes blazing with all the tempests of the winter sea.

Down in a bed of bluebells had they lain, the *hee-fayrie*—the great Tamlane of legend—bare of clothing beneath the cloak to find a place between her naked thighs. And she had wrapped her arms about him, bereft of all shame or maidenly hesitation.

Recalling her dream, Amarantha touched a hand to her breast and then to her flushed cheek.

She awoke from her reverie to discover that she had come to the end of the drive. She turned left and wandered away from the path to the village. She did not want any company to distract her from her thoughts—simple as they were. Also, on this morning of glorious renaissance, it would be obscene to look upon the damage to the ancient greensward caused by the Maypole and the scorching balefire that had burned there yestereve.

It was better to contemplate her internal fires, which were also magically renewing. The attraction that could sometimes ignite between a man and a woman had been between her and Tamlane from their first meeting. But while cautious suspicion on her part should have smothered the spark, instead it had somehow fanned it to greater life. Even their different personalities, which might have been a bar, did not cause either contempt nor blend themselves into some common, mundane liking—the former being the usual fate of her relationships with the men who entered her life these days.

Instead, their differences had kindled one another. It was a new future she looked at this morning.

It was also potential pain, she admitted with a small flutter of alarm.

Amarantha put a hand to her cheek. But there were many signs that the future could bring magnificent joy, she told herself. Did she not tingle in every limb with a mixture of anticipation and anxiety? And did she not fail to predict from one moment to the next which emotion would be transcendent? It was her heart and not her head that held sway now, which was the way that great loves went.

That was all well and good, her sensible side argued, but how could she be certain that there was something more than attraction between them? Surely genuine love—for so she wanted to name this emotion—required the soil of honesty to take root in. Delicate seeds would not grow in stony ground.

Of course, countered optimism, who was to say that the ground was sterile? It had not been salted, only abandoned for a time after Ian's desertion. Perhaps it simply needed a season to lay fallow, to heal. Mayhap her heart knew truth better than her senses, and it would give her what she needed now that the time was propitious.

And perhaps it did not know best. Perhaps it was distracted by Tamlane's many charms.

Amarantha made a sound of frustration and turned about on her heel. She paced back toward Talland House, casting the last of her crusts aside to her avian entourage that followed her with fluttering coos of greed.

"That is the last of it. You may cease your chase," she told them, when the birds continued to eye her hopefully and flap agitated wings. "This madwoman has naught else to give you. Begone."

Of course, she wasn't truly *mad* and therefore irresponsible, and the only sensible thing for her to do was to discover the truth about Tamlane's affairs. Now, more than ever, she was determined to find out what Tamlane Adair was doing with the connivance of French smugglers—if that was what they were. It still seemed to her that smuggling must be the Frenchmen's chief occupation, for though there were many Frenchmen in the world, they did not journey to small towns on the Bodmin Moor . . . in secrecy . . . during the dark of the moon. If the French were there, it was for profit.

But Tamlane . . .

Amarantha thought of his quick mind, his odd yet consistent scruples, the direct honesty that looked out of his magnificent eyes when he spoke of his faith. Tamlane cared about his parishioners, she was certain. Profit was not what motivated him to act. No, it was not money that lured him. It remained to be discovered what Tamlane's relationship to the French was, and how Maxwell Taxier fit into the complicated puzzle, but she was as certain as the sunrise it was not greed that moved him.

The door to the house opened with a cheerful bang and Cyril Stanhope stepped outside. The day was so pleasant that he, too, had abandoned fashion's shackles and was without an overcoat.

"Amy, dear, I have been looking for you. I am thinking of taking a small trip to wild Langarrow," he announced without preamble.

"Langarrow?" she repeated, startled from her inner contemplation. "But, Uncle, wasn't that the—"

"Yes! Buried in sand for moral turpitude," he answered cheerfully, his eyes sparkling. "I didn't mean that literally, of course. After all, we don't need a trip to Saint Guron's well to foretell the future, do we?"

Amarantha blinked twice and made an effort to banish Tamlane's distracting features from her mind. Her attention was obviously needed here, for her uncle was in far too jovial a mood for a man about to abandon his research and set forth in travel—something he heartily disliked and never did impulsively. And his references to Cornish magical sites this morning were—even for him—unusually obscure. He was obviously planning something of sufficient import that his precious translations could be set aside.

"I am not so certain," she answered at last. "Saint Guron's help would be most welcome, I think. I would like to know what the future held for me. But please speak plainly. Where were you thinking of going, if not to see Langarrow?"

Uncle Cyril chuckled at what he assumed was a jest.

"I've had a letter from my friend Cookworthy in Helston. He's found some deposits of china clay. Apparently, there is some interest from a chap in Wooster who thinks he can use soapstone to make porcelain—the real stuff that won't crack when you pour hot tea into it. They have been attempting to manufacture some crockery and having a deal of success with the venture!"

Amarantha stared in consternation. Langarrow, Saint Guron—and now porcelain. She arranged and rearranged the words in her mind but still made no sense of them.

"And King Arthur made teapots there, I suppose."

"Don't be daft, girl. Of course he didn't! The leader of the Celts wasn't a bloody potter."

"Then what do you want with porcelain from Helston?" she demanded.

"*I* don't want anything with it! But *you'll* be wanting some fancy porcelain soon. By June at the latest, I should think. Much better to have some pottery made here than in some heathen land, so I'm off for Helston. What do you think? A teapot and a dozen cups? No, better twenty. And some dishes—platters and such. Ah well, Cookworthy will know just what we need. Do you like the blue porcelain, or the one with the colorful herons and trees?"

"Colorful herons and trees," she answered, giving up all hope of understanding her uncle. A search for colorful native porcelain sounded safe enough, and it suited her to have him away for a while. In any event, she had more important things to contemplate.

"You don't mind staying here alone, do you?" Uncle Cyril asked suddenly. "I am sure that Tamlane will visit often and Mrs. Polreath will be here to keep you company. Or—I've just thought—you could come with me. We would only be gone for a week or so. Unless we went to Saint Catherine's. 'Tis a special place. The Knights Templar—"

"Thank you, but no," Amarantha declined hurriedly. She knew how these journeys of her uncle's worked. He'd find some inn he liked and squat there indefinitely while he pored over his notes and sampled the local grape or rye gleanings. She could not risk being away next Sunday night. "But, Uncle! Before you go—"

"Yes, dear?" he asked with a frown.

"I have heard that there are some standing stones near a wood and a creek north and west of here. Where might they be—specifically?"

Cyril's face brightened.

"You're getting caught up in the spell, aren't you? The moor is a fascinating place. I shall take you to the local dancing stones when I return. They are said to be the wicked maidens of Blesland—"

"I should like to visit them soon and hear the tale, but not just now," Amarantha interrupted. She added inventively: "It would spoil it to know the story before I see them. Once I've been there, I will know better what questions to ask of you on another visit. It will also take some time for me to sketch them and I do not wish to detain you when you have such excellent weather for travel."

"Oh, very well." He looked slightly disappointed at being deprived of the treat of showing off some of his favorite monuments. "You must go north from the Trethevy Quoit. There you will find a stream that broadens out into a largish creek. Follow it downstream until you see the wood. The stones are an obvious outthrust sitting at the top of a small hillock. Just have a care with the wild berry vines on the south bank of the stream. They can be nasty. Sheep have gotten so tangled that they starved to death waiting for rescue."

"I shall be careful," she promised sincerely.

"Ask Tamlane to go with you," her uncle suggested. "He knows the area quite well, and I've seen him up there a time or two."

"Do not be concerned. I plan to see him there," she said with an innocent smile that would never have fooled her parents but passed easily by her childless uncle.

"That is fine then. It's an excellent and private place for a bit of trysting. Well then, I shall be off forthwith. No time to waste. What a splendid day for travel." Cyril smiled back at her and then strode briskly away. Apparently her unanticipated—and to her, *unknown*—need for porcelain had seized fiercely upon his brain. Amarantha hoped that he was not growing soft in the head. His Arthurian fixation was quite distracting enough. There would be no living with him if he started cluttering up the house with pottery.

He was correct about it being a glorious day for travel, though. Amarantha decided that she did not even need a cloak with the sun resting on her in a warm mantle. She would walk off some of her restlessness by heading at once to explore the path to the standing stones.

The way to the quoit was quite well known to her now, and from there it was easy to head due north until she found the creek and then travel west toward the narrow belt of woods that bisected that part of the moor. She was grateful not to have to cope with any fens or bogs along the way. They were not dangerous if you were careful about where you set your feet, but they were eerie places where the ancient Celts used to drown their dead, and she did not care for them.

At first, the shade offered by the trees seemed attractive. Beneath the wood, the land was still damp and littered with fallen leaves and twigs, which snapped underfoot and filled the air with aromatic scents. But it was not an entirely welcoming place when one ventured deeper. The moor's tiny forest was not a pleasure garden deliberately cultivated to encourage people to saunter in its shade. In many places the trees' roots had heaved themselves out of the rocky soil and were waiting beneath the drifted leaves to trip the unwary, and low-growing branches snatched at her skirts with mean fingers that delayed and tore at her clothing. There were also places where branches—thick as her wrists—had woven themselves into a wall that no creature larger than a spider could penetrate.

There was also much scuttling about in the shrubbery, and while she knew that it was likely rabbits or harmless field mice moving about in the undergrowth, still she did not care for the atmosphere. There was too much movement in a place that felt empty of all companionship. She did not believe in spriggans and dragons and such, but there might be some wild pigs about—or even a feral cat.

In any event, she decided, stopping abruptly at a patch of brambles, it wasn't necessary to go deep into the forest for cover. The less overgrown edges of the tangled woods would offer plenty of concealment after dark.

Amarantha gladly left the dark wood and returned to the waiting sunshine. Ahead of her was an isolated hillock. The dancing stones showed their crowns at the top on a talus slope, which was not especially steep, but had some loose scree on its weedy banks. Amarantha made a note that she would have to use care as she climbed, for a carelessly placed foot could send rocks scattering and make an awful racket in the silence of the night.

Amarantha scrambled quickly upward and paused at the crest to regain her breath. She had been expecting something grim and solid like the quoit and was therefore pleasantly surprised by the standing stones. They were not especially large and forbidding. No longer erect, they canted slightly like inebriates, some of them actually touching one another as though they were too drunk to remain standing on their own. Or perhaps they *were* maidens frozen in some pagan dance.

They certainly looked gay. The stones wore thick coats of colorful lichens and had bright shoes of new green moss with tufted leek bows. The landscape about them was meager, barren but for some red-tinged bracken and a few stands of exuberant gorse. The eye had no choice but to be drawn to the vivid stones' stationary revels and once there, their color made her smile.

She circled the stones once, deciding where she might best take shelter and still watch the proceedings on Sunday night. One of the stands of gorse seemed most likely. It would be difficult to conceal herself behind the stones themselves, and the land was quite bare of other cover in the immediate area around them. But the gorse was thick and did not make too much betraying rustling if one was cautious.

Feeling suddenly peckish and regretting those carelessly cast-off crusts, she turned about and began retracing her steps toward the stream. Much care was needed in descending the talus slope, and it was not until she had reached the bottom of the hill that she realized she was no longer alone.

Percy Aldridge and two other men were waiting below, sitting quietly atop their mounts, dress swords sheathed and looking out of place on the empty moor. In spite of the sun's warmth, they were buttoned up in correct, formal attire with brass buttons gleaming. Their expressions were also correctly formal.

Amarantha felt at a disadvantage, dressed carelessly

149

and approaching on foot, but could think of no way to avoid them now that they had seen her and were so obviously waiting to speak to her. She gritted her teeth and walked toward them. She might dislike their presence in this place so close to Sunday, but there was no need to appear foolish or frightened by running away. Indeed it would be most unwise to show any weakness, for she sensed that Percy Aldridge was the type to exploit fear in others.

"Good morning, Mister Aldridge," she said politely, but without enthusiasm, coming to a stop four paces away. Their mounts did not look particularly mean, but she had a theory that horses took on the temperament of their riders and did not want to get too close lest she be bitten.

"Mistress Stanhope." His bow was punctilious. "What are you doing out here? Are you alone?"

Amarantha raised an eyebrow and replied coldly: "Walking. What are you doing out here?"

She did not intend to answer his other question, finding it offensive.

Percy Aldridge flushed at hearing his own impertinent question thrown back at him, and he began to scowl.

"We are on our way to Padstow," he said stiffly. "Mistress, it is not safe for you to be walking about alone. Did your uncle not tell you that a prisoner has escaped from Bodmin gaol?"

Her uncle hadn't mentioned it, but Tamlane had. She had simply been distracted that morning and forgotten the possible danger. Not that Amarantha had any intention of conceding the point to this man.

"The escape was mentioned. But I understood that

the man had stolen a horse and fled the area."

"We cannot be certain of that. There are also dastard smugglers lurking out here on the moor. Until we apprehend them, it is extremely foolish of you to be wandering alone."

"No," Amarantha contradicted him. Her anger was held in check with an effort. It wasn't what Aldridge said that angered her; it was *how* he said it. He was like a strawberry seed lodged in the gums—annoying and impossible to ignore.

"No!" Percy Aldridge mottled and his voice rose an octave. "What do you mean, *no?*"

"No, it is not dangerous during the day. And, no there aren't any smugglers on the moor."

"I tell you there are smugglers everywhere! Their villainy is legend!"

"And I am telling you that there are no smugglers here," Amarantha said calmly. "Uncle Cyril and I walk the moors daily, and I have *never* seen a smuggler. It's a pity really. They are, as you say, quite legendary and I should like to have a glimpse of one. And a giant, too, but I don't suppose I ever shall."

Percy Aldridge stared at her as though she had started speaking in tongues.

"They don't go about smuggling during the day," he said huffily, doubtless deciding that she was stupid.

Behind him, one of the other Preventives had to bite back a smile.

"In any event, I am certain you have seen them and are simply unaware of it. Many of the common folk are involved in the illicit trade," he told her.

"If they do not smuggle during the day then I am quite safe for now, so you need not be concerned."

She smiled broadly and added insincerely: "But I thank you for thinking of me. It is reassuring to know that you are here to protect us. If you will excuse me now . . ."

Amarantha went to step around the excise men, but Percy Aldridge again stopped her.

"Wait."

"Why?" Her voice was now arctic.

"We will escort you home," he said shortly. "I want a word with your uncle."

"Uncle Cyril is in Helston, so you will have to wait until next week to see him. The three-man escort is also unnecessary."

"I say an escort *is* necessary."

Finding the argument tiresome, Amarantha decided to end it.

"A single man shall surely be escort enough." Before Aldridge could reply, Amarantha smiled up at the younger of the excise men who had shown a brief flash of humor. "I would not dream of keeping you from your work, Mister Aldridge. But perhaps this gentleman—Mister—?"

"Guthrie," the young man supplied.

"Perhaps Mister Guthrie can be spared for an hour."

"Certainly." The tone was not gracious. He clearly did not like being thwarted, but there was no way to protest without looking ridiculous. "Guthrie, you will see Mistress Stanhope home and then ride on to Padstow."

"Sir!"

Without a word of goodbye, Aldridge and the second Preventive rode on.

Amarantha *tsked* and said: "He forgot to bow. His mother would be mortified at his lack of polish."

Guthrie turned his head and gave a strangled cough.

Left alone with the young excise man, Amarantha began to feel less annoyed. It occurred to her that this was actually an opportunity that could be exploited, if she was careful about extracting information.

She tilted her head to one side and studied the Preventive.

Amarantha liked what she saw. Guthrie was young, squarely built, brown-skinned and perhaps attractive in a rough sort of way. He would also be of mortal height once he was removed from his equine perch.

"I suppose you feel it your bound duty to follow me to Talland House?" she asked with a small smile.

"Yes, Mistress, I do." He didn't sound terribly apologetic. "Mister Aldridge is quite correct about the escaped prisoner. He was to be transported to the madhouse and must be reckoned as quite dangerous."

"Then come along. Perhaps you would care to dismount and walk beside me," she suggested. "I shall get a crick in my neck if we continue to converse this way—and I quite refuse to have you trailing about behind me like a faithful hound."

"Certainly." Guthrie swung down from his saddle and then gathered his mount's reins close to the bit. "Shall I put you up in my place? We are a distance from the village and there is no need for you to tire yourself."

"Thank you, no. I prefer to walk." Amarantha

pushed a stray strand of hair off of her face, noting the admiring glance from her companion as he focused on the dark streamers that moved gently in the breeze. "You are new to Blesland, Mister Guthrie, are you not?"

"Yes, I was sent down just last weekend." His eyes returned to her face, and she made herself smile at him.

"I should not have thought—even with dangerous smugglers lurking in every bush—that there would be enough work for three of His Majesty's excise men in tiny Blesland. Surely the soldiers at Bodmin are protection and deterrent enough for this small neighborhood."

"We are here only temporarily. Once we have rid the area of France's lawless wickedness I shall be sent on to Helston."

"Indeed? How ambitious. I do hope then that there will be more of you."

"You do?" Guthrie was startled. Probably no one had ever told him that they wanted more tax collectors in their area. He asked ingenuously: "But why?"

"Certainly, I do. Three men will never suffice to rid the area of all the wickedness that abides here. Have you not heard of the many different evils that stalk the moor?"

"No," he said slowly. "I hadn't heard of *many* evils. Just French spies and smugglers."

Amarantha held up her hand and began to tick items off on her fingers.

"Well, there are spriggans—evil imps those. I think I heard some today over in the wood. And there is the famous Beast of Bodmin, a fierce fanged cat of some sort, one gathers, that can carry off children and slay grown men. And don't forget the giants. Jack the Giant-Killer lived here, you will recall. But not all of Cornwall is so dangerous. Helston, they say, is very nice," she said, dropping her hand and turning the conversation. Perhaps with enough sharp conversational turns in a short space of time, Guthrie would stumble and let some information slip.

"Yes, it is." He paused. "Mistress Stanhope?"

"Mister Guthrie?" She picked up another stray tress and brushed it over her shoulder. The distraction worked. His eyes followed her unbound hair. "You were saying?"

"Your conversation is a bit dizzying. Are you making a game of me?" he asked with touching dignity.

"A game? Whatever do you mean?" So, he wasn't entirely stupid. Amarantha kept her expression innocent as she lifted her face to the blue heights overhead and let the sun bathe her face. "Would you rather speak of the weather? It is rather glorious today."

"No, I—"

"Excellent—so over-discussed, the weather. Instead, do let us talk about Helston. I plan to visit there next May."

"Not this May?" he asked, trying gamely to follow her.

"No, for I have missed the furry dance. Not that I am pining. I am certain that nothing could be more impressive than Padstow's Obby Oss."

"Obby Oss?"

"A May Day sea monster," she explained. "Have a care for those daffodils! The heedless flowers will grow right where one wishes to walk, but I cannot bear to see them trampled upon."

Guthrie obediently pulled his mount aside and skirted the plants.

"Well, I do not know anything about this furry dance, but Helston holds other attractions for me."

"Hmm? The soapstone perhaps?"

A stray breeze wafted over them, and Amarantha turned her head so that her hair would catch the wind and settle over Guthrie's sleeve like a dark veil.

"*Er,* no." He stared hard at his coat as if uncertain of what to do with the dark strands that nestled there. "I was thinking of the change in society. I like to be with people—and a little less of Mister Aldridge's stifling company will be entirely welcome."

"You are not the only person to think so." She sidestepped a large stone, removing her locks from Guthrie's sleeve. "Though we are but a small village, Mister Aldridge has succeeding in driving most of the inhabitants away from the tavern. He is damaging the villagers' livelihoods."

"That is most direct, Mistress Stanhope." Guthrie was less growing less startled by her conversation.

"So is Mister Aldridge," she said with a sigh.

"I imagine that he has rather spoiled sport in the region." Guthrie sounded nearly apologetic. "I have been out on patrol at night in Blesland all this last week and never seen a soul abroad. You must lead a rather restricted social life and perhaps that is somewhat my fault."

"Ah. This is true. I am not surprised to hear that no one is abroad at night. But we mustn't blame you.

Or even Percy Aldridge. It is not your presence that keeps people in their homes at night."

"No?"

"No." Not trusting her face to remain innocent this time, Amarantha kept her gaze fixed on the patches of wildflowers near her feet, allowing her hair to veil her face.

" 'Tis Satan."

"*Satan?*" He said the word as though it had no meaning.

Amarantha couldn't blame him, as it had been her first reaction as well. Nevertheless, she felt compelled to attempt planting the seeds of nervousness in Mister Guthrie's young mind. A fear of going abroad on the moor could be most useful. There was no hope of instilling any sort of terror in Percy Aldridge—the man lacked all imagination—but perhaps young Guthrie would prove more fertile ground. And if he brought the subject up in the village, she could count on the Bleslanders to corroborate her tales, however wild.

"Yes. The devil. Mephistopheles. *The Father of Lies.* He travels the moor in a sable coach pulled by a team of headless horses." She kept her voice matter-of-fact.

"I see." He sounded incredulous. "And have you seen this coach?"

"Good heavens, no! Who in their right mind would go abroad on the moor at night? As you've seen, no one here does."

"I can't imagine who would venture out voluntarily," he said frankly. "It is an eerie place once night has fallen. Still, there are some—myself for instance—who have a compelling need to be abroad, and I have

157

never seen a sable coach or headless horses."

"Then I rejoice for your present fortune. And I'm most sorry for my earlier comment—I didn't mean to imply that *you* were insane. You have your orders from Mister Aldridge, and I don't imagine that he minds going out at night if there are a great many of you."

"There are only three of us. For now. Another man may be coming later. And Mister Aldridge doesn't go out at night. I was actually speaking of your rect—"

"No? *He* doesn't? But he makes you go in his place? How very—*odd.*" Amarantha interrupted hurriedly, allowing her disapproval of Percy Aldridge's supposed cowardice to show. She did not want to discuss Tamlane. She did not trust herself to remain neutral enough if questioned about him. Her cheeks had a habit of betraying her when the rector's name was mentioned.

There was a pause as Guthrie debated commenting further on his superior's habits, but in the end he turned the subject back to a safer topic.

"You uncle is in Helston now?" he asked directly.

"Yes." They turned onto the path that led to Talland House. "Look, a yew tree. How fortunate. Yew fights evil you know. It will protect one from demons and witches."

She broke off a twig and tucked it behind her ear and then offered Guthrie a second piece.

"No I didn't know that." He accepted the stem but seemed unsure of what to do with it. Amarantha plucked it from his hands and inserted it into a spare buttonhole.

Guthrie blushed.

"My uncle is a folklorist."

"He has folklorist friends in Helston?" Guthrie probed.

"Uncle Cyril has friends everywhere. But this trip is not social." She turned away and resumed walking.

"No? He has business concerns there?" Guthrie was definitely doing some prying of his own.

Amarantha had to work to suppress an evil smile.

"No," she answered casually. "He is there to purchase porcelain."

"Porcelain? Dishes and such?"

"Yes." Amarantha stopped at the drive to Talland House.

"I don't quite understand. Why go to Helston?"

"Neither do I understand his journey, Mister Guthrie. But that is one of Uncle Cyril's most attractive points. And why not Helston?"

"But there is no porcelain for sale in Helston," he objected. "Not unless—"

Not unless it was smuggled, was what he meant. Amarantha smothered another wicked smile at Guthrie's suddenly still face. What a stroke of good fortune! With any luck, this would send the three Preventives off post-haste to Helston to hunt for porcelain smugglers and keep them there until after next Sunday.

"There is certainly porcelain there now. My uncle had a letter telling him about it. If you will excuse me, Mister Guthrie, I am home now." She gestured toward the house. "I won't keep you any longer. Thank you for you kind escort. Do you have a care as you go."

"Certainly, Mistress," he answered. But his reply was distracted and he mounted hastily. The bit of yew fell unnoticed from his buttonhole and was left in the lane to be carelessly trampled.

"Good day. Have a safe journey."

"What?" He looked suddenly guilty.

And well he should! she thought. *What a cad to use her careless words to try and trap her uncle.*

"To Padstow," she reminded him. "That's where you are going, isn't it?"

"Oh—yes. Thank you, Mistress Stanhope. A good day to you also." Unlike Percy Aldridge, Mister Guthrie remembered to bow, but he rode off just as quickly as his superior had.

"And give my regards to Helston," she added under her breath.

She waited until Guthrie was out of sight, then turned up the drive to the house. She began calculating. A day would be lost in Padstow. It would take a day's hard riding to reach Helston—two if the roads were bad. And they would need at least a day to investigate and ride back. There would be no way that they could return before Sunday night.

Of course, they might not all go. But she had a feeling that the ambitious Mister Guthrie was going to press hard for the chance to uncover Helston's porcelain smugglers, and even one less Preventive in the area was an improvement over the current situation.

Amarantha decided that she would take another walk after lunch and pay a call on Rector Adair. He should be told of her uncle's desire to purchase porcelain and the excitement this aroused in Guthrie's breast.

Of course, she would take Taxier with her. Tamlane was apt to fuss if he knew she was out walking alone, and for some reason she was of a mind to please him this morning.

Feeling at once cheerful and full of purpose, Amarantha took up her skirts and walked briskly toward the house. Perhaps Pendennis would have baked a star-gazey pie and she could take a slice to Tamlane.

Chapter Seven

Stars bloomed overhead and the moon was still bright enough to cast a faint shadow, but the heavenly luminaries were being rapidly overtaken by another unseasonable squall. If the clouds became too thick or the rain too hard, Amarantha knew that she would have to use the lantern she had brought with her in order to find her way home. Which would be unfortunate because the light would surely attract the attention of anyone else who was out on the moor.

As it was, the night vapor rising from the creek threatened to become a problem. If it over-spilled its banks, it could easily blanket the lower wooded moor from the Dancing Stones to Talland House and force her out from the arboreal cover and onto higher ground, for she dared not risk wandering into a fen.

The thought called for some sotto-voce cursing. Why hadn't Tamlane just confessed when she'd visited him earlier with news of Guthrie's questions? If he had, there would have been no need for her to be out here now, on Sunday night, trying to find out some answers herself. She did not want to get lost in the mist, yet she did not dare to be seen by the Preventives—or the smugglers either! Though she did not think of the law-breakers as being the desperate cutthroats portrayed by Percy Aldridge. They couldn't be! She was convinced that Tamlane would not be involved with truly violent people. Still, at the very least, there would be a dreadful scandal if she were seen out at this time of night.

It was annoying that the wet weather had chosen this evening to descend upon the moor. Of course, she should have anticipated the event. It had been a wetter than usual spring. In two decades, the residents said that they had not had such late storms. But the moment that she had an urgent need to be out at night—*viola!* Rain appeared every time. Perhaps it was an ill omen.

"Bah!" An aggravated Amarantha climbed up the small rise to the talus she had walked during the day and stepped onto the path near the stream, which was more or less level and offered a limited view. She paused for a moment to catch her breath and to consider what next to do.

The standing stones were but ten minutes' level walking from where she was. If she didn't seek the protective cover of the wood. If she did, the way would be a great deal slower and she would likely be overtaken by the coming rain before she could get back to the house. And if the mist delayed her at all, the threatened drenching was a certainty.

"Bloody hell," she swore crossly, weighing speed and convenience against prudence. Prudence was still in slight ascendancy. The Preventives were more dangerous than fog. She had Uncle Cyril's cloak wrapped about her so she would not get cold, and she was wearing sensible shoes and a specially hemmed dress, which rose well above her ankles and left her free to walk without tangling herself in the low-growing shrubbery that carpeted much of the moor. As long as she stayed away from the berry vines—and did not wander into a bog—the wooded creek path was the more sensible course.

As if to mock her decision, the sky spit out a small spatter of water and waited for her reply. When she didn't move, it dropped more water upon her. Amarantha's teeth clenched in annoyance as the world around her began to drip.

This is all Tamlane's fault, she thought again. Why hadn't he responded differently to her inquiries, her clever probes? But he and Taxier had heard her tale of Uncle Cyril and the excise men out in silence, and then after an exchange of pointed glances, had made innocuous comments and sent her home. And both men had avoided her ever since! She had every right to be angry about his pigheaded refusal to confide in her—and now it was raining! If her stupid heart had not already been involved, she would simply leave the blasted moor and never see the man again.

But her heart—the fickle, senseless thing—was involved and would not permit her to leave without knowing the truth about the man it held in affection.

"Very well! The moor it is," she muttered, starting briskly for the standing stones. She didn't care much for the woods anyway. The trees looked like bent old men with arms outstretched to grab her, and called to mind all the talk about the escaped prisoners and the beast that stalked Bodmin Moor. These nonsensical—but still very unpleasant—thoughts made her regret her decision not to borrow a pistol from her uncle's gunroom before starting out on her adventure.

"Ridiculous! Why am I out here in the rain and dark? I should know better. Men and their political causes! '*I could not love thee, dear, so much*—' " she groused as she trudged along. "As if women did not have honor and did not know very well what love was!"

Life was growing more difficult by the day. First had come the impulse to live again, to be involved with others' affairs. And then her heart had reawakened from its long sleep and began telling her of its need for affection. Unwished for—and at times, like now, completely unwanted—the need spoke out strongly and demanded recognition.

Stupid heart! Did it not understand that she had been slighted by the object of its affection? Trivialized! Deemed unworthy of confidence. And what was the sense of indulging her heart if she were to die of an inflammation of the lungs? Or, worse yet, to have her spirit wither away because it was starved for respect and confidence but destined to receive none from the man who did not trust her.

"I should leave right now. Before he knows that I am here. With my ill luck I shall be discovered wet and sniffing. Shall I betray myself in this fashion? Why not simply strip naked and stand in the square proclaiming my mindless infatuation for the man? It could not be more humiliating." But in spite of her harsh words, she didn't leave. Her feet continued to guide her toward the hillock where her heart knew Tamlane waited.

However, she had taken only a dozen steps more when there came a shout from up ahead followed by rifle shot.

Amarantha's heart gave a painful bump and then began galloping like a frightened horse. She could practically hear pursuing hooves clattering under her ribs as it raced with alarm.

"Tamlane!" she gasped, all ire forgotten.

There were more shots, louder ones that seemed to fly at her out of the dark, and Amarantha dropped her lantern and dove for the sheltering wood. But she didn't turn back east toward the protection of home. Instead she continued to run toward the ragged outthrust of the stone hillock where the standing stones were. Her terror-enlarged heart was in her mouth, and she regretted eating a heavy meal of stewed mutton, which seemed to weigh on her stomach as much as an entire wooly sheep would. But danger or not, she had no choice but to go on. It wasn't mere curiosity that drove her to action now. Other, stronger emotions compelled her will.

There was more shouting in two different directions, but the words were being drowned out by a rising wind. It was an uncanny thing that howled like a pack of wolves on the hunt.

Or could it be that these were real hounds that the Pre-

*ventives had set upon the smugglers? They used them in
Scotland to hunt fugitives.* Amarantha gave a small sob
and began running at an angle for the fog-bound
stream. Her previous fear of the woods was forgotten.
Rain would help confuse the scent, but only running
water would baffle true hunting hounds. Tamlane
knew this and he would surely head for the creek.
She would try and intercept him and—and—do
something!

Of course, the Preventives would also know this
and would likely race for the creek too. *Why hadn't
she brought a weapon!*

Once in the woods, the way was rough. The trees
were tangled and presented a narrow but dense bar-
rier whose roots were treacherous in the dark. She
stumbled often, but fear kept her mainly on her feet
until a black horse suddenly burst out the tangled
wood and nearly ran her down.

For an instant, she thought the devil had come
upon her. Amarantha cried out and dodged the
wicked hooves that thundered by.

"Mistress Stanhope!" The horse's rider was barely
in control of the beast, but he managed to check its
headlong flight and come back for her. It was only
as he drew near her prone form that she recognized
Maxwell Taxier.

"Mistress Stanhope!" he gasped again. He had his
right hand clapped over his left shoulder and he was
hunched in the saddle. "Are you hurt? You must flee
at once. Get up before me!"

"Taxier? Where is Tamlane?" she demanded, attempting to regain her feet but finding herself tan-

gled in her skirts and unable to rise farther than her knees. "Is he hurt?"

A crash answered her, before she could do more than turn her head, a second black horse and dark cloaked rider was bearing down upon her. Fortunately, Tamlane had complete control of his mount and leaped over her half-prone body with a disciplined bound.

His horse was well in hand, but his emotions were another matter. Tamlane's expression was hidden by darkness, but his voice was plain enough in its anger.

"Amarantha! Are you daft, woman?"

"Thank God!" she breathed, a large measure of her fear falling by the wayside now that he was there and obviously unhurt. She untucked her skirts from the brambles' embrace and rose. Dignity was forgotten. Placing a trembling hand on his boot she said: "I was so afraid that you had been shot."

Tamlane didn't answer for a moment. When he spoke again, his voice was calmer and there was only a hint of exasperation lingering in his tone.

"If this night doesn't end in total disaster, it will be no thanks to you, you disobedient girl. How bad is it?" Tamlane asked Taxier riding forward.

Amarantha dropped her trembling hand and stepped back a pace.

"A graze only. Have you a handkerchief? I must stop the bleeding or the dogs will take the scent." Taxier's voice was weak, suggesting that he lied about the seriousness of his wounds. "The others? Did they get away?"

"I believe so. If they make it past the berry vines, they will be fine. You are the last. What possessed thee, man, to ride this way?" Tamlane took out a handkerchief and folded it into a pad, which he thrust inside Taxier's shirt. He pulled off his neckerchief, and tied a rough bandage over Taxier's holed smock. That done, he reached into his left pocket for a flask which he uncapped and held to Taxier's lips.

"As if I would leave you to face the Preventives alone. Besides, if they take my scent I will lead them to the others."

"Drink. You should have gone on. I was in no danger. I know these moors well—and the ship will likely be well off before the hounds arrive."

Taxier looked down at Amarantha's worried face and out of kindness didn't argue. Instead he took another draught from the flask.

"Well, there's no blinking at facts. I won't make it to the ship now, lad. The boat will be away by now if they have any sense," Taxier said when the flask was pulled away. His voice was still far from strong and the rain pattering on the leaves overheard nearly drowned it out.

"Another drop?" Tamlane asked, holding up the flask. "There's still a swallow left."

"Nay, I'll be drunk as a wheelbarrow if I have any more of that noxious French brew. I'm already a bit lightheaded."

"Sorry, but I have no scotch." Tamlane turned to Amarantha and offered her the flask.

"No." She was quite dazed enough by the night's events and did not want any brandy to confuse her.

"My little puritan," Tamlane said as he shook his head and pocketed the flask. He turned back to Taxier. "No, my friend, you won't be going over the sea this time. But I believe that we can still carry the day. Come, let us contrive a little."

Tamlane looked down at Amarantha and smiled suddenly, his teeth white in the darkness.

"Your presence may turn out to be a blessing after all, gypsy."

Amarantha finally regained some of her wits and demanded: "Why?—I mean, why are you here? What are you doing—truly? I don't believe for one minute that you are smuggling."

"At this moment, I am giving you some much needed occupation. Get up in front of Taxier," he instructed, reaching out a gauntleted hand to assist her. "Since you have thrust yourself into this affair, you may make yourself useful."

His long fingers closed on her wrist and, with a sharp tug, Amarantha found herself swung up into the saddle. She didn't argue with Tamlane's order. With a lame arm, Taxier would not be able to control his horse if it bolted again. Obviously, she would have to ride with him.

"Is this wise?" Taxier asked, but Tamlane and Amarantha ignored him.

Having no lady's sidesaddle, she settled herself as best she could astride the stallion and took up the reins. Taxier looped his good arm about her waist. The lame one was left trailing. He was breathing hard. It was tight in the curve of the saddle and a heavy burden for the beast, but he looked a strong animal and sound of wind. He would carry them safely if they did not have to go too far or fast.

"I can perhaps guess at your part in this affair,"

Amarantha said. "But why is Taxier here? He isn't any more a smuggler than you are. And I don't believe that either of you is recruiting for the Jacobite cause. However stubborn you usually are, the two of you aren't that dimwitted."

"Neither of us is really a smuggler—as you well know," Tamlane said impatiently. "But my explanation about going out at night to grapple with the devil isn't accepted by everyone, so I use smuggling as a likely reason for meeting up with others from France who bring news of the exiles and help with those who once worked for the cause, but now need assistance escaping. No one hereabouts cares about smuggling, but there are some who might object to helping the Jacobites who have remained in England."

"The *cause?*" she repeated. "Tamlane, the Stuart cause is dead! It died at Culloden."

"The cause may have died there, but some of the men didn't. Nor did their families. The reprisals being taken in the highlands are worse than you can imagine. Nor are they selective. Mere suspicion of involvement carries a death sentence these days. People are being turned out of their homes daily and left to starve. Others are imprisoned or executed."

"I am here because a bill of attainder has been sworn out against me in the north," Taxier said hoarsely. "My great crime was that I gave shelter to some Jacobite soldiers who were near starvation, and I spoke out against the English inhumanity in punishing whole families for one person's acts. The rector is helping me to escape, as he has so many other victims of the reprisals. I'm sorry, Mistress, that I

171

couldn't tell you this before. I know that it was a terrible abuse of hospitality."

"We had hoped that he could start a new life in the south, but he may be too famous—or notorious—for this. Those in power do not welcome dissent, and they mark the rebels well." If Tamlane was concerned about revealing these secrets to her, he gave no sign. Nor did Taxier—if that was his true name—protest the revelations. Apparently he had decided to trust her now that the situation was desperate.

Amarantha digested this.

"Where are we going?" she asked finally. "To find another ship?"

Taxier exhaled in relief and leaned against her. His body was trembling.

"Thank you," he said softly.

"You are going back to Talland House," Tamlane said. "It is the closest, if you stay in the wood. The rain has driven back the fog. Keep to the stream for as long as you can. The dogs are headed west, but they will eventually come back this way. Let's not give them an easy trail."

"Where are *you* going?" Amarantha was proud that her voice was even. She wanted to scream, but knowing that there were Preventives in the woods and two men's lives were in her hands prohibited any such foolishness.

"I'm going that way." Tamlane gestured upstream.

"But that's where the Preventives are!"

"I'm going to draw them off so you will have time to get away." Tamlane reached into his cloak and pulled out a pistol. "This is bait which will be irresistible."

Amarantha felt herself pale.

"Tamlane, you can't—"

"Now, love, of course I can. Have faith! There are only two of them just now and they'll never get near me," he said briskly. "Ride for the house. I'll be there soon, I swear it."

He leaned forward and caught her hand. He brought it swiftly to his lips and pressed a kiss into its palm. The fleeting touch was still hot enough to sear her chilled skin.

"God is with us—never fear," he said, then turned his horse away. In only a moment he was gone into the night.

Taxier moaned softly and slumped heavily against her back. Reminded of his injuries, Amarantha turned his horse toward Talland House. Around her she could hear only the wind and the stream as it stumbled down its stony course.

Rain began to fall in earnest. Though Taxier trembled violently, Amarantha welcomed it. The two of them riding double couldn't outrun the hounds set to hunt them. They had to pray that water washed out their tracks, or that the dogs truly had followed the others toward the sea.

The horse's hooves seemed very loud, until they entered the chattering stream, and then all noise was swallowed in the water's loud voice.

"Do not let them follow Tamlane! Let him lose them on the moor. Let them be eaten by the beast of Bodmin and crushed by giants, or drown in a bog," she prayed aloud. If they caught Tamlane, there would be no mercy—not even for a man of God. They would hang him—just as they had hanged all the other patriots who had died at Tyburn and Creiff.

"He shall be fine," Taxier mumbled. "The men of the north called him *ceo*—the mist. He took many fugitive men over the fens and bogs and never once was caught. He has eluded more hunters than an old fox. I think Divinity is truly looking after him."

A shot rang out. Though she flinched, Amarantha did not cry out.

"The hunt is on." Taxier laid a cheek on her shoulder and brandy fumes bathed her face. He said again: "Never fear. The hand of God is upon him. All will be well. Ride west with the stream. No one will follow."

"I pray that is so!"

A little farther on, Taxier swore and wrapped her bunched skirt about his lamed arm. His movements were sluggish and obviously pained.

"I'm sorry, Mistress." His words were now slurred, barely audible. He quaked like a leaf in a storm. "I am bleeding again and dare not leave a trail for the hounds to follow."

"Never give it a thought," she said with a levity she did not feel. "I never liked this dress anyway. We shall be at the house soon and we'll see you put right."

Taxier did not answer.

When they came out of the cover of the wood, Amarantha abandoned the stream and struck off cross-country in the most direct path for home that she knew. The moon showed through occasional breaks in the fast-moving storm clouds and gave her enough light to stay headed in the proper direction. She dared not risk a gallop or even a trot, for Taxier was now wholly supported by her spine and she feared he had swooned.

They should stop so that she might bandage him again, but she did not dare to pause as she did not know how close behind them the Preventives might be, and if Taxier fell from the horse's back, she would never be able to lift his heavy form into the saddle.

Now away from the noise of the stream, the moor was full of mysterious rustlings and eerie moans. They were unnerving, but better than human voices or the sounds of pursuit and gunfire.

She almost rode past Uncle Cyril's home. The moon had disappeared again and Talland House showed no light. It was barely discernible against the screen of dark trees, revealing itself only by the regular roofline that blotted out the night sky. The smell of lilac was her next clue that home was near. It blended beautifully with the scent of rain and heated horseflesh.

Amarantha was too weary to weep with relief, but no sight—except Tamlane riding out of the woods—had ever been more welcome to her eyes.

Chapter Eight

"Good girl!" Tamlane was suddenly there in front of the dark house, just as he had promised, and he immediately lifted the unconscious Taxier down from the horse. "You lost them in the wood. With any luck, it will be hours before they double-back and find a trail."

"He's been in a deep swoon since the quoit," Amarantha gasped as she slid from her mount's back and landed on tired legs. She was not accustomed to riding astride and had to clasp the bridle to stay erect. She was breathing hard, as sometimes happened when she exerted herself in the rarified air of the high moor.

"I feared as much. The ball passed straight through

his arm but it left a nasty hole that was bleeding fiercely. Mrs. Polreath!"

The housekeeper unshuttered a lantern and stepped off the terraced entry. She was, for once, absent a broad smile. Peering over the horse's back, Amarantha could just make out that standing behind her was an even less happy Trefry. His face was never welcoming, but by the lantern's pale light his expression was positively repulsive.

"Trefry, you will take this horse and mine and stable them at the cottage," Tamlane said to the gargoyle. "Rub them down thoroughly so they are not in a sweat. You will then undress and go to bed. I gave you leave to retire for the night before I departed for dinner at Talland House and you have been asleep since then."

"Ez."

Mrs. Polreath stuffed wadded wool into Taxier's shirt while Tamlane gave his instructions. Her hands were all brisk efficiency and her manner not in the least fluttery or uncertain.

"Take him upstairs so I may have a better look at his wound," she ordered. "I can do naught for him down here."

"Should we send for a surgeon?" Amarantha asked, at a loss for what else to do. She had never dressed a wound before.

"There is none to send for, dearie. And even if there were one about, we wouldn't dare risk it."

"Go at once, Trefry. We've no time to spare." Tamlane turned and started for the house. Amarantha could only marvel at his strength. He carried Taxier

177

with the ease of a mother cradling an infant.

"*Ez.* Mistress?" Trefry prompted her. "Cumuz on now."

"Yes. Sorry." She made her fingers loosen on the reins. Trefry took the exhausted horse's bridle from Amarantha and led it and Tamlane's mount quickly away. Their hooves were silent as they passed over the damp grass and into the wet dark.

Amarantha's legs were still shaking, but she commanded her knees to stand firm and started immediately for the house. Tamlane and Mrs. Polreath had already disappeared inside the dimly lighted doorway, and she was alone in the rustling darkness.

Blood. Blood was the first thing she saw when she stepped inside—blood on the entry tiles. Bloody pearls were everywhere it seemed, grotesque and bright in the candlelight, which wavered wildly over the soiled floor making the thickening clots shimmer.

Horrified, Amarantha followed Tamlane, Taxier and Mrs. Polreath up the stairs, staring in dismay at the trail of gore that was left behind them on the treads. In spite of the extra bandaging, as they rounded the corner a few drops cascaded down Taxier's trailing arm and landed on the point of the newel post making the wicked spike glitter like the end of a bloodied spear.

"Bloody hell," she said appropriately. Taxier had bled through both the handkerchief bandage and wadded wool and his bloodied shirt could sop no more gore. In the dark, his wound had not seemed so bad and she hadn't worried. Now she wondered if he would live.

"Indeed." Tamlane's voice was grim and strained.

Apparently the combination of Taxier and keeping his footing on the slippery stairs was straining his muscles after all.

Amarantha started after them and then halted abruptly. Her own cape was sodden with a mixture of rain and blood. She shrugged off her wet wrap, leaving it to fall where it willed.

"Bring him in here," Mrs. Polreath commanded, opening a vacant bedroom's door. She turned to Amarantha, holding a branch of candles aloft as she leaned over the railing. "Dearie? Why have you stopped? You aren't about to faint are you?"

"No." At least, she hoped not. She had never been prone to vapors, but was quite unused to seeing so much blood. Amarantha lifted her eyes from the crimson drops on the slippery treads to stare at the housekeeper.

"The blood must be cleaned up before the Preventives arrive," Mrs. Polreath said gently. Her eyes were compassionate as she added: "They will be doing a house-to-house search looking for wounded men and will be here soon. Can you manage it on your own? Tamlane will assist me with Taxier."

"Yes, I understand. I must change as well. There is blood on my dress." She glanced at the stain that reached from ribs to knees and felt ill.

"Use it to mop the floor and then hide it. I'll clean it later."

Hide it? Amarantha's stomach might threaten rebellion, but her mind was not so clouded that she couldn't reason. Indeed, though fear trembled through her flesh, already her mind was suppressing it, commanding her nerves to quiet themselves. The habit of years of logical thought was coming to her aid. Though her heart wished to be with Tamlane, her mind was able to consider what had to be done to keep him—and all of them—safe.

"That won't be enough to fool the Preventives if they come here. They have dogs. They will smell the blood." Feeling more than slightly ill at what she must do, Amarantha climbed the stair until she reached the newel post. She reached down, dipped her fingers in Taxier's blood which had dribbled on the stairs and then smeared it with gore already on the up-thrust spear. Mrs. Polreath made a sound of protest and Amarantha explained: "We won't be able to move Taxier. If they search the house and find him we will have to somehow explain his wound."

"Yes?"

"It is obvious what happened. He fell on the newel post while examining the whitewash and was gored." Amarantha looked up into the housekeeper's eyes. "I have warned uncle repeatedly about the danger of this stair. We shall have to replace this tread first thing tomorrow and have these newels removed."

"The newel post. That will have to do." Mrs. Polreath nodded and started for the chamber where the ripping of cloth could be heard. "You are correct. I fear that there won't be time to hide him in the cellars even if he is well enough. Mister Aldridge doesn't like your uncle, and this house will be suspected as a likely harbor of fugitives."

It wasn't what Amarantha wished to hear at the moment, but she nodded an acknowledgment of the facts.

"Bring me his shirt and I will burn it too. That will

explain a large fire and the smell of burning cloth. I fear it will leave a heavy stench in the air." Amarantha stood on the landing and began pulling her own soiled gown from her body. It was difficult as the lacings were wet and she was trembling with cold and shock. Fortunately, whatever her body's failings, her mind was growing steadily more clear and cold in its calculations.

The first problem to face was the gore. She must not track any more of it about. The blood on the stairs didn't matter, but the drops in the entry and on the doorstep had to be removed or hidden. They left a clear trail that plainly contradicted her tale of a fall on the newel post.

Finally freeing herself of her soiled skirts, Amarantha dropped to her knees in her petticoats and began to scrub at the blood in the entry. Unfortunately, the stone floor was porous and the crimson drops had been swallowed into the tiny rock mouths. The traces of blood could not be completely expunged.

"Bloody hell!" Amarantha stood up. She commanded herself. "Think! Why would there be blood on the floor down here? Why?—Because I ran through it and tracked it to the door when . . . when I ran outside. I went outside to—to get Penkevil because—because—*think!* Because Taxier needs another shirt. If he isn't dead."

Shaking badly from the cold, Amarantha climbed back up the stair. Facing downward she deliberately stepped in Taxier's blood. She then walked with care toward the front door, placing her own bloodied shoes atop each stain, leaving a clear shoe print behind. With great care, she opened the door and stepped into the single drop of blood that sullied the granite doorstep.

"What shall I do now? My shoes are a mess. I will track blood everywhere I go." Amarantha shook her head and answered herself. "Take them off. You do not need them in the house."

Fortunately, the night was warming and the rain lessening to little more than a mist, because in her undressed state the wind was able to pierce her petticoats and chemise and rub up against her already chilled flesh with invisible fingers. She remained outside only long enough to remove her shoes, and then retreated back inside the house and closed the door upon the weather and the hostile forces that might be lurking there.

"Dearie?" Mrs. Polreath appeared at the top of the stair. Taxier's bloodstained shirt was clutched in her hands. She stared a moment at Amarantha's undressed state, but made no comment.

Amarantha held up her arms.

"Hurry. Just drop it." Her voice was harsh.

The sodden shirt fell heavily. Amarantha caught it and then wrapped it in her discarded dress. It had to be burned as there was no place in which to bury the things that the dogs could not find them. There were telltale powder burns on the fabric of the shirt that would give lie to their tale of the newel post if examined closely, and her own dress was stained with both blood and creek soil.

She hurried to the kitchen and stirred up the fire, feeding it until it glowed strongly. The delay chafed at her, but the fire had to be powerful in order to consume the damp fabric. As she waited for the fresh wood to catch, she spotted the teapot, which Mrs. Polreath had obviously abandoned when the rector arrived. The tea was still warm so Amarantha poured out a cup and gulped it down. It was a partial anodyne against the cold inside her.

The abandoned crockery gave her an idea. Quickly she gathered together cups and saucers and put them and the teapot onto a tray. She thrust a taper into the fire and then set it into an ornate brass holder. Walking carefully with her load of delicate crockery, she crossed the dark hall and into the red drawing room. She had to move cautiously though the gloom, as the garnet drapes were drawn over the windows against the night, and the oak paneling made the chamber as dark as a cave. Though it wavered madly in the draught of disturbed air, the single candle remained lit and lent sufficient light that she was able to find the side table without incident and safely let go her fragile burden.

Kindling was already laid in the hearth, so it was only a moment's work to set it to burning. Next, she lit the branch of candles on the mantel and then poured out three cups of tea, placing the crockery about the room. As a final touch of realism to her deception, she pulled Mrs. Polreath's embroidery frame over to the chair nearest the fire. She left the door wide open.

"Excellent," she murmured. It was just like putting on a theatrical. This time, the play was about the rector coming to tea.

Grimly pleased with her handiwork, she hurried to the kitchen and began the tedious task of burning her gown. Time was fleeting, but she did not allow herself to move too quickly and snuff out the fire. They hadn't time to build another. She took up a knife, and, inserting the point in the fabric, began tearing it into strips starting at the seams. The sound was somewhat sickening, for with all the blood about she was able to imagine that some part of her was still inside the gown and also being torn to shreds.

"Dearie, wash your hands and then go dress yourself. Wear something dark and bind your hair. I'll tend to this." Mrs. Polreath was pale but calm as she joined Amarantha by the flags. She held out her hand for the knife.

"Taxier?"

"He still lives."

Amarantha surrendered her blade and said urgently: "We were having tea in the red drawing room—you, the rector and I—when we heard the scream. We left our cups and went to see what had happened. Taxier had fallen off a stool and was gored by the newel." Amarantha plunged her hands into the pail of water, which was always kept near the hearth in case of stray sparks. She scrubbed at her hands hurriedly in the tepid water. Taxier's blood had dried into a brown crust under her nails.

"The teapot—?"

"It's in the drawing room. I also lit the fire and some tapers." Amarantha told her hurrying away.

Now for the second part of the drama. The Bloodshed. For the next act of the play, she fetched a footstool from the library and climbed the stair carefully, avoiding the blood with her bare feet. She used great caution on the slippery treads lest Fate decide to make her lie into truth and leave her impaled on the deadly newel. Amarantha left the stool on the landing, tipped over on the floor. She stepped back to observe the effect. It told an obvious, if untrue, tale.

Time was disappearing at an indecent speed, but unable to stay away for another moment, she took the time on her way to redress to look in on Tamlane and his patient.

The small room was lit by a single branch of candles, which were guttering angrily on their table near the casement. Though dim and uneven, they provided enough light to show that Taxier's pale chest was moving up and down in shallow respiration. Tamlane knelt beside the bed as he finished tying off a thick bandage. His profile was grim and a bit pale, but Amarantha thought it the most beautiful thing in the world.

"Will he live?" she asked quietly.

"I believe so. He lost a deal of blood, but the wound is clean. The ball passed straight through the shoulder without hitting the bone," Tamlane said, rising to his feet.

"He had that much fortune then."

"Yes, though 'tis little enough—" Tamlane turned toward her. His stopped speaking in midsentence and his eyes widened slightly as he looked her over. His pupils dilated and his breath caught.

Belatedly, Amarantha recalled that she was undressed and her petticoats rendered indecent by moisture. Had she any nerves to spare, she would have blushed. Instead she spun away, heading for the safety of the shadowy hall.

"I must dress."

"Wait. You shall have a fall if you go about in the

dark." Tamlane took up the candles and was quickly beside her. He did not touch her with his hands, but it was unnecessary, for his eyes were quite heavy enough upon her bare neck and arms again revealed by the candle's wavering light. Amarantha dared not meet his gaze, though his next words were delivered as unloverlike as Uncle Cyril giving an Arthurian lecture. "Is everything cleaned up downstairs?"

"Nearly. The blood would not come off of the stones so I made it look like I walked in it. After I have dressed, I will go to the stables and wake up Penkevil and Tregengon. I'll tell them Taxier fell on the newel post and needs a new shirt. I hate to involve them, but can't see anything for it. 'Twas the only way I could think to explain the blood in the hall."

Tamlane frowned.

"I can go for you. You are chilled, lass, and like to get ill."

"No. Those are my footprints in the blood. I must have a reason for being outside—Also for my cloak being wet. And I must dress!" she said, hurrying away, torn between joy at his concern and embarrassment at her state of undress.

"I will assist you," he said calmly.

"No. I—"

"Don't argue." Tamlane took her arm in a firm grasp and thrust her into her chamber. Setting the candles on a dressing table, he pulled open the wardrobe and inspected its contents. "What will you wear?"

"Something dark. The green dress," she decided, pointing to a plain gown that had been hemmed to a length easily worn without panniers and would not require extensive lacing.

Tamlane pulled out the chosen dress and, gathering up the skirts, threw the yardage over her head. A few deft twitches had the gown in place and he began pulling on the laces with practiced tugs. It did not escape Amarantha's attention that he was familiar with female apparel.

"You've done this before," she said, unable to hide the note of accusation that had crept into her mind in a flash of searing jealousy.

"Yes. For a time before he escaped to France, Prince Charlie was disguised as a woman." Amarantha gasped and he asked solicitously. "Is that too tight?"

"Charles Stuart?" she repeated, astonished momentarily out of her cold and horror—and even her embarrassment. "*You* dressed the prince? As a woman?"

"Yes. I was with the prince for a time. I had been called in to tend to some of the dying after Culloden. Someday I will tell you the entire tale." Tamlane tied her laces and then turned her about for a quick inspection. He reached for a ribbon and quickly tied back her hair. "It is a shame to bind up these lovely tresses, but you will do so now. You had best get on to the stables and tell Penkevil and Tregengon about Taxier's *fall*."

"Yes—oh! I almost forgot. I have put out the tea things in the red drawing room. We were having tea there when we heard Taxier scream. He apparently fell on the newel post while examining the whitewash."

Tamlane smiled suddenly. It was an illuminating grin that lit his eyes and set them dancing.

"As I said, you will do nicely. A lesser woman would have panicked twenty times over this night."

"I should like to panic, but it would not be useful," she said frankly.

"Keep up your courage, love. We are nearly there."

Amarantha looked into his shining eyes. They were bright with excitement. He still smelled vaguely of the outdoors and radiated an appealing aura of warmth and confidence. She realized that this was an inopportune moment to feel longing for Tamlane's arms, to want to be held and even kissed, but the urge was there and nearly overwhelming. Giving in to the impulse, she rose up on her toes and brushed a light kiss over his lips.

"Remember, Taxier fell off the stool while examining the whitewash. Have a care not to trip on it when you come down. I left the footstool on the landing," she said hurriedly as she raced for the door. She did not spare the nerve or time to look into Tamlane's face for a reaction to her kiss. She did not wish to see his countenance if he were shocked or disgusted with her brazen behavior.

Back in the entry, Amarantha picked up her discarded cloak and took up Mrs. Polreath's abandoned lantern. Once outside, she paused long enough to thrust her feet into her shoes but did not bother to lace them.

Though Penkevil and Tregengon were of an incurious—even simple—nature, and did not speak much English, she still rehearsed her words as she walked toward the stables so that they would be believable.

"Penkevil!" she called loudly, as soon as she had the stable door open.

But it was not Penkevil who answered her. It was a sleepy Pendennis.

"Mistress? What is wrong?" His sleep-flushed face appeared over the loft rail. He squinted at the lantern she held aloft.

"Where are Penkevil and Tregengon?" she demanded, shaken to see the cook looking down at her. *How could they have forgotten about Pendennis?* The cook was of another stamp altogether—bright, observant and apt to ask pointed questions!

Amarantha swallowed hard. They would have to change their story now and say that Tamlane had only stopped in for a late visit and been offered tea, which Mrs. Polreath prepared.

"They've gone to the tavern and will likely pass the night there. What is it, Mistress? Is Mrs. Polreath ill?"

"No. No, it is Taxier. He has fallen on the newel post and gored himself. I need a clean shirt for him," she ended lamely.

"Ah! That *illy* stair! I'll come at once. He'll need carrying back to the stable like as not."

"*No!* Don't come! I mean, Rector Adair has already carried him upstairs. He is too badly hurt to move right now, so you aren't needed."

"The Rector? *Werzetoo en?*"

"He came for tea." Amarantha looked into Pendennis's honest gray eyes and willed him to believe her lie. If he did not, there was little hope of convincing the suspicious Preventives of this tale.

"Tea?" he repeated thoughtfully. He disappeared into the loft and there was the rustle of fabric as he hastily donned his apparel. "Tonight? In the storm? With your uncle from the house? I think he had best have been for dinner, Mistress, and stayed on after dark to quiet your nerves. Unless you are afeared of the village gossip that will come of this story."

Amarantha exhaled slowly. Pendennis wouldn't betray them after all! Relief made her feel slightly light-headed.

"Gossip in the village? I think that is the least of our worries at present."

Pendennis's feet appeared on the top rung, and he quickly descended the ladder. He had a man's smock thrown over his shoulder.

"Aye. You've the right of it. Are the Preventives here yet?"

"No, but they can't be far behind us. Thankfully there was a heavy rain that will have washed away the trail of blood."

Pendennis nodded.

"Come, we'll go the back way. 'Tis closer." He took the lantern from her trembling hand and struck out across the muddied suntrap.

Moonlight was fading into gray morn, and illumined by the faint lantern light, Pendennis looked disembodied, more like a ghost floating through mist than a flesh-and-blood man. In many ways, though she had not believed it before, the moor's night shadows were comforting. The truth could be easily lost in them and the counterfeit made to appear more real.

They barely had time to gain the warm kitchen and for Amarantha to put off her cloak and knock the mud from her shoes, when a heavy knock sounded at the front door.

"They're here," Amarantha said softly. "It could be no one else at this hour."

"Courage now," Pendennis said, handing her the

smock for Taxier before heading for the entry hall. "Mrs. Polreath and I shall manage this. You take the back stair and stay with the rector and Taxier until we call you. Remember that you are the mistress of this house. Act the part well."

Amarantha didn't answer his retreating form. She took the lantern and went up the narrow treads as fleetly and silently as she was able.

The rector was waiting for her at the head of the stair and immediately took her cold hands in his own. She thought that he wished to say something to her, but they had no time for private speech with each other as the summons from downstairs came immediately.

"Dearie?" Mrs. Polreath called up. "Can you or the rector spare a moment? Mister Aldridge is here and wishes to speak with you."

"I'll go." Amarantha whispered, bending down to tighten the laces of her shoes.

Tamlane nodded and set a hand on her head. He repeated his earlier belief: "God is with us. There is nothing to fear."

"I've told him about the accident, but he will not wait!" Mrs. Polreath said plaintively as Amarantha appeared at the top of the stairs. She was standing like a sentry at the base of the staircase, arms slightly akimbo.

"I'm sorry, Mrs. Polreath. Did you say that Mister Aldridge is here? At this hour? Has he brought a doctor or perhaps a surgeon then?"

Two pairs of familiar eyes turned upward at her words, and Amarantha allowed herself to check on the landing and start in honest surprise. She had expected to see Percy Aldridge and the other Preventive standing below in the entry—but not young Mister Guthrie. The inquisitive excise man should have been safely away in Helston. She was taken aback by his presence but managed to say in credibly feigned bewilderment, "Are you trained as a surgeon, Mister Guthrie?"

"Nay," Guthrie answered, his tone abnormally harsh. His eyes held a mixture of disappointment and accusation. "I am not."

Amarantha swallowed and ordered her nerves to return to calm. Neither of the men appeared at all normal. Part of the strangeness was seeing them at night with their clothes wet and muddied and their expression grim and—in Percy Aldridge's case—maliciously triumphant. But there was something else amiss. After a moment, she placed it. The men were armed with muskets. It was a grave social breach to carry firearms into a private home, and would only be done if they intended to make an arrest.

They would all have to be extraordinarily careful.

"Where is Rector Adair?" Aldridge finally demanded. "His man said he was here. If that is true, let him show himself."

"Rector Adair is busy tending to a wounded man. If you must speak to him, you may come upstairs to the sickroom." Mindful of Pendennis's advice, Amarantha was coldly disdainful, drawing further upon her experience at the London theatre where she had never missed a season. Her repertoire of favorite plays contained a number of history's more haughty queens. "Mrs. Polreath, have Pendennis prepare more tea. I am sure that the rector could use a cup.

We were never able to drink the first one. Bring it to the drawing room. I shall be down shortly."

"Yes, dearie. And I'd best have Pendennis start preparing some broth as well. Oh dear! Oh dear!"

The two men started up the stairs as soon as Mrs. Polreath was out of their way. Amarantha deliberately did not warn them about the slippery treads or fallen stool waiting in the shadows until they were upon them. Guthrie tangled his feet in the footstool's legs and fell hard against the wall. Aldridge did not fall, but was forced to grab the bloodied newel to steady himself.

"God's nightgown!" he swore, disgusted by the smear on his hand. He pulled out a handkerchief and tried to scrub his fingers clean.

"Have a care!" Amarantha said sharply, turning her back on the men and leading the way to Taxier's room. "One casualty on the stair is quite enough. As it is, Mrs. Polreath will never get the blood up off the wood. And I will thank you, Mister Aldridge, to not blaspheme in the rector's presence. Or my own."

"There is blood all over the entry as well." Guthrie said, mounting the stairs at a more gingerly pace. His voice had taken on a note of curiosity. "How came that to be?"

"I am aware of the blood. I hadn't a light when I went down the first time and tracked the mess all over the floor. I fear that all the stones shall have to be taken up and replaced." Amarantha started down the dark hall at a dignified pace, refusing to be hurried by either the silent Percy Aldridge or her panicked heart.

"Why is the rector here?" Aldridge asked.

"Because Mister Taxier is here." She replied coldly, stopping in front of the guest chamber door and putting her hand on the latch. She made it clear that she was offended by the question. "Where else should he be, but tending to the wounded man?"

Guthrie flushed.

"No, you misunderstand. Why is he in this house with your uncle away? It is a most unusual occurrence."

"It is not the least unusual. The rector—as he often does—came to have dinner and stayed for tea." Amarantha pushed the door open. "Rector Adair, it is Mister Aldridge here on supposedly urgent business."

Her tone made it very clear that whatever the business was, it was an inconvenience to her. Never in her life had she sounded so petulant and unpleasant. She reflected that it truly was a pity that no lady could ever appear on the stage, for surely the art of dissemblement was in her blood.

"Mister Aldridge. Mister Guthrie." The rector rose from his bedside chair. He had obviously enjoyed many of the same plays she had seen, for he was also playing the role of an arrogant monarch displeased with an importunate fool.

"Why are you here, Rector Adair?" Aldridge asked Guthrie's question again. He was wasting no time on pleasantries, and Amarantha was glad to see Guthrie wince at his superior's rude tone.

"I am here because it is my duty," he chided coldly. "Mister Taxier is badly hurt and may not live out the night."

"You came because he was hurt, is that it?" Aldridge asked, slyly.

Amarantha stared a warning at Tamlane. Aldridge already had the answer from Trefry, Mrs. Polreath and her.

"No, I came to dinner. Not that this is any business of yours."

"But it is my business." Aldridge walked around the bed. He stared at the clean smock laid out at its foot. "If you were here to dine, then what did you have for dinner?"

"Oyster soup, pilchard and leek pie, pease pudding." Tamlane said promptly. "But you will be so good as to explain how my dinner arrangements are any of your business?"

Aldridge paused, clearly not expecting so pat an answer.

"Guthrie, go downstairs and ask the cook what he prepared for dinner. Then find the housekeeper and ask her the same question. Question them separately. If they are lying, I want them found out immediately."

Guthrie nodded once and then left the crowded room.

"While we are waiting, let's examine this wound." Before Amarantha could stop him, Aldridge had caught up the blankets and pulled them down, exposing Taxier's pale, bandaged chest.

Amarantha gasped and reached for the blankets, but the Preventive caught her sharply about the wrist.

"Remove your hand at once!" Tamlane's voice cut like the crack of a whip as Amarantha twisted away, raising her own hand as a claw to strike at the Preventive's face with her nails.

"How dare you lay hands upon me! I shall have you horse-whipped." Amarantha welcomed the rage that poured through her, driving off all cold and fear. As Aldridge stepped back, she dropped her hand and snatched up the covers. She replaced them with care, tucking them gently about Taxier's body.

"I am going to examine this wound. Stand aside," Aldridge declared, but he was obviously shaken by the display of righteous anger from two people who should have been quaking in fear at being arrested for sheltering a smuggler.

"You will do nothing of the kind." Tamlane said coldly. "We have only just stopped the bleeding. It would be murder if you touched him now—and I would swear it in court. You are overstepping your bounds, tax collector. Have a care what you are about."

"He will touch no one in this house," Amarantha spat out. "I cannot believe his impertinence! Leave at once or I shall have you arrested for trespass as well as flogged!"

"Patience, girl." Tamlane, amazingly enough, suddenly sounded amused. "Hear the man out before you summon the executioner. If I am not mistaken, he thinks that he is hot on the trail of some smugglers and as long as he doesn't harm Taxier, it is our duty to listen."

"I am aware of what the idiot thinks. He has told me at some length of his stupid obsession." A part of Amarantha was appalled at her behavior. Never had she been so rude to anyone. Even her uncle was rarely this impolite, and only when he had been imbibing too freely.

"I *am* on the trail of this vile gang of smugglers and this time I shall have the whole lot. And we will stretch the neck of every last one of yo—"

"Enough." Tamlane interrupted. "Present your proof, ask your questions and then leave. I have to remind you once again that you have over-reached yourself, so have a care."

Guthrie's feet sounded in the hall. He stepped into the doorway but came no farther. He looked only at Percy Aldridge as he broke the news. Amarantha watched his face. It seemed to her that he appeared somewhat relieved by the message he carried.

"It's as the rector said. The cook and housekeeper both said the same thing. Oyster soup, pilchard and leek pie and pease pudding. They dined at seven."

Aldridge frowned.

"Did you question them separately?"

"Yes. They gave the same answer. Then everyone went to—"

"Silence!" Aldridge turned to the rector. The inquisition continued over the sickbed. "Finish, Rector. What did you do then after eating?"

"We went to the red drawing room," Amarantha said immediately. "Later, the rector, Mrs. Polreath and I had tea there."

Aldridge looked at Guthrie who nodded agreement. His young face betrayed his growing unease. If this story were true then he and Mister Aldridge had committed slander and trespass against the two most powerful families in the village.

"That's what the housekeeper said as well. And the tea things are still laid out on the table. There is also a fire in the hearth."

"I don't believe it."

"Then you are a fool," Tamlane told him. "For everyone else shall."

"And I suppose you were here all evening?" Aldridge sneered. "You never went out once."

"Yes, we all were in the drawing room together until we heard Taxier cry out when he fell on the newel post."

"Fine. If that is your tale then cling to it. There are other ways of finding out the truth." Aldridge looked down at Taxier, his expression unmoved by the white countenance.

"I will not allow you to question this man," Amarantha warned him. "Not tonight."

"There's no need. We have caught one of the smugglers," Aldridge said haughtily. "He got tangled in the brambles and couldn't escape with the others. My man will have him out by now and be escorting him to the gaol immediately. Be assured that the wretch will be persuaded to talk and tell me everything I want to know. Then I'll be back for Taxier—and the rest of you."

Amarantha did not allow herself to flinch or show in any manner that his words affected her.

"If you have a prisoner, then what in the name of all that is holy are you wasting your time here for?" Tamlane asked in the voice of reason. "You had best be off at once and question your prisoner about his activities."

"I do not consider that my time has been wasted," Aldridge said coldly. "Guthrie, you will remain in this house. No one is to leave until I return. Rector, you will also stay here."

"Certainly I will stay until Taxier is either out of danger or gone to his reward. This man is near death," he reminded Aldridge with all the dignity of his calling.

"Mistress Stanhope—"

"I have had quite enough nonsense for one evening," Amarantha said shrilly. "I am exhausted and retiring to bed at once. Mister Guthrie may stay where he pleases—so long as he is quiet and does not disturb Taxier or the staff. I suggest the red drawing room, Mister Guthrie. The fire is made up in there and Mrs. Polreath is preparing more tea." She added spitefully: "Unfortunately, I fear it will be a long night for you as I don't believe that there was any smuggler in the berry vines. You have simply caught yourself a straying sheep."

She turned and swept out of the room, forcing Guthrie to step out of the doorway or be trampled. Amarantha did not slam her chamber door behind her, but it was closed with audible force. Not pausing to consider her actions, she went directly to her casement and pulled it wide.

The apple tree that grew next to the house was well maintained, but one sturdy limb had been allowed to grow right up to the wall and was but half a body-length below her. Amarantha did not permit herself a moment of hesitation but launched herself immediately into the tree's blossoming embrace and began to climb down its solid trunk.

There was no time to spare. She knew Tamlane well by now and reasoned that the moment he could get free he would go to rescue the supposed smuggler. She was determined that he would not go alone.

Amarantha dropped to the ground, and, snatching up her skirt, ran all the way to the stables. She must borrow some men's clothing from Penkevil who was much her size, and then hasten to Penrose Cottage. They would need horses if they were to catch up with the "smuggler" and the Preventive who was taking him to be questioned at Bodmin gaol.

She did not allow herself to consider what would happen if the poor Jacobite was already held fast in the gaol. If he were already imprisoned behind its stout walls, it would require bloodshed to see him freed. She did not try and guess at the soldiers' numbers—all that mattered was a great many of them were garrisoned there and they all had firearms.

"I pray that you are right, my love," she muttered as she ran. "We shall need God's help this night!"

Chapter Nine

Avoiding the suntrap's uncovered windows where alert eyes might see her pass, Amarantha ran by the back way, pushing her way through the thin honeysuckle and lilac hedge that separated her uncle's house from the rear of the stables. It struck her as incongruous—even nightmarish—to be at a task so dire and yet have the smell of the bruised blossoms' innocent fragrance thick in the night air like a lover's heady perfume.

Amarantha found that her breath was inclined to heave in and out like bellows when she ran hard, but she made certain that she was as silent as the mist as she neared the stables so that she would not attract Percy Aldridge's attention as he left Talland House on his gruesome mission. Given his suspicions of them, he would be certain to pause long enough to investigate any careless footsteps or rustling in the shrubbery, and her daily store of inventiveness had about run dry. There really wasn't any explanation she could imagine to account satisfactorily for her presence outside the house.

She arrived at the barn unmolested by man or dog, and found that Pendennis was also back in the stables with the lantern lit waiting calmly—for all the world as though he were expecting her arrival. A winded Amarantha sent him up to the loft to find some suitable toggery for her to wear while she caught her breath and retied her slipping shoes.

Though Pendennis gave her a worried look as he presented his findings, she took up the borrowed clothing without explanations being asked or offered. There wasn't time for details, and it was better that he not know anything of what she intended. His conscience was bound to trouble him for the many lies he had already told; she didn't want to burden him with any more secrets.

No longer afraid of what nightmare creatures might be waiting in the dark, Amarantha ran on to Penrose Cottage without a backward glance. The vegetation, though in places quite thick, was kind and did not trip her while she fled by on seemingly winged feet.

It seemed only a moment until she was at Tamlane's house. There, neat as a dream—or perhaps a well-crafted play—was Trefry, opening the narrow door to the cottage as she approached, apparently expecting to see someone coming at a wild pace through the night.

However, the dream quality of her venture failed at that point, for the fact that she was not the expected party was obvious from the ugly factotem's widening eyes. She would have preferred to keep her illusion that this was all just a theatrical farce but, as always, Trefry was there to spoil the moment.

Fearing that any discouragement might bring about a change in her crazed ambition, she gave him no time to express his disapproval of her unexpected appearance.

"A Preventive has been left to guard Taxier and the house," she told the old man as she pushed inside the cottage and headed for the library where welcome firelight glowed. She would make her final change of attire of the evening with the comfort of a warm hearth. "But I know that Tamlane will escape as soon as he is able. We must ride at once for the gaol. One of the men—the smugglers—was taken prisoner and Percy Aldridge has said that he will begin questioning him immediately as he arrives at the garrison. Wait out there! I must change without delay."

Amarantha closed the door partway and began to disrobe behind it. She was very tired of lacing and unlacing gowns and knew a moment's envy for men's simpler clothing.

"What are ye doing?" Trefry asked, for the first time using proper English when he addressed her.

"I am putting on a smock and breeches," she said crisply. "I shall leave my gown in the secret cupboard for now, but you must either hide it or return it to Mrs. Polreath. For now, go saddle two horses. We must be ready to leave the moment Tamlane arrives."

Trefry made a wheezing sound that might be either laughter or the shocked gasp of a diseased lung.

"And the rector knows what ye are about?" he demanded. "Wearing breeches and chasing after smugglers?"

"No. Not yet. We hadn't time for private speech." Amarantha pushed her skirts to the floor and picked up the breeches. She had never worn them before, but they seemed a deal less complicated in construction than a gown. The garments might have been a bit neater and made of a softer cloth, but she supposed that she should be thankful they were a near fit for length.

Trefry wheezed again: "Well! An ye both live to marry, it happens ye'll be well suited to the rector's way of living."

"Married?" Amarantha paused, one shod foot tangled in her breeches.

"Aye."

"Married?" she said again. She hadn't progressed that far in her thinking. *Married? To a rector who routinely broke the law?* Frankly, she had had no thought to marry anyone. There was absolutely no need to. Certainly she cared for Tamlane but—

Amarantha looked at the *Book of Common Prayer* that sat open atop Tamlane's desk. It was open to the section headed Solemnization of Matrimony—a pointed reminder of his calling, and an omen of sorts.

She blinked several times.

Of course, being a man of God, he would probably insist upon marriage. Bloody hell! Of course he would! What had she been thinking? This was not some London rogue. The laws of man he might be willing to break, but Divine law was another matter. Tamlane would never take her as a lover—particularly as she was a lady and he was a friend of her uncle's. No, he would insist upon the legal ties before involving either of them in an affair of the heart.

"Bloody hell," she sighed, this time cursing aloud, and then said for a third time, "But marriage?"

This was a complicated matter. She hadn't time to consider it just then, and even if she had, Trefry was not the person she would choose to confide in. She would have to set this aside and consider it another time.

"I don't see nuptials on the horizon," she said repressively. "We are not yet to that degree of acquaintance."

They had merely kissed and she had allowed him to see her nearly unclothed while he dressed her and tied up her hair. And now she was preparing to break the law for him. Could she truly protest that they were only acquaintances?

"Nay? Happens ye are a bit short-sighted for a female," he answered rudely. "Some men need a wife. Rector'll have ye here at Penrose Cottage as soon as he might—and a good thing it shall be. Too unsettled he has been of late—making no plans, just drifting from one mad start to another. Any road, *'Better to marry than to burn,'* the Bible says. Happens it's right about this, too."

"Nonsense. You surprise me, Trefry," she said, pushing her foot through the narrow tubes where the legs went and pulling them up over her hips. It was a bit of a struggle. The breeches seemed to make no allowance for her curves. "In any event, I would expect you to be upset at the prospect of having a female in the household. Especially on a night like tonight."

"Upset at yer being here? Nay, that I am not. Mind, rector'll be angry enough for any two men when he finds ye here, but I'm thinking that he'll take yer help for all that."

"Of course he will. In any event, he hasn't a choice. I'm coming," Amarantha said firmly, fastening her unfamiliar garment. She added breathlessly, "Go saddle the horses."

"Happens there is too much at stake for him to do otherwise," Trefry went on, ignoring her command as he settled in for a long chat, apparently not comprehending the urgency of the situation and making Amarantha want to pull her hair out with frustration. "Whether Jacobite or smuggler, if that poor soul speaks to Aldridge during questioning then the rector, Taxier and meself will be betrayed and have to flee this very night. It follows that Cyril Stanhope and all his household would be suspected, too. The rector'll not allow that to happen if he can do anything to prevent it. He'll use whatever poor tool comes to hand."

The dire prognostication threatened to renew her panic, which was a bad thing when she was struggling with over-tight breeches.

"I hope you are correct that we can prevent it. Let us hope that I am not a poor tool." Amarantha's brave words were muffled as she pulled the rough smock over her head. It smelled rather dreadfully of animal, but she supposed that she would simply have to endure it. She then took up her gown and went to the secret cupboard. She repeated brusquely, "So do stop chattering and go saddle the horses."

"I am correct, but he'll not like it. With the soldiers about, happens ye may have to shoot the poor man before he talks an ye fail to rescue him. Still, that would be a kindness to what will await him, poor soul."

"Trefry, you are a veritable Job's comforter." Amarantha tucked up her leaking skirts and attempted to shut the cupboard door upon them. They fit as tightly as she did in her borrowed breeches.

There was the welcome sound of familiar footsteps in the hall and Amarantha found that once again her heart was made to labor.

"No, I do *not* like it, you infernal bagpipe. But still your loud tongue and go saddle the horses anyway." Tamlane's voice was deep and calm.

" 'Tis done," Trefry answered. "She can have mine. I'll go to the village on foot. 'Tis the more normal course any road."

Amarantha speedily opened the library door and faced Tamlane. Expecting an argument, she told him firmly: "Neither do I like this, but needs must when the devil drives. I *am* going with you and nothing you have to say will dissuade me, so you had best save your breath for riding."

His eyes traveled down and then up her boyishly clad form. She could make nothing of his expression. Perhaps after seeing her in petticoats, no attire would appear too strange.

"That is most unfortunately true, and it is marginally safer for you to accompany me than to have you galloping about the countryside on your own, so I shall take you," he said coolly. "Have you a weapon?"

"No."

"Can you use one?"

"Of course. I hunt."

"Then we'd best get you a pistol. Trefry will lend you a dark cloak and you may keep it in the pocket."

Surprised at his ready acceptance of her company, Amarantha fell back from the doorway to let Tamlane through. He went to the secret cupboard where her dress hung, thrown over his broadsword as a convenient peg. He reached inside and, shoving her voluminous skirts aside, extracted one of a pair of dueling pistols and a powder horn. He began loading the weapon.

Amarantha felt momentarily let down. The evening had already gone on for an eternity, and only her jittery nerves kept her from collapsing with exhaustion. She had girded herself for battle with the rector, expecting to be summarily dismissed—to once again be ordered out of harm's way—but, as always, Tamlane had surprised her. He had not even commented on her breeches, either to condemn their immodesty or to praise her ingenuity in securing them.

"You will, of course, do exactly as I say." His tone was stern but mild.

"Of course," she agreed softly, and added to herself: Unless it means leaving you in harm's way.

Tamlane shot her a glance as though hearing her thought.

"You left via your casement?" It wasn't really a question.

"Yes, the apple tree seemed the most prudent route for me to take under the circumstances."

"A popular choice this evening. I must remember

to thank Cyril for his foresight in leaving the tree there. Congratulations. You are obviously an enterprising woman. That is the first step to being a useful tool." He handed her the loaded weapon and then took out the second pistol. He began loading it as well.

Amarantha hefted her pistol and felt its weight. The weapon was heavy and spoke of power. The feel of it in her hand bolstered her flagging will. They *would* succeed in rescuing this arrested man. The appalling scenario of a merciful killing of the poor prisoner that Trefry had suggested would never come to pass. They would ride hard and manage to intercept Aldridge and the other excise man before they reached the gaol.

"You are smiling, lass. It worries me. This is all quite illegal you know, not some game for the well-bred bored of the *ton*," Tamlane told her. "There will be no mercy because of your gender, or even for the justness of this cause. They will likely hang you if we are captured."

That was true. They would, for the Preventives would call them lawless for what they were doing. But whatever the excise men's belief in the law they served, she knew Tamlane to be a man of integrity and immense dedication to what he believed was the moral right of the situation. He answered to his faith—and probably his prince's cause—before the laws of the English.

Now, faced with the same circumstances, she was making the same choice. She would follow heart rather than mind or law.

The prince. This thought did not please her. Tamlane had obviously been close to Charles Stuart. So much had been lost to the Jacobite cause. The very thought of it raised bitter spectres in her mind. But that unhappiness was of the past, and she would not allow the thought of old defeats to tarnish her judgment. Tamlane was not Ian. He was not an innocent led away to the Jacobite war by romantic notions. And, most importantly to her, Tamlane was not abandoning her while he went off to fight his war. The decision of what happened next was wholly hers.

The responsibility was hers as well.

He had a plan, she assured herself, and they were acting out of careful thought and prudent judgment.

Or he was. She was there because she loved him.

Amarantha exhaled slowly and examined this notion.

She loved him. And it was true love. For the first and last time she was bound to another at the heart. Such love was an irreversible fact, and those who trafficked in such matters of the heart must face the circumstance with honesty. For Tamlane and her, there was too little occasion to do anything else. There would be no time for weaving self-deceptions and rosy dreams. Their love would either end in bliss or tragedy—there would be no middle ground.

Of course, her feelings for Tamlane were not the only subject that demanded honesty. She could not mislead herself into believing that her aid to the Cause was any longer of a merely passive nature. Innocence had ended when she helped Taxier flee from Aldridge. She had now accepted a weapon with the intention of using it, should it be necessary. She might kill—or die—this night. This was not a dream or a play. It was important for her mind to be clear in its thinking. She repeated it to herself. *She was in love, and she was ready to slay or die if it was necessary to defend Tamlane.*

The fact left her grim but unshaken in resolve.

But what of Tamlane? What were *his* truths? She knew his politics, but not his heart. She believed that he was not indifferent to her. Trefry certainly thought he was interested in her—that he even intended marriage.

To add weight to the assumption of serious intent there was the fact that rectors did not trifle with the affections of nieces of old friends. They did not snatch careless kisses in taverns, or appear with them in public without a chaperone. So, she would have to assume that this was in fact his ambition.

And what was her reaction to the notion of a betrothal, assuming she lived through the night?

Firstly, it remained to be seen whether he cared for her more than his cause. Presuming they lived to see the dawn, she decided that this was the answer that would choose their future destiny for she was not prepared now—or ever—to be espoused to a man who already had a demanding mistress. And there was none more demanding than Highland politics.

Their courtship might well be a protracted one, for she suspected that Tamlane would have to wrestle with his conscience over this matter. And because of his morals, they would not have the lovers' way of persuading the heart.

She sighed.

"Amarantha?" The rector's green eyes rested upon

her, their expression thoughtful. "Are you under-standing me, lass? This isn't a game."

"I am fully aware of this fact that I am breaking the law and am prepared to face the consequences." Her voice was steady as was her gaze.

"And you are not frightened?"

"Terrified," she told him and laughed shortly. "If I were not so chilled from the rain I should be per-spiring like a draft horse on a summer's day."

"Good," he said firmly, surprising her again. He put up the second pistol. "Fear will make you cautious and sharpen your wits—not that I will permit you to be too near to danger. Do as I say and all will be well. Let us depart."

Tamlane took up his hat and then strode for the stable with the erect bearing of the soldier he had once been. All casual elegance was gone. His dark hair was subdued to neatness, confined by a band at the nape. Amarantha was able to walk at his side, matching him pace for pace because of the freedom of her breeches. A glance up at his face showed that his eyes were bright, his expression one of assured excitement. With such a man at her side, anything seemed possible.

Her nerves trilled. She was going off to war. Few women had ever stood in this position. They gave life, they did not take it from others. How reckless she was!

Trefry was waiting outside with the horses and had an extra cloak, hat and muffler ready for her.

" 'Tis not that cold," Amarantha objected.

"Wrap the muffler up over your lower face. I do not want you recognized. Be careful not to speak either. I would prefer not to make this into a killing affair—which we shall have if your identity is made known to the soldiers." Tamlane settled the cloak about her, waited as she stowed the pistol in its capacious pockets and donned her hat, and then he bent down to give her a leg up onto her mount.

Amarantha found herself tossed up into a man's saddle for the second time that night. She discovered that sitting astride was a quite convenient position when she was wearing men's clothing.

Tamlane mounted quickly.

"I know a shortcut to the gaol, but it is through rough terrain and you must stay directly behind me, especially in the fen. To stray off the path would be inconvenient and, in places, perhaps even fatal."

"I shall be right behind you."

"Like a shadow?" He brought his horse closer to her.

"Yes. Just like your shadow."

Tamlane leaned toward her.

"It is still dark. See that my shadow is not lost among the other shades."

He put a gauntleted finger beneath her chin and tilted her face up to the moon. He stared intently, as though seeing her for the first time, or perhaps trying to memorize her features. He looked at her eyes and then her mouth before he lowered his lips to hers.

"I never imagined this would come to pass," he muttered.

"Nor I."

Their kiss did not feel like a first-time greeting or even a second. It had all the passion of an experienced and secure love and answered some of Amarantha's questions. Tamlane was not conducting an idle flirtation. There was genuine desire there—however hard he might fight it.

"This is damnable timing," he said, lifting his lips from her own.

"But it may be all the time we have. My only regret is that we do not have even a moment to spare for more," she said honestly.

Tamlane's teeth flashed in a brilliant smile.

"Now, love! You must have faith. I promise—there will be time for more." His hand dropped to the reins and he pulled his mount about. "Come now. We must ride swiftly. Trefry?"

"Ez?"

"You know what to do if we are delayed."

"Aye. Mrs. Polreath and I will do our part."

Though she tried to recall later what route they took, Amarantha could never completely reconstruct it in her mind. She could summon the clear memory of a narrow pass filled ankle deep with water, with stony banks as steep and deep as a grave. And there was a white ruin with empty arched windows crumbling slowly back into the rocky earth from whence it first came. The roof was long gone and the shell of the house did not hold back the moonlight, which forced its way through the thinning clouds and showed them the terraced garden stairs down which they rode at a reckless pace.

The rain had ceased and mist was beginning to form on the ground that stood wither-high on their mounts. She knew the earth was still there below them because she could hear the damp crunching of last autumn's leaves beneath the horse's hooves and smell the spice of their broken veins of sap when they passed over them.

There were other rustlings as well in the trees around them, but they did not frighten her—bears, wolves, or even the Beast of Bodmin could not worry her with Tamlane riding at her side.

They heard the sound of fast-running water once off to the south and it, too, was lovely in its fearsome noisiness. It babbled hollowly around carelessly placed stones, which blocked its chosen route as it rushed on to a rendezvous with the sea.

They passed through the fens as well, and though Amarantha did not fear the passage under Tamlane's guidance, still she could not enjoy the eerie place. The water lilies looked like giant frogs squatting in the brackish water and the mares' tails poked up out of the mist like an army bearing hostile spears. The hummocks of invading bog mosses were safe enough to traverse, but it never escaped her attention that to stray off them was to invite disaster. It was a relief to emerge on the far side of the fens where they could again set a cantering pace over solid earth.

"Silence now," Tamlane whispered. "We are nearing the gaol. Do not fire your pistol unless you absolutely must."

Amarantha nodded and straightened in the saddle.

They heard voices long before their quarry came into view, and paused long enough to pull their mufflers up and their hats low upon their brows before venturing close enough to see who was wrangling so loudly at the edge of the fens.

Aldridge and the other Preventive were easily recognized by their gleaming buttons, which twinkled beneath the waning moon as they argued what path to take. The prisoner between them was turned away but Amarantha was certain that he was not anyone that she had seen before. He was not dressed in the smock of a villager and had an earring pierced through the one ear she could see, so she had to assume that he truly was one of the Frenchmen smugglers. It made no difference to their own plight who he was, if he knew their identities, but she was still relieved that it was not one of the Jacobites or villagers who had been taken prisoner.

Tamlane drew out his pistol and, true to her promise to be his shadow, Amarantha followed his example without protest. The rector nodded at her and thus conspicuously armed, they rode boldly out into the small clearing.

"*Bon soir. Je regrette, m'sieurs,* but you will immediately surrender this man to me." Tamlane extended his pistol so that it pointed at Percy Aldridge's head. "We have an urgent appointment elsewhere and must be off with the tide."

Amarantha did not blink at Tamlane's sudden transformation into a French smuggler, but merely followed his lead, pointing her pistol at the other excise man, who sat in stunned stillness. She was pleased by her hand's steadiness. She had never pointed a weapon at a human being and had wondered whether she would be able to do it without trembling.

"You will untie the prisoner and return the reins to him," Tamlane instructed. "Do it now, or you shall instantly die."

Three heads turned in his direction, and Amarantha saw Tamlane stiffen in surprise. Before anyone had time to respond to his command, there came two sharp reports from the woods to the west and both excise men crumpled to the ground without a single cry.

"Bloody hell!" Amarantha's mount started violently at the pistol shot, and she was momentarily occupied with controlling her equine's hysteria. By the time she had authority restored, she found herself surrounded by armed smugglers showing varying degrees of hostile posture.

"Friends of yours?" Amarantha asked quietly of an immobile Tamlane. She was trying desperately to ignore the two bodies half-hidden in the mist that eddied beneath them. She had certainly been deceived in thinking that Tamlane's acquaintances were not prone to violence.

"No," he answered, his voice equally quiet. He never took his eyes from the man in front of him or lowered his pistol. "I've never seen them before."

"You mean to say—" she gasped, suddenly appalled. She looked once at the man they had rescued. He was grinning widely. "Then he isn't . . . ?"

"No, he isn't. And, yes, we've fallen among the heathen. These are genuine smugglers."

"Bloody hell," she muttered.

"Indeed."

Chapter Ten

Dawn chose that moment to light the horizon with her pearl pink light. It was only a lessening of true dark, but for all that it was a weak thing, Amarantha welcomed it. Her experience was that nothing looked quite so impossible by the light of day.

Her pistol was still in her fist but hidden by her cloak. It didn't seem an opportune time to call attention to her possession of yet another weapon so she left it there. There were quite enough weapons in the clearing already. A quick glance showed an impressive inventory of daggers, brass-studded clubs, and a variety of firearms and swords on display.

The apparent leader of this band was a giant fellow with—was it possible?—pink eyes and a shock of astonishing white hair. He might have some questionable sartorial aspirations to piratical fashion, dressing in a slash-sleeved shirt and bright galligaskin breeches—stuffed to fullness with either wool or straw—but it was no fop's practice *gauche* that he carried. His large fist held a menacing piece of curved steel called a cuttoe that could behead a person with a single stroke. The sight of it made Amarantha feel a bit ill.

"Bonjour," Tamlane finally said, lowering his pistol. "I see that our presence was not required after all."

"You came to save *mon ami*? But why? Who are you?" The leader's English was thick and barely understandable. Amarantha wondered whether he suffered from some defect of the tongue.

"A sympathizer," Tamlane answered shortly. "And as a friend, I suggest that you depart immediately. Now that the sun is up, the cowards at the gaol will be out *en force* to search for these two and to see what all the shooting was about."

The rabbit-faced giant considered Tamlane's words.

"This is sound advice. Yet I still have some question. One of my other men has disappeared somewhere and I feel that perhaps you might enlighten me about him, *non?*"

"I am afraid that I know nothing of this other man. This is the only one captured by Preventives."

"Vraiment? And yet, is that not blood on your shirt? That does not suggest such innocence to me."

Tamlane did not glance at his exposed cuff, but Amarantha did, and in the growing light, the crimson stain was evident.

"There has been much blood spilled tonight." He

shrugged indifferently, shocking Amarantha with his callousness. She was sure that he feigned this heartlessness, yet the performance was convincing. London had lost a great actor when Tamlane Adair was called to the holy orders. Or maybe years of war had truly hardened his nature.

"Perhaps it would be best if you accompanied us back to our ship. We could offer you passage downcoast, *oui?*"

"That would not be wise. It is dawn. The boy and I shall be missed if we do not return soon."

"Boy? This does not look like a lad. My eyes work quite well, *monsieur*, and this is not a male."

At a nod from their leader, one of the men leaned forward and pulled off Amarantha's hat, exposing her long hair. Amarantha felt herself flush under the sudden scrutiny and then grow pale, but she did not look away from the leader or put up her weapon.

"Come. We shall not harm you." The leader's smile was rather more awful than his frown for it displayed his rotting teeth. Amarantha had to repress a shudder and fight not to look away from it.

"*Bien.* If you wish, I will ride with you a while. I have some news for you to share with The Brothers," Tamlane said, putting up his pistol.

Amarantha very reluctantly followed his example. Only the knowledge that she couldn't shoot them all before they retaliated kept her from taking aim on the leader then and there.

They traveled overland toward the coast with the glow of the new sun casting long gray shadows ahead of them. They were not paralleling the road to Padstow—or any other that she knew—but Amarantha remained firmly unconcerned. The strangers were ignoring her now and Tamlane was calm. In fact, he looked quite supremely confident as he spoke with the ruffians; therefore she resolved that she would be calm and confident too, even if the murdering smugglers seemed to be asking some very pointed questions about the numbers and placement of soldiers in Bodmin, and Tamlane was answering them without any hesitation.

The men spoke in a thickly accented form of French, which was rather difficult for Amarantha to follow, but Tamlane seemed quite comfortable with the dialect and expressions, and answered them with ease and a deal of charm, which belied any notion that they had fallen among murderous thieves. She supposed that it was also a propitious sign that they were not deprived of their weapons or in any way molested or bound. Their custodians had already demonstrated that they felt no compunction about killing enemies and would not boggle at a spot of theft or physical abuse if they felt in any way threatened by their prisoners.

Nevertheless, Amarantha couldn't fail to be aware that their situation was not a happy one. Even if the company were more congenial, this was not a morning when they had time to spare. By now the soldiers billeted at the gaol would have gone to fetch Guthrie at Talland House and told him of the prisoner's abortive appearance—and the Preventives' failure to show with their captive, especially as it seemed that they might have already captured one of the real smugglers.

It followed that a search for the missing excise men

221

would have been mounted at dawn, with or without Guthrie's knowledge or assistance, and unless pains were taken by the smugglers to hide the bodies of Aldridge and the other poor man in the fens, they would be discovered soon—and after that, there would be a giant hue and cry raised across the entire moor. The land smugglers who had taken charge of the illicit cargo would likely be caught if they had not already hastened away and there would be mass arrests and hangings as the tortured named accomplices.

Amarantha bit her lip. It was quite probable that Mrs. Polreath and Pendennis had been able to keep the anxious Guthrie from seeking out Tamlane and Taxier in the pre-dawn hours—and certainly, he would not have invaded *her* chamber in the early morning—but very soon the other soldiers would come to Talland House to question all of them about the reason for Aldridge's night visit. Their absence, when specifically confined to the house by the dead man, would be hard to explain. They might even be suspected of his murder.

There was also the unfortunate fact that Uncle Cyril would be returning home soon, and would be greeted with the news of a missing niece—now branded as a fugitive—a wounded suspect ensconced in the spare bedchamber, and a house in general turmoil.

Amarantha groaned softly.

"How fare you?" Tamlane asked quietly after glancing around quickly to see that they would not be easily overheard. He had been at pains to present the impression that she spoke no French, doubtless hoping to lessen her danger in the smuggler's eyes by cloaking her in a shroud of seeming linguistic ignorance.

"Quite well." It was a lie. She was—though not frightened, of course—exhausted and beginning to grow uncomfortably warm under the cloak and muffler. The unaccustomed sensation of perspiration dampening her clothing was growing more unpleasant with every passing minute and she regretted her glib words about sweating like a draft horse.

Tamlane leaned closer and explained. "There is no need for concern. We are not going to be taken aboard the ship but rather we are being escorted to a hideout where some of the smuggled goods were stored. They say that they will leave us there unharmed while they go on to their ship."

Amarantha studied his face. It was calm, even happy. His green eyes sparkled like polished jewels. Except for the shadow of a new beard, he looked as if he might have just risen from a sound night's sleep and was riding out for a day of tranquil fishing.

Men, she decided, were very strange and illogical about the possible effects of war and danger.

"And you believe this? It can't be so simple. What would prevent our making an outcry if we took such a daft notion in mind as to go to the gaol and tell the soldiers of what has passed? They dare not trust us. At the very least, they will take our horses, or leave us tied up inside some quoit or ruin while they escape." Amarantha's voice was quieter than her companion's, for she had no wish to be overheard by the nearby riders. Though murder for bad manners was an extreme reaction, she did not put it past this band of armed bullies.

"I gather that this place is an ancient church that has been abandoned because of the encroaching sand. I believe that I know it. If it is the same ruin, it is so buried now that it can only be entered through a transept in the roof. They propose to lower us down inside on a rope and then leave. We will eventually be able to escape by digging our way out, or our horses will be seen and someone will come to our aid." Tamlane sounded quite blithe and Amarantha couldn't help but stare at him. Courage in the face of adversity was one thing; this was dangerous naiveté. Or perhaps the euphoria she had heard overcame men before they rushed into battle.

"*They* say," she whispered. "Isn't it as likely that our horses will simply be stolen by some passer-by—or never noticed at all?"

"You are still lacking in faith," Tamlane scolded.

"What I—*what we*—are lacking in is *time.*" It was an effort, but Amarantha made her voice remain low and calm and her expression serene. The woods were growing tighter, forcing the smugglers to draw nearer to them. She asked urgently: "Have you forgotten that Aldridge is dead? That the soldiers from the gaol will be out *en masse*, searching the neighborhood and wishing to interview us—particularly as Aldridge confined us to the house? And what of Taxier?"

"Pendennis and Mrs. Polreath shall tell him what to say." Tamlane's voice was low and quick. "As for us going missing, I took a precaution there and left instructions with Trefry and Mrs. Polreath about what they should say if we were gone until morning. Don't worry about Aldridge's instructions. He had no authority to confine us."

"What—"

"Not now." Tamlane straightened and lowered one eyelid in a wink. "I have a plan which I shall explain to you later. Courage, love. Just a little more effort and then you may rest."

Amarantha prayed that was the truth. Her muscles ached from knees to shoulders and the man's saddle was bruising to her unaccustomed flesh. Even if they were abandoned in a stone church, it could not be as uncomfortable as continuing atop this horse in the company of unpleasantly pungent men.

They emerged out of the covering woods into an alien landscape that looked like an oceanless beach. There were a few ragged sheep grazing placidly on the rangy weeds that grew in the dunes, but other than a carelessly flitting cabbage moth and a breathy wind, which sighed sadly as they passed, they were utterly alone on the waterless shore.

They rode through a low hedge of cow parsley and confronted an exceptionally tall dune, which sported a regular roof at its sandy peak. There was a solitary sheep grazing on the stony crown with an air of pleasant lethargy and utter indifference to their presence. They might have been invisible spirits for all the attention it paid them.

This was the smugglers' proposed prison. She supposed it could be worse, but the air of isolation was so complete that she feared that in spite of the grazing sheep, which doubtless belonged to some farmer, no one would ever pass by there. That meant that they would have to dig their way out, and she could only stare in dismay at the volume of sand that stood between them and freedom.

They circled the building until they came upon the east face where a transept and part of the clearstory were visible. The few windows, which were left unburied by the encroaching sand, had the blank appearance of something long dead and abandoned by men. The narrow casements that looked out at the world—all but one—had been webbed in a filthy cataract of jumbled spider's silk adorned with dust and chitin. Gritty winds had blasted away any exterior decoration that had not been buried leaving the building scoured like old whalebones on a beach.

But as they drew closer, Amarantha saw with pleasant surprise that there were wallflowers there too. The cheerful blossoms were sunning themselves in the dawn light as they peeped shyly out of the fissures in the old wall and eaves. And there was also the hollow cawing of hoarse-voiced rooks filling the musty air that escaped the church. They packed the air with ugly, angry echoes. The harsh cries nearly drowned out the steady cooing from some nearby doves who were sheltering under the stone eaves and studying the group with avian alarm. It greatly relieved Amarantha to know that they were not completely alone in this seemingly lifeless place.

One of the Frenchmen said something and the company halted. Tamlane answered shortly while Amarantha stared into the distance, saying nothing and making no eye contact with anyone—particularly not the white-haired leader who so repelled her with his mean eyes and peculiar speech and awful sword.

"Down you get, love," Tamlane said cheerfully,

leading his mount to a bit of scrub and tethering him as firmly as possible.

Amarantha, though exhausted, was grateful that he had not offered to assist her from her own mount. Perhaps it was foolishness, but she did not want to call attention to her gender by appearing helpless in front of these rough men. Her sex would be seen as something to exploit, not protect, and she had no illusions about her fate if she were taken off with these beasts.

With that ugly thought firmly in mind, as soon as she was on the ground, her hand returned to her pocket where her pistol rested. Tamlane might trust these men, but she did not.

The sand was loose underfoot and shifted up over her ankles as she led her own mount to stand beside Tamlane's. The bush was a sorry piece of scrub and would not hold the horses if they took it into their heads to wander away. Though burning to point out this fact to her determinedly dense swain, she remained silent while their captors were near enough to hear her.

"This way. Just past the pigeon's nest there. See the opening?" Tamlane asked.

Amarantha nodded and began scrambling up the dune, which was dry and shifting underfoot in spite of the previous night's rain.

There came an indignant squawk and she looked an apology at the irate fledglings whose breakfast they had interrupted, but didn't stop her climb until she reached the one cleared window. She checked at the opening however, taking a small, suspicious breath of the cloudy air and then recoiling. The scent emanating from the hole was not an attractive one being a mixture of bird droppings, dust, and something less pleasant—mice. A great many of them.

"Must we really?" she asked beneath her breath. "I'd prefer a nice, clean quoit or cave."

"Aye, we must. Follow me now. It isn't far to the floor. There is a rope down to the bottom. It isn't a long drop and I shall be waiting to catch you."

Amarantha might have lingered regardless of Tamlane's encouragement, but one of the ruffians had come up behind her, and she didn't doubt that he would bodily assist her into the musty hole if she did not take herself there immediately. Caught between the two direful odors, she readily chose the safety of Tamlane and the musty church.

Tamlane disappeared into the dark opening, silencing the rooks' dispute, and only a moment later she could hear his boots scraping over the floor. Not wishing to risk being taken by the Frenchmen, should their leader suddenly change his mind about a hostage now that Tamlane was inside the church and unable to aid her, she hurriedly levered herself over the sill and clasped the crusty rope. She had lowered herself but a half a body's length when Tamlane's arms were wrapped about her knees and began easing her to the sandy floor. He gave her a brief hug before releasing her.

"Thank you." She barely had time to let go of the rope before it was whipped back up into the sunny opening.

"*Au revoir, mes amis,*" said the rough voice.

"And may you be in heaven a half an hour before

the devil knows you are dead," Amarantha muttered back, causing Tamlane to chuckle.

"Au revoir," Tamlane answered loudly, but the shadowy silhouette was already gone.

"You are entirely too friendly with the wrong sort of people," Amarantha said wearily, parting from Tamlane and looking about for a clean place to sit. The filthy floor covered in various bird and rodent droppings was not her first choice. The sight was discouraging. There they were, alone at last and able to converse, but Amarantha couldn't imaging trying to discuss any of her troubled thoughts with this dashing, soldierly Tamlane. To begin with, the setting was so far from love's dream that sensibilities absolutely forbade any discussion of the tender emotions. Instead she complained, "In case you haven't noticed, they have profaned this church by using it for smuggling. And what you did by discussing the soldiers with them might even be called treason by some less than understanding persons. Of course, if they are alrcady going to hang you for smuggling and being a Jacobite sympathizer, what matters a new crime or two? Particularly as we will be dead of starvation before we can be arrested."

"I had a feeling that you would grumble if I brought you with me." He grinned at her.

"How perceptive of you. Have you also noticed that your cheerfulness is giving me a headache?"

" 'Tis a lack of breakfast making you swoonish," Tamlane said heartlessly. He reached into his cloak and pulled out his flask. "Here, sit on this pew and rest for a moment. Drink this last bit of brandy down. It'll put some spine in you."

"We shall be resting for a great while longer than a moment—unless you happen to have a ladder hidden in your pocket as well." Amarantha collapsed on the dirty pew with a grimace and began rubbing her legs. The bench was marginally less soiled than the floor, but still far from clean. After a moment, she took Tamlane's advice and helped herself to a swallow of brandy. It wouldn't refresh her the way a meal or sleep would, but it might help to dull the ache in her legs. She could not recall ever being so tired.

Tamlane's attitude continued to puzzle her. He had been furious when she had been insulted by harmless strangers at the Obby Oss, but here she was—kidnapped by murderous ruffians and abandoned to starve—and he seemed nearly jovial. The man was an enigma to her.

"No, alas. My forethought did not extend quite that far or I should have provided breakfast as well. Still, luck generally favors me. I believe that all will be well." He smiled at her, as though amused by her rational observations.

"If we haven't any way out—and no breakfast—then why are you so bloody cheerful?" she asked, stripping her muffler away from her face. Her chin was hot and itchy and she was tired of the smell of unwashed body.

"There are two reasons—actually three. The first is that I lied from beginning to end about where the soldiers were stationed and how many there were."

"Did you?" Amarantha looked up into Tamlane's dancing eyes.

"Yes, I did. In fact, so great was my misinformation that I fear our violent friends are going to encounter an entire garrison of soldiers on their way back to their ship if they continue on that route. So, Lady Disdain, there is no call to speak of treason. There is also not one suspicion in anyone's mind about Jacobites in Cornwall, so do try not to put any there. And as for smuggling . . ." Tamlane shrugged. "They may suspect me, but there isn't a shred of proof. Not one ragged thread. In fact, this little occurrence is fortuitous. The authorities now have someone else to chase and I shall be forgotten."

"Hmm." She didn't smile, but Amarantha was pleased. She hadn't liked Percy Aldridge—and the English soldiers were hardly their allies in this situation—but these smugglers had killed him and the other Preventive in cold blood, and she wanted to see them punished for their crimes before anyone else was murdered.

Then an unpleasant thought occurred.

"But what if they speak of us when questioned?"

"What if they do? We are innocent victims—kidnapped on our way to Saint Catherine's and left to a heartless fate in an abandoned church—which by the way, they did not profane as it became unsanctified when it was abandoned."

"So, you believe the soldiers will rescue us?"

"I don't doubt that they shall make the attempt if they become aware of our entrapment. We, of course, shall be long departed by then." He strolled casually toward the vestry.

"We shall?" Amarantha asked hopefully, trying to make out Tamlane's expression in the gloom.

"Of course. We shall be back on the road to Saint Catherine's by then."

"But how? And why Saint Catherine's? Are we meeting Trefry there? Or more Jacobites?"

"No, we shall not meet Trefry—and there are no more Jacobites. Do strive to forget that there ever were any, will you?"

"But—"

"The how of the escape should be easy enough. That is my third reason for feeling pleasure. There is no need for digging. We shall depart by ladder." Tamlane tugged open the narrow door and, after pulling away a dense curtain of gray cobwebs with a gauntleted hand, he removed the said wooden object from its now unholy crypt.

"A ladder!" Amarantha jumped to her feet, her heart thumping against her ribs and her exhaustion forgotten. "But how came it to be here?"

"You can't truly imagine that I left this place unexplored as a boy, do you? I brought this thing here when I was twelve or so. Left it here as well and got flogged for misplacing it." Tamlane looked fondly at the old ladder. "I was sent away to school soon after that and never came back to retrieve it."

Amarantha laughed in disbelief.

"Of course you explored these ruins! Playing in rat-infested rubble would be even more entertaining than salting snails."

"Just so." Tamlane carried the ladder across the room and laid it against the wall beneath the open transept. He said cheerfully: "I believe that our companions are well on their way by now and will not witness our escape. Shall we depart and seek out some sustenance? There is a house not too far on, and I know the people there."

"Yes, let us leave at once. The air in here is foul, and I do not think that the birds like us at all," she answered, returning the stare of an angry rook who had landed on the end of an aisle pew and was approaching boldly with an outthrust beak.

"Age has not improved the place, I must say. Give me the flask and have a care as you go. Test each step. The wood is old and may not be entirely sound." He took up a position beside the ladder where he might brace it, but also catch her if the rungs should give way. "I am quite glad that you had the sense to borrow breeches. A dress would have been confoundedly in the way. Of course, we shall have to procure a gown for you somewhere. You can't arrive at Saint Catherine's dressed as a boy. The priests are liberal there, but this might put even them off."

Amarantha chuckled happily as she mounted the ladder. Sudden relief made her giddy and inattentive to Tamlane's final words.

"Can you imagine climbing this wearing panniers? I should never fit through this casement."

"The view from below would certainly be different," Tamlane said dryly.

Amarantha clambered gleefully into the open air, and looked up at the bluing sky. The morning sun was strengthening, and a slight but refreshing breeze was sighing through the dunes. Fortunately, the smugglers had kept their word—no doubt because they couldn't take the horses on board the ship—and their mounts had been left behind to break their fast on the scrub.

In only a moment, Tamlane stepped out beside her onto the sand. The fledgling pigeons were not happy to see them a second time and ignored her repeated apology for intruding upon them. She hurried past the nest into the bright sunlight that carpeted the sandy tussock, breathing deeply of the clean air.

Amarantha removed her heavy cloak and flung it over her saddle, and then looked down at her drooping shirt. She prayed the rest of her did not appear so soiled and wilting in the unforgiving morning light. Tamlane was correct, they would have to procure new clothing before anyone saw her and reported to the world of her lowly—even scandalous—state.

"Ugh! I am filthy."

Tamlane shook his head and smiled slightly. He reached in his pocket and pulled out some cord.

" *'Sweet is thy voice and fair is thy face,'* but the clothing is a sorry sight. You look like an untrained groom after mucking out the stables. Still, it is apparent that you are a female for all your dirt. Bind up your hair again, Amarantha, and hide it beneath your shirt."

He handed her the cord.

"There is no danger of you overwhelming me with insincere flattery, is there?" She brushed ineffectually at her grimed sleeves and then gave up the hopeless task so that she might confine her escaped tresses. "However, the songs of Solomon are better than Proverbs, which you quoted at me last time, so I suppose that I must rate this as an improvement. Still, if you do not mind, I would rather not face any more scripture on an empty stomach."

"Fair enough. No more scripture until after we break our fast." Tamlane stooped to give her a leg up, and this time Amarantha accepted the aid. She had no choice, her poor muscles were all but done in and she could not mount on her own.

Tamlane's hands lingered a moment on her calf, giving her a small caress, but then he turned briskly away and reached for his own mount. Amarantha felt bewildered. He sometimes treated her as a woman that he wanted, and the rest of the time as some casual traveling companion.

"Tamlane, where shall I find a dress? There aren't any shops, are there, that would have made-up clothing? Is there a seamstress perhaps?"

"Not around here. But have some—"

"—faith?" she groaned, trying to slide into a more comfortable position in the saddle.

"Precisely. As it happens, I have a friend with a sympathetic wife who lives but two hours away. We shall be able to put you to rights at *Carn Brea*."

"*Carn Brea?* The rockpile?"

"Yes. It is an odd sort of house. With your new passion for ruins, I think you will enjoy both the architecture and my friend, Harry Trelawny. He is a bit of an odd one as well."

Amarantha snorted. That was an amusing description coming from Tamlane's lips. She was convinced that no one could be as odd as Blesland's Rector Adair.

Chapter Eleven

Amarantha thought *Carn Brea* was aptly named. It was certainly built of stones—round river rocks piled randomly atop one another for wing after connecting wing with no thought for design or the servants who would have to traverse the ill-laid passages. It was also a puzzle. She thought that perhaps some of the house was derelict, for parts looked positively ruinous and overgrown. Amarantha hoped, for the occupants' sake, that the stones in the occupied portions of the house were better chinked than the outlying walls, else it would prove drafty and wet in the winter.

Yet for all that it was lacking in anything approaching formal lines, the house, once seen closer up, was also oddly charming, nearly magical in the pagan sort of way that old ruins were—a home for a family of sprightly pixies perhaps. Overrun with many species of wild red and pink roses, and riotous golden honeysuckle that hadn't known a pruner's sheers in many a long month—perhaps even a year—the basking gray and brown stones seemed warm and alive to the wonders of a spring day.

Birds and moths of every species had made a home in the unkempt garden where the air was fresh and sweet. They were not in the least disturbed by the human invasion, but kept right on with their full-throated warbles and aimless flittings as the small party rode by.

In spite of the ever-present worry and exhaustion, Amarantha had to smile at the colorful sight.

"How well this place suits you," Tamlane said quietly. "It is a little fey—certainly grown too wild and full of thorns—yet also beautiful and without artifice."

Amarantha's already warm cheeks deepened another shade as she looked over at her companion.

Tamlane also was a bit wilder in aspect than usual. His hair was now unbound and disheveled by the breeze, his clothes smudged with dust and cobwebs, and there was the definite shadow of a beard sneaking onto his cheeks. Yet, for all that he had no plumed hat or metal visor, he still rode upright like a gallant knight or brave cavalier. Doubtless, it was a soldier's training. She could only envy his strength and confidence and wish that they were her own. Her own posture was depressingly wilted.

"I am relieved that I do not remind you of the Trethevy Quoit or the ruins of King Arthur's Hall," she answered lightly.

Tamlane smiled and shook his head.

"Nay, those places are far too massive in weight—too masculine and too ancient. It is not a place where wildflowers would grow into their finest forms, or where innocent butterflies would pass their days."

Uncertain of how to answer this flirtation—if idle flirting it was—Amarantha looked away and changed the subject of their conversation to something less likely to cause a blush. It was growing more difficult to remain on guard while in Tamlane's company and not betray her warm feelings for this enigmatic man. This was hardly the proper time or place to discuss matters of the heart, especially when she was still so uncertain of what she wished for from this man, or he from her. It was a quandary without an obvious solution when he likely would not have her for a lover—and she was uncertain that she wished to be a wife.

With this thought in mind she said: "You still have not told me why we are going to Saint Catherine's. Will the priests there be able to help us in some way? Or is Uncle Cyril perhaps on his way there? I seem to recall that he mentioned the place before he left for Helston."

"Cyril mentioned Saint Catherine's? How odd. I've no notion of seeing him here—though his presence would certainly be welcome."

"Oh." Amarantha tried not to be disappointed. She would welcome her uncle's presence too.

"But be of good cheer, lass. The priests shall help us." Tamlane's smile was suddenly a bit wry. He added, almost as an afterthought: "I had not thought that we should come to this moment in such a way.

I made these plans only as a remote precaution. Still, we must follow where destiny leads."

"You are beginning to alarm me," Amarantha told him, adding flippantly: "What shall we be doing at Saint Catherine's? Pretending to take the orders? Masquerading as monks? Hiring priests to chase smugglers? Becoming smugglers?"

"Vows we may take perhaps, but orders? No. Neither of us is eligible. And you would most certainly be noticed at once as being female." He shook his head. His tone and expression were again amused. "In any event, I think holy orders would ill-suit you, Mistress."

"I quite agree. Frankly, I am astonished that the temple is still in existence. It was founded by the Knights Templar, was it not?"

"Yes, back in the twelfth century. It was built by the brothers as a refuge for those traveling across the moor. It has gained a rather unsavory reputation in recent years—just as the lowlands in the north where so many go to make consensual rather than church-sanctioned marriages—yet the men who live at Saint Catherine's are still ministers ordained. And there are times when it is best that marriages be performed without the posting of the banns. And it is a kindness to families of suicides to give those poor souls who take their own lives a burial someplace other than a crossroad."

This explanation, for some reason that she did not care to explore, made her feel vaguely uneasy. Tamlane, as a man of God, surely could not feel as acquiescent about the activities of this place as he seemed.

Of course, she had said more than once that Tamlane Adair was a very strange sort of rector and more tolerant of human foibles than was a normal parson's wont.

"I am relieved that Saint Catherine's reputation has been overstated. It would be most inconvenient to arrive and find smugglers already there. I am, however, still unenlightened as to what these holy brothers may do for us. Perhaps, while we are still alone, you had best explain fully—"

She was interrupted by a salutation from an apple tree.

"Hello, Rector Adair! Have you come to see Da?" asked a shrill, piping voice from above.

Tamlane exhaled and smiled broadly at the quaking leaves. Almost, she thought, he seemed relieved at the interruption.

They pulled up their horses at the edge of the small orchard and after a moment a young face spattered with pale freckles and crowned with a shock of red hair appeared among the quaking, blossomed branches.

"Hello, young Trelawny," Tamlane said. "Yes, we have come to have a word with your father. Is he about?"

"Aye, he and Mum are still at table."

"Then perhaps you should come along and tell them that we are here." Tamlane held up an arm, and the young scamp obligingly lowered himself from his tree limb and onto the horse's back. It took only a moment to settle him in the saddle before Tamlane.

"This is a big prancer," the boy said reverently, running a tiny hand down the horse's neck.

"Aye, that he is."

"Would he like a carrot, do you think?"

"I imagine that he would. But just one," Tamlane added hastily. "Last time you gave Black Peter a bellyache with all those apples. He was windy for days."

"I was just a baby then," the boy excused himself. "I am seven now and know just how to care for horses."

"Hmm." His tone was skeptical, but Tamlane didn't challenge the statement. "And what have you been about, young scamp?"

"Naught." The boy craned his neck back and smiled angelically. His face was far from pristine and his smock was badly rumpled. He looked a complete urchin—not that Amarantha was in any state to be making judgments about others' appearances.

"Does he run very fast?"

"Like the wind," Tamlane assured him patiently. "And you have had no visitors here?"

"Not in a score of days. There was a stupid lad come to the house Monday afore last," the boy said helpfully. "He had a barres nose."

"Barres?" Amarantha asked.

"A codfish," Tamlane explained. "And what did the stupid lad want?"

"Dunno. Water, he said, but that didna make any sense to me. Mum watched him dithering about in the yard, getting hung up in the briars and stomping on the berries, and she went out and brung him in for tea."

"Dithering, was he? But over what?"

Amarantha shot Tamlane a glance. She sensed that this was no idle catechism and that he was quizzing the boy for specific information about visitors to the area.

"He'd upset his hayrack and made a great mess in the road. He was shook up and asking to come in for a drink of water, but Mum said tea was better and he should come inside. After that he was in a great twitter."

"Was he now?" Tamlane asked with interest. "And how very careless of him to upset a hay wagon on such a straight bit of road."

"Aye, that it was. He must be blind not to see that rock he ran over."

"And what happened then?"

"So, Mum gave him tea instead of water, but he kept saying that his da would no' want him stoppin' in for tea. . . . Who are you?" the boy asked, shifting his smile to Amarantha. He added ingenuously: "Your horse is very nice, too. Does he run like the wind as well? What's his name?"

"This is Amarantha Stanhope, and her horse is called Gallant," Tamlane answered before Amarantha could say anything. "Now then, pay attention, lad. Why did the stupid boy think his father would object to him having tea here?"

"On account of the spilled hay in the road—You're awfully clean for a groom. And you look like a girl," the imp told her.

"That is because I am a girl."

"*Coo!* Girls can't be grooms."

"Certainly they can. I just don't think that any sane female would want to be. But come now! I am curious. What of this spilled hay? What has that to do with not taking tea?" Amarantha asked, beginning to be intrigued and a little amused by the conversation. It was also helping to distract her from her fatigued muscles. "Surely, it takes only a little longer to drink tea than water, and then he would have help to put his mess to rights."

"It has naught to do with tea. But the silly gowk forgot to tell Mum that his da was under the hay when the wagon tipped. The old gent was fair angry and red as apples by the time Da, the stupid boy and I got back to unbury him and right the horses. The barlinney went on like it was a boleigh!" He added reassuringly: " 'Course it wasn't any such thing. The ponies were not hurt at all. It was only a wheel come off and the haft being twisted around."

"A translation please," she said, smiling at Tamlane.

"*Barlinney* is a fire-eater, and *boleighs* are places of slaughter. Matthew Trelawny, mind your English. Mistress Stanhope hasn't quite the way of the *kernow* yet."

Amarantha choked back a laugh.

"Indeed, I have not, but I am learning quickly. I like the sound of this *barlinney*. So, in spite of the overturned hayrack, this was a fortunate happening, was it not? No one—no person—was injured?"

"Nay. I was afeared the one pony might have strained his foreleg, but there was nothing amiss after all. I do not see why the man was so angry with us."

"I imagine that he was a great deal annoyed that his son waited to take tea before mentioning him. Hay is very uncomfortable, you know, as well as being quite hot and heavy," Amarantha explained, a small tremor of laughter passing through her tired body.

"Aye, that's what the angry man said. He told the stupid boy not to ever go off and have tea again when he was buried under hay in the middle of the road."

"Sound parental advice," Tamlane agreed dryly. "And this has been your only visitor? There have been no soldiers or excise men about? Not this morning?"

"Naw. Just the stupid boy and his father. No one ever comes here." Matthew sighed heavily. "At least, no one with horses."

"Good—far too many bad people have horses— and here we are! Down you get, young Trelawny. Pop in and ask your father to come out to us as soon as is convenient." Tamlane lowered the child to the ground. "Then come back and I'll let you put up the horses. They need a rubdown and some hay."

"I'll be back directly!" the boy promised with enthusiasm.

"*Barres* nose, *barlinney, boligh,*" Amarantha recited softly as she watched the boy's retreating form.

"You would do well to forget the first one," Tamlane said, dismounting.

"Certainly not! I am saving that one for Trefry. He always says mean things to me. I should like to pay him back in the same coin."

Tamlane shook his head and assisted her from the saddle. He set her gently on her feet and held her until she found her legs. Amarantha was glad to lean against his stronger frame and absorb some of his strength.

"I can see troubled times ahead," he said, lowering a cheek to her escaping hair where he turned his head back and forth and bestowed what felt like a kiss on the mussed tresses. Her heart certainly believed in the caress for it began to beat erratically and make her feel lightheaded and overly warm even though they stood in shade.

"I am prepared to beat my spears into plowshares any time that he is ready," she assured Tamlane, her voice a bit breathless.

" *'Answer not a fool according to his folly,'* " Tamlane muttered, releasing her and starting for the house.

"I believe I told you before that I do not care for Proverbs on an empty stomach," Amarantha snapped at his back, slightly bereft now that his arms had been withdrawn. She had to wonder whether she—and her heart—had imagined the light caress.

"You are to come in now," their young escort told them when he reappeared in the shadowy doorway with two carrots clutched in his fists. "Mum and Da are coming out directly. Does Gallant like onions as well as carrots?"

"No, he does not. And there is to be no feeding produce to the horses beyond that one carrot—understood?"

"Aye," the little voice was dejected. " 'Tis just that we have lots of onions about the house just now."

"No onions," Tamlane repeated. "Just hay and carrots."

"I can feed them hay?"

"Certainly. They would be honored to be fed hay from your hand," Tamlane lied. "Go and accept their thanks."

Matthew laughed delightedly.

"You truly trust these people?" Amarantha asked softly as Matthew scampered over to the horses, his treat proffered up like gold or incense.

"With my life. Come now, all will be well. Trelawny

245

and I were boys together and fought side by side in Ireland. His wife is a good sort as well. Very loyal and obedient." Tamlane stepped over the sill and disappeared into the gloom.

"You fought in Ireland? With the Catholics?" She stared at Tamlane, bothered that there was still more about him that she didn't know.

"Aye, with the gallowglass. For a brief time only. But hush now. We'll speak of this later."

Later. The things they needed to think about and speak about were growing apace.

Feeling some trepidation at meeting strangers while dressed in her borrowed garb, Amarantha was not reassured by her first glance at their proposed refuge. Housewifery was most obviously not Mistress Trelawny's passion. The house seemed as ill-kept as the abandoned church where they had started their day.

"This place reminds you of me?" she demanded, staring in amazement at the clutches of vervain and dill that grew thickly on the door's badly fractured sill.

"The flowers only."

"So I should hope! This building is a ruin."

Amarantha was dismayed and deeply disappointed at the depth of dust and detritus accumulated on the entry floor. Even through the obvious path where the family traveled to and from the door, there was sufficient grit and dead leaves under her shoes to cause a faint crunching when she walked.

The room was only dimly lit by a pair of windows, which were nearly covered over in flowering vines, and nothing else, the rotting shutters being half-torn from their hinges and ancient panes of glass broken and scattered on the floor. The exuberant honeysuckle had also invaded the damaged walls with its lovely tendrils and was rampaging up the stones and apparently through the roof. Faint as the sun's penetrations were, there was still sufficient light to show suspicious stains of darkness on the floor, which spoke of perpetual dampness, and some ugly scorch marks that marred the walls not yet invaded by flora.

"There was a fire!" Amarantha exclaimed, as the meaning of the damage finally dawned upon her.

"Aye. In Cromwell's day. The family has never bothered with repairs as this is but a rear entrance to the house and it was too large to keep up properly once the family's fortunes were overturned by the Puritans."

"That would explain the garden as well." Amarantha stepped carefully over a patch of trefoil, which had sprung up out of the cracked floor, and began regarding the room in a more kindly light. In her opinion, anything that had survived Cromwell's armies deserved a measure of respect.

"Aye, they spend their time on the vegetable and herb gardens. The flowers must fend for themselves."

There was a squeak of hinges and two figures entered the scarred chamber through a warped doorway whose header had settled heavily on one side.

The woman—Mistress Trelawny, Amarantha presumed—rather resembled one of the weathered sculptures of saints that adorned ancient cathedrals in the north. She was colorless as stone in her plain dress with an indistinct face made memorable only because of its worried forehead, which was presently corrugated with lines of concern. She also possessed a broad nose that looked as though it had been rubbed flat by years of the moor's wind.

However colorless the mistress of *Carn Brea*, its master was stood as ample compensation for the eye. There was nothing indistinct or saintly about this man. He had a thatch of violent red hair, only just turning to gray. It was also obvious where his son's freckles originated—indeed he had enough to spare that he might liberally endow a dozen offspring and still not have to go without. He wore a painfully bright waistcoat, striped in deepest plum and emerald, and—Amarantha discovered, to her nose's dismay—he was redolent of onions. The harsh root smell about his person was pungent enough to bring tears to her eyes and make her empty stomach roil.

Amarantha turned an anguished gaze upon Tamlane and pleaded silently for him to ameliorate her nasal distress by taking his boyhood friend elsewhere—preferably where there was a breeze.

"Harry!" Tamlane said warmly, ignoring her unspoken plea by stepping farther into the room. "I am sorry to descend upon you without warning, but my fiancée and I have had a spot of trouble with a band of smugglers on our way to Saint Catherine's and I need your assistance."

Fiancée! Amarantha started violently at the title before she realized that Tamlane would have to make up some excuse to account for her unchaperoned presence in his company at this early hour, for obviously they would have had to have left Blesland before dawn to have traveled so far. There really was not any other explanation that he could give that would not cause a dreadful scandal if their circumstances ever became widely known, particularly as they were going to Saint Catherine's.

Still, she did not like the lie. Talk of marriage made her most uneasy, and eventually they would be found out in this and be hurt by the lack of honesty.

"Tamlane!" Mister Trelawny surged forward, his hand outstretched. "Don't be daft, man. And who would you be coming to in a time of need if not your oldest friend?"

Tamlane clasped his friend's fingers and the two men pounded each other on the back, apparently not at all discommoded by the powerful aura that enveloped them.

"Nowhere—for I want your advice. But perhaps while we speak your sweet Constance might discover something for my fiancée to wear? I fear that she finds her current mode of dress most disturbing."

"Certainly, certainly—but your *fiancée*, did you say?" Bright blue eyes were turned in Amarantha's direction, finally taking in her soiled shirt and breeches. "Well Heaven preserve us all! This *is* a female."

"Aye, that she is. Amarantha, my dear, this is my good friend Harry Trelawny, and his wife Constance."

"Hello. It is very nice to make your acquaintance," she lied, taking only shallow breaths and not bothering to curtsy. It would have looked undignified in her borrowed breeches.

"Well bless me!" Harry looked blank.

"It's a long story, Harry. I shall tell you about it if you offer us some food," Tamlane suggested.

"Of course. Constance, my dear, could you—?"

The prompt was unnecessary. Constance Trelawny was already at Amarantha's side and brushing at her borrowed clothes with fussiness completely out of place in the filthy room.

"You poor child! Come with me now and I shall find you a dress. We'll have you out of those nasty breeches in a trice—and may the blessings of Saint Brigit be upon us!" Constance took Amarantha's arm in a firm grip and began hurrying her toward the door. She continued to talk fretfully in a faintly Irish accented voice as she ushered her unexpected guest down the hall. "And we'll get you a nice cup of tea, dear. Smugglers! What is the world coming to, I ask you!"

As much as Amarantha wished to change clothes and escape from her pungent host, she wished that she might remain long enough to hear what tale Tamlane was concocting for his friend's delectation. She strained with all her might to listen and just as they turned the corner of the narrow passage and emerged into a clean and well-lighted room, Amarantha heard Harry Trelawny say: "Smugglers did this to you? Nonsense! I'm not believing a word of it. Boy-o, I want the round tale immediately—and there'll be no ale for you until I have it. Smugglers—*pshaw!* And what the devil are you wanting at Saint Catherine's?"

What indeed? Amarantha also wished to know. Tamlane's silence made her very nervous.

For a long moment after the women departed silence reigned. Much of Harry's bluff manner fell away with the retreating footsteps, and he waited quietly for his friend's answer.

"Well the cat's in the cream pot this time, and no mistake." Tamlane smiled wryly at his suddenly serious companion.

"With you it was ever thus. It's your Jacobite friend, isn't it? The one called Taxier?" When Tamlane didn't answer, Harry added, "Just recall that it's me yer talking to, and let me have the tale with no bark upon it." Harry jerked his head toward the door. "Let's be off to me study where we'll have some peace."

"An excellent suggestion. But first, Harry, you must know that Amarantha Stanhope is indeed my fiancée, and we are going to be married as immediately as I can reach Saint Catherine's. She just doesn't know it as yet."

Trelawny looked at him sharply.

"But whyever? How is this possible? The bride not know your intentions? This is most unusual, Tamlane. . . . And a Stanhope, you say? Any relation to old Cyril?"

"Aye, she is his niece." Tamlane seated himself in a comfortable chair and propped his boots on the empty grate. He ran a hand over his chin and grimaced. "Harry, I must borrow your shaving tackle after I have dined, for I am as grizzled as a boar and about as hungry as one too. I fear I may give Amarantha a disgust of me once she is washed and changed back into a lady."

Harry ignored Tamlane's request for blade and bath.

"His niece? Have your wits run amuck, lad? You

cannot be running off with a lady—to Saint Catherine's no less. 'Twould be a prodigious great scandal." Trelawny flung himself into the other chair and began to swing a leg. "Why, your bishop would likely defrock you! Not that this would be any loss. I still can't believe you signed on with the enemy!"

"I doubt it will come to defrocking. We leave that to you Catholics. Anyway, no one wanted the Blesland parish to begin with. . . . Harry, lad, I see that you haven't lost the habit of fidgeting," Tamlane teased. "That restless foot is a dead giveaway that you are worrying."

"Not around you, I haven't lost it," Trelawny retorted. "You make me nervous as a cat and that's a fact. So tell me how this all came about, for I cannot make heads nor tails of it so far."

"I can make clear everything except my own idiocy," Tamlane warned. "But what has happened to my reason in the last fortnight, I am at a loss to explain. And this lapse of reason is chiefly responsible for my current difficulties."

Harry smiled broadly. "But, lad, that is the only clear part of this tale! Even smudged and exhausted, she is clearly a lovely thing. What splendid eyes and skin!"

"Aye, she's that. Beautiful—and also stubborn as an old highland pony. She'll not like being married out of hand this way. Indeed, I've no clear notion that she wants to be married at all. She's an heiress, you see, and much pursued by greedy men. She has told her uncle that she wants no part of married life."

Harry laughed.

"Leave it to you to find a beautiful heiress in the

most godforsaken village in Cornwall! But never mind her part in this tale for now. Tell me instead about your Jacobite."

"Well, to begin with, there was not just one. There were three of them. . . ." Tamlane launched himself into a hurried explanation, but the whole time he spoke he kept an ear cocked toward the door, listening impatiently for the sound of feminine footfalls that would herald Amarantha's return. He could not be easy until she was again safely in his presence.

Amarantha carefully folded her dirtied smock and added it to the bundle of borrowed clothing, which she planned on returning to Penkevil if—*when*—she got back to Talland House.

Her present attire, also borrowed, was not entirely to her taste, being very plain and made of simple fabric, but over this she was not inclined to worry. Even sackcloth, one supposed, could not be too plain for calling upon holy brothers—so long as it was made up in skirts rather than breeches, and showed no bosom.

She had broken her fast on some bread and cheese—and the inevitable tea, which Mistress Trelawny seemed to view as a universal palliative—and she was feeling more in fighting trim. Amarantha did not wish to appear rude to her kind hostess, but she was anxious to rejoin Tamlane and discover just what he had disclosed to his boyhood friend, and to hear of his true reasons for journeying to Saint Catherine's before returning home.

As soon as she was able to make a polite escape, she had her reluctant hostess take her back to the men. The two friends were discovered at the harvest table in the larder with the untidy remains of a meal spread out between them. They rose immediately as they heard footsteps in the passage and turned with an expectant air to await their arrival. No entrance at a ball had ever seemed so formally greeted.

Amarantha saw at once that Tamlane had scraped off his whiskers and brushed his coat, and was looking withal much neater and even rested as he lounged with his habitual careless ease.

Though her thoughts were mainly upon Tamlane's transformation back into the country rector, Amarantha could not help but notice Harry Trelawny's likewise altered behavior. Her host adopted a smiling manner as soon as the two ladies entered, but Amarantha was aware of a new and intense scrutiny of her, which he hid beneath the polite curve of his thick lips.

"Well, good luck and godspeed to you both—and the blessings of the Virgin Mary and Saint Nicholas upon you. We shall see you again before darkfall."

Amarantha looked in question at Tamlane, but his gaze shifted away.

"Shall I not wait for you here?" she suggested.

"Nay. We shall return here after our business at Saint Catherine's is done," he told her. "I would take you home directly, but since we have had no word about whether the smugglers have been apprehended I dare not risk exposing you to either the soldiers or the criminals they seek."

Amarantha was disappointed, but she didn't argue in front of their hosts. It was apparent to her that Tamlane would not speak freely while Mistress Trelawny was present. She did not despair. There would be time for discussion when they were on the road to Saint Catherine's.

"Hadn't we best be off?" she suggested, hoping to escape from the odor that was clogging her nose. It was not just her host who filled the air with reek, but the numerous bundles of onions, bunched in smelly bouquets and hung from hooks in the rafters. She said a brief prayer that if they must indeed return to this house and spend the night that she be assigned some remote bedchamber. She would rather cope with invading animals and a leaking roof than the ferocious stench of aging onions.

"Aye, that you should. I've had Matthew hitch up the pony cart, so you needn't worry about riding any farther. And we'll have a grand supper waiting for you both upon your return. After all, this is cause for celebration."

"Hush, Harry. You talk too much," Tamlane scolded.

Increasingly puzzled, in a fever of curiosity about what had Tamlane had told his friend, Amarantha tucked her hand into Tamlane's sleeve and gave him an unobtrusive pinch.

"We shall see you soon and you may then drink our health," Tamlane promised his friend. Finally obedient to her prompt, he started for the door. Amarantha pulled him along as though she expected him to dawdle.

"Goodbye, lad. And the best of luck to you both."

Amarantha looked back. Harry Trelawny's mouth was prim, but his eyes were dancing.

"You have very strange friends," Amarantha muttered beneath her breath as she turned away from her host. "Laughing at our danger and living in onions. It seems that all our outings are strange ones, Rector Adair."

"My dear, you can have no notion of how very strange this day is apt to be," Tamlane retorted.

Chapter Twelve

"But we cannot!" Amarantha stared at Tamlane in shock and—she had to admit—something that was close kin to actual horror. She didn't accuse him of jesting, for his face wore a particularly determined look that she was coming to know and dislike intensely.

"Yet I fear that we must. There is no other solution."

"But surely—"

"No." The single syllable was uncompromising.

Amarantha, too disturbed to face her would-be suitor at that moment, looked doggedly at the buttons of Tamlane's plain coat and tried to decide what she might best do. She found his clothing was of little assistance in this dilemma. The fine, but unadorned, garment gave evidence of his unpretentious personality, but not of his thought or even occupation—past or present—and was no help to her in this moment of great need and counsel. Besides, the buttons moved up and down with every respiration, reminding her of who and what waited beneath the coat. And of the priest who awaited her decision in the front of the church.

She did not cry, tears being both ruinous to the complexion and completely unproductive, but so palpable was her distress that she had to turn away from Tamlane and put some space between them so his presence did not clutter her thoughts with confusing impulses and make her weak.

Amarantha began a brisk pacing in the narrow space at the back of Saint Catherine's seeking to find some manner of restoring equilibrium of spirit that did not involve either weeping or vapors or heavy drink.

She frowned. There was no comfort to be found in the plain stone walls that surrounded them. They were hard and unforgiving and offered no solace to her shocked sensibilities. Never had she seen a building she liked less, but that was hardly the fault of the architect. Her world had become a nightmare of confusion, exhaustion and saddle-caused pain. At that moment the beauteous Hampton Court would probably appear hideous.

Tamlane—that inconsiderate brute—had said nothing on their journey to prepare her for this upset. He had ignored her questions and spent much of the time singing gay songs for her while they rode the path of dwindling trees and thinning shrubs that led from *Carn Brea* to Saint Catherine's.

She understood now why he had been evasive when questioned about their plans. No doubt he had feared that she would run away from him if he told her of his arrangements before reaching the temple—and the thoughtless beast would have been proven correct, too.

Probably.

It did not seem possible that just yesterday she had been going about her usual routine, filled with innocent anticipation at catching Tamlane sneaking about on the moor. In just a single day and a night she had become part of the *dramatis personae* of some divine play—a farcical drama! She had also become a liar, a criminal, a runaway, and a kidnap victim—and now apparently betrothed to Tamlane Adair, rector of Blesland! Absurd!

"This is what comes of trying to save people from their just fates," she muttered. "Meddlers have retribution wrought upon them. I should have left him to the Preventives."

It was bitterly ironic that she had finally found a man to love and instead of being content to have an affair with her, as any man of the *ton* would be—well, any man not desperate for a rich wife, and many of them would also have been happy to indulge her as a mistress—he was insisting on marriage. Marriage: the eternal promise to love, honor and obey regardless of a husband's activities or one's own better judgment!

Of course, it wasn't love—or even simple desire—that had led them to this sorry pass. No, it was nothing so romantic or hopeful that they might build a future upon. She hadn't even the tatters of romantic illusion to pull about herself.

"Amarantha," Tamlane said gently as he watched her hasty perambulations. "Mistress, do you imagine that I enjoy being at the mercy of circumstance? That I would choose to marry this way when I know what a scandal it will cause for us both? But people have short memories and the gossip will pass. I believe that your uncle would urge you to do the sensible thing."

Amarantha snorted.

"No doubt he would. But what is the sensible thing, Rector Adair? Uncle Cyril, even with his careless regard for social customs would scarcely advocate such a course of action as you suggest."

"Perhaps you do not know your uncle as well as you believe," Tamlane suggested evenly.

She snorted again.

"I do not think that I know you as well as I believed either."

"Possibly. Probably. But think you that my reasons for an immediate marriage are frivolous?" he asked, still striving patiently for reason.

"No, nothing about this situation is frivolous. And I do not imagine that you are enjoying this contretemps—any more than I am enjoying being at the mercy of scandalous fate." Amarantha spun about and continued pacing. "But it is not this alone which troubles me. Scandal I am prepared to face if I must. We are speaking now of marriage. This is—is—*forever*. I do not wish to do *anything* for forever, especially not marriage to a man I barely know."

"I am fully aware of this sentiment of yours." For

the first time he sounded harsh, even angry. "But I do not comprehend why this common act would trouble you. Neither do I understand this sudden missishness. Your actions have led me to believe that you are not indifferent to me and were of a mind to have an intimate relationship grow between us."

Though she took exception to his use of the word *missish*, she found that there was no way to answer this question about her intentions without sounding immodest and entirely lacking in morals. She *had* wished that they would become lovers, but she would be boiled in oil before she admitted it.

"Well?" he asked.

Amarantha at last raised her eyes to his and tried to explain some of the other turmoil clouding her brain. It was once again the time for truth, but there was only so much she could reveal without stripping her pride bare by baldly enumerating her confusing mix of fears, feelings and sudden carnal impulses.

"I . . . I have a great regard for you, Tamlane, and you are correct that I have considered the possibility of a more intimate relationship between us. But this regard makes me feel most disadvantaged when making any decisions in your presence. All that I know for certain is that I am not prepared to marry this day. Surely, there is something else we might do to gain some time for reflection." She laid an appealing hand upon his sleeve, and he immediately covered it with his own fingers.

"We have no time, love." His voice gentled. "I am sorry that it should be thus, but the circumstances compel us to haste. We must wed and immediately."

Amarantha pulled back.

"I do not see why."

"Then you are either weary past all reason or being willful ignorant," he said with less indulgence of tone.

"Your eloquence and sympathy are to be marveled at. It would serve you right if I began weeping," she snapped.

"Please do not. It would give rise to even more gossip."

"Gossip be hanged!" she flared. "I will not—*will not*—be bound in the shackles of matrimony because of those stupid smugglers kidnapping us! Neither of us should be tied for eternity to an indifferent partner because of a wicked trick of circumstance. I will not do this!"

Tamlane's face had hardened at the word *shackled*, then he laughed harshly, saying: "*Indifferent!* Can you truly believe that I have no feeling for you? That I am unaware of this great attraction that flows between us? *Regard*, you call it! What a tame word that is. Amarantha, I can feel it when your eyes are upon me. I toss in my bed every night with your face in my dreams. You have been an affliction," he said with near bitterness. "Mistress Stanhope, I assure you that were you in my arms this very instant, I could not be more aware of you than I am. I am far—*far*—from being an *indifferent* partner in this union."

Amarantha looked deeply into Tamlane's eyes, trying to see into his heart. But though she searched diligently, he remained an enigma. His thoughts, as always, were unknowable. She had only his inadequate—even angry—words and the knowledge that the man was a consummate actor.

"You are speaking of *lust*—and that is not what I

refer to when I speak of regard," she said, dropping her gaze. She would never admit to having lustful thoughts of her own.

Tamlane exhaled loudly.

"My apologies. I would not have spoken of this to you before we were wed, had circumstances not compelled us to have this conversation."

"Tamlane, because of the smugglers we are caught in a fierce current of unlooked for events, and, true, it is sweeping us along at a dangerous pace—" she began.

"This current is no more powerful than the one which already caught us," Tamlane said firmly, calmly, relentlessly. "I was already swept off my feet and being carried to this place—and not by mere lust. *Oh, how I prayed it was mere lust!* But Mistress, this attraction is made up of many other more powerful things. Destiny intends that you be at my side— whether you and I will it or not."

Amarantha caught her breath, uncertain whether she should feel insulted by his comment or flattered and hopeful.

"Believe me, Mistress, our wedding is hastened but a little by these damnable circumstances," he said earnestly. "We would have ended up at the altar by summer's end regardless."

"That is by no means a true statement. I have had no thought to wed any time soon—especially not to a man in orders who already has a damned mistress," she blurted out without thinking.

"What?" Tamlane was confounded by the accusation. His voice was a study of stupefaction as he forgot their whereabouts and repeated loudly: "*A mistress!*

263

That is a vile lie. I am a man of the cloth now! I have nothing of the sort!"

Amarantha winced.

"I am not speaking of some woman, but rather of your precious *cause*—the Jacobite rebellion," she said in a lowered voice, mindful of the waiting priest's attentive ears. "You were committed to her long before you met me—and I doubt that you shall soon renounce her."

Tamlane looked stupified.

"I thought it to be your cause, too, at least in your heart."

"No." It was difficult, but Amarantha forced herself to meet his stunned gaze. "It was the cause embraced by my family because they had no choice but to fight or give up their home, but it was never mine. I sympathize with your loyalty—and understand why you do what you do. Truly! But I could never place the games of kings and politicians ahead of my feelings. Perhaps it is because I am a woman, but I could never do what you men have done. I would never abandon my family and home and seek out war."

Instead of being angry or insulted by her assessment, Tamlane looked suddenly thoughtful.

"I see. And you believe that I will lead you into danger by my past affiliation with the prince," he said slowly. "But, Amarantha, I assure you that this whole adventure is very out of the ordinary. It is a bizarre confluence of events that shall never pass again. It is true that in the past when I was young and angry that I was a soldier for the Jacobite cause in Scotland—and for a time in Ireland. But that crusade ended long ago. I am a man of God now. *I study war no more.*"

"Is it truly ended? Can it end so long as you have family or friends being persecuted? It does not seem so to me." She shook her head. "It is not that I object to danger, Tamlane. I would face it willingly if it came to us. But I do strongly object to being placed in its path because of your love for something other than—than your wife."

It was as close to a demand and a plea for reassurance as she could come.

Tamlane said slowly: "I do not care for the prince more than you. In fact, I do not love him at all. This rebellion was never about the right of the Stuart kings, but about justice and freedom for our kin. How can you not understand that?"

Amarantha waited, breath stilled, hoping he would say more. If he proclaimed a great love for her she would believe him, for Tamlane would not lie. But he said no more and after a moment she spoke again.

"But you are still loyal to this cause of justice and freedom," she said sadly. "And I do not know what to do. Had we a little more time, we could . . ."

"Could discover ways to test my devotion to you?" He smiled wryly. "Ah, lass, how would you have me prove that you are wrong in your assumptions? How can I ever give proof that you would believe? There is no window into my heart through which you may peer, no spyglass to see into my thoughts and emotions."

"I know this." Amarantha found her throat growing tight and feared that she might end up weeping after all. Things seemed hopeless, and she was so very tired.

Tamlane possessed himself of her hand and chafed the cold fingers gently.

"I can do no more than offer you my word that I take the marriage vows seriously, and that I would never place the needs of strangers ahead of my wife— or my children."

Amarantha began to feel a little dizzy. She did not know whether she should believe him. Her heart wished that the things implied in his words would be true, but her mind was less certain that they actually were.

"Can you not have just a little faith, love?" he asked her quietly. "You have taken so many risks this last day and night, can you not take one more?"

"I don't know," she answered, shutting her eyes and trying to think her way through the clouds of exhaustion that fogged her brain.

He released her at that.

"Then what will you do, Mistress? Will you abandon me at the altar then? Destroy my alibi? Have Taxier arrested and executed? Bring scandal—even danger— to your uncle and all in his home?"

"Oh! You are cruel!" she gasped, putting hands over her face. "Why do you thrust this burden upon me?"

"Belike I am cruel—but, Amarantha, I am cruel only when necessary. And what I am telling you is only the truth of the situation after all. No one thrust it upon you except you yourself. Had we returned home last night, all would have been well. But we did not. So now the soldiers who came looking for us have been told that we left last night in order to make a runaway match. They will assume it is because you are already with child and could not wait any longer without showing that you were breeding. If I know anything of gossip, this story will have already spread through the village."

"Oh no! But I have not been here even a month! Surely such a tale would not be believed!"

"No one will care about that small fact. Gossip is always believed because people wish to believe it. They will say that we met during my travels. They will likely assume we eloped because your uncle did not approve the match between an heiress and a vicar and this was our opportunity to escape—and possibly that we needed to marry before the bishop heard of my moral lapse and I was dismissed from orders. Which, I must add, I shall be if we return unwed." Tamlane's voice was relentless.

"Don't say any more," she pleaded from behind her fingers. "This is too awful to contemplate."

"That much scandal is already a fact. But if we return married, then at least Taxier wasn't out smuggling—he simply had an accident on the stair, the Preventives ran into that other band of smugglers—not our Jacobites—and our being out where we were kidnapped was not because we were smuggling or aiding Jacobites, but because we were eloping. It is a scandal—but not a hanging matter. But, love, without this confirmation of our alibis, *l'affaire* Taxier becomes something else altogether, something deadly that endangers all of us." He added harshly, "Our fate is in your hands."

"Bloody hell. And I *wanted* to go with you to keep you from harm," she lamented bitterly.

"Indeed, you insisted upon it," Tamlane agreed.

"And now is your great opportunity to actually aid me. Come! Prove your good intentions."

"Be quiet a moment. If you laugh now, you beast, I shall box your ears!"

Tamlane sighed.

"I am not laughing. Have your moment, Mistress. Have two even. But we are not leaving Saint Catherine's until we are married."

In that moment she almost hated him. Amarantha turned her back on Tamlane and tried vainly to think.

How had she failed to notice that danger was so close? Had she been so shocked and exhausted by her experience at the dancing stones, and then with the smugglers, that she had been unable to reason this horrible situation through on her own? Tamlane's arguments were all very clear once stated. Once any thread of their alibi began to unravel, then the whole tapestry of falsehoods came apart.

Leaving aside her uncle and Taxier's fate—which she could not readily do—there was still Tamlane's destiny to consider. He had not said that he would hang with Taxier should the man be discovered a Jacobite, but Amarantha knew it was so.

Her feelings and vows of a spinster existence were now outweighed by other life-and-death considerations, and they could not be allowed to interfere.

And had she not also sworn that if ever faced with a deadly circumstance, she would not turn her back on the man she loved? She had not been thinking of bestowing her hand in marriage when she made the vow, but rather her virtue, yet did not the argument still apply?

"It must," she whispered to herself, straightening. She would keep the thought steadily before her, to help her do what she must.

And perhaps it was splitting hairs rather finely, but she saw a difference between wedding Tamlane and any of other men who had proposed marriage to her. She was not breaking her promise, she reasoned. Her integrity was not compromised. She had not rejected love when she'd made her vow, just marriage with any who sought her for reasons other than true regard and passion. In her world, love and marriage were rarely partnered. Weddings were for property, profit or heirs. Such an arrangement had offered her nothing, therefore she had rejected it.

But in this case, she could be certain that she was not being sought for her fortune, her property or an heir. And Tamlane apparently did have strong feelings for her.

And, she admitted, the thought of an affair with Tamlane had been only an idle dream. For Tamlane, there would never have been an expression of affection between them without marriage. It was marriage or naught.

The question she most urgently wished answered was whether he could make a marriage when there was no *love*. Surely not! There had to at least be the hope that the feeling would someday grow between them.

And in the meantime she knew that there was at least passion on his part—as well as her own.

"Does your heart not tell you that this is right?" he whispered, his breath tickling her ear, so near was he standing.

She shivered.

"My heart speaks senseless gibberish."

"Aye, and mine as well. No doubt we'll learn to understand this new language in due time."

"I shall probably regret this," she whispered mostly to herself. "But my heart has waited an age to be lost to something. This is certainly a worthy cause. Maybe I shall—this once—act and not count the cost. But, Tamlane, if you are untrue to your word, I promise that I shall make your life unending misery. You'll have no peace this side of the crypt—I swear this on my parents' grave."

Tamlane touched a finger to her cheek and waited for her to open her eyes. He smiled gently.

"Of course you will, love. And maybe even if I keep my promise." He smiled a little. "Truly, I expected nothing less from you."

"You were reading about this—marriage—before we left Blesland, weren't you?" she asked irrelevantly.

"Yes . . . I was reviewing the vows and seeing if I was ready to take them."

"And were you?"

"Aye, I was. I am. Are *you* ready?" he asked her.

No!

"Yes," she whispered.

"Then let us begin. We must wed before dark."

Amarantha allowed him to take her hand and move her toward the altar where the priest and a witness awaited them. Their footsteps rang out from the paving stones and filled the chapel with reverberations. She could smell the salt from a nearby estuary and burning wax. It made her tired eyes burn.

"I am sorry that there is no music or bridal clothes,"

Tamlane said as they halted before the altar.

"It doesn't matter," she answered.

"Dearly beloved," the priest began immediately as they turned to face the gray stone altar. Two small candles flickered there, their brightness unneeded with sunlight streaming in upon them. The pale cleric had the look of an owl with large, unblinking eyes unused to the light of day, and a voice just as high and unnerving as any night fowl's. "We are gathered here in the presence of God to unite this man and this woman in holy wedlock. . . ."

Amarantha closed her eyes again and concentrated on staying erect on her trembling legs. Her mouth had granted permission for this to happen, but the rest of her mind and body seemed unable to comprehend her actions.

Tamlane kept a close eye on Amarantha's complexion while they went through the wedding rituals. Her pallor was most unhealthy and he knew from her limping gait that her legs pained her. Her hands plucked restlessly at the borrowed gown of plain homespun that did not suit her, and her posture was strained as if she continually fought the urge to flee.

It hurt him that she had accused him of being cruel, yet she did not know just how much cruelty he had been prepared to use should the occasion have called for it. He had been willing to contrive this marriage by some very unsubtle means had it been necessary.

To begin with, he had slightly overstated the morals of the brothers at Saint Catherine's. There were some, like the cleric performing the ceremony, who were willing—for a generous fee—to marry a couple, even against the bride's wishes and protestations.

Still, he had been brutal enough with his words, and he would offer her nearly any recompense for this shattering of her maiden's vision of what a romantic courtship should be. Indeed, he had hardly covered himself in glory in the day and night just passed. And that was after he had promised to keep her safe!

The bruises to her body would heal quickly, though perhaps not the buffets to her feelings. Perhaps this ceremony was a just cure for her curious nature that had led them to this impasse, but he felt ashamed that her bridal was passing unmarked by friends or family, or even a floral wreath or veil. Her clothes were borrowed, except for her shoes, and the only ring he had to offer was a worn and over-large band that he wore on his farthest left finger, for there had been no time to procure another.

Then, were that not insult enough, he thought with a grimace, he would return her to *Carn Brea* where she would be exposed for a night and another morning to the odor of onions that she found so objectionable, and then subject her to another long ride back to Blesland where they would be met with many questions and great deal of wild and unpleasant speculation.

It was entirely a memorable nuptial—which was most unfortunate! Tamlane suspected that this was one moment that would never be looked back upon with fond thoughts. It was not a propitious start to a marriage to have the bride loathing the very remembrance of her wedding day.

Still, once Taxier had been wounded and Amarantha was there in the woods, there had been no turning back from the path before them. There was nothing they could do but plough onward and trust that providence was looking out for them. He was right, he assured himself, to be resolute about pushing for this marriage. It solved so many problems. And, in time, Amarantha would see that he had been correct when he insisted upon it.

Too, he was not a complete dastard. There *was* something gentlemanly he could do for her. He would put aside his own inclinations and not insist upon consummation of this union until Amarantha was more used to him . . . and they had a comfortable bed that did not reek of onions.

The wait would probably kill him. His body had been in distress since their first meeting. But he swore that he would not push her any further until she gave some sign that she was ready to be a wife in more than name. It was the least he could do for his gallant bride.

Tamlane suddenly realized that silence had fallen and the cleric was waiting for some response from him.

His *"I do"* was emphatic enough to draw Amarantha's gaze.

He tried smiling in reassurance at her, but her expression remained closed and pale. Tamlane realized that he might have a long wait before he was welcomed to his wife's bed.

Chapter Thirteen

The lonely bleating of a stray sheep was the only sound to be heard outside the silent church, and its forlorn call did nothing to lift the mournful mood that enveloped Amarantha.

"Don't worry, little lamb," she said. "The daily sacrifice has already been to the altar. You should be quite safe for now."

Tamlane shot her an unreadable look, but said nothing of her frail attempt at humor. She didn't blame him; it was hardly the subject of rollicksome jest. Still, she felt she deserved some word of praise for not weeping or being unwell, or in any other way disgracing herself in what some would see as a useless, feminine manner. For a few moments at the end of the short but pointed ceremony she had thought that she might have done both—and then fainted besides.

To Amarantha's newly married eyes, the landscape around Saint Catherine's had turned as somber as a graveyard—which, she finally noticed, it was—and the countryside was completely deserted except for the orange light of a waning sun. She suspected that this was a perpetual state of abandonment, for who would wish to come and visit poor, disgraced suicides of centuries past and the very strange holy men who continued to live and worship here?

"The trap is this way," Tamlane reminded her, taking her arm in a gentle grasp and helping her as he would someone very elderly or invalid. "It won't be long now until you may sleep."

Amarantha stared at the narrow road to *Carn Brea* where the pony and cart waited unstabled or fed since the brothers did not run to such accommodations. The path was a scar on the dreary moor, a manmade wound that was only half healed and scabrous with patches of determined weeds that sought some open ground in which to grow. Eventually, the flora would reclaim the moorland from the holy brothers. Saint Catherine's was dead and decaying, and at the moment she felt vindictive enough to take satisfaction in the church's ruination.

Tamlane was being very brisk and efficient as he handed her up into the cart and checked the pony's tack. He even whistled beneath his breath while he worked, which she found quite annoying of him when he had to be every bit as weary and saddle-sore as she was. There was no need to pretend that he was feeling jolly about this bridal expedition. His protestations of attraction to her aside, the situation was hardly what could be termed an ideal one for a man of the cloth.

But the man was peculiar. Perhaps he *was* feeling happy. Mayhap, in his oddly optimistic universe, he saw them as having had Divine help in escaping evil fortune and felt the need to give joyous thanks for their salvation. Wasn't that what the psalm said— *'Make a joyful noise unto the Lord.'* Maybe he saw their marriage as something determined by Heaven and therefore propitious, in spite of the scandal that was surely now erupting in Blesland.

Or perhaps he simply found the scent of drying onions invigorating and was looking forward with pleasure to spending the night rolling about in them. It would be just like Tamlane to decide to pass his first night as a married man—

"Oh my God in Heaven!" she uttered faintly, staring at Tamlane with shocked eyes as the full import of what had just happened in the church rushed in upon her.

They were married! That meant sharing a home— sharing a room—sharing a bed whenever Tamlane wished!

But he couldn't be expecting a wedding night, could he? At least, not tonight! The rector was strange and unpredictable—but not completely insensitive and lack-witted. He had to know that this was all too—too—upsetting. Never mind that she had once wished for them to be lovers! It was different now. Terrifying even.

"What is it?" Tamlane asked, reaching for his pistol and looking about rapidly to see what had alarmed her. "Is someone watching us?"

"Just you," she whispered to herself, staring at the ring which shackled her finger in the traditional manner of bond between a wife and her husband.

They were married!

"Lass?"

" 'Tis naught. Perhaps you should keep the ring. It is too large for me and I may lose it."

She held out the band and turned her face away before he could detect her betraying blushes and guess that this was mainly a gesture of repudiation. If the disturbing notion of what this occasion usually connoted hadn't entered his head, she would not be the one to put it there.

"That was rather a strong curse for *naught*," he said lightly, taking the ring from her. "Are you certain that nothing is amiss?" He climbed aboard the cart and picked up the reins. He did not touch her, but such was her awareness of him that she felt his scrutiny on her face.

"Of course everything is amiss. I have just sustained a great shock. The entire situation is infuriating," she said in a rallying tone, still refusing to look his way, as her color had not subsided. She enumerated her complaints: "I haven't been in my own clothes since yesterday evening, or my bed since the night before. I miss my uncle and Mrs. Polreath, and Pendennis's lovely dinners—and my comfortable cot that has well-aired linens, which I doubt *Carn Brea* possesses as its air is quite polluted even with the holes in the roof where all the night pests might fly in!"

"Hmm. This is hard indeed."

Tamlane was tactful and didn't mention that as his wife she would not be enjoying Pendennis's dinners, or her own cot, when they returned to Blesland and took up residence at his cottage, but the knowledge that this was the case made her feel angry and a bit panicked.

She added sharply: "And have I mentioned that I am truly unenthusiastic about the odor of drying onions? I have also just been married against my better judgment, embroiled in scandal—and let me tell you that I feel positively faint when I think of having to explain this advent to Uncle Cyril—and I do not have any smelling salts with me either! So to avoid the public spectacle of a woman having vapors in an open cart, perhaps it would be best if we did not converse until I have had some sleep and a time for quiet reflection."

Tamlane sighed.

"Conserve your strength, lass. You haven't the energy for a proper set of vapors, nor have I the will to deal with them."

"Tamlane!" Amarantha's hands balled into fists.

"Peace, lass. I'll admit that you've a long list of grievous complaints. And I am right sorry about the onions. But you shall have a clean bed and a good meal soon enough. And after that things will not seem so very unpleasant."

"I care less about the meal than I do about sleeping," she said, finally able to look at Tamlane without coloring. "Rest I must and shall have. My spirits are worn down until I am churlish and ill-tempered. In fact, it might be best if you take back your pistol as I am apt to do you harm if provoked. It would be a shame to be widowed as soon as I am wifed."

"You shall have both food and rest," he promised

with a wry smile. "Fate is smiling upon you, in spite of how the situation now appears. And you keep that pistol, lass. We may yet have need of it."

The reminder was sobering and distracted her from personal ills.

"Do you think the smugglers have followed us here?"

"No."

"The soldiers then?"

"Nay. We are being looked after and all will be well."

Amarantha blinked and tried to imagine what he meant. But try though she did, she could not think how Tamlane arrived at his conclusion.

"How so? Unless you are thinking that every day not in the grave is a good one and are feeling generally grateful to be alive."

"There is that favorable point to be certain. But I was thinking of smaller, domestic things. You are most fortunate that I do not snore. Some wives suffer greatly because of this," he teased, hoping for a smile.

A fresh wave of color washed into Amarantha's face and then drained immediately away, leaving her feverish and shaken.

"No," she said flatly.

"No?" he asked, confused and alarmed at her sudden pallor.

"*No*, we are not sharing a room."

Tamlane sighed again.

"I am sorry from the bottom of my heart, lass, but we shall have to share a room and a bed. The Trelawnys have but one chamber to spare, and for me to sleep anywhere else would arouse more speculation and comment than either of us would care to endure. Harry is a dear friend and would walk through the gates of Hell to defend us, but he is also a confoundedly curious one and, when inebriated, apt to speculate—aloud—and offer much unwanted advice. If I know my friend, he began celebrating the moment we left and will be in a state of advanced inebriation when we arrive. If you wish to sleep tonight, my presence at your side is a requirement. And truthfully, lass, until I know that we are safe, I'd not let you from my side anyhow."

There was a moment of silence and Amarantha said, "Take me back to Saint Catherine's."

"Why?" Tamlane asked, startled.

"Because I have decided to commit suicide. You may as well leave me there. After all, eternity in a lake of burning fire could not be any worse than this."

He laughed at her pronouncement and whipped up the cart.

"I adore your sense of the ridiculous, love. Not every woman could jest in the face of such adversity. Such gallantry of the spirit is rarer than rubies."

"Jest?" Amarantha stared at Tamlane with a fascinated eye and decided that it wasn't impartial Fate who was meddling in her life. It was cruel Nemesis.

Flames hissed on the hearth where a spitted chicken was roasting. The heavenly smell filled the air and nearly masked the odor of drying onion, those having been cleared away from the table so that they might enjoy an abbreviated wedding feast.

Though not usually inclined to drink, Amarantha threw caution to the wind and followed her host's example and imbibed freely of the port he offered his guests. Tucked into a settle and seated near the warmth of the hearth, a state of blessed numbness finally reigned within her.

Tamlane was less careless of the amounts he quaffed, but seemed quite relaxed in his friend's teasing company and their humble surroundings. Perhaps his years as a soldier had inured him to all hardship. Certainly, if he had any regrets about their sudden marriage he was making no public show of them.

Of course, in his own strange way, Tamlane was a gentleman. It would not be in his nature to hold his wife up to ridicule. For this she could only be thankful, as she hadn't the strength to endure any more adversity.

The bridal meal, though held at the wrong hour of the day was nearly festive and there was even a small bowl of strawberries for a bit of sweetness among the roasted meat and boiled vegetables. Surely the berries were the first of the season, for they were not plentiful or large—or even very ripe—but Amarantha was still touched at the gesture and the generosity that prompted it, and smiled gratefully at her shy hostess.

Constance Trelawny seemed fascinated and pleased by the strange events that had been visited upon them. Amarantha supposed that to an outsider, unacquainted with the facts and possessed of great sentiment, their marriage, brought about by wild circumstance, might seem a very romantic thing. Put into a song or verse, it would make an epic tale. But when experienced in fact, the whole adventure was depressingly *un*romantic. Still, she was a lady and had been raised to know the proper method of telling believable social lies, so she smiled at her hosts and gave the pretense of being content with what had come to pass.

Perhaps, in time, she truly would be.

Constance was kind enough to serve as her maid when it was time to retire, though Amarantha hardly required any assistance to disrobe from her extremely plain gown and use the modest basin to bathe in. Though Amarantha had been careful to guard her tongue—and as far as she could, her expression— while donning a borrowed and extremely modest night rail, her hostess seemed to have picked up on her perturbation of spirit and made a kindly intended effort to set her guest at ease.

As Amarantha climbed into the narrow bed, an attempt—exquisitely embarrassing for both of them— was made by Constance to make clear what was expected of a wife on her wedding night. Fortunately, Amarantha was able to reassure her that this ritual had been explained to her before and she had no fears on this score.

"Then if this does not trouble you, what is it that makes you frown and stay so silent?" Constance asked quietly, obviously perplexed.

"Marriage to the rebel rector of Blesland," Amarantha muttered without thinking.

"Do you not approve of Rector Adair's activities with the men of the north who fought for the prince's Holy Cause? The true king had no better supporter!"

Constance sounded shocked and more than a little hurt.

Amarantha closed her eyes, wishing that her sweetly naive hostess would depart. She was too weary to continue guarding her tongue from every thought that passed through her brain.

"My approval or disapproval does not seem to enter into this affair."

Constance gave a small gasp and Amarantha forced her eyes open one last time. She made an effort to repair the damage of her somewhat caustic reply.

"Never mind me tonight, Constance. I haven't slept in two days and am so weary that I know not what I am saying. Tamlane's past is a fact. I knew his sympathies before we married and aided him of my own free will. I care very much for him and esteem his sense of honor. Accommodations will have to be made."

Just not tonight, she added to herself.

A movement in the doorway brought her head whipping around. It was, as she had feared, Tamlane, and he had donned his languid disguise as he lounged in the tiny doorway. From the half smile he wore, Amarantha suspected that he had heard her words to Constance Trelawny. She wondered what there was in them to be entertaining. Surely not her expression of esteem! Perhaps the notion of compromise amused him.

"Good evening, my dear," he said, stepping into the room. "Mistress Trelawny, I cannot thank you enough for welcoming us to your home. We are both very grateful for your hospitality."

With his generous bulk crowded into the tiny

chamber there was no room for their hostess, and with a quiet murmur of assurance and pleasure at having them at *Carn Brea*, Constance hurried away.

"It does not seem that you and Constance share much of a personality," Tamlane commented, settling cautiously onto a crude stool and reaching for the bootjack Harry had lent him.

"It would seem not," Amarantha said morosely. "In fact, I rather fear that I have offended her."

"No, just startled her a wee bit. She would never dream of making *accommodations* for her husband. Harry Trelawny is her lord and master, his word and will second only to God's—who doubtless speaks through him anyway."

"How fortunate for Harry." Unable to hold back the tide of weariness any longer, Amarantha allowed her eyes to close upon the plain chamber. Not even the sight of Tamlane disrobing had the power to keep her awake.

"I suppose that you envision me making accommodations in this marriage as well?" Tamlane asked.

"Yes," she agreed, too close to Morpheus to make a less direct reply.

Tamlane's voice came once more from far away. She could hear an undertone of amusement in it.

"And I suppose that you would prefer to not have me lavishing affection upon you tonight."

"You may be affectionate if it pleases you to be, just do not wake me while you are doing it," she tried to say, but Amarantha did not know if she replied so bluntly in fact or just in her dreams.

* * *

Tamlane looked down as his sleeping bride and smiled ruefully. This was not at all how he had imagined his wedding night would be. He had not been with a woman for three years, not since taking his vows to the church, and his recent time spent in Amarantha's company had rekindled old, carnal thoughts. Fired by the body, when he had imagined marriage, he had seen his first night with his wife as a time for reawaking his own passions and for introducing her to the pleasures of the marriage bed. And in his dreams, Amarantha was awake—a bit shy perhaps, but welcoming. And eventually she was passionate as well.

Instead, he was in a small drafty chamber, condemned to sleeping on a narrow cot with a woman in a coma. The object of his desire was deeply asleep and wearing plain homespun and profound purple bruises beneath her eyes rather than a night rail made of silk and trimmed out in lace and a welcoming smile.

However, she was now truly his wife, and he had the right to share her bed, her thoughts—and someday, God willing, they would share children. With that thought, he could be content.

Tamlane finished undressing and then eased himself beneath the blanket. Amarantha grumbled as he slid an arm under her cheek and put another around her waist, but did not protest when he tucked her body into his own.

He took a deep breath of the tresses that tickled his nose and found that they still held the faint scent of sunshine and wildflowers. Her closeness made his body stir but he was weary enough to ignore the pangs of awakened desire. Tamlane sighed contentedly and, with Amarantha held close, allowed his own body and mind to slip into healing sleep.

Chapter Fourteen

The pale streamers of dawn light were creeping over the window sill and through the chamber's honeysuckle curtains when Amarantha opened her eyes and rejoined the wakened world. Her first moments of alertness were disorienting, but she was far from alarmed by the foreign surroundings. The gentle beat of Tamlane's heart was a lullabye beneath her ear, his arm about her waist was the warmest of blankets, and his body curved to her own made the most comfortable of cots. From this safe cradle she watched the new day mount the sky through the narrow casement at the foot of the bed, and floating along on a tide of dreamy detachment, she considered what she would do about Tamlane.

The matter, even after a night's repose, was a complicated one and she made careful note of her options, attempting to lay all her thoughts out in logical order. This was perhaps difficult to do when the object of her consideration was serving as the very pillow she laid upon, his scent filling her head with pleasant thoughts and daydreams, but she still made an effort to seek reason and look into her heart with clear and truthful sight. That organ of care and feeling had been a most painful place to visit for some time now, but she went regularly for she knew that she could not long survive if she was divorced from her heart's needs and wishes. At such an important moment, her heart—along with reason—had to be consulted about what was best to do.

She was not so innocent as to fail to realize that to remain with Tamlane in a conjugal bed beyond this moment was to precipitate the final act that would make their union complete in the eyes of the law—and more importantly, at least to Tamlane—in the eyes of God. If she stayed in this bed until he awoke she would likely be forced into a decision, in short, to give consent to love making or else deny Tamlane his connubial rights.

With another, less scrupulous man it might be otherwise, but to agree to sharing physical love with Tamlane was to consent to the marriage, something which she was still not entirely certain that she wished to do. And yet she found, much to her surprise, that she did not immediately wish to repudiate the union either. Something about it felt correct. Her body certainly approved.

Amarantha sighed and snuggled a little closer, absently toying with the crisp chest hair upon which she lay.

If only she had been allowed a bit more time to arrive at some conclusion! Even a day of solitude in which she might consider what was best to be done would have been enough. It was hard to look past the resentment of the fact that she had been compelled to the altar, to consider calmly the larger question of what she might in time have wanted to do.

She supposed that it might be possible to supplicate for another day's grace—or even a week's—by pleading exhaustion or nerves. But to refuse Tamlane now would be to set an unfortunate precedent, which might well overshadow their future—supposing they still had one after she rejected his affections.

And, she admitted to herself, it was cowardly and unfair to ask him to continue on with the belief that they would be man and wife if she did not truly intend to be his bride. If an annulment was to be sought, for the sake of both of their reputations, it had to be agreed to immediately. She could not hold out false hope.

An annulment. Amarantha closed her eyes and tried not to shudder at the thought of what that could mean.

An annulment was not so easy a thing to achieve, particularly if they waited several months or a year. But even supposing that the events of the previous day could somehow be reversed, would she truly want them to be? What would she be taking back beyond her freedom? Boredom? Loneliness? For that, without doubt, awaited her in abundance if she continued on with her solitary existence as the niece of a folklorist and scholar in this tiny corner of Cornwall—or even as a determined spinster in London.

The notion of a life without family in London she discarded immediately, which left Uncle Cyril and Cornwall. She was fond of her uncle, but without Tamlane's wit and company, tiny Blesland would surely be insupportable. Her spirit would shrivel up and die a little more with each passing year.

And could she bear to see him in the village, to meet him as an acquaintance only, and know that he might have been hers? To watch dispassionately if someday he married another and brought her to live in his home? See him raise children with some other woman as their mother?

"No," she whispered.

More horrible still, could she support life if her rejection of their marriage later led to his arrest and execution? Or to Taxier's? Or her uncle's?

Amarantha tightened her fingers as she rejected the horrific notion and tried a different path of thought, one less fraught with emotional images.

Perhaps it would help to think of herself as entering into a love affair rather than a marriage. For that, she might be able to have some enthusiasm. This was not something that she enterprised lightly, but it was something about which she had given a great deal of thought.

Too, she had been looking at all this from her own perspective. But what of Tamlane? What might he be thinking? What might he want of her—of a lover? Of a wife? These questions needed to be answered before she decided anything final.

He had not said that he loved her—that he desired

her, yes, but only very reluctantly. There had been no romantic words between them, no declarations of undying love. No plan for a shared future.

Yet the fact that he had not said anything about love did not mean that he could not in time come to feel deeper emotions for her. For many men, love was not the visitation of poetic lightning that women would wish, but rather something that came with time and better acquaintance. They grew familiar with and trusted a woman, and then love would follow. Desire was a place to start. Much could be built with it.

And in the meanwhile, her own feelings were surely strong enough to support their union. This was not how she would have chosen to enter an affair, driven there by circumstance and avoidance of arrest, but—

"That is a mighty frown which mars your lovely countenance," a deep voice said into her unbound hair, which had somehow freed itself in the night. "And I believe that my breast has been bereft of hair in that patch beneath your hand."

Amarantha immediately loosed her hold on his chest fur and turned her face upward to stare into the most beautiful eyes she had ever seen. They were clear and pure as spring and lit with joyous spirit. His lovely mouth was curved in a wry smile as he awaited her reply.

In that instant, her decision was as clear as his gaze, and the smile she gave back to her lover was blinding, having in it all the hope for their future that she had saved deep inside her heart when the rest of her was grieving for the loss of a false love.

"Good morning," she answered. Her own voice was pitched low and a bit raspy with lingering sleep.

Tamlane blinked, apparently startled at the change that had been wrought on her mood during the night.

"Poor lass. Are your muscles still protesting their day and night in the saddle?" he asked solicitously. "I could request Charlotte to fetch some embrocation to you."

Considering, Amarantha flexed her legs experimentally and felt no pain.

"No, they don't hurt," she said, feeling more cheerful by the minute. It was good that their first bedding would not be done with her body already in pain. "I feel quite remarkably well."

"Splendid." Tamlane, clearly puzzled by her answers and mood, returned her smile and then made to throw back the covers. He said briskly: "Then we shall leave directly after we have broken fast. It would be best that we return to Blesland as soon as possible. I need time to work on my sermon, and we must reassure everyone that we are well. Mrs. Polreath should be well nigh hysterical by this time."

He was leaving their bed?

But he couldn't! Not when she had screwed her courage to the sticking point!

"Wait." Amarantha stilled his hand as it clasped the covers. She had touched him many times before, but she was aware now that his skin was bare and the flesh of his body—like that of his hand—was warm and entirely naked. This time, she was touching her lover.

Her heart gave an excited bump, but unlike all the earlier frantic beatings, this one did not come from terror.

She watched as Tamlane's expression grew arrested. Through all her jumble of foreign emotions, she was able to discern a thread of amusement tickling her heart. How she loved to surprise this man! He so often amazed her; it was delightful to sometimes have the upper hand.

"There is something I must know." Amarantha swallowed and braved herself to go on. She wasn't sure if she was giddy or terrified.

"Aye." His hand was very still beneath hers, but also very tense.

"Was this marriage all a ploy? Do you plan to seek an annulment to this union later?" she asked, all innocence.

"No." The syllable was certain. He added, frowning: "And you shall not seek one either. We are wed. That is the end of it."

Amarantha's heart went from canter to gallop.

"Ah well! You say this now, but perhaps it would be best to make certain of that fact. I am not so sure that you will not cast me aside when this moonlit madness has passed off of you." She allowed her hand to slide upward over his wrist and onto his forearm when the dark hair tickled her fingertips. That hair was something that belonged only to males of their kind. She marveled, too, at his heat, which grew stronger every moment and radiated into the cool room. "And how do I know that you are actually *capable* of being a husband to me. It seems that with the men of the clergy it would difficult to judge if—"

Tamlane sat up abruptly, forcing her upright as well. His arms were tight about her waist and she could feel them clearly with only the cloth of her woolen night rail between them. His eyes began to gleam as he studied her face in the sweet morning light that flooded the room.

"Madame wife, are you actually suggesting that I am so cowardly a knave as to flee from your bed at this or any other moment? Or—words nearly fail me—that I am not potent?"

"It has happened before," she said with feigned mournfulness. "There has been much poetic literature devoted to the subject. Uncle Cyril has collected volumes upon it. Apparently any noose compared to the shackles of matrimony is preferable to some men. Especially Scotsmen—they often drown themselves to escape their women. And there must be *some* reason that so many men join the priesthood. It can't all be godliness. Perhaps you wish a wife only to allay suspicion of these masculine shortcomings among your parishioners."

"Amarantha!"

She giggled, unable to sustain a dignified front in the face of his outrage.

"You are teasing me," he said reproachfully. "That is unkind. And unwise. For what if I do not accept the rules of this game and wish for more than mere flirtation? In spite of my calling, I am not some marble saint divorced from all human impulse."

"I am not teasing. Teasing is purposeless." Amarantha leaned forward and brushed her lips over Tamlane's mouth. Such boldness nearly caused her heart to arrest itself. "And you are certainly not made of cold stone. Everything about you is wonderfully warm and alive."

Tamlane was nearly frozen with surprise. She would have thought him turned to that marble statue had not the linens about his waist begun to stir and rise.

"Mayhap you don't understand what . . . what . . ." he began in a strangled voice.

"I understand," she assured him, burying her face in the curve of his neck. Boldness could only take her so far, and her nerves were failing at last. She added a bit desperately: "Tamlane, now is not the time for you to be stubborn and pursue an argument. Do please be a bit perceptive. I cannot do this all alone."

"I am not so certain that a little stubbornness might not be a good thing," he answered with a sigh as he buried his face in her unraveled hair. His hands caressed her waist and the flare of her hips. Then he confided: "But I am not of a mind to fight this battle alone either. And I have found that when I think myself most resolved upon a course, you somehow manage to lead me astray."

"That is man's lament since Adam—and no more valid now than it was then," she scolded. Her words were completely mitigated by the soft kiss she gave him. "How unfair of him to cast all blame upon Eve. Have women so much power?"

"Aye, but woe to the man who admits it to the wrong woman!" He laughed softly and lowered them back into the linens and turned her so that she was beneath him on the narrow cot.

"In any event, I am the helpless one. I feel that I have surrendered my will, that I could drown in your eyes, and that was never my intention," she confided. "I never thought to feel this. Was I not so intoxicated I would be terrified of you."

Amarantha shut her eyes and breathed in deeply. The scent of Tamlane and warming honeysuckle filled her head. It was a heady mixture. With every breath she inhaled, it seemed that she drank down bewitching perfume that bade her to forget all modesty and breeding.

"Ah, lady! That smile would move even a statue to unholy thoughts. I do not know whether I should ask of what you are thinking, but I am grateful for it."

"Why I am thinking of you, of course," she answered, opening her eyes and looking up into Tamlane's face. His cheeks wore a hectic flush and she could see a pulse tripping in his throat.

"Of course." He grinned suddenly. "This should not shock me—even though you have been hostile and suspicious of me from the start."

She laid a finger against his lips and shook her head.

"You must not tease either." He kissed the silencing finger. She added breathlessly: "I am also hoping that I am not too unpleasant a sight to look upon. I know that I am not at my best."

"You please much more than just my sight, lass," Tamlane assured her fervently. He lowered his head and his own dark locks mingled with the tangle on the pillow until they were as one. Amarantha put her arms about Tamlane's waist and prepared to become his lover.

Their lips met and his breath joined with hers. A long-fingered hand plucked at the ties of the night rail and pushed it from her shoulder. His lips traced from cheek and throat down to tender bosom where the tiny rose of nipple peeped over the plain nightgown's simple edge.

Amarantha

Tamlane paused to marvel. Her skin was lustrous as fine pearl.

"How could there be such passion here and I not see it?" he muttered.

"You have been distracted," she whispered. "And I did not want you to see it."

"Distracted to the point of blindness it seems. The sun is not half so fine a sight." In truth, he suspected that this attraction to his wife was very like the sun—or perhaps the sea. For the sun rose but once a day, but his passions were like to be as the tide and ever moving from heart to head, from body to brain.

Amarantha took in the words, and though wishing that he spoke more of feelings than of physical things, was nevertheless pleased.

A hand slid up under her night rail and he urged it to her waist. He rolled carefully between her legs, being watchful not to put too much weight upon her. With a sigh of pleasure, he kissed the midline between her breasts and then rising from her, settled on his knees. With gentle hands, he urged her legs a little higher, then set his hand against the heart of her. She was warmer than summer sun and slicked with dew.

"I wish that there was some gift I could give you that would be half so fine," he whispered.

She stared up into Tamlane's eyes and wanted to say: *Be in love with none but me forever.* Instead she smiled and said: "Perhaps someday there will be."

With a throttled groan, he set his flesh against hers and forced his way inside. He felt her slight flinch and made to stop, but Amarantha put hands to his flank and urged him to continue.

Wild then with the need of years, and nearly drunk with the sight and scent of the most intriguing woman he had ever met, Tamlane surged into the welcoming heat of her body. He made an effort to slow himself, to touch Amarantha gently and see to her needs, but the years of abstinence and now weeks of constant desire for this woman were not to be overcome in the moments before fulfillment. His body had mastery of the moment. He gasped wildly, an oath and a plea, and then he poured himself into her, giving everything that was within him to give; affection, need—and though he did not know it yet—heart and soul as well.

After the first instant, Tamlane did not try to resist the tide's relentless pull, but launched himself gladly into the bright sea of bliss where he found for the first time, not just the transcendental pleasure of earthly passion, but the complete peace of his heart's true home.

Chapter Fifteen

The urge to leap out of bed and trek to Blesland seemed to have left Tamlane. He knew that he should rouse himself and go out to seek the day, but he found the sensations of satiated contentment too appealing to immediately surrender for the dubious comfort of porridge and more of his friend's pungent company.

But his curiosity, once aroused, was a restless beast and not long content to be still. Long before his body was ready to surrender its delighted state, it was pricking at him with a dozen questions it wanted answered. After a few last blissful moments, Tamlane reluctantly opened his eyes, and, rising up on one elbow, he looked down into his wife's face and tried to see into her mind.

Amarantha still wore a light flush of color and her own eyes were closed. Was it bliss, or embarrassment that caused this? He couldn't judge. So many things about his new bride were a mystery to him.

"Are you well, love?" he asked tentatively.

"*Very* well." Amarantha opened her eyes. Her expression was a trifle dazed but also determined.

"Why do I feel that, in spite of your words, you were not entirely prepared for what just happened?" he asked gently.

"I doubt that any bride is ever completely prepared," she said evasively, turning her head toward the window and moving restlessly. He decided that she was definitely blushing from embarrassment. "Hadn't we best arise?"

"Presently. The day shall await our convenience for another moment yet." His eyes feasted happily on her disheveled state.

"The day may, but I put no such dependence upon your friend," she said, rallying. "He seems to me one of those depressingly chipper people who must be up with the sun and insisting that the world be up and about as well."

"Harry Trelawny is both an early riser and profoundly tactless, but not entirely stupid. He would not intrude on this of all morns." Amarantha snorted and Tamlane found himself reassured. Thus encouraged by her apparent normal mental state, he went on, "I fear that there was little pleasure for you in what just happened—"

"It was very pleasant," Amarantha said hurriedly. "But surely there is no need to discuss it."

"There is every need," Tamlane said firmly. "Be not

shy with me, Amarantha. It is something that all husbands and wives must discuss if there is to be any happiness in the marriage bed."

"It is not! My mother and father did not speak of such things, I am sure." Amarantha scowled at him. It was not the look of first love, but he liked it nonetheless.

"Are you certain of that? Surely you were not present at such intimate moments," he teased.

"Of course I wasn't there. Nevertheless I knew my parents well, and they would not have spoken about this. Now be so kind as to let me up." She pushed at the large hand that was settled possessively upon her stomach.

"Not until you tell me why you insisted upon this consummation when I know quite well that you are full of doubts about this marriage and detest your surroundings too much to think of them as bridal bower. Come, lass, speak to me. I usually have fine instincts, but would infinitely prefer some instruction about your feelings on this occasion."

She rolled her eyes.

"Why do you never ask me any simple questions— like what I might like for breakfast? Or you could inquire after my plans for the day," she asked in exasperation, then turned her face completely away before he could see the stain that was laid over her cheeks and think her wanton and depraved for her reasoning.

How could she explain her heart? She could hardly tell him that she hadn't been consummating their marriage, but rather had taken him as her lover.

"I shall doubtless ask you these things many times,

but at the moment my own question seems rather more important. In any event, there will likely be porridge for breakfast. There is surely no need to rush about for that."

"Porridge." The word was so mundane that Amarantha found the courage to look him full in the eyes, and recovering from her moment of inexpressible shock at her actions and what they meant—and the topic of conversation that had sprung from them— she said deliberately: "Very well, I *seduced* you this morning because—what's the matter? Are you choking?"

"Nay, it was just a sneeze trying to escape," Tamlane lied, making an effort to keep his face still. " 'Tis the dust, I fear."

"Hmph! As I was saying, I seduced you because while I have doubts about the wisdom of the course you have chosen—and my own qualifications to be a rector's wife—I have never had any doubts about wanting you. Nor am I a coward. There now! The matter is that simple. Now let me up!" Amarantha heaved mightily against his arm and made to roll from the cot. Her gown was rucked up at waist and she made a hasty effort to pull it back down to a modest length but was hindered by the loosened ties at the neckline which let the gown slip off her shoulders and bared her breasts. She hadn't hands enough to maintain decency and also fend off Tamlane.

"Not just yet." Tamlane ruthlessly retrieved her and dragged her back onto the cot, inadvertently pulling her gown right back to an indecent level. "I wish to discuss this *simple* matter of wanting me a little further. When did this happen? I thought you were suspicious of me."

Annoyance filled her bosom.

"There will be blizzards in hell before I speak of this again," she answered, spitting a loose tress from her mouth. "And I was bloody well justified in being suspicious, wasn't I?"

Tamlane chuckled. "You sound quite cross, lass."

Amarantha stared up into his face through a tangle of hair and asked in disbelief: "Are you being playful? Jesting even?"

"I believe that was my intention, yes. This is a fine joke after all, and I feel quite happy. Surely you will not begrudge me my good mood."

He felt happy. That was something—not romantic of course—but still rather wonderful to hear. It made her own ambivalence about the moment seem rather less important.

Amarantha cleared her throat. "I am glad that you are happy. But now is not a good moment for levity or a heavy hand upon me. To be blunt—"

But she was given no opportunity for direct speech as just then a weighty knock fell upon their door.

Amarantha groaned.

"Did I not say that this would happen?"

"Tamlane! Roust yerself, laddie," Harry Trelawny called through the door. "We've company coming. The boy says that a squad of soldiers is coming up the road from Blesland, and I have a notion it is you they'll be wanting to see."

Tamlane muttered a word that rectors were not supposed to use, then finally released his prisoner.

"I'm coming," he said at the door. Then, in a lower

voice: "This does not mean that we are through speaking about this matter. I will not forget my questions." He began to dress, pulling on clothing with a speed that spoke of much practice at the art of hurried dressing.

"We are through speaking for now," Amarantha muttered, beginning the hunt for her borrowed gown, and praying that Tamlane would leave her so that she might use the chamber pot and wash herself. Men! They were thoughtless, heedless—

"You aren't going to do anything rash, are you?" she demanded uneasily as she saw Tamlane check the priming on his pistol and slide it into a cloak pocket.

"*Rash?* Of course not," he answered with a sort of sublime certainty as he pulled on his boots and opened the door. He smiled at her briefly, a straying lock of midnight hair falling into his eyes, and she was suddenly aware that they now actually had a shared future—for the moment a bit uncertain—but still a future stretching out before them. *For better or for worse*, she had promised.

"Dear God," she breathed, struck again by what she had done.

"Amen." As was his wont, Tamlane added: "Have a little faith, love. All will be well, I promise."

She looked at Tamlane's retreating back and most of her wrath left her. Mayhap he had been a bit heavy of hand this morning with his teasing, but he was lovely to look at—so gallant and gay—and truly it boded well that he wished to speak to her at all. Many husbands and wives lived out their married life in polite silence, never doing more than nodding when they met over the coffee cups.

Thinking of coffee made Amarantha realize that she was hungry and so she made haste to dress. Porridge was not her favorite food, but she must have something in her stomach before she met up with the soldiers. If she was to be arrested and thrown in gaol, she preferred that it not be on an empty stomach. It was difficult to be courageous when starving.

A warm bath would have been ambrosial, but an ewer of cold water and a handkerchief was all there was to wash away Tamlane's spent seed and the slight traces of her virginity.

Still, it was better than what she had had yesterday morning when they were trapped inside the buried church. Borrowing a page from Tamlane's texts of the philosophy of the wonders of everyday fortune, she decided to be content with this.

The morning, as she ventured out into it, she found to be very still with motionless wisps of clouds stalled on the horizon like bits of sheep wool snagged on a brambled bush. Bees droned with a sleepy monotony, and the air smelled a bit like warm honey and mown hay. Everything was placid. It seemed impossible that anything important should be changed from yesterday.

Amarantha put up a hand to shield her eyes. The path back to Blesland wound like a snake and was obscured in parts by woods, so the company of soldiers was not immediately to be seen. She walked briskly to meet Trelawny and Tamlane where they stood at a bend in the road, consulting each other and the sun.

Amarantha should have been nervous, but she

wasn't. She actually felt quite sanguine. Even if the soldiers discovered them, and they were arrested and hung from a gibbet in Blesland Square, she thought that she would not regret this adventure. Not that such would ever happen! Luck was with them. Her newfound optimism came as a bit of a shock, but she embraced it gladly and gave silent thanks to Tamlane for inspiring her. He was a previously unexperienced mix of sensibility, calculated risk and faith, and she was now caught up in his assumption that all would be well. . . . Amazingly, she had faith, too.

Perhaps making love had not been what she anticipated—but it was still very pleasant, and made her feel very close to Tamlane. The scent and feel of him was still with her. She would be glad to repeat the experience when they had a more comfortable bed and more privacy—if they ever had a chance.

Of course, nothing unfortunate would happen today. Tamlane was right. The soldiers—no matter what the smugglers might have said—would never suspect a holy rector of Cornwall and a lady of conspiring with Jacobites. The very idea was preposterous. She hardly believed the truth of it herself, and she had been through the entire adventure.

"Good morning," she said, offering both men an easy smile.

Tamlane cocked a brow at her, but answered with equal cheer.

"Good morrow, wife. Have you dined?"

"Yes, thank you." She looked at Trelawny. "Your wife is an excellent cook. I have never enjoyed porridge more."

Trelawny smiled at her with approval.

"I see that a night's rest has improved your spirits. You were looking a mite wan yestereve."

Amarantha felt herself blush, but agreed readily to this suggestion that it was sleep that had improved her spirits. There was no possibility of her admitting to anyone that it was her decision to remain with Tamlane that had renewed her. Battling against herself had been exhausting.

"We wait here for the soldiers?" she asked. The urge to touch Tamlane was strong, but she firmly resisted the impulse.

"Nay. Let us back to the house and see about saddling the horses," he said.

"That varmint of mine shall have the task done," Trelawny prophesied. "The lad does know his horses."

"Nevertheless, I think I shall have a quick look at the tack and then we'll be on our way." Tamlane started back for the house. His heels crunched noisily through the remains of last autumn's leaves that littered the side of the path. "There is no need for the soldiers to come into your home. We can meet them on the road."

"Lad, you know that I would never mind—"

"But your wife would," Tamlane said firmly. "There is no need to bring back painful memories of what happened in Ireland. We will be off at once."

"Nonsense, laddie!"

But Tamlane proved more stubborn than his friend, and he and Amarantha were under way only minutes later, with Amarantha's borrowed breeches rolled into a small bundle and tied to the back of the saddle.

They had not gone far when the jingling of bridles was heard on the still air and the small patrol of soldiers came into view. Their demeanor was not somber, as she had expected, and it grew even lighter once their attention alighted upon them.

"Hullo there, rector!" One of them called. "We have been searching for ye."

"Hullo, Jamesy," Tamlane answered with lifted hand and charming smile. "Have you come to wish us well? Or is Cyril Stanhope after my blood?"

"Mister Stanhope?" The soldiers exchanged glances and then looked shyly at Amarantha. She was not up to her usual standard of dress, but the soldiers were not likely to notice the poor attire.

"Wasn't it he who sent you after us? I must tell you that you are too late in coming. My wife and I took vows yesterday at Saint Catherine's." Tamlane lifted Amarantha's gloved hand and gallantly saluted her wrist.

The soldiers blinked and exchanged another round of glances.

"Nay, it wasn't Mister Stanhope, but rather Cap'n Sharpe," Jamesy finally answered. "After Mister Aldridge was found shot down dead by smugglers and that other Preventive—Guthrie—in a swivet that you had gone missing and might be attacked on the moor as well. We were all afraid after that poor madman from the asylum was found with his neck broken and his clothing stolen. Cap'n turned us all out to hunt fer ye."

Not really listening, Amarantha found comfort in the pistol she had secreted in her pocket. It would not be possible to shoot all of the men, but the threat would probably be sufficient to let them escape. They could ride for the coast and seek immediate passage on some outward bound ship. . . .

"We are right glad to see you both unharmed," Jamesy added.

Amarantha blinked, unsure if she had heard correctly.

"Mister Aldridge is dead?" Tamlane appeared quite shocked at the news. Amarantha was shocked, too, but only at their good fortune.

"Aye, he and another Preventive. Only Mister Guthrie survived."

Amarantha turned this fact over in her mind. Guthrie had not sent soldiers after them to make an arrest, but rather because he feared for their safety.

"And it was smugglers? Are you certain?" Tamlane frowned and said slowly: "There has been no violence in Bodmin before this. The brotherhood has been largely cautious. Could it not have instead been one of those escaped madmen they have been warning us about?"

"Aye—that's what I thought," one of the other soldiers said eagerly. "Must be one of those crazies from Bodmin town what did this. There's no call for the *gentlemen* to turn violent. Blesland has never done them any harm. Any road, there would be no call for them to steal a dead man's clothes. It had to be one madman turning against another."

Amarantha did not point out the fact that the escaped prisoners had not been armed with pistols; it was barely possible that they had stolen a firearm from someplace and used it on the Preventives. As she had no wish to tarnish the soldier's shining theory with irrelevant fact, she remained silent on the subject.

"Has there been any sign of smugglers in the area?" Amarantha asked, speaking for the first time. Her voice was steady. No one would guess that she was having to suppress the urge to bite her fingernails.

"Mister Guthrie said as how Mister Aldridge was convinced of it, and was sending us some prisoner to look after until he could question them. But Guthrie never saw the man for hisself and the man never come to the gaol. And now the two Preventives are dead, and another gone to Helston, so we've no one to say for certain what happened."

That meant that somehow their kidnappers had avoided the soldiers. Amarantha was ashamed to be relieved that this was so. She wished the murderers to be punished, but if they were captured and talked of what had happened on the moor, it would put them all in danger—especially now that she and Tamlane had implied that they had no knowledge of Aldridge's fate.

But surely, by this time, those men had escaped back to France and would return no more! It was difficult to grasp, but it seemed that the danger had passed.

"Tamlane, we must hurry home." Amarantha looked at her love and said appealingly: "I wish to see my uncle and explain about . . . about all this. And we must not be away from home at such a time. The village will be uneasy."

"Your uncle was still away from the house when we left yesterday," Jamesy told her. He grinned impudently at Tamlane. "So your blood is safe from Cyril

310

Stanhope for another day, Rector. And, Mistress Stan—*Adair*—Mrs. Polreath said if I saw you that I was to tell you that the poor man, Taxier, is doing much better. It looks as how he is going to live after all. In fact, his first words to her when he opened his eyes was about how he was going to fix that damn— *er, uh*—blasted newel post for good and all."

They all laughed.

"Oh! I am so relieved that he is doing well." Amarantha allowed herself to relax and smile broadly. It seemed too amazing to believe, but it looked as though all was going to turn out well. "We were fairly certain that he was out of danger before we left, but it is still very good news."

"So, are you to give us escort back to Blesland?" Tamlane asked.

"Nay, we are to ride on to Padstow. The navy has set up a blockade there, but that may be lifted now that you have been found safe and no smugglers discovered. Best they go back to Penzance where the real smugglers are. Of course, if ye are afeared of meeting up with that madman . . ."

"Nay, I don't fear that," Tamlane said honestly.

"Very well then, we'll be off. You might send yer man around to the gaol with word that ye and yer wife are unharmed so the searchers may be called back to their regular patrol."

"I shall do so at once," Tamlane promised. "Good day to you, gentlemen. Many blessings upon you."

"Good day, Rector," Jamesy answered, and the others nodded their heads. "We shall see you on Sunday."

" 'Til Sunday then."

And with that they parted company. Amarantha waited until the soldiers were well away before speaking again.

"Tamlane Adair, you are the luckiest man I know."

"The Lord looks after His own, lass," he answered with a smile that reached all the way to his eyes and made them sparkle.

Amarantha wondered whether her heart would ever cease to stutter when she watched him smile.

"That is what they say about the devil as well," she told him.

"Aye, so it is," he agreed affably. "Do you think your husband a devil, wife?"

Husband. Wife.

"It is in the early days yet," she answered with a less than amused smirk. Thinking of what lay ahead, she said, "Ask me again in a week."

Tamlane looked at her consideringly but made no comment.

Chapter Sixteen

The air finally began to stir with the nightfall as the sea released its pent-up breath and a fresh line of clouds rolled in over the moor carrying the promise of heavy rain to come.

Amarantha and Tamlane had made good time and were but a league or so from Blesland when dark and drizzle began to fall. They were on a lonely stretch of moor, decorated with bracken and bogs that caught the setting sun's eerie light and swallowed all but the red glint of waning sun. Their surroundings were far from felicitous, but it was not the Dantesque scenery that caused Amarantha alarm.

They had fallen into a tense silence some minutes before. Nothing was said, but Amarantha sensed Tamlane was also alert to the feeling of danger that rode on the stirring air. There was a strong sensation of being observed by hostile eyes, and she wondered briefly whether their kidnappers had not, after all, sought their ships and departed for their homes in France, but had instead followed them to Saint Catherine's and were now lying in wait for them.

But reason dictated that it would be otherwise. After committing the murder of His Majesty's excise men, only fools would linger for the manhunt that was bound to follow. Also, there was no way for the smugglers to predict which road she and Tamlane would have traveled when they left *Carn Brea.*

Yet, there was enough of this sense of antagonism in the air that Amarantha found herself reaching for her pistol and scanning the encroaching shrubbery with a cautious eye.

As they entered a stretch of stunted woodland, Tamlane calmly withdrew his own pistol and carried it at the ready under the shelter of his cloak. They still did not speak to one another of the danger in the air, but so close were their thoughts in that moment that speech was unnecessary.

Amarantha's brow furrowed in annoyance as her stomach gave a gentle grumble, which broke the near-silence that haunted the trail. It defied belief, yet she was hungry again! It was ridiculous that in this moment of tension when they were leagues from food or shelter and about to be caught in the rain that her gut was rumbling emptily, upset by its missed meal. Was this what adventure did to her? If so, she would have to avoid it in future. She was tired of starving to the point of making unladylike noises.

"There is an old tomb less than half a league this

way. It is empty now," Tamlane said softly, also breaking the silence. "Let us take shelter there for the night."

"Could we not press on? I should like to have a real roof over my head and a stout door between us and the world," Amarantha answered in an equally soft voice.

Tamlane shook his head.

"It is about to come down hard, and I do not want you contracting an inflammation of the lung by riding in the damp night air." He smiled at her. "And you will surely not deny that you are sore from riding so awkwardly in your skirts. It is best we stop and rest."

"Aye, I am a bit sore," she admitted, not adding that part of that was his doing. She was willing to bet that most brides were not deflowered and then asked to ride all day in an uncomfortable saddle. If he had forgotten this matter, she had no intention of reviving their earlier conversation.

"Come then. This tomb is large and we may build a fire out of the leaves and twigs that have doubtless accumulated in it since last fall." Tamlane turned and pushing through a narrow belt of shrubbery, started across an open space. Though he still rode through the twilight with the easy grace of a sportsman, he did not put up his pistol or relax his vigilant study of the landscape. A belted knight on the way to war would ride out thusly.

Of course, a true knight of the realm would not be sleeping in a pagan tomb like a common beggar. But then, neither would a true lady.

"We go from strength to strength. Or do I mean from ruin to ruin?" Amarantha laughed softly, causing Tamlane to wince and shake his head. "You did assure me that marriage was a sound notion, did you not? That there would be fewer disagreeable consequences if I agreed to wed you?"

"I know, lass. I know! First onions and now a tomb. But I promise that I shall have you in Blesland tomorrow and into a comfortable bed by nightfall."

"I am sure that is your intention, but I have to wonder whether luck has abandoned us. I always get rained on before something bad happens." She squinted at the lowering sky, which was spitting cold black droplets at them.

"Surely not! And even if that were true, you cannot expect me to believe that something bad happens every time it rains."

"Lately, it has."

Tamlane glanced at her. His look was skeptical.

"Give me an example of this evil happenstance," he demanded.

"Let me see . . . The first night I followed you—"

"What!" Tamlane was clearly startled by this news. He frowned direfully and dropped back to ride beside her so that he might read her face in the gloom. "You followed me? More than once?"

"Yes," she admitted without blushing.

"You little gypsy! You should be thankful that I did not catch you."

"Well, I was thankful," she said candidly. "Especially after you met up with that Frenchman. He looked vaguely sinister all muffled up like that. And, of course, it was obvious that you were up to something nefarious."

"Frenchman?" Tamlane's voice was nearly strangled. "You saw one of them?"

"Did I not just say so?"

The silence that followed her question was of the kind frequently termed *"pregnant with meaning."*

"Just when did you follow me?"

Amarantha studied his vexed profile and had to smother another smile.

"The first time was after you came to dine," she told him.

"The first time?"

"Yes."

"In other words, from the first day we met you began spying on me?"

"Yes." Amarantha flipped the hood of her cape over her head and tried to huddle more deeply in its folds. It smelled stale with perspiration, but the weather was growing quite chill, and it seemed wise to take such shelter as the hood offered, regardless of the olfactory assault.

"You certainly did not trust me at all," he sounded vaguely offended.

"You should be pleased with my perspicacity! I have good instincts for dissimulation. Not that you bothered to try and hide what you were doing—or supposedly doing. If you had not left me so piqued at our encounter I should likely have never thought of following you."

"Hmph!" Tamlane grunted. "We stray from the subject. And what bad thing occurred then? I suppose that it was too much to hope that your uncle caught you sneaking home with the dawn and gave you a thrashing."

"Yes, that would be hoping for entirely too much," she answered cheerfully. "Uncle Cyril is not that observant and sleeps quite soundly once abed. Too, I don't think that he is the sort of unimaginative man who thinks that beatings are at all useful. He has certainly never suggested any such thing."

"Have you ever been thrashed?" Tamlane demanded.

"Never," she told him. "My father was not a violent man."

"Then do not sneer at its efficacy. We will try it first. Perhaps I may find it a useful tool," he said grimly. "But do go on and tell me what bad thing happened to you. Since I saw you the next day in church and you had the bloom of roses in your cheek and were bright of eye, it was not illness—or a sleepless night filled with remorse—that overcame you."

"Well, if you are going to threaten me, I don't think I shall tell you anything at all," she said, peering into the increasing gloom. She was grateful for Tamlane's extraordinary night sight, for she couldn't see much of anything in the dark about them, and all there was to hear was the sighing of the wind and patter of cold rain. "I am not some child or chattel to be ordered about and misused on a whim."

"I am not threatening you—and you *shall* tell me everything you have been up to." He made no comment about her other observation.

"It sounded like a threat," she said doubtfully.

"No, it was more in the nature of a possibility. Actually, it is a probability if I ever find you creeping about at night."

"Hmm. As long as *you* never give me cause, I think

that I can safely promise not to be about on the moor at night. It's a plaguey uncomfortable place." Amarantha suddenly realized that she had lost the sense of being under hostile observation. She looked about quickly. "Tamlane?"

"Aye, I think that we have lost whoever was following us. Perhaps they were on foot and could not keep up over the open spaces."

"I hope so. I don't think I am ready to start shooting people right now. It is hard to be bloodthirsty when I am so very hungry."

Tamlane groaned. "Again?"

"Well, it is only natural," she defended herself. "I always dine at this hour."

"Never mind your stomach. You will eventually learn that there is no place for appetites when adventuring. Instead, tell me more about what happened that night on the moor."

"Well, I got very muddy and wrecked not only my brocade dress but also Uncle Cyril's cape, which I had borrowed. Mrs. Polreath went around sighing like a martyr making me feel guilty for days—which was ridiculous! I told her to just throw the gown away and not bother cutting away the stains and then rehemming the thing. But she persisted in sewing the thing back together because there was enough material in the side panels to hide the mend with a flounce."

"I see. That doesn't sound very much like punishment to anyone except Mrs. Polreath."

"I didn't say that I was *punished*, merely that something unpleasant happened."

"And the next time you followed me?"

"That was the only time really—except the night when Taxier was shot," she assured him, finding it politic not to mention the day that she had searched his house, or her trek out to the dancing stones to inspect his place of rendezvous.

"I am glad to hear it. That was quite dangerous enough. Ah! Here we are." Tamlane pulled up beside a greater patch of darkness and dismounted from his horse. "Bring your mount in with you. There is room inside to stable them and they shall help to warm the air."

"They'll warm the air with horse breath," she muttered, throwing a painful leg over her saddle and sliding down to the ground. Her muscles squawked but managed to hold her upright. She rested her cheek against the saddle briefly and willed her body to motion. The first step was particularly painful. "Bloody hell."

"Are you hurt, lass?" The concern in Tamlane's voice was refreshing after the hectoring tone he had adopted while she was telling her story.

"No more than usual," she lied. In fact, her legs were very tired and ached all the way through the sinews and down to the very bones.

"I've a flint. We shall have a fire directly," Tamlane's voice assured her from out of the darkness of the tomb. "And I borrowed a nip of whisky from Harry, so you may have some liquid comfort immediately."

"I'd rather have oyster soup," she said, straightening with an effort and taking hold of her horse's bridle. She walked slowly toward Tamlane's voice. She did not relish sleeping in a cold tomb, but standing out in the increasingly icy rain was not appealing either.

"You'll find the whisky more effective," Tamlane assured her. There was a sudden spark and then the crackle of leaves being fed to a flame. The tiny light that sprang up was bright after the dark of the moor night and gave her a beacon to follow.

The ancient burial chamber was large but not so grand as to comfortably stable two horses, two people and a fire. Neither equine shied from the flames, but they were made uneasy by the fire's pale smoke and kept as close to the mouth of the tomb as they could and still take shelter from the rain.

Amarantha was exhausted, but she made an effort to unsaddle her mount before collapsing. However, her nervous horse was not entirely cooperative, snorting and twitching and slapping his tail about until after a moment, she dropped her tired arms and stepped away from the hair whip.

"Stupid beast! Stay the night in harness then and rot from saddle sores. You and Trefry deserve one another," she added spitefully.

"Sit down by the fire, lass," Tamlane said gently, pulling her away from the horses and putting a familiar flask into her hands. He guided her to the small pile of leaves and twigs that were burning merrily on the floor. It gave off very little heat, but the light was welcoming.

He shed his cloak and carefully lowered her down upon it. Amarantha would have liked to have protested the aid, but her body simply had reached the end of its endurance and she could not at that moment realistically claim her independence from his steadying arm.

Throwing caution to the wind, she uncapped the offered flask and helped herself to a mouthful of highland lightning. As expected, it scorched a path from lips to stomach, but it did help push back the cold and hunger with its liquid flame.

Her pistol was now confoundedly in the way, so she withdrew the heavy iron from her pocket and set it in a corner far from the fire. Pulling her smelly cloak tightly about her, she sipped more cautiously at the whisky that second time and watched Tamlane as he efficiently stripped the horses of their saddles and blankets. Gallant didn't try slapping his tail at Tamlane.

"It would be better if I were a man, would it not?" she asked. "I should be less of a burden if I were stronger. It is odd, but I never knew that I was so weak."

"Better as a man? Certainly not." He turned and smiled at her. His eyes were warm and approving. "I would not have such pleasure of you were you of my own sex. With another man, such an adventure would be mundane indeed, while this has been wholly unique."

Amarantha thought about what had passed between them that morning, their lovemaking. She recalled how, in the moments of passion, Tamlane had stiffened and then cried out before collapsing upon her. His entire face had been altered by that instant of impassioned fervor. That was, for her, wholly unique as well.

"That is true, I suppose," she agreed, speaking to

herself more than Tamlane. "For you, this is all probably boringly familiar—the smugglers and soldiers and so forth. But you did seem to have—um—*pleasure* of me. Perhaps that is some recompense. I certainly hope so. I had never realized that my stamina was so limited. It seems that I am always hungry or tired. At this moment I feel a true burden to you, which I never expected to be. It is all very lowering."

Tamlane glanced down at the flask in her hand and then turned away to finish his task. When he spoke, there was a smile in his voice. "They say *in vino veritas*. But I think there may be more of it in whisky. Do not get too garrulous, my dear, or you may regret your confidences later. I know your dignity must be dear to you, so closely do you clutch at it, and there is no need to be maudlin about this subject. God made you with a frailer body than that of a man. Accept that. It is the natural way of things."

"I believe I resent that." Amarantha took another small sip from the flask. The whisky wasn't as painful to swallow now, and it was suffusing her body with a warm glow.

"That women are frailer than men?"

"No. That is pleasantly true. How ridiculous I should look with bulging sinews. I should not want to have your body—unless I were a man, of course."

"Of course." There was a choking sound that might have been stifled laughter.

"I was speaking of my veracity. I do not need wine to tell the truth. I have never lied to you. At least, if I have lied, I do not recall it," she added conscientiously. "Perhaps I do not always speak the thoughts which are in my head, but for that fact you should be grateful."

"I most assuredly am, for plainly they have been less than flattering."

"Oh, not entirely so. . . . I have found many things about you to admire."

"You unman me with such praise."

"Ha! That I could so easily best you!" Amarantha smiled to herself and took another swallow of anesthetic. "I do not see how you can say that I am so very dignified, not when you are forever calling me a gypsy—which is unfair, I think, as after our first meeting I was at pains to appear neat and attractive whenever we met. That I have lately worn some very ugly clothing and been disheveled is hardly my fault."

"Thank you," he said gravely. "I am flattered at your thoughtfulness and I acquit you of blame for your recent wardrobe. Ah, have I *often* called you a gypsy?"

"Yes."

"Hmm. How strangely rude of me." A saddle hit the floor.

"It is because I make you angry."

"Angry? Nay. Perhaps you have been the cause of anxiety and some madness—but not anger. And I do not think you have lied to me either. By now I have a fair estimate of your character and deceit is not your vice." Tamlane walked a half pace to the fire and then joined her on his cloak. He extracted the flask from her grasp and took a small sip. "Nor will you ever lie to me, will you, Amarantha? Whatever your reservation, you will always tell me the truth. They say a virtuous woman is above rubies—but I think an honest one is to be just as highly valued."

He saluted her and then raised the flask again.

"I can't think why I should lie to you," she said slowly, surprised, watching closely the muscles in Tamlane's throat as he swallowed his native brew. The firelight laid a patina of golden honey over his damp skin. Without caution or thought she asked him: "I wonder. Do you taste of salt or sweetness?"

Tamlane froze for an instant and then lowered the flask slowly. He looked into her eyes as he recapped the whisky. His gaze was unblinking and seemed to spark with tiny red embers. She knew that it was caused by the light the fire cast over them, but the effect was still enchanting.

"Do you truly wish to know, lass?"

Amarantha found that he suddenly had an unexplainable power over her. His very stare seemed able to reach inside and make parts of her clench tight and yet other parts of her melt. The longing for something she could not put a name to made her feel a little unsteady.

"I don't know. I seem to always be divorced from my good sense these days. But you do look lovely."

"Ah, lass! The things that are writ upon your face! There seems to be more than truth in whisky. Are you bent on tempting me again? I should think that you would be content with your first seduction. Or is it the drink?" He added meditatively: "I'd no thought of taking you again without a proper bed beneath us, you know."

"*Taking me?* Oh!" She colored and managed to blink. She said hastily: "No, let us not do that again just now. It was very pleasant, of course, but there is no need to repeat the experience immediately."

Tamlane frowned, causing her to likewise furrow her brow as she unknowingly mirrored his expression.

"What is it?" she asked. "Are you upset? Am I being rude?"

"Aye, I am upset. I feared that you had had no pleasure of our union, and now I know it is so," he answered regretfully. "But, lass, I promise that it will not always be thus. Indeed, with the fires that burn inside you, I suspect that with enough coaxing this floor of stone could seem the softest of cots if I exercised a little care."

"Nay. I do not think it," she said, shaking her head apologetically. The swinging action made her feel slightly dizzy so she ceased immediately. "I am not so wanton as you must imagine me after this morning. That was an aberration, I'm sure. I was thinking of you as a lover and not a husband, and it affected my judgment."

"Were you affected pleasantly by that thought?" Tamlane asked softly after a moment's contemplation.

"Yes. But I am not thinking of you as a lover now. And this floor is *very* hard and I am sore from riding. I know that I was very brazen when—when we awoke." She attempted again to explain herself. "But I am not usually this way. I've been riding all day and just now it would take a magician to enchant me, so let us not think of—of—it. Perhaps some day in the future I shall wish to attempt it again."

One eyebrow flew up and his teeth gleamed as he smiled.

"A magician, is it? And you no longer think of me

as your lover? That's a slight, lass—a mortal wound to my heart."

"Nay—" she said hastily.

"Madame, you have teased and insulted me once too often. I think this challenge must be answered at once," he muttered, reaching for her. His smile was playful. "Let us discover if I cannot work this lover's magic upon you. I'll wager you a new brocade gown that I can."

"Tamlane," she said, but the protest was feeble for a part of her longed to have his arms about her.

"I ask just a kiss, lass. Surely you would not deny your lover a mere kiss? What harm could there be in this?" he murmured coaxingly, as he took her hand and drew her near. The soft fumes of whisky bathed her face as their breath mingled. Heat came from his body that rivaled the fire for warmth and was far more beguiling.

She looked up into his catlike eyes and found she could not utter the words of denial that would hold him at bay. Perhaps Tamlane *could* still work some powerful spell upon her. Craving a release from her weary state, would it be so wrong to permit him to try his magic upon her again? Even a brief return to the excitement of the morning would be welcome.

"Ah," she breathed softly, relaxing into the comfort of his enfolding arms.

"Wilt thou be mine?" he asked, a hand tracing the line of her back with clever fingers. "Speak now, love."

Had he been the smallest measure less appealing to her senses, she would have refused. But he was a lodestone that attracted her, doubtless made beautiful by Fate to tempt her—and who was she to resist such divinely wrought design when he asked for a kiss? So, instead of being sensible and refusing his overture, she gave in to her body's prompting and whispered, "I will not deny you a kiss."

Unlike that morning, when he had been filled with urgency, his lips now moved with exquisite tenderness as they brushed against her mouth, then her cheek and then down the column of her throat. Unknowing, she let her head fall back and her damp cloak slip from her shoulders. Had she been able to think, she might have noticed that Tamlane's usually graceful hands tremored slightly as they touched the neckline of her gown and brushed over woolen-clad breasts.

Whatever the state of his hands, his lips knew what they sought, and she found them truly magical when they returned to her mouth, pulling all will and thought from her mind and body with a kiss more stupefying than the tincture of poppies. Desire raced through her body pushed by her racing heart, which pounded a painful tattoo beneath her ribs. And she had her answer: Tamlane was both salt and sweet under her lips.

As he had predicted, in that moment, she did not know or care whether it was stone or feathers beneath her. All she wanted was for this kiss to continue, to draw him into her body and somehow extinguish the fires that had begun burning there. This new craving was like the need for water on a hot day, or air to one who was buried alive. It was a dark enchantment.

Distantly, she was aware of the thought that this new need might not be an entirely convenient thing.

To desire so intensely was to make oneself vulnerable, as an addict was to a drug. Disturbed at this notion, she rolled her head away from his lips and turned her face into the shelter of his neck while she attempted to collect her senses.

"Nay, do not hide from me, lass."

"Tamlane, wait. . . ."

But then his hand cupped the back of her neck, his long fingers burying themselves in her loosened tresses. He pulled her head back slowly and tasted heavily of the pulse that throbbed in her neck. His teeth as they scraped along her skin made her shiver. When he returned to her mouth to finish his spell, she ceased thinking.

"Madness," he muttered, lifting his head. His voice was unsteady.

"Aye," she agreed. "But 'tis sweet insanity."

She pressed her mouth against his but suddenly he stiffened, turning his head from her lips.

"There's danger here."

"Surely not," she coaxed, again seeking his lips.

But with cruel suddenness, he pulled completely away from her, spinning about to face the tomb's entry, where he stared fixedly at the horses' ten legs.

So bemused were her senses that it took Amarantha a moment to rejoin unpleasant reality. At first, all she was aware of was a feeling of wrongness and being cold now that Tamlane had turned away and left her bereft. But as the returning aches from her days riding made themselves known, and the stone floor ceased to be a bridal bed, she regained sufficient sense to realize that two horses—or even three— would not possess a total of ten legs between them.

Nor would one set of legs be clad in workman's rough woolen clothing.

Amarantha gasped and looked about for her pistol, but there was no urgent need for it as Tamlane already had his out and pointed at approximately knee height.

"Show yourself." Tamlane's voice was rough and Amarantha wondered whether it was frustrated desire that had lodged that new note there. It was childish of her, but she rather hoped it was, for it pricked her pride that she could have been so involved in the kiss and he'd still retained at that blissful moment sufficient awareness of his surroundings that he heard above the noise of the fire and storm—and, she had to admit, some sighing and moaning—the sounds of an intruder outside the sepulcher.

The man outside coughed once and then called out: "Rector Adair? Tammie? Is it ye in there? Dinna shoot me new breeks. 'Tis Jimmie, it is. Jimmie Gordon, yer cousin. May I be comin' in tae ye?"

At the sound of the thick Scottish brogue, Amarantha turned amazed eyes upon Tamlane. In spite of her frustration at the untimely interruption, which had recalled her from a blissful state, and her pained body which had reawakened to its many ills, she knew a moment's amusement at Tamlane's look of long-suffering resignation. He shoved once at his misshapen breeches where his arousal was slowly subsiding and then answered roughly.

"Jimmie Gordon. You are worse than a banshee and about as welcome as the plague. Come inside if you must, you thief—and don't take anything from the saddles as you pass."

"Bless ye, Rector. There's nowt tae take here, I shouldn't think, belonging to a holy man and all. And surely ye dinna think that I'd ever take bread frae my kin." A short and skinny man with the long face of a rat slid past their restless mounts and joined them by the dwindling fire. His gaze shifted back and forth rapidly as he looked between Tamlane and Amarantha, and he twitched uneasily as he shifted his weight from foot to foot. He was the very picture of ill-ease and succeeded in alarming Amarantha into total alertness, banishing all romantic notions.

Tamlane shook his head and gave the intruder a withering stare.

"I am not worried about our bread, for we have none."

Feeling the lack of enthusiasm at his presence and perhaps sensing that he had interrupted something of import, Jimmie rushed into further placating speech.

"Any road, it isnae the night for doing mair than settin' by a warm fire, and as a just man, ye'll agree, Tammie. It's fair dreepin' wi' rain I am and like to be carried off with illness. Hello, Mistress. Jimmie Gordon at yer service. I be the rector's cousin on his father's mother's side."

"As distant a cousin as Cain," Tamlane said, lowering his pistol but not putting it away. "And this is not just any woman, Jimmie. This is my wife, so you will be very careful about what you say and do around her, won't you?"

"Wha? Yer wife? Ooh! Certainly I shall hae a rare care then." The rat face smiled broadly, and Amarantha saw that there was after all a slight resemblance to Tamlane. It did not lie in their physical bodies, but in the charm and power of those twisting lips. Jimmie Gordon looked almost appealing when he smiled. "Sae, ye are me new cousin. This must be a sudden happening. But it is delighted I am tae meet ye— um—"

"Mistress Adair will do," Tamlane supplied unhelpfully.

"Now, Tammie, dinnae be sae hard and unforgiving. That's nae way to treat family. Let bygones be bygones. Ye ken that I didnae mean tae leave ye alone tae fight those *sassanach*. It was detained I was by unavoidable circumstances arising frae me business concerns."

"Fighting? Then he is another Jacobite?" Amarantha asked her husband, watching Tamlane's nervous cousin with a fascinated eye. A small pool was forming around him and the water was none too clean as he had a deal of mud on his boots. The man had obviously been walking over open moor. It didn't seem possible that he was the hostile presence she had felt earlier, but his appearance did raise a suspicion or two in her mind. And from Tamlane's unenthusiastic welcome, it raised some questions in his thoughts as well.

"Don't debase the term." Tamlane's voice was dry. "Jimmie is what we would call an opportunist. He was at Prestopans and Falkirk, but it wasn't out of devotion to the cause of freedom. Rather, he was busy reaping personal reward."

"Well now! A man has tae look after his own wellbeing—has he nae bonnie wife tae dae it for him," Jimmie excused himself, with another ingratiating smile. Amarantha had to admit that he had nice teeth.

"And what were you doing at Prestopans and Falkirk, if not fighting, Mister Gordon?" Amarantha asked him, attempting to be polite even though the circumstances of their meeting were so bizarre.

Jimmie cleared his throat and rolled an anxious eye at the ceiling as though seeking inspiration there. "Weel, ye might say that I was helping with the distribution of goods among the soldiers."

"Or, you might say that he was robbing the battlefield dead. Sit down, Jimmie, and don't try and wheedle with my wife. She has no patience with liars."

Amarantha was shocked enough at this announcement to remonstrate.

"You were robbing the dead?" she asked, disbelieving, a bubble of horrified laughter trying to escape her throat. She looked to her husband for a retraction of his words. "I do not believe it. Tamlane, surely you jest. That's—that's—a dastardly thing to say!"

"Believe it," Tamlane said. "And, aye, I think we may call it dastardly."

Jimmie *tsked* loudly.

"Well now, it wasnae if the *sassanach* needed their wee things after they were gone frae the earthly warld, was it? And why should Scotland nae profit frae this tragic loss of life?"

"The point—apparently too fine for you to have grasped, Jimmie—was that *Scotland* did not profit from your ventures. Only you did. And it was not only the *sassanach* whom you divested of goods—nor were your victims all dead when you reached them."

Amarantha shivered and tried not imagine the act these words implied.

"Weel, that isnae entirely true, Tammie," Jimmie answered, seating himself by the small fire. He was so close in their cramped surroundings that his legs touched Amarantha's puddled skirts, which she tried to move from his muddied boots without showing any obvious distaste for their guest.

"Isn't it?"

"Nay. Did I nae spend that money in dear auld Scotland? Did I nae help the poor publicans and merchants tae stay in business in a time of war? And it wasnae as if I were robbin' highlanders. It was only them frae the lowlands and Borders that I—uh—visited. They were all *sassanachs* in their black hearts." Jimmie eyed Tamlane's pistol with some misgiving. "Are ye going tae put that barker away?"

"No, I don't think I shall. There is simply no knowing who or what may come into this place seeking shelter from the rain."

"Aye, true enough! Ye always were a cautious one, Tammie." Jimmie clapped his hands together and rubbed them vigorously. "Well, Tammie? Would that be a wee flask I see sitting there by yer leg? Let us have a toast and I shall drink tae your very good health. It's perishin' thirsty I am."

Tamlane sighed in resignation and handed the flask to his unpopular cousin. As his arm brushed over Amarantha's she could feel the tension in him and wondered whether it was outrage or distrust. Was his cousin so treacherous as to lull them while others surrounded the tomb in preparation of robbery?

"Do you know, Jimmie, I had thought that after

Culloden that I would never see you again."

"Weel, you always did hae the most unholy luck." Jimmie uncapped the flask and drank noisily, quaffing the fiery whisky as if it were cool water from a mountain stream. Amarantha was secretly awed. Her stomach would never tolerate such an assault without rebelling.

"Aye, and sometimes it is luck for the ill," Tamlane muttered. "What are you doing in Cornwall, Jimmie?"

"Oh, just a wee bit of trading in foreign goods."

"Free-trading with the French?"

"Nay! I've nae taste for the sea. I am doing a bit of land transportation for my employer."

"Land smuggling." Tamlane sighed, watching Amarantha's eyes grow wider with every damning revelation. "Have you misplaced your ponies in the storm? Or did they get passed on before the excise men arrived."

"I saw them off safe enough. Not that the excise men will be troublin' me none, being dead as coffin nails now."

Amarantha knew that he might have heard this news from many sources, but she had a sinking feeling that Tamlane's cousin was involved with the same smugglers who had kidnapped them. Bodmin Moor was small and simply could not sustain more than one band of smugglers.

"They're not all dead—and there will be more," Tamlane warned.

"Aye, likely there will be—but not for a wee while yet. And if my luck holds, they may die as well. A dangerous place the moor is." This time Jimmie's smile was unpleasant.

"Mister Gordon, are you not afraid that you will die and meet up with the devil for what you have done?" Amarantha asked curiously.

"Nay! I've nae fear of the King of Horrors. I was hand-fasted with his daughter for one lang year. Auld Nick holds nae terror for me now." He grinned unrepentantly. "Any road, I never did hae much use fer the kirk's teachin's. They smother a man's soul, sae they do. I believe Tammie here is the first of our kin wha ever entered the church. It's a wee bit unnatural for us Gordons. We think it might be the corruption of the Cornish blood frae his mither," he confided. "Best watch yer young'uns for the taint and beat it out of them at once if they show any signs."

"Are you absolutely certain that you two are related?" Amarantha demanded indignantly of Tamlane.

"Ye waud nae think it tae look at us," Jimmie answered. "But we share the same blood, we dae. Only Tammie there grew tae tall and got kind of awkward and gowkish—and mean."

Amarantha found the situation too ridiculous to be taken seriously. Likely she was having a dream, or some vision induced by the whisky.

"You might have mentioned this familial connection before, love. Now I shall have to watch out for taint in our children," Amarantha chided. But she was only jesting. Clearly Tamlane was nothing like this wretched man and was likely mortified by such a relative. "Are there any more like him likely to descend upon us?"

"Nay! That there are not." Tamlane turned an apologetic gaze on Amarantha and murmured: "I should have told you of my family—and planned to later, once you had recovered from our trip. Add Jimmie to my list of sins of omission and I'll pay the ransom later."

"But it is such a long list already. Can you afford your cousin? I think he might cost you more than a brocade gown."

Finally Tamlane relaxed and smiled.

"Brazen gypsy! I won that wager. Go to sleep now, love, if you can. He'll be gone when you wake up in the morning."

Amarantha touched Tamlane's cheek, pleased to see the return of his smile. For an instant, they both ignored Jimmie Gordon's unwanted presence.

"I told you something bad always happens when it rains," she whispered, sliding down to the floor and trying to find a comfortable place among the rough stones that poked through the thin cushion of Tamlane's cloak. Desire had curled back in on itself, taking away the pleasant anodyne of the fiery kisses. Now she was again cold and tired, and had a new ache in her loins and breasts to contemplate.

She found it very easy in that moment to heartily dislike Jimmie Gordon on his own behalf, but also on Tamlane's.

"Henceforth I shall heed your warnings," Tamlane said gently, smoothing back her hair, which he had mussed with his careless fingers.

Jimmie would have to be dealt with later—probably roughly—but for the moment, Tamlane ignored his cousin's over-attentive gaze as he repeated: "Sleep now. You are tired."

"I am tired, but a light sleeper. I do hope nothing

wakens me," Amarantha warned, but obediently closed her eyes since it was obviously what Tamlane wanted. She very much doubted that she would do much sleeping, caught between the twin perils of unforgiving stone and Jimmie Gordon's muddy boots, which were steadily stretching out across the available floor. Still, she could make a pretense of slumber if it pleased Tamlane.

Her lover's hand on her brow was very pleasant and soothing, but she had to admit that she would far rather that he had continued to caress her in other, less restful ways. She might have been covered with bruises in the morning from lovemaking on the ground, but she suddenly had the conviction that it would have been worth it.

Perhaps she truly was wanton.

"Goodnight, Tamlane." She reluctantly added: "Goodnight, Mister Gordon."

"And muckle deep sleep tae you, Mistress. Ye've nae need to fear anything. Jimmie Gordon is here tae guard ye."

Tamlane snorted.

Unable to think of a single polite reply, Amarantha elected to remain silent.

Chapter Seventeen

Tamlane had briefly considered ordering Amarantha to trade places with him so that she would be as far from Jimmie Gordon as possible in their stony shelter. But it was a cold night and their clothing damp, so he decided it was better for her health that she remain close to the fire while she slept, even if it left her in close proximity to his less than honest cousin.

Tamlane was already resigned to the fact that he was going to pass a sleepless night. His clamoring body could not seem to accept that it was doomed to return to its celibate state until he had Amarantha installed in his home and in a bed laid out with proper linens. The obstinate organ, which led so many men astray, refused to accept this edict, and was protesting the abrupt end of their lovemaking, feeling that it had been promised more than a wakeful night on a cold stone floor. Given this uncomfortable state of semi-arousal that stubbornly persisted, staying awake to keep a weathered eye out for his treacherous cousin's wandering fingers was no great matter.

Tamlane sighed. He could only wonder at his ill luck in having Jimmie Gordon wander into their shelter in the middle of the deserted moor. What baleful fate had contrived this? What were the chances that his cousin would find work as a land smuggler in his own tiny corner of Cornwall? Amarantha already took a dim view of past activities for *his cause.* Jimmie's disreputable presence was hardly likely to soften her opinion of his connections to activities in the north and the people with whom he consorted.

And should he be caught, having her husband's relative hanged in the public square would not be pleasant either.

"Tammie?"

Tamlane grunted discouragingly.

Jimmie cleared his throat and whispered: "A few of us hae come down south in recent months and started a business concern which may interest ye. We might be willin' tae let ye in on a few things if ye were sae inclined tae join us."

"I'm not inclined. And it would be best if your *concern* went farther south. There are more soldiers in Bodmin than ever before, and there will be more excise men as well now that murder has been done."

"Perhaps aye, but perhaps nay. Mayhap the soldiers will find some poor soul to blame for the murders, being they are no' too diligent or particular."

Tamlane stared at his plainly dressed cousin, recalling the poor inmate the soldiers had claimed had been killed and robbed of his clothing.

Taking his silence for interest, Jimmie went on.

"But, Tammie, only consider it! Ye have the perfect position for this job. It would be easy money, so it would!"

That was true, but Tamlane had no intention of jeopardizing his position by working with a treacherous rat like Jimmie Gordon, particularly not now that he had a wife whom he had promised a life of peaceful uneventfulness.

Jimmie continued to talk in glowing terms about a possible future in free-trading, but once he discovered that Tamlane was truly disinclined to discuss their past, the future, business, the weather, or even news from the north, Jimmie settled into a corner and disposed his body to sleep.

Jimmie Gordon was often given to dissimulation when what he wanted could not be had by force or coercion, and Tamlane feared that he would have to do his tiresome cousin a violence before the night was through. It was regrettable that Amarantha might have to witness the unpleasantness, but fate had not been kind to them that evening.

Tamlane slitted his eyes to mere lines, deciding that he might as well get the next ugliness out of the way immediately. He began feigning the deep breath of sleep, and awaited events that he knew were to follow as certainly as tomorrow's sunrise. Not only did he recall an entire litany of his cousin's bad habits, which included theft and murder of business partners, but he was understandably suspicious of the stubbled jaw that never dropped onto his breast, and

341

the lack of heavy breathing from a man who was a notorious snorer.

Tamlane was not kept waiting long for Jimmie's worst impulses to present themselves. As soon as Tamlane began a loud, rhythmic breathing, Jimmie cracked open an eye and started reaching stealthily for the pistol Amarantha had discarded.

"Jimmie, as a cousin—however distant the connection—I feel it is time for some sage advice. You are of an age and profession where the application of a reasonable degree of caution would not come amiss," Tamlane said softly, not bothering to open his eyes any wider.

Jimmie gasped and snatched back his hand.

"Damnation! Ye scared the puff out of me, Tammie!"

"Just so. I should not want you to be misled by my recent calling to the holy orders," Tamlane explained. "Though it is by and large a less violent profession I follow these days, I shall still be obliged to break every finger in your hand if you reach for that pistol again."

"Here now, Tammie!" Jimmie blustered. "I was only thinking that it was unsafe tae have the thing near the lassie while she slept."

"I think it is far safer for all of us for the pistol to remain where it is. Oh, and Jimmie, I would have to do more than break your fingers if I found them anywhere near my wife's person. I just mention this in the interest of clarity and to forestall any possible misunderstandings."

"The thought never crossed me mind," he said righteously, and perhaps truthfully—Jimmie was much more interested in women's possessions than their bodies.

"How fortunate. Then you shall not be disappointed by the loss." Feeling the tightening in the form beside him, Tamlane looked down and saw that Amarantha's eyes were open. Her expression was one of discouraged resignation. He made a mental note to assure her later that his unpleasant cousin would never be coming to Penrose Cottage for visits.

He might also buy her that new brocade gown.

"There'll be nae thowless freaks frae me, laddie," Jimmie promised cheerfully. "That lassie is safe as a spinster in a kirk."

"Good, for your tricks would all be quite useless. She would not hesitate to shoot you, and I could not but encourage the notion." Tamlane smiled a little at Amarantha's raised brow. "Now go to sleep before I am made to do something inhospitable and put you back out in the rain."

"Ah, Tammie! You'd no' dae that. I'd catch my death of cold belike."

"Aye, but that is still better than catching your death by ball and powder, don't you think?"

"Ye've grown intae a hard man, Tammie." Jimmie sighed heavily and slumped back into his stony corner.

"Aye, and one that is also a little daft, so do not press your luck."

After that exchange, everyone closed their eyes and pretended to sleep, but it was doubtful that anyone other than Jimmie, who almost immediately began to snore, passed a restful night.

* * *

True to Tamlane's prediction, when Amarantha opened her eyes to the soft dawn light creeping into the tomb, she discovered that Jimmie Gordon was gone. All that was left to prove he had ever been there was a large muddy stain on the floor and a shoe print on the hem of her skirt.

She could hear Tamlane outside doing something to the horses' tacks that involved a deal of jingling but apparently didn't disturb the beasts as they continued to chomp contentedly at the available grass. Amarantha smiled. Tamlane's spirits were irrepressible; he was whistling a jig while he worked.

Feeling as stiff as an eighty-year-old rheumatic, Amarantha rolled to her feet and staggered to the tomb's mouth. The rain, as it always did after these spring storms, had retreated with the morning and had left behind a sky washed pure and blue, and a moor bursting with wildflowers. The bright light abraded her sore eyeballs.

"Good morning, lass. There is a small stream out yonder where ye might have a wash, if you care to brave the cold waters." Tamlane, for once the soul of tact, did not turn to greet her.

"Good morning." Her voice was creaky, her head hurt, and she felt obscurely embarrassed by her disheveled state, even though he had not looked at her in daylight and her appearance was in no way her own fault. And, she acknowledged, he had seen her looking just as shabby on other mornings in the course of their adventure. Still, they were lovers now, and she did not wish for him to see her looking like an old birch broom.

"Your cousin has departed?"

"With the night."

"Willingly?"

"Willingly enough." Tamlane's tone was wry.

"Good. I know that I promised to love, honor and obey, but I don't think those vows were ever meant to encompass people like your cousin."

Tamlane laughed.

"Poor lass! I have used you very ill—but have a quick bath and all will seem better. There is no need to be nervous for we are quite alone now, but would you like me to come with you?"

Not prepared to examine herself too closely until nature's most urgent calls had been satisfied—or Tamlane either, though from the water glistening on his forearms she concluded that he had already enjoyed an alfresco bath—she walked as hurriedly as she could on her aching legs toward the sound of rushing water. She called back over her shoulder: "No thank you. I shall manage on my own."

The water in the tiny stream was not so cold as to be a penance, and she found a lavender bush from which she could take some flowers to rub against her dampened skin in the place of soap. There was also a convenient twig that she used in place of a toothbrush, but Amarantha found bathing in the open moor to be a most uncomfortable experience. She had surrendered many of her London ways, but she could not help feeling that her mother would have said that ladies did not bathe outside—even if they desperately needed to and there was no one to see them.

Amarantha looked about hurriedly as she smoothed her skirts back over her damp legs. She did not sense any observation from the dark hummocks around her, but after their visitor creeping upon them last night, she was no longer certain that she would know whether someone was nearby.

However distressing the experience, one good thing came of her hurried bath: the painful tingling of her bare skin which so distracted her that she forgot her other aches. By the time she had re-clothed herself and plaited her hair, she was moving about without noticeable stiffness or pain.

She cast an eye at the advancing sun and hurried back to the sepulcher. She tromped over wildflowers with careless heels, feeling both guilty at having tarried as long as she had at the water's edge, yet also relieved to be sufficiently refreshed as to face with equanimity the idea of another day in the saddle. After the three nights she had just passed, she felt she was owed some compensation. Particularly as she was unlikely to have any breakfast until they reached Blesland.

Tamlane had finished with the horses and was sitting atop a flat stone, relaxing in the warmth of the rising sun while he awaited her return. Nothing in his posture suggested that he was in any great haste to resume their travel, so Amarantha slowed her pace to a measured walk and allowed herself to observe Tamlane openly.

"Feeling rejuvenated, lass?" he asked, turning his head as she approached. "There's nothing like an open stream on a bright morning for curing a bad head."

"Is that was ails me?" she asked.

All thoughts of breakfast were forgotten. Amarantha found her heart beating heavily as she looked at him, and it was not from her hasty stroll on the moor. Seen head on, Tamlane's familiar smile was bracketed by the noticeable lines of weariness that framed his mouth in pale gray bands, but it was still a smile that held all the warmth of the midday sun. His body was lean, roped with muscles, his limbs long but of perfect proportion. And his eyes were as beautiful as the spring. Surely this was a machination by the gods to lure a reluctant woman to the altar!

She stared at him in helpless fascination, marveling at the change that had come over her. This transformation of heart was completely unexplainable. In spite of their present unpleasant circumstance—and the ones just past, and also those waiting in the future—the attraction to her husband was growing stronger every moment she was in his company. Every time she looked at him, he was more pleasing to her sight.

And even if she could by some means exorcise these feelings, she would not do it, for they told her that after the long dark where her happiness had hibernated in the cold of isolation, she was now awake and prepared to feel again.

Ah! But still, if only she knew what was in her lover's heart when he smiled at her this way! If she knew it was love behind that smile, she would throw all caution to the wind and happily proclaim her own heart's sweet emotion. It would be a relief to tell him.

But as it was, she did not feel brave enough to tell him what she was feeling. How agonizing it would be to declare oneself and be met with silent pity!

"Come and set with me for a moment. Have you

ever seen a more glorious sight?" Tamlane asked, holding out his hand to her.

"No, that I have not," she said softly, putting her fingers into his palm and allowing him to draw her onto the stone before him. She shuddered delicately at the pleasure of having Tamlane pressed close to her again. At his urging, she leaned back against his chest using him as a chair. The moor was beautiful that morning, but it was not the wonders of the rain-washed landscape that enthralled her.

"Are you warm enough, lass?" He folded his arms about her waist.

"Yes."

"What opinions are with you this morning, lass?"

She did not answer at once. The scene before her was tranquil, but Amarantha found that her thoughts were not.

Did he care for her? her reason asked.

Did he reach for her because he loved her? demanded her heart. *Or was this just lust? Or, a more lowering thought still, was this attentiveness simply duty and compassion to an unwanted wife foisted upon him by fell circumstance?*

No! She could not think that. If he did not love her yet, she would teach him to! She had to. There was no other choice. Her heart and hand had been given to this man, and she would never accept another in his place.

Perhaps sensing her disquiet, Tamlane turned from his contemplation of the horizon and looked down into her upturned face. He asked again: "What say you this morning, love? Who am I today—your unwanted husband, or your lover?" His hand moved from her waist to cup her left breast. "Be not so silent."

Her eyes widened. Tamlane was flirting with her—perhaps planning to seduce her!

"Which would you like to be?" she asked, made reckless by her wild heart's beatings and a strangely hopeful mind.

"One day, I should like to be both. But for now, I suppose that I would rather be your lover, for as your lover I might persuade you to take pity on a desperate man and come lie with me before this adventure's end."

She swallowed.

"If that is what you wish, then I shall look upon you that way."

"Good."

Tamlane at once set her on her feet, then also dismounted his perch. He immediately knelt in the velvet grass and shrugged off his cloak to make a simple bed. He looked up at her then and held out a hand.

"Come here, love."

Pressure was building in her. Her heart's tempo increased to a frantic beat, and her skin warmed with a vivid flush. She could even feel her heart pounding in the pads of her fingers and the deep recesses of her body. Resistance to this summons was an impossibility. Amarantha once again tucked her hand into his palm and allowed him to pull her to the ground where he laid her gently upon his cloak.

She did not loll with yesterday's innocent abandon. Her body was taut, filled with awareness of what was to happen. Around her the scent of crushed hellebore rose in the air.

"I had wished that our second time would be in a comfortable bed," Tamlane said ruefully, running a hand over her stiffened torso. "Truly, it was my intention to wait until we had returned home, but my poor, weak flesh is having none of it."

"You wished this no more than I," she said and found herself smiling tremulously. "But this is a deal better than a tomb. Or a root cellar."

"So it is."

"And I am making no complaint."

"Therein lies the temptation."

Tamlane lay down on his side and folded her into his arms. He again drew her against his body and then covered her mouth with his own. This time, he did not stop with a brushing of the lips, but asked her to let him inside. Surprised, but willing to do as he wanted, Amarantha parted her lips. Tamlane loomed over her, his broad shoulders blotting out the sun.

The kiss was intimate. She could taste him as she never had before. Their breath mingled until it was one. Their hearts united in a thundering pace that brought color to their skin. It was a kiss that made her want to wrap herself around him like a cloak, to lay sensitized hands boldly upon his bared flesh. There was no place in her thoughts for delicate words or gallantry. In that moment, she was no longer a lady and she did not want a gentleman.

Her recent experience with male clothing stood her in good stead. Even as they kissed, she was able to strip away the annoying layers of wool and linen that stood between her and the skin she wished to know better. She needed to run her hands over his back and shoulders, to learn the textures of skin with fingertips and palms—even lips and tongue—to savor the heat that grew between them.

She knew a moment's amused relief that Tamlane was not truly the buckled knight she had imagined him as, for a dress sword between them could have been a most dangerous obstacle when in such desperate haste. As it was, the lacings of his breeches were threatening to become snarling restraints.

"Undo them, or cut them!" she ordered in frustration, wondering where her maiden's blushes had gone, and a little shocked at how her body's wantonness could command her speech.

Tamlane was exultant at this reaction and wanted to laugh at her aggravation, but his own need had his muscles clenching to the point of pain, and he was every bit as eager as she to rid himself of the cloth encumbrance. One final wrench had the knee laces stripped away, and the offending breaches were kicked aside. A quick tug had his shirt pulled over his head and cast carelessly onto a bank of dew-drenched flowers.

Amarantha's own clothing was dealt with as ruthlessly, and it was a relief to have the scratchy wool no longer abrading her tender flesh. Tamlane's eyes swept down her slender body so supple and gently curved, and the approval in his gaze was as arousing to Amarantha as any words might be.

He looked then at her mouth; the lips flushed, parted, undefended, and had to groan at the unspoken invitation.

"Kiss me," he said, threading his hands through her hair.

And she did without hesitation. All he asked for, she gave. Her lips opened without any maidenly uncertainty at the touch of his tongue, offering him whatever he might want to take. Taste made him giddy and he drank greedily. Desire redoubled with every hammering blow of his heart, which he felt all the way to his loins. He wanted to kiss all of her, but that mouth held him enthralled until he did not know whether it was blinding desire or lack of breath that made his head spin like a drunken man's.

He realized that Amarantha was straining against him, trembling with the same desire that drove him to the edge of riot and madness. Though it felt like he was being separated from his skin with a blunt knife, Tamlane pulled his lips away to allow them to gulp down some much needed air before going any further. He realized that if he did not slow down, it would be over before it began, and this time he was determined that Amarantha should find her pleasure too.

"I'm not sure if this is heaven or hell," he muttered, staring in wonder and disbelief. "I cannot recall ever feeling this way."

"I don't care what it is so long as it leads somewhere." Amarantha's voice was ragged. The tide that raged through her body was so fierce she had no names for the feeling. It was furious oceans and rampaging wildfires—and her body knew that somehow Tamlane could still them if he tried. He had conjured the torment with his kiss; he could banish it, too.

Not knowing what else to do, Amarantha took hold of his hair and pulled his lips back to her own, where she could taste more of him.

But this ploy failed her, for all the renewed kiss accomplished was to fuel the fires with fresh tinder and to let the rising tides creep further into her body. Driven by instinct, she moved her hips against Tamlane. When he shuddered and settled himself more intimately against her, she knew that she was questing in the right direction. Not wishing him to escape, she wrapped her legs about him and attempted to hold him fast.

Once again, Tamlane tore his lips away, but this time he did not speak. He rose to his knees, pressed her legs back, making room for himself, and then traveled swiftly down her body, stopping only when he reached her breasts. Amarantha exhaled sharply when she felt the edge of his teeth scrape lightly over her nipple. Radiance burst like a noonday sun vaulting over a dark horizon and bathed her in heat from breasts to loins.

"Tamlane!"

Long fingers traced the line of her open thigh, then sought the sultry heat at her core. More sensations burst upon her, making her gasp and press herself against his hand. It was pleasure beyond endurance. Amarantha opened her eyes, pleading wordlessly with Tamlane to end this distress, and she found in his gaze the same heat and torment that blazed in her own body.

"Now," she said, knowing where the act would end and wishing it to be over so that her body could return to calm. She knew now why passion was so often likened to madness. At that moment, she would do anything to escape the fulcrum on which she was wracked.

"No." Tamlane's voice was altered—harsh and straining. Lust had seized his mind and body. A layer of perspiration sheened him from forehead to knees. He was in splendid agony, but also determined that Amarantha should not be left in need by his urge to haste. He told her, "This time you will find pleasure in our union."

"Tamlane! I shall find death in this union if you do not cease—Ah!"

Tamlane again moved his hip against hers, pressing his aroused flesh to her own. He rocked against her, grinding pelvis to pelvis, but it was not enough to end the torment for either of them.

"Stop this right now!" she demanded, sinking her nails into the flesh of his forearms, the only part of him that she could easily reach. Again her legs attempted to trap him and pull him back where he belonged.

Tamlane closed his eyes and engaged in a pitched battle for another few moments of self-restraint. He won, but upon harsh terms. Knowing that the next skirmish would be lost to desire, he moved swiftly down her body, reluctantly bypassing the soft curve of her belly which called sweetly to him, and settling himself between her restless legs.

He was grateful that Amarantha's eyes were again closed and her beautiful, tormenting hands, safely clenched in the folds of his cape. What he wished to do was shocking, wicked, and at that moment of passion-induced insanity, also inevitable.

His hands shook as he touched the soft curls, and then he slid one finger inside her. He groaned as her muscles tensed around him. He slid his thumb over her nub and was rewarded with another strangled gasp and the arching of her spine. He caressed her for a fleeting moment, then lowered his head to her heated flesh. The view, the scent, the desire was dizzying.

The brush of his tongue called forth the sun. Amarantha let go of the mangled cloak and caught her hands in Tamlane's hair. The light fell down upon her and blazed until it blotted out all thought, all memory, all sense of place and time.

When Amarantha returned to her senses, it was to find Tamlane again atop her. His expression was taut and his eyes blazing. Understanding now what torment wracked him, Amarantha pulled him close.

"Now," she told him. "Or you shall surely die."

"Yes." Tamlane admitted that she was right. Part of him wanted more of her hands and her sweet mouth exploring his body, but above all that was the blinding need to be gloved in her heat.

Hard flesh invaded her body, but this time she was prepared for it and welcomed him. He drove into her until he could go no deeper, then pulled away. But not too far. His body forbade that their flesh separate until the act was complete. He held her tightly, his body wild with hunger, rocking until finally desire likewise overtook him and bathed him in the same incandescent ecstasy he had given to his lover.

The silence between them was peaceful as they enjoyed a few last moments of loving touches.

Tamlane was still in a state of bliss, but he frowned at the marks on Amarantha's silken skin, which showed plainly in the sunlight that gilded them. Every bruise was a reproof against the lust that had overtaken him. Unfortunately, he could not be entirely repentant about what had just passed. Nothing in his life had ever been as sweet and compelling as the siren song that called him to his wife. Such passions had summoned gods and princes to their dooms—who was he to stand against them?

Still, he was angered that any pain caused by him should have marred her delicate body. And since he knew that his own willpower was at low ebb—indeed, his body was already making plans for its next encounter with his lover—it behooved them to make haste for Blesland, for he swore that he would not take her again on the stony ground of the moor. She deserved better than this.

Tamlane gave Amarantha a last caress and then rolled over to search for his clothing. Some of it was a distance away, having been cast off with considerable force. He rose to his feet and went to retrieve his shirt. It was damp and bore the green stain of broken stems that had bled into the cloth. He next spotted the edge of his breeches at the top of a small pile of boulders. They were snagged on an outcropping of silver rock and missing their lacings.

Tamlane smiled and shook his head. *Madness*—that's what it was. They were bloody lucky that no one had come upon them.

He bent down to retrieve his battered clothing when he heard Amarantha gasp and give a tiny scream. He spun about immediately and felt a chill of terror race through his body as a giant, beastly shadow rose menacingly on the stony wall beside him. It bristled with spikes and had six-inch fangs and carried a garrote in its vicious claws.

Chapter Eighteen

Tamlane cast about quickly for his pistol, but realized it was still in his cloak pocket, which was—thanks to his libidinous behavior—lying uselessly beneath Amarantha. Wasting no more time or breath on self-recriminations for his distraction, he snatched up a large rock with chiseled edges that might approximate an axe, and uttering a battle-cry, vaulted over the stone pile prepared to do combat with the monster that loomed over his wife. Leaping toward the source of the deadly shadow, Tamlane swung his arm in a wide arc, ready to dash the brains from the creature's hell-born body.

The attack was short-lived, quite the briefest in history. He skidded to a stop on the mossy ground, smearing his feet with vivid slime, and dropped his arm before the echoes of his war cry had died on the air. It was quite apparent that his battle prowess was not needed in this instance.

Fate was making a game of him. The low morning sun and a marauding cat were responsible for the long shadow that had distorted the wall. His imagination had done the rest. Tamlane had only a glance of the feline's tail, for it was retreating smartly with his knee laces clenched between its teeth. However, that one quick peek was sufficient to assure him that they were not being stalked by the Beast of Bodmin Moor.

"I take it that you are unharmed," he said, feeling rather foolish. His sharp stone was cast away with a grimace. He felt a melodramatic fool.

Amarantha's bare belly—now trembling with laughter—bore two muddy paw prints and a single thin scratch—probably caused when he startled the cat.

"Quite—but thank you for coming so promptly to my rescue." Her voice quavered as she rose onto an elbow and looked him up and down. Her hair did little to veil her body, "How very timely you are. I am so glad that you did not bother with formal attire."

Tamlane glanced down at his own naked body. He supposed that the sight of him flying through the air with nothing more than a scream on his lips had been fairly amusing. The trouble was that he did not feel amused. And now that the danger was passed, all the excitement of the moment was beginning to manifest itself in physical ways—and not in laughter. In spite of his wishes—and Amarantha's giggling—his loins were beginning to stir and rise.

"Damnation," he muttered, staring in disbelief. He addressed his nether region in tones of purest exasperation: "Have you no sense? Have you no shame? Did you not hear what I just said to you?"

But obviously it had not heard his prohibitions, for it simply continued to grow. And grow. And all the while Amarantha looked on with rounded eyes.

"Lass?" he asked, looking up hopefully.

Amarantha shook her head in amazement and tore her fascinated gaze away from his manhood.

"Try the stream," she recommended, eyes twinkling. "It is quite cold enough to be a distraction."

"Aye. But the fact is I've no wish to be so distracted that way—and you may stop laughing now, you heartless woman. 'Tis cruel of you to be amused at my appearance. Do you not care that I was rushing to your aid?"

"I'm sorry. Truly, it is not your gallant impulses which are amusing."

"No?" he asked, lowering his voice and his brow. "Then what, pray tell, is the cause of this laughter?"

"N-nothing. It is just that this is the first time that I have had a clear look at you." Amarantha excused herself. "You certainly are—*um* . . ."

"In need? Beautiful to behold? The quintessential man?"

"Red. You are very red."

Tamlane stared at her consideringly. Her laughter begged retaliation—preferably of sensual nature, since it was his aroused body that so amused her—but he had promised himself that he would not ever again take her on the cold ground.

His body throbbed sharply at this unhappy reminder of his vow and Tamlane decided that this promise of limited abstinence should not include any mating that *didn't* happen on the ground. That left a great many other possibilities open.

His conscience clear, he took a step toward her.

"Tamlane!" Reading the intent in his face, Amarantha rose quickly to her feet.

"Come here, love," he said softly. "I need you."

"No, thank you. I am through being a lover for now, I think." She retreated laughing, trying to snatch up her gown and shoes while pacing backward.

"Come here, wife," he growled, tensing his muscles for another long spring.

"No, I want to bathe—"

Tamlane pounced. Amarantha had time for only a brief squeal before she was caught up in Tamlane's arms. His grip was barely loose enough to allow breath, though when she would next draw it, she did not know for Tamlane's mouth came down upon hers and as always, her heart and breathing faltered.

Tamlane eventually sensed her swoon and left her lips to return to his favorite hollow in her throat where he could feel her pulse hammering at the skin. He loved to think of this telltale tripping beneath his lips, for it told him clearly of his lover's arousal.

"You have a choice," he told her, his voice a low murmur. "Agree to be mine this instant, or I drop you in the stream for that requested *bath.*"

She shivered as she felt his teeth scrape along her shoulder.

"I'm yours."

Amarantha closed her eyes and let her head fall back. Her clothes and shoes dropped from her hands. It seemed to her that the heat from the sun could not compare to the fire that burned between them, and it was not in her to resist Tamlane when he wanted her so badly. It perhaps was not in her to resist him ever. She did not understand the magic wielded by this man—this lover—who by rights should be nothing more than an interesting acquaintance she socialized with in the company of a chaperone. He was still largely a stranger to her, yet he was also the lover she had sought diligently, until she finally decided that the ideal man did not actually exist.

She moaned as he rubbed against her. Trying to steady herself when her world was in a spin, she wrapped her legs around Tamlane's hips and sank her fingers into his hair. She groaned again when he ground himself directly against her tender flesh. Familiar longing flooded her, the tides of desire rising rapidly.

Sensing her capitulation, he lifted her higher, this time drawing her nipples into his mouth where he could lave and nibble at them at will. Gone was his thought of searching out a leafy bower, or some mossy stone table where he might lay her down before ravishing her.

He scraped her lightly with his teeth, and desire, like a streak of lightning, traversed her body from breasts to loins making her eyes snap open and her body go taut. Her speculations and search for answers about Tamlane's appeal were forgotten. She stared down at her love, their gazes locking; her own drowning with desire, and his more than a little wild with ever-growing need.

"I believe I promised that I would not take you again on the hard ground." His voice was low and rough.

"Then don't take me there," she answered, desire making her both practical and forgetful of modesty. "There must be some soft ground somewhere."

Tamlane laughed, a bit victorious and certainly joyous of her immediate capitulation to his lovemaking. It was not gentlemanly to glory in her surrender, but still he reveled.

"There's none around here, love, but that needn't concern us. I have another, simpler notion." Slowly, he let her weight slide down his body until she was resting against the head of his shaft. He lifted a brow. "What say you, aye or nay?"

Amarantha made a noise of surprise and agreement.

"But can you stand?" Amarantha knew that she could not. Arousal made her first weak in the knees and then completely boneless.

"I can do anything if it will get me inside you," he muttered truthfully, turning so that his legs from the buttocks downward were resting against a convenient boulder. With the flames of renewed passion licking at his flesh he was unaware of the cold radiating from the stone.

He began to push into her softness. Amarantha shivered as little by little she settled onto him. He felt huge. He felt wonderful. This iron strength was all hers to enjoy. The thought made her giddy.

His grip shifted around to below her rear. Fingers sank into her flesh and he began to force her up and down in slow counterpoint to his rocking hips. He would have growled his pleasure to the sky above them, but his jaws were locked together, his whole body bracing for the climax rushing down upon it with the speed of a gale-driven storm.

"Tamlane!" Amarantha arched her back and began to shudder.

The instant he felt Amarantha contract around him, his body let go, pouring out its excitement and battle readiness in a dizzying rush.

Then it was over. Suddenly, his legs ceased to be pillars of strength and began to tremble. It was all he could do not to collapse onto the ground. His manhood might not have been quite prepared to leave off its favorite activity, but the rest of his body demanded that he cease at once or die where he stood, ankle deep in itching, green moss.

Reluctantly, Tamlane eased Amarantha's body from his own and set her on her feet before leaning back against his stony prop. He was aware of the cold now that reason had returned. He also noticed that her legs were trembling.

Tamlane shook his head in amazement. This was dangerous. It was distraction beyond any he had known or heard of.

"We bathe. We dress—and then we ride for Blesland," he said weakly, pushing away from the boulder. "And please, for the love of heaven, put on your gown before I do something else to you."

Recalled to her naked state, Amarantha blushed. It was difficult to see it stain her skin as she was already wearing the hectic flush of arousal.

"What might you do?" she asked curiously, as she looked about for her discarded gown and shoes.

"Something that would ruin our knees and leave us helpless cripples for the remainder of our lives." Tamlane took her arm and guided her toward the stream.

"I don't think I would enjoy that," she said, wincing as she stepped upon a sharp pebble. She hopped on one foot while tugging on a shoe. "But then, I did not think that I would enjoy being taken in a tomb. On the ground or—um—"

"While being juggled in the air?"

"Yes! But I did enjoy it," she confided shyly.

"I am so glad." Tamlane smiled a little. "I thought perhaps you had. Nevertheless, I do not want to spend another night on the open moor, which is likely to happen if we continue to be distracted by these carnal things."

Carnal things. Amarantha frowned, her light mood leaving her. There was no arguing with the fact that what had passed between them was indeed carnal, but it had felt like something much more important to her. Something soul shaking! Surely what they had done was not *commonplace*—could not be had with any random person.

But perhaps she was wrong. Maybe Tamlane had done this before—perhaps even frequently. He had denied having a mistress, but that did not preclude some former relationship. In fact, given the society they came from, it would be marvelous if he had *not* had a lover. Thinking of Tamlane sharing such a moment with another woman made Amarantha feel a bit ill and also wrathful.

"Amarantha, are you well?" Tamlane asked with instant concern. "You have grown pale."

"Yes, I am well," she answered immediately, lifting

her chin. "It is just that this scratch has begun to hurt."

"I shall bathe it for you," Tamlane promised, again feeling guilty. "The cool water will stop the stinging."

"That isn't necessary." Amarantha freed her arm from his grasp and began pulling her gown over her head. When she finally emerged from the prickly swaddling it was to find Tamlane watching her with a furrowed brow.

"I hate to spare the time when home is so near, but perhaps I should catch a fish and let you have some breakfast. You truly look quite pale."

"I'm not hungry," she said firmly, her tone growing slightly remote. "Let us be on our way before you talk me into having a *missish* decline."

"After we bathe. You shall be uncomfortable else." Tamlane's frown deepened. "I shall put you to bed immediately as we return home, and I shall see that you have a meal brought up and you have a rest before we deal with the Preventives or your uncle. Indeed, there is no reason for you to be distressed by anything. I can tell everyone of our marriage."

"Thank you," Amarantha found it easier not to argue. Once again, her thoughts were in turmoil and she longed for a period of quiet reflection.

She was not, however, so given to distraction that she failed to give some wifely advice.

"Do wash your feet, Tamlane. They are quite a horrid shade of green."

Blesland looked wonderfully unchanged as they rode through the village square. They were greeted by many of its inhabitants, including soldiers, with smiles and waves. Amarantha was relieved to notice that while their gazes were curious and some grins a bit sly, the villagers were also friendly, which suggested that if there were a great deal of gossip, it was not of a hostile nature.

Once they reached the far side of the hamlet, Amarantha and Tamlane debated briefly about their destination. He wanted, perhaps irrationally, to immediately install his wife at Penrose Cottage, but Amarantha had other plans, which she enumerated coolly. Of first immediacy was seeing her uncle and Taxier for news and collecting her clothing.

Tamlane acquiesced only because Amarantha's color had improved during their ride, and because he knew that Pendennis could be relied upon to instantly prepare a substantial meal. He had teased Amarantha about her constant appetite, but the fact was that after a day and more without food, he was also feeling peckish enough to eat his *sgian dubh* and enjoy it. She, with her more delicate stomach, would be feeling the lost meals keenly.

Too, Tamlane simply did not want to mar the day by having an argument with his wife and ending it with enforcing his wishes. Nothing could cause greater—and perhaps more lasting—resentment in a woman than feeling that she had been coerced into the married state and made the promise of wifely obedience under great duress.

Tamlane would have preferred a quiet arrival at Talland House, but it was not to be. First to be endured were the tears of joy from Mrs. Polreath, who came trotting from the house the moment they turned their mounts onto the drive. Behind her came

Pendennis, his arm supporting a much mended Maxwell Taxier. Fortunately, neither of them was crying. Maxwell was, in fact, wearing a broad grin.

"Oh, dearie!" Mrs. Polreath cried. "Mister Taxier saw you coming from the window upstairs. It's very relieved we all are to have you with us again. We were so frightened when we heard what had happened to those poor Preventives and feared that you might have met up with those bloodthirsty smugglers."

"I am quite well, Mrs. Polreath," Amarantha said, accepting Tamlane's hands about her waist as natural when he lifted her down from her horse's back. "We had quite an adventure, but I assure you that I am unharmed—save for a scratch which I received from the Beast of Bodmin Moor."

"Dearie!" Mrs. Polreath's eyes grew large, and Pendennis *tsked* softly.

Maxwell Taxier laughed, though it caused him to wince when his shoulders shook.

"The Beast of Bodmin, was it? Rector, you are getting careless in your old age," he teased his friend.

Tamlane grimaced.

"This adventure has certainly aged me a decade and more! I feel in my dotage. Has Cyril Stanhope returned yet?"

"Aye, he has," boomed Cyril's voice as he also appeared in the broad door. He looked once from Tamlane's unlaced knee to his niece's borrowed gown and frowned. "And I am waiting, lad, for an explanation. What do you mean taking my Amy off to Saint Catherine's? Great God, man! I'd have let you wed her. I intended that you wed her!"

Cyril strode down the step and embraced Amar-

antha and then wrung Tamlane's hand in an unprec-
edented display of affection.

"You shall have your tale," Tamlane promised. "But
after we have eaten. Your niece has been complaining
of hunger since Saint Catherine's."

"Oh, dearie, come inside at once. Pendennis shall
fetch you some pilchard and leek pie." Mrs. Polreath
shouldered the men aside to put an arm about Amarantha's waist and guided her inside. Amarantha con-
trolled a grimace at the offered menu, but didn't
complain. It was absolutely wonderful to be home
again.

"Don't worry about the horses," Cyril said. "Tregengon and Penkevil will see to them directly."

Amarantha craned her neck around her uncle's tall
form and spotted the two men waiting silently. She
smiled shyly and was pleased when they grinned back.

"Dearie?" Mrs. Polreath dropped her voice. "What
is this awful brown thing you are wearing? It looks
like something stitched for a scullery maid."

"I haven't a notion," she said gaily. "They told me
it was a gown, but I don't see how the word can apply
to anything so infernally uncomfortable. It is closer
to a hair shirt or sackcloth—Good heaven! What is
all of this?"

"Why it's porcelain obviously!" Uncle Cyril answered enthusiastically as he joined them in the dining parlor. "Just look at the many designs I have
chosen for you."

"For *me?*"

"Of course for you, girl! Did I not tell you that this
porcelain was why I was going to Helston? Only now

I suppose that I must give it to you early since you went off and wed without me."

Amarantha recalled then, much to her consternation, Uncle Cyril's strange explanation of why he had gone to visit Helston. Strewn across the dining table was an enormous selection of oddly matched crockery bearing some very strange mythological creatures that her uncle had doubtless intended as a bridal gift for her and Tamlane.

He had, however, mentioned the month of June. Doubtless that had been the expected bridal date. Had everyone expected her marriage to Tamlane while she remained in the dark? Amarantha sighed and then peered again at a lumpy teapot.

"You may keep it as long as you like," she told Uncle Cyril.

"Thank you, Amy, but there's no need. I shall come have tea with you often. Look at this. They are still experimenting with designs," Cyril explained, seeing her flabbergasted expression. He picked up a cup that was rather squat and not entirely circular. "Look! He made one with a *Lorelei* on it as a special favor to me. Mrs. Polreath, Amarantha will have tea in this cup. I don't suppose that the stair can be called *Lorelei* any longer though, since someone cut off the newel posts."

Amarantha stared at the half-woman half-serpent curled about the irregular hemisphere. She had never seen anything uglier, but hadn't the heart to say anything to her proud uncle.

"I can see that this is a *Lorelei*. Thank you, Uncle Cyril. I'll think of you every time I see it," Amarantha said, allowing Tamlane to tuck her into a chair at the littered table. They exchanged a brief glance filled with laughter. Their moment of private amusement made Amarantha feel rather better. Since the moment she had realized that she was not the first woman in Tamlane's life, she had been experiencing an odd mixture of pain and jealousy. His careless words characterizing their relationship as something carnal had made her again aware that Tamlane had not—even in the throes of passion—said that he loved her.

And given that one unhappy tidbit, her cruel, overactive imagination had supplied the image of another woman—someone petite and auburn haired and Scottish—whom Tamlane *had* adored and even loved. No doubt she had carried his heart to some lonely highland grave and he would never be able to love again. That was why he had never married.

Though it was a piteous portrait and should have aroused sympathy for Tamlane in her bosom, it was the picture of the unknown woman in his arms that had wedged in her brain and it quite blighted her morning—even ruining her appetite.

However, her body, once offered the badly required food, insisted that she eat. In aid of that, it flooded her mouth with saliva and set her stomach to beseeching rumbling. Not wishing to spoil her stomach's long anticipated pleasure, Amarantha fixed her gaze upon the strange porcelain that was now hers and listened as Tamlane gave a severely expurgated account of their adventures, which did not included Harry, Jimmie, the missing lace from Tamlane's breeches, or their witnessing the Preventives' demise at the smugglers' bloody hands.

She ate what was placed in front of her without care or awareness, but found presently that she was feeling a deal stronger. Determination returned and she vowed to her imagination that though she might not be the first love of her husband's life, she was going to be the last and *best*—even if she had to travel all the way to the highlands and dig his heart out of that other woman's grave!

Chapter Nineteen

Tamlane eventually answered enough of Cyril's questions that he was able to escape to his own home and begin to attend to the business which awaited there. He was, however, attending to things alone. Amarantha had remained at her uncle's.

It bothered him that he had left his wife at her uncle's home, but practicality dictated she stay with Mrs. Polreath and pack her clothing before coming to Penrose Cottage—a process that plainly disturbed her, most likely because it was one more confirmation of the fact that she truly was married now and would be leaving her home to come to her husband. Given her continuing resistance to this notion of being a wife, it was best that Amarantha have an able assistant to see that the packing was actually completed in a timely manner. In this, Mrs. Polreath could be counted on to act with promptitude and thoroughness.

And, his possessive feelings aside, it was likewise advisable to have private speech with Trefry before presenting Amarantha to him as his new mistress, and see that his factotum make some preparations for receiving her politely—if not enthusiastically. Trefry had seemed resolved to Tamlane's eventual union with this woman, but the henchman's mood could be unpredictable—at times even misogynistic—and in her present frame of mind Amarantha was likely to peel a strip off of his hide if he did anything to cross her. Trefry would respond in kind and a nasty skirmish would ensue. Amarantha would likely wish to return to her uncle's and remain there until Trefry was dismissed from service.

Tamlane grimaced. No, it did not suit his humor to have the harmony of his household destroyed by a tangle between the two of them on their first day of sharing the premises. Prevention was absolutely necessary.

There were other matters awaiting his attention as well. Tamlane did not delude himself that their troubles with the law were past. However, it seemed that the hand of Fate had elected not to settle upon them this time. He had expected the Bleslanders' help in this difficult time, but he was receiving aid from some unexpected quarters as well. Thanks to Mister Aldridge's obnoxiousness and the convenient corpse of the murdered inmate, which suggested the murders were the act of a madman rather than smugglers, Cyril claimed the soldiers in Bodmin were not being terribly diligent about finding the Preventives' killer. And so, though there would doubtless be questions about what had really happened that night in the minds of whoever was sent to replace Percy Aldridge, it seemed that Mister Guthrie and Captain Sharpe were determined to officially protect Amarantha and Tamlane to whatever extent they could. Guthrie's reports on the matter would particularly influence London's decisions about administrating in Blesland.

" 'Tis the luck of the devil we've had." Tamlane supposed that he would have to cultivate the wretched boy to a greater extent than he had his superior.

He smiled wryly at the thought. This benevolence on the part of the Preventive was doubtless due to his wife's influence with the young man. Clearly the boy was taken with her, and while this admiration was perhaps slightly annoying to the possessive part of Tamlane's nature, it was also very convenient. And certainly he could not fault the young man for his taste in females. Amarantha was undoubtedly worthy of any amount of admiration.

Amarantha.

She was certainly never long from his thoughts these days. Give his mind a moment free of occupation and there she was ready to leap into his memory!

There was one other thing in regard to his wife that was preying upon Tamlane's mind. It had disturbed him that Amarantha had returned his ring immediately after the wedding ceremony. It was perfectly true that the band was too large for her petite hands, but he knew that this was not the entire reason that she had rejected it. Unfortunately, he suspected that the remainder of the explanation for her refusal to wear his ring was not a simple one. His wife was given to deep thoughts that she did not readily share.

Of course, he was prepared to give her some time to adjust to the change in her estate, but it had become an ambition of his to see her wear a wedding ring. It was only a token—a mere symbol—but it was a visible one. And he was acquainted enough with his wife to know that she would not be a hypocrite. That band told the world that she was his wife. When she wore it, she would be proclaiming her acceptance of this status and would act accordingly.

He told himself that all he need do was get a ring on her hand. After that she would embrace the part of his spouse. Explanation could come later.

"Is that all that is needed?" he asked himself mockingly.

Tamlane shook his head at the task he had set himself. The ring was a polite version of a shackle—and Amarantha would doubtless see it that way. He needed an irresistible lure—something too wonderful to refuse. And he had just the piece of jewelry to do the trick. It was a gaud that had belonged to his mother, and the only thing she had refused to donate to the Cause during the uprising of '19. It was a showy piece brought from the Eastern lands and cut down to fit his mother's hand. The ring was set with a deep indigo sapphire surrounded with a ring of sparkling but pale female sapphires. Supposedly it had been made for a ruler who had had many wives, each represented by one of the stones. It was thought to bring magical charisma to its owner.

His reserved mother had often said to her husband

that the ring's decorative history was an accurate portrait of his early life when he had been pursued by the bold Scottish lasses of his village.

And his father had never denied the stories. Indeed, he had been only too happy to expound upon the charm of his family line, even though it had earned him many scoldings. Such behavior had been incomprehensible to Tamlane until recently. Now he understood his father's childish impulse to provoke a response in his quiet and undemonstrative mother.

However, Tamlane decided that he would not tell Amarantha the part of the tale about the sapphires' power just yet. She might object to wearing it on grounds of the symbolism of the stones' faithless former owner, as well as that of the wedding band as which it was to serve.

Of course, sorry soul that he was, he thought that some display of jealousy would be a good sign. One had to care at least a little in order to find the passion for jealousy. Maybe he would mention the story to her after all—invent some tales about dozens of old loves. Perhaps she would be so taken up with possessive rage she would at last let slip her guard and give him some indication of her hidden feelings.

Tamlane began to whistle under his breath and began walking briskly through his gardens. He was certain that his mother's ring was in the strong box in his bedroom. He would find it straight off. Captain Sharpe and the soldiers at the garrison could wait a little while longer for a report of their adventures. . . . In fact, Trefry could carry a message to the garrison for him. It was more important that he return to Talland House and assist his wife with her packing. Tonight she was going to live the part of his wife—she would sleep under his roof and in his bed.

Amarantha looked for a moment at the gaping emptiness of the trunks she had so recently unpacked and, feeling mocked by it, turned toward the windows to stare out at the day. Mrs. Polreath was eager to be of assistance, so Amarantha decided to let the housekeeper have the unassisted pleasure of folding up her voluminous skirts and putting them away for their brief travel to Penrose Cottage.

"Dearie?" Mrs. Polreath asked as she swaddled Amarantha's favorite green brocade in an unneeded sheet of muslin. "Would you like to have a bit of a lie down? I'm sure there is plenty of time for you to have a nap before the rector returns."

Amarantha glanced at the bed. It looked wonderful all made up in its tidy counterpane, but she was too agitated in spirit to seek the balm of sleep, however much her body craved it.

"No, thank you, Mrs. Polreath. It is probable that Tamlane shall have no difficulties with Captain Sharpe or Mister Guthrie, but if there are questions to be answered, I prefer to be wide awake when they are asked." This was the truth as far as it went, but it was Tamlane and the specter of their marriage causing her the most heart burnings and restlessness.

Anything had seemed possible to achieve when they were out in the wilds of the moor. But now that they were back among family, and the traditional conventions hedged them in, Amarantha was feeling overwhelmed by the task that lay ahead of her. What would they say to each other over the breakfast dishes? Where would she sleep? In her own chamber? With Tamlane? Who would help her dress—her husband? And these were just the private matters that needed sorting out. What of her public role? No rector's wife would have ever been watched with such curiosity as the Bleslanders would her.

She would be expected to sit in the front of their tiny church every Sunday and listen attentively to her husband while he preached. It would be her duty to go out among the sick parishioners and offer them ease and comfort from their afflictions. These were two responsibilities that she was completely unsuited for, and she feared that she would be wholly inadequate in both the role of town comforter and as an attentive helpmate. Amarantha Stanhope—Adair now—*a rector's wife!* It couldn't be.

"How did this happen?" she whispered.

"I'm sorry, dearie? Did you say something? I could not hear you above all the rustling. I do so love these crisp brocades."

"It was nothing, Mrs. Polreath. I was simply talking to myself." Amarantha forced herself to smile.

"Are you nervous, dearie?" Mrs. Polreath asked kindly. "Because you needn't be. I know that some silly women talk of the pain of the first time in the marriage bed, but I assure you that this is all great exaggeration. And Tamlane will be all consideration, I'm sure. 'Tis a natural enough thing, after all—not complicated. One needn't be clever or experienced to manage it."

Amarantha blushed and hurried to stop the explanations before they grew too embarrassing. It was strange that she should be able to be intimate with

Tamlane but find such personal matters an agony. It had been painful with Constance Trelawny and now Mrs. Polreath—and even more upsetting to discuss with Tamlane. She could only pray that he didn't feel the need to initiate another discussion of these matters.

"That is not the problem, Mrs. Polreath. I have no reason to be nervous. Tamlane and I have already— *er*—"

There was a soft gasp from the inside of the trunk.

"You have consummated the relationship? In the wilds? Without a bed? But that's—" Mrs. Polreath emerged from the interior of a trunk with eyes wide and mouth slightly open. "Dearie, have you splinters in your backside? Is that the trouble? For I can fetch a needle and an embrocation—"

"No! I am quite well." Amarantha flinched at the very thought of being administered to in this manner. She was perhaps fortunate after all. Her moment of mortification could have been greatly compounded if she had actually required Mrs. Polreath to dig splinters out of her buttocks.

"Well, dearie, this is highly unusual," Mrs. Polreath said, rallying after a moment. She went on encouragingly: "But I am certain that things will improve from here forward. You will find your tasks in the marriage bed quite a bit more pleasant when there is an actual bed to have—uh—a marriage in."

Amarantha had to stifle a spurt of laughter, though it had its roots in hysteria rather than true amusement. Her difficulty was not with the physical aspects of their marriage, but she felt completely unable to explain this to the well-meaning housekeeper.

Women were not supposed to feel confident about such things—unless they were immoral harlots, of course. But Tamlane's presence seemed to be sufficient to turn her wanton.

Amarantha sighed. That was one more lowering thought to consider when she had the time.

"Come now, dearie. Speak to me," Mrs. Polreath said gently. "Your mother is not here so you must make do with me. I shall answer anything that I can. . . . Is it perhaps childbirth that you fear?"

Childbirth! Amarantha pushed the notion away immediately. She was not ready to contemplate the arrival of a baby.

"I am certain that you are correct about the bed, but it is not that aspect of being a wife which concerns me. It is . . ." It was so many things that she simply did not know where to begin. Mostly, it was lack of confidence that was undermining her will. It was the fear that Tamlane would find her lacking as a wife and helpmate. If he loved her, there would be some forgiveness of her shortcomings, more patience with her gaffes and flaws. Without love, she feared that he would soon grow angry and impatient with her errors.

However, Amarantha was not prepared to talk about this with anyone. The embarrassment of confessing that one's husband did not love one was far more excruciating than discussing the expectations of a wife in the marriage bed. But, looking at Mrs. Polreath's kindly, expectant face, clearly some explanation of her heavy spirits would have to be offered, or else the sweet woman might take offense. So instead of discussing her heart, Amarantha spoke of her earlier concerns regarding entering the public arena as a rector's wife.

"I fear I am unsuited to be a rector's wife," she confessed. "I have never gone to visit the poor or sick, or tried to bring comfort to one who is in grief. What if I never gain the skills? What if my very nature precludes such activities? I am also not terribly pious either—no one in my family is."

Mrs. Polreath's face eased into a smile as she reached for another gown and a muslin swathe.

"Nonsense, dearie. You are worrying for naught. Why, you have been a great comfort to your uncle! And we have all seen how brave and generous you are. The villagers will welcome you with open hearts and arms."

Amarantha stared at her, confused. *Brave and generous?*

"Dearie, the moment you knew that Taxier was a Jacobite you threw yourself into the breach to defend him—facing all the perils of the moor! The smugglers and Preventives! The Beast of Bodmin! Even the Evil One himself! Of course, no one knows that Taxier was part of the Troubles, but they know that you were brave enough to run off in the dead of night and marry the rector."

Amarantha strangled a snort.

"That was not courage, Mrs. Polreath," she said gently. "I am afraid that I never gave the perils a moment of thought. Had I believed that the Beast of Bodmin was waiting for me, I would probably not have gone out that night."

"Of course you would have, dearie." Mrs. Polreath looked at her. For once her gaze was not misted with sentiment. "You would have gone to protect your uncle's reputation. And you would have gone because Tamlane was there."

Amarantha nodded reluctantly. That was probably true, but she was glad that she hadn't had any such imaginative horrors cluttering up her mind. The real dangers had been quite worrisome enough to chase all sense from her brain.

That was how she had ended up at the altar of Saint Catherine's.

"Of course you would have gone. You have fallen in love with Rector Adair, have you not, dearie?"

"Yes, I have," she admitted softly, her hands clenching in the folds of her skirts. Her heart began to thud and she felt slightly faint. Putting this feeling about Tamlane into words and expressing it to someone else made it real, gave it more power over her. Amarantha fought panic.

What was she going to do?

"Dearie, you've gone all pale." Mrs. Polreath put down her bundle and hurried to Amarantha's side. She took her arm and urged her to the bed. "You have a little lie down now. You've been too long without a proper sleep and it's making you vaporish and nervous when you needn't be. Why the only bar to your happiness that I can see is Trefry—"

Amarantha groaned at the name and sank onto the bed. Perhaps Mrs. Polreath was right. Maybe she did need to have a brief nap. The very thought of facing Trefry unnerved her completely. The Beast of Bodmin wasn't real, but the beast of Penrose Cottage was quite alive and apt to make her life a misery any time that she erred from her role as the perfect wife.

"Now, dearie! Don't you be concerned. Rector Adair will sort him out. And if the nasty brute is the least bit unkind you come and tell me, and I shall give him what for! It is high time that he give over a bit and let someone else have care of the rector and that lovely house. Just because he was the family *ghillie* for all those years—"

"He was a family servant?"

"Aye. And he served with Tamlane's father in the uprisings of '15 and '19 as well as with Tamlane in the one just passed. It's where he got his unattractive nose. The poor man broke it in every battle."

Amarantha digested this. Such years of dedicated service to a family—especially to a master who embraced a political cause that was not one's own—deserved a large measure of patience. Particularly if the reward was a scarred countenance. She could only hope that she discovered some patience somewhere.

"Mrs. Polreath, I have a sudden headache."

"There! There! You just rest yourself a space and I shall brew you a tisane. After a small sleep you will feel much better."

"I hope so," Amarantha muttered, closing her eyes. "I am not at all enjoying being out of sorts. I haven't the proper way of being unwell either."

"Amarantha, wake up, lass," the gentle voice coaxed, and a soft hand brushed back her hair. "It is time to have a bit of dinner—and I have prevailed upon Pendennis to prepare something other than pilchard and leek pie."

Amarantha's eyelids fluttered open and settled on Tamlane's face. The shadows made it seem that he was smiling tenderly. Almost, she could believe that this was the expression of a man in love.

Of course, she reminded herself, he was nothing of the sort—not yet—and she would have to be careful not to be led into false hope by a wishful heart.

"It is nearly full dark," she said, sitting up slowly as she untangled her limbs. Someone had laid a coverlet over her while she slept.

Tamlane slipped an arm about her back and cradled her to him while he fluffed a pillow behind her. Amarantha went willingly into his embrace. He smelled sweetly of lavender soap and had also changed his clothing. In his arms, everything seemed wonderful and uncomplicated. She wished that she could stay there forever and never have to face the sly questions and expectation of the outside world.

"Aye, you've had a long rest, lass. Is your headache gone now?"

"Yes, thank you. It is," she said a little breathlessly as Tamlane brushed a light kiss over her brow and tucked hair back behind an ear. "I am much restored."

"That is good, for I have a present for you and would like to give it to you when you are in the humor for such things."

"A present?" she asked, her curiosity aroused.

"Aye. A bride gift," he said deliberately, setting her against the bolster and turning away to strike a tinder. After a moment, a candle's light pushed back some of the evening gloom that had invaded the chamber.

Amarantha curled her legs under her and waited curiously to see what Tamlane had brought for her. She was no longer flinching at the mention of being a bride. Her mind had apparently ruminated during her sleep and finally accepted the situation so that she was able to make a reasonable accommodation for that word.

"This was something that my father gave to my mother. It is the only jewel she kept. All the rest—even her wedding band—went to those who defended the Stuart cause. But this she held too dear to part with, and my father never asked her to surrender it, for his heart, too, was bound up in this ring. It is the only reminder I have of them and a thing which I hold quite dear."

Tamlane reached into his pocket and pulled out his mother's sapphire. The soft light of the candle made the blue gems blaze with unearthly fire. He held it out.

"It's beautiful," Amarantha said softly. However, she did not move to take the ring or meet Tamlane's searching gaze.

There was silence for a long moment.

"You would not take the wedding band I gave you. Will you not accept this token from me in its stead?" Tamlane asked.

Amarantha felt her lower lip tremble.

"Not yet," she whispered.

"Why not?" he asked baldly. "Do you still reject the idea that I can be both your husband and lover?"

Hot tears filled her eyes. She blinked furiously, trying to stem the tide of tears, for it made her angry that her eyes should betray her this way.

"I refuse it because it is a symbol of a great love, and it should not be given for any lesser reason," she said in a gruff voice.

"And you will not accept it because though you have shared your body with me, you do not share your heart. You want me as a lover, but you do not *love* me." Tamlane's voice was stark, his brow drawn. "I had feared that this was the case, but prayed it was not so."

Unable to face him, Amarantha dropped her head. Burning tears fell upon the coverlet, leaving tiny splotches as testimony of her sorrow. So much for pride. It had met Tamlane's unhappiness and lost the battle.

"That is not the difficulty," she told him, forced to honesty. "It is your own feelings that I fear are lacking. I cannot wear that ring when you have no tender thoughts for me."

Once again Tamlane was left staring in stupefaction at an accusation that amazed him.

"My feelings?" A pause, then he repeated, "My feelings?"

"Yes!" Amarantha snapped, raising her head. "*Your* feelings! The emotions which should belong to you—and your wife!"

"Are you jesting?"

"*Jesting?*" If her voice had been less strangled, the question would have emerged with all the shrillness of a falcon's cry. Her fists doubled up and she knew a shocking, completely unladylike impulse to hit him.

Tamlane eyed her clenched palms and then studied her face.

"I am sorry," he said stiffly. "My word was ill-chosen. But how can you not be aware of the sentiments I hold for you?"

"I am unaware of any of your feelings because you

have never declared yourself to be in possession of any—save only annoyance and lust!" Her own annoyance had grown to the stage where it dried up her tears and allowed her to look at her husband without flinching.

Tamlane stood abruptly and took a turn about the room.

"I see. Then I must apologize," he said formally. "I have to confess that I thought these things to be self-evident."

"Your feelings are not evident to me." Amarantha looked about for a handkerchief, and finding none, used the already tear-marred coverlet to dry her cheeks.

"No?" Tamlane glared at her. Abandoning formal periods he added, "But confound it, Amarantha—they are plain for any sensible person to see!"

Amarantha dropped her coverlet and shook her head in bemusement. How could Tamlane be so wise and yet so stupid?

"I fear you have married a very unintelligent woman, Tamlane, for I am quite in the dark about your sentiments." Feeling more hopeful, she pushed the rumpled coverlet aside and rose to her knees. "Please speak plainly to me so that I may know what everyone apparently does."

"I shall try to be direct. I must tell you that I have no experience with this and find it very difficult to talk about." His green eyes stared at her suspiciously, plainly wondering whether she was tormenting him as punishment for his high-handed arrangement of their marriage. Amarantha worked hard to conceal the sudden smile that tried to form on her lips. It was too soon to give in to hope and the happiness Tamlane's speech promised.

"Surely this is as important as discussing the physical aspects of a marriage! And you did not allow my squeamishness to be a bar to *that* conversation," she reminded him. "Let us now have that same honesty and openness of thought you say that you value."

Tamlane grumbled something obscene and took another turn about the room. It amused her when he forgot himself and behaved in an unrectorlike manner. Perhaps he would after all understand when she also fell short of perfect behavior.

"Very well. I am ready," he announced, ceasing his perambulations and drawing himself up straight. He cleared his throat. "It happens—once in a great while—that a man finds the woman of his imaginings. If he is a very fortunate soul, he will be permitted to marry her and they will have the opportunity to live out their lives together. I must count myself as one of the fortunate few to have found such a woman to esteem."

He looked at her hopefully, asking to be spared any further elaboration. Unfortunately, Amarantha was not feeling merciful. Her doubts had fattened themselves on his silence on this matter until only the most direct declaration would slay them. She wanted the words—all of them.

"That is a very gallant speech," she told him. "But what does that mean?"

"You are being vindictive and ridiculous!" he growled. "I am saying, wife, that I love you!"

"Then just say it."

"I just did," he muttered.

"Say it again."

"I love you!" he shouted. Then moderating his voice, he asked: "And you, Amarantha? What do you feel toward me—resentment that I forced you to this marriage? Fondness and desire for a lover, but not a husband?"

In reply, Amaranth rose off of the bed and flung herself into his arms, confident that he would catch her.

"I love you, too, you daft creature! As a lover—and a husband. Do you really believe that anything less than love would have drawn me out into the rain and the dangers of the night moor? I assure you that my curiosity is not that insatiable. I just needed to know that you loved me, too, before I could truly be your wife."

She would have said more, but Tamlane's lips smothered her own, and as always happened, his kisses quite destroyed her powers of speech. He did not have the knack of gentle-mannered wooing. His embrace was most authoritative and quite over-powered her with its strength.

But he was not unaffected by their closeness. The beating of his heart and the sudden heat rising from his body spoke truly of the desire that was overtaking the gentleman rector.

A step brought them back to the bed and he laid them down upon it, Amarantha beneath him. He settled himself upon her.

"Dinner?" she asked breathlessly.

"It can wait." He caught her face between his palms and cradled her while his eyes roved over her face. "So, you are ready to be my wife?"

"Yes."

"And you love me?"

"Yes."

"I am more grateful than you will ever know." Tamlane rolled onto his side and searched for her hand. The sapphire band was placed on her finger and followed by a kiss. "Thank you, love."

In reply, Amarantha reached over and tangled her fingers in his hair, mussing the neat locks. She tugged his mouth back to her own.

Tamlane didn't wait then for speeches or invitation. Amarantha's skirts were pushed up and his breeches down with an expeditious hand. He settled back upon her and entered her body in one heavy surge.

Amarantha exhaled and arched involuntarily at the sudden invasion. She had not been prepared but her body was willing to be fired by the desire he always summoned in her. She enfolded him eagerly.

Tamlane groaned softly. It was a rueful mix of pleasure and guilt and his accent was marked when he spoke. "Sorry, lass. It's a selfish beast I am sometimes. You make me half mad."

She smiled and shook her head.

"I'm not sorry. You make me half mad, too." Amarantha drew his head back down so she could resume their kiss.

Dinner was forgotten.

NIGHT VISITOR

MELANIE JACKSON

All self-respecting Scots know of the massacre and of the brave piper who gave his life so that some of its defenders might live. But few see his face in their sleep, his sad gray eyes touching their souls, his warm hands caressing them like a lover's. And Tafaline is willing to wager that none have heard his sweet voice. But he was slain so long ago. How is it possible that he now haunts her dreams? Are they true, those fairy tales that claim a woman of MacLeod blood can save a man from even death? Is it true that when she touched his bones, she bound herself to his soul? Yes, it is Malcolm "the piper" who calls to her insistently, across the winds of night and time . . . and looking into her heart, Taffy knows there is naught to do but go to him.

__52423-6 $5.50 US/$6.50 CAN

IONA

MELANIE JACKSON

Isolated by the icy storms of the North Atlantic, the isle of Iona is only a temporary haven for its mistress. Lona MacLean, daughter of a rebel and traitor to the crown, knows that it is only a matter of time before the bloody Sasannachs come for her. But she has a stout Scottish heart, and the fiery beauty gave up dreams of happiness years before. One task remains—to protect her people. But the man who lands upon Iona's rain-swept shores is not an Englishman. The handsome intruder is a Scot, and a crafty one at that. His clever words leave her tossing and turning in her bed long into the night. His kiss promises an end to the ghosts that plague both her people and her heart. And in his powerful embrace, Lona finds an ecstasy she'd long ago forsworn.

___4614-8 $4.99 US/$5.99 CAN

MANON
MELANIE JACKSON

Alone and barely ahead of the storm, Manon flees Scotland; the insurrection has failed and Bonnie Prince Charlie's rebellion has been thrown down. Innocent of treason, yet sought by agents of the English king, the Scots beauty dons the guise of a man and rides to London—and into the hands of the sexiest Sassanach she's ever seen. But she has no time to dally, especially not with an English baronet. Nor can she indulge fantasies of his strong male arms about her or his heated lips pressed against her own. She fears that despite her precautions, this rake may uncover her as no man but *Manon*, and she may learn of something more dangerous than an Englishman's sword—his heart.

Lair of the Wolf

Also includes the eighth installment of *Lair of the Wolf*, a serialized romance set in medieval Wales. Be sure to look for future chapters of this exciting story featured in Leisure books and written by the industry's top authors.

___4737-3 $4.99 US/$5.99 CAN

Across a Moonswept Moor

Julie Moffett

An enchanted dagger points Fiona to Ireland in search of her missing cousin. Then a midnight visit to Celtic holy ground slides her into the seventeenth century—and into the arms of the most gorgeous male she has ever encountered. The hot-blooded barbarian called Ian orders her about as if she were a soldier. But his kisses leave no doubt he thinks of her as a woman, and soon she knows she would trade a thousand bubble baths for one of his sensual massages and give up chocolate to melt in one of his passionate embraces. For although she has traveled across three centuries, it has taken only a moment for her heart to recognize she has met her match.

___52448-1 $4.99 US/$5.99 CAN

A Double-Edged Blade

JULIE MOFFETT

Lovely British agent Faith Worthington is sent on a mission to expose a ruthless IRA terrorist. But a bullet to the thigh knocks her back to seventeenth-century Ireland . . . and into the arms of rebel leader Miles O'Bruaidar. Known as the Irish Lion, Miles immediately suspects the modern-day beauty of being a spy. He takes Faith as his hostage, only to discover her feminine wiles are incredibly alluring. But desperate to return to the future, Faith has no time for love—at least not from a mutton-feasting, ale-quaffing brute like Miles. Yet with each passing day—and each fiery kiss—Faith's defenses weaken. Torn between returning to her own time and staying with the charming rogue, Faith knows her heart has been pierced to the quick, but she wonders if their love will always be a double-edged blade.

___52369-8 $5.50 US/$6.50 CAN

Dorchester Publishing Co., Inc.
P.O. Box 6640
Wayne, PA 19087-8640

Please add $1.75 for shipping and handling for the first book and $.50 for each book thereafter. NY, NYC, and PA residents, please add appropriate sales tax. No cash, stamps, or C.O.D.s. All orders shipped within 6 weeks via postal service book rate. Canadian orders require $2.00 extra postage and must be paid in U.S. dollars through a U.S. banking facility.

Name _____
Address_____
City_____State _____Zip _____
I have enclosed $ _____ in payment for the checked book(s).
Payment <u>must</u> accompany all orders. ❑ Please send a free catalog.

TESS MALLORY
HIGHLAND DREAM

When Jix Ferguson's dream reveals that her best friend is making a terrible mistake and marrying the wrong guy, she tricks Samantha into flying to Scotland. There the two women met the man Jix is convinced her friend should marry--Jamie MacGregor. He is handsome, smart, perfect . . . the only problem is, Jix falls for him, too. Then a slight scuffle involving the Scot's ancestral sword sends all three back to the start of the seventeenth century--where MacGregors are outlaws and hunted. All Jix has to do is marry Griffin Campbell, steal Jamie's sword back from their captor, and find a way to return herself and her friends to their own time. Oh yeah, and she has to fall in love. It isn't going to be easy, but in this matter of the heart, Jix knows she'll laugh last.

___52444-9 $5.50 US/$6.50 CAN

To Touch The Stars

Tess Mallory

Eagle is enjoying the quiet serenity of Station One when suddenly it is attacked by a rebel spacecraft. Before he can defend himself, he is pinned by a beautiful droid who demands to know the whereabouts of a child. Skyra will let nothing—and no one—stand in the way of finding her little sister, for Mayla is the only hope of freedom for the rebels. But the more time she spends with Eagle, the more she feels something stronger than compassion for her prisoner, something that makes her burn with delicious turmoil when she envisions his sleek muscular form. And only in his arms does she find an ecstasy like none she's ever known, one that lifts her high enough to touch the stars.

___52253-5 $4.99 US/$5.99 CAN